Margie's Murder Mystery:

Dropped Dead In Kona

by Gerry Stimmler copyright 2010

Eleanor Avenue Press, Saint Paul, MN

For Ruth

This book is essentially an 'author's proof,' which means it contains typos and minor mistakes not typically found in a published book. Rather than destroy the book, the author has decided to release the book 'into the wild' for readers to enjoy. See the inside back cover for the BookCrossing.com information and please let the author know when you find this book and when you set it free again.

Disclaimer: This is a work of fiction. It's not based on a true story and none of the characters are real. In other words it's a big fat lie.

In the Beginning

I remember I was in the middle of one of those pleasant dreams you hope really aren't dreams at all because they're so damn warm and wonderful.

We were on a train in one of those sleeper cabins. Not one of those sterile American ones with gleaming aluminum and sticky vinyl, but one of those European models with rich, dark mahogany and gilded trim and soft, cloth seats. We were steaming along through a moonlit fairy land of silver streams and glowing pastures dotted by thatch-roofed cottages and thunderous castles and rock walls and hedgerows.

Ahead of us was a tunnel through a soaring range of snow-covered mountains and there was music. Brahms I think. Or Beethoven. Of course it might have been John Williams; I'm not well versed in classical music. In any event Margie was at the open window looking out and a soft breeze played with the fabric of the long white negligee she'd bought for our honeymoon and she looked spectacular with her soft curly blonde hair reflecting the moon glow.

Margie turned, smiling and reached out her hand to me. I moved forward and we...

You know actually the dream really has nothing to do with this story.

Anyway, I was in the middle of what I've already said was a fabulous dream when I heard a voice. You know it's funny, you're in a dream and you hear a voice, but it's not a voice in the dream. It's like God is calling . Or your mother. Or your wife.

"Joe!"

It was Margie, my wife. I tried my best to ignore her because like I said the dream was getting pretty hot!

'Joe!!"

There was that voice again. Louder. Determined. I felt the dream begin to fade. I tried to hold on but...

"Joe!!!"

The dream dissolved and I opened my eyes to a nighttime world of black on black.

"What?" I said, rolling toward Margie's shadow next to me.

"Shush," Margie scolded.

"What is it?" I asked softly, hoping my voice was now at a more acceptable level.

"I'm not sure," Margie's whisper was barely audible – and very sexy. "Something woke me."

I pushed up on my elbows and cocked an ear toward the door to the hallway. Nothing.

All I could hear was the distant surf and the 'clackity-clack-clack' that stupid thorny plant outside our bedroom makes in the slightest breeze. Of course my hearing isn't superhuman like Margie's so I couldn't be certain there wasn't something I was missing.

"I don't hear nothing," I said ungrammatically and lay down and pulled the thin blanket over my bare shoulders. "If it's a burglar, Magoo will bark."

At the sound of his name, Magoo, our oversized flop-eared Yorky who sleeps between us on our king-size mattress and takes up twice as much acreage as either

Margie or me, wriggled and stretched then flopped back down.

Margie however was not so easily dissuaded. "Something's wrong," she insisted.

"Go back to sleep," I said firmly as I burrowed back into my warm pillow, trying desperately to reenter that dream. There was something especially good about to happen and I wanted to find out what it was.

Of course I knew I'd never be allowed to go back to sleep. I felt Margie throw off the covers and slip out of bed. I felt Magoo rise and follow her, though I'm certain he was hoping she was headed to the kitchen for a late night snack.

With a groan of protest, I pulled myself from the bed found my slippers and robe and followed the fading shadows of Margie and Magoo into the living room.

By the time I arrived in the living room Margie was already tiptoeing through the open doors that lead out to our small yard, spacious lanai, and oversized pool. Magoo was still with her, though likely he was disappointed to discover the kitchen was not Margie's destination.

By the time I reached the other side of the living room Margie was out beyond the pool standing tippy toe on the low rock wall peering over the tall hibiscus bushes that separate our home from the fourth fairway of the Kona Coast golf course. Her filmy nightgown billowed in the soft breeze and clung to her lean frame. A sliver of moon lit the scene and danced off Margie's blond curls.

Hmmm. Perhaps getting up in the middle of the night wasn't going to be so bad after all.

I skirted the pool and stepped behind Margie opened my robe and gathered her in to shield her from the cool night air. She pulled the robe close and her warm flesh heated mine but her attention and gaze was focused beyond the hedge.

I rested my cheek against hers and looked out into the night.

As I already told you, our house sits above the fourth fairway on one of the Big Island's prime golf courses. It has a panoramic view of Keauhou which includes much of the golf course, the lower portion of Alii Drive, the roof tops of half a dozen well-manicured condo developments, Keauhou Bay and, of course, the vast, deep waters of the Pacific ocean. It's a gorgeous view night or day and in the quiet night air under the moon glow everything seemed warm and wonderful and very normal.

I yawned and belched softly – an action I immediately regretted since I knew it would make it harder to turn Margie's attention in the direction I was headed.

"Charming," Margie admonished but took no revenge.

"Sorry," I offered lamely. "There's nothing out there, Margie. Come to bed."

I tried to guide her gently away. She resisted.

"There is too something out there!"

"Where?"

She pointed into the darkness. "In the middle of the fairway."

I squinted at the spot she point to. There was, in fact, a large object in the middle of the fairway but it was impossible to tell what it was. I was quite certain it was simply exposed lava, which is a common obstacle on Big Island fairways.

"It's only lava," I said and nuzzled Margie's neck.

Margie didn't pull away, but she was determined.

"It is not lava," she said and wriggled free of my robe corral and pushed through the bushes. "It wasn't there yesterday."

"Margie…" I meant only to complain, but it came out more of a whine and then I too pushed through the bushes and followed after her and Magoo.

Margie marched quickly toward the object; I dragged along behind. My thinking was that if I held back it would be just that much less of a walk back to the house and my bed -- which would now be cold and uncomfortable – once Margie saw that the object was merely exposed lava as I'd told her.

Margie reached the 'lava,' and stopped. I heard Magoo growl softly, something he seldom does.

"I told you!" Margie called back in triumph without turning around.

"Okay, what is it?" I said without hastened my pace.

Margie put her hands on her hips and turned. "Come and see!"

I strolled down casually until I stood next to Margie and looked down. I do not know what I thought I'd see, but I assure you I did not expect to see what was there.

"Holy shit!" was what I said, though that doesn't reflect my full range of emotions.

There on the ground before us lay the body of a woman. An attractive woman in life, she appeared to be in her mid to late thirties, with short blonde hair and a fair complexion. She was completely naked and her thin body was wildly contorted. It seems odd to say it, but the way she was laid out reminded me of one of those Egyptian wall paintings where the arms and head and legs are all unnaturally skewed. And I remember thinking that it looked as if she'd been *thrown* to the ground.

5

Her eyes were open and stared sightlessly up at me and Margie and the sky, and a single dark spot – a bullet hole? -- was clearly visible in the middle of her forehead. There was, however, no visible blood.

Now, you don't find dead bodies every day so it took me awhile to absorb the scene and when I had, I glanced around nervously, wondering whether we were really alone. But there was no one around. As far as I could tell we were alone.

"We'd better call 9-1-1," I said.

"'Ya think?" Margie taunted, squatting down next to the body.

"Don't touch it!" I snapped.

"I'm just looking," Margie said, annoyed. "I think her neck's broken."

I looked again at the position of the body. Unless the woman was an owl, her neck was definitely broken.

"'Ya think?" I said, mimicking Margie's taunt.

Margie looked up and stuck her tongue out at me and then stood up.

"Why would someone shoot her AND break her neck."

"I don't know," I said, looking down at the body again. "Maybe they were really mad. A better question is: 'Why did they dump her here?'" I looked around again.

Margie looked at the ground. "I don't see any tracks or footprints."

I looked down too. I could see our footsteps in the grass but no others.

"Let's go make that call. I'm not sure it's safe out here."

"You go. I'll stay here with her."

I thought that was not a good idea. "No one's going to steal her!" I reasoned.

"I know. I just think I'd better stay. I'll be fine. Magoo's here."

I looked at tiny Magoo, who sniffed the body and growled softly again.

"Yeah, he'll be a big help. Listen, Margie, I am not leaving you here."

Margie crossed her arms and turned to me. It was too dark to see her eyes clearly, but I knew the look. It was the 'I'm a big girl and survived just fine before you came along' stare.

I stood my ground and met her eyes. Time ticked by. Margie finally dropped her arms in surrender.

"Oh, okay. I'm cold anyway. Come on Magoo."

And so the three of us turned and headed back to the house, leaving the naked corpse in the middle of the fairway looking up at God.

I don't know what Margie was thinking as we hurried along, but I was thinking how glad I was it wasn't me out there -- or Margie.

As we pushed back through the bushes it started to rain lightly and by the time I got off the phone to the police, it was raining hard -- one of those tropical downpours that come out of nowhere and end as quickly as they start.

I went to stand behind Margie just inside the living room out of the rain. She had her robe and slippers now, but I put my arms around her and put my chin on her shoulder and together we watched the rain.

"Glad you decided to come in?"

Margie sighed. "We shouldn't have left her in the rain."

"You didn't know it was going to rain."

"Still..."

Margie was quite a moment. "Why do people do things like that?"

I pulled Margie close and didn't answer. The truth of the matter was, I didn't have an answer and figured no one really did. I just held Margie and wondered if someone would be missing holding that woman on the fairway the same way I was holding Margie or if maybe the person who used to hold that woman on the fairway was the person who left her there.

Margie shivered in the damp air and I pulled her tight. Together, under the roar of the rain, we heard sirens.

Detective Lo

We stood together under a big police-issue umbrella in the middle of the fairway lit by half a dozen headlights and flood lamps as they lifted the body – now entrusted to a large zippered black bag – onto a gurney and wheeled it to a waiting ambulance.

A young officer stood near us and offered some additional protection from the rain with yet another umbrella. I noticed he kept glancing at our robes, which seemed a little odd, so I finally asked him: "Is there a problem officer?"

He gave me a pleasant grin. "No, sir," he said. "It's no big deal, but you've got each other's robes on."

I looked down at my robe; the monogram read 'Hers.' I looked over at Margie's monogram which read 'His."

"No," I said. "They're the right robes."

It took a moment, but the patrolman finally smiled and gave me a thumbs up.

Detective Lo, an imposing native Hawaiian and the head of the homicide division for the County of Hawaii, made his way over and took up a spot in front of us with his notepad and pencil. Another young officer held yet another police-issue umbrella for him. The rain had started to end, but it was still falling at a steady clip.

"You heard the shot?" Lo asked Margie without any introduction. Since we already knew the detective quite well, we didn't take offence. At least I didn't take offense.

"I'm not sure," Margie said. "Maybe. Something woke me. I guess... Why do you suppose anyone would want to kill a sweet looking woman like that?"

"Mrs. Thomas, please. Just answer the questions," Detective Lo said.

"And where are her clothes?" Margie was clearly upset by the lack of clothing on the victim. In fact Margie had become more and more agitated about the whole thing once the shock of discovery had worn off.

"I'm sure they'll find them, Margie," I said consolingly.

"So you didn't hear a shot?" Detective Lo asked. He was not the kind of man who was easily sidetracked.

Margie shrugged. "I just woke up all of a sudden. I don't know why."

"Did you hear anything after you woke? Footsteps, voices, a car?"

Margie furled her brow. "No. No I didn't. It was very quiet. I sat in bed listening and I didn't hear a thing. That's when I woke Joe up."

Lo tapped his pencil on his pad and looked at me.

"She got up and I followed," I offered. "We came outside and I followed Margie here. There wasn't anyone around. Magoo would have heard them."

Detective Lo looked down at Magoo who was huddled close to Margie's leg and unhappy with the wet grass and falling rain. The umbrella wasn't much help to him.

"And you don't recognize her?" the detective asked.

"No," we said together.

"You're *sure* you don't recognize her?" Detective Lo repeated.

Margie pulled away from me, crossed her arms stiffly over her chest and took a step toward the detective.

"And just what is that supposed to mean?" she snapped.

"It's just..." Detective Lo started.

"It's because of last time, isn't it," Margie scolded, her hands coming loose and moving to her hips. "Well, that was completely different. Totally different."

I put my hand on Margie's shoulder and tried to hold her back, but she was worked up.

"Well, Detective, if you hadn't been so focused on Joe back then, you might have figured out who the real killer was earlier and solved that murder *before* Joe nearly got blowup and drowned and run off the road and before we got hijacked down at the volcano and nearly murdered and before we got trussed up and shanghaied and nearly thrown overboard and almost smashed on the rocks in that runaway cruiser..." Margie should have taken a breath here, but didn't. She's got a terrific set of lungs. "And let me tell you something else..." Margie took another step toward the detective, her hands flying and her eyes wide as she continued reprimanding the detective.

I'll save you the trouble of listening to the rest of her lecture and instead try to give you some background on why Margie's got her undies in a bunch just now. I certainly don't want you to get the wrong impression about Margie. She's not one of those difficult people who barks at everyone and everything. In fact, Margie is the warmest, kindest, most considerate and generous person I've ever known.

10

The reason she's miffed is because of what happened the last time we found a body. Yes, it's true; this is not the first murder victim she and I have discovered. We found our first murder victim just a day after we first met.

You see, I'd come to Hawaii with Jillian, my wife, for a much needed vacation with the hope of reviving a stale, failing marriage. Jillian and Margie were old college roomies who'd stayed in touch and we – Jillian and I -- were going to be house guests of Margie and Frank – Margie's husband. What I didn't know was that Jillian and her lover – who as it turned out was Margie's husband Frank -- were planning a little 'accident' for me while I was here so they could collect on a two million dollar insurance policy that I knew nothing about.

In any event, Margie and I discovered our first murder victim floating in her swimming pool shortly after we met, and when we called the police I told Detective Lo that neither Margie nor I knew who it was. Of course it turned out that I had had an encounter with the murder victim at the airport in Honolulu where I had taken his picture – actually, I was taking a picture of the hula girls and he was in the background. He didn't like being in my picture and we had had a quarrel about whether or not I could take a picture of anyone I chose to take a picture of in a public place. But being the stalwart gentleman that I am, I eventually erased his photograph from my camera to pacify him.

As it turned out, the murder victim in the pool was a hit man hired by Margie's husband. Why Frank killed the guy is kind of complicated, so I won't go into that. The important point is that when Detective Lo discovered I'd had an argument with the man, I became a murder suspect. Being labeled a murder suspect was a stroke of luck for Jillian and Frank because it made it that much harder for Margie and me to figure out their plan to kill me. A plan that almost got Margie and her best friend Amanda killed as well.

But, as you can tell things didn't work out for Jillian and Frank. Frank drowned at sea and my ex is serving 30 to life in a Texas prison. This is funny because people think that if they do bad things in Hawaii, they get to serve time in Hawaii. The fact is it's cheaper to send them to Texas. Yeah, Texas. Doing time there has got to be twice as hard as anywhere else. I apologize to all those Texan's reading this. But that's my opinion right or wrong.

Anyway, back to my digression.

Obviously things *did* work out for Margie and me, because while we were trying to unravel the cause of my many near fatal accidents, we spent a lot of time together and eventually discovered we were absolutely crazy about one another. And so once Frank was dead and Jillian was imprisoned and I got a divorce, we got married!

As I look back on things now, I can't imagine what my life would be like if my ex hadn't tried to kill me, and in some small way I'll always be grateful to her for that.

Of course Margie knows that I have put all this behind me and buried the hatch with Detective Lo, but Margie's still got an axe to grind so I thought you should have all this background so you can understand why Detective Lo is asking if we're *sure* we don't recognize the dead woman and why Margie's so pissed off at the inference behind his question.

There. Now as they say, 'back to our regularly scheduled show.'

"… and it's your fault that we were nearly killed!" Margie finished out of breath.

I gave Margie a hug. "Let it go, Margie. Detective Lo didn't mean anything by it."

"I'm just doing my job, Mrs. Thomas," the detective said earnestly.

"We know that," I said, though I knew Margie was still angry.

"Are we done now, detective?" I asked finally.

"Yes, I'll call you if there's anything else." Detective Lo started to leave then stopped. "I'd appreciate it if you didn't discuss this with anyone. The less information that gets out the better."

"We won't tell a soul," I said in my most accommodating voice.

Margie gave me a dirty look. I guess maybe I was being too cooperative. Anyway I thought it made sense to stay on the good side of Detective Lo. He'd locked me up once as a suspect, and I certainly didn't want to go through that again.

The rain had finally stopped, so I thanked the young officer who'd shielded us with the umbrella and turned Margie toward the house and quietly we made our way home with Magoo close behind.

Yes, They're Real

A murder in Kona is a really big deal. Most of the time the paper is filled with much tamer stuff like disputes about highway construction and land development and which cruise ship is going to dock on a specific day.

For those who don't know, Kona -- it's actually Kailua-Kona, but everyone just calls it Kona -- is a sleepy resort town on the west side of Hawaii. It's south of what is referred to as the *Gold Coast*, so named for its fabulous weather, spectacular beaches, and luxuriously expensive resorts.

13

Hawaii, again in case you didn't know, is the largest island of the Hawaiian Islands. It's often referred to as the *Big Island* because people tend to call the Hawaiian Islands 'Hawaii' when in fact the Hawaiian Islands include six major islands: Kauai, Oahu, Molokai, Lanai, Maui, and Hawaii -- or as I've already said, the Big Island.

The west coast of the Big Island is the dry side. In fact, Kona gets only about 10 inches of rain a year – which technically makes it a desert. Hilo, the largest city on the island and the county seat, on the east coast of the island gets about the same amount each month which means it gets a yearly total of 120 to 200 inches! In fact, Hilo can get as much as 10 inches in a single day! Not surprising, it's very green there.

Kona however is the most popular tourist destination because of its persistent sunshine, beautiful beaches, and those luxury resorts I mentioned. It also has calm waters, great snorkeling, the Ironman, fishing tournaments, world-class golf courses, which tend to be associated with those pricey resorts, and last but not least, and certainly not to be underestimated, the most gorgeous and romantic sunsets on the planet – bar none.

I wish I could do a passable job of describing Hawaii to you, but I can't. I don't think words are enough. Even pictures don't do it justice. I tried to describe it to a friend in Chicago once and when I was done she responded. "So it's like L.A. without the smog and the people?"

Well, yes, I guess it's sort of like that, but not really at all.

Travel posters will help you get the idea as will scenes from motion pictures that were shot in Hawaii– like Jurassic Park and South Pacific. But looking at pictures you can't feel the trade wind on your face or smell the mix of volcanic soil, plants, flowers, trees, and ocean all drenched in tropical sunshine.

Hawaii is not just a treat to the eyes, but to all the senses. So I guess I won't try to describe it any better than that. Your dreams will have to do until you make the trip yourself. Suffice it to say, I came, I saw, I stayed.

On the morning following our discovery of the murder victim, I was sitting in my usual spot outside by the pool reading the morning paper and enjoying the quiet, simple pleasure of living while Margie finished up her laps in the pool.

Margie's a marvelous swimmer and does one hundred laps every morning before breakfast. I watch. And no I don't feel guilty about it. I don't feel the need to exert myself that early in the day thank you!

So as I said I was reading my paper when I heard the front door open followed by the clatter of tiny sandals crossing the living room tile. I knew who it was even before I heard the soft, sensual voice call the traditional "Aloha."

I lowered my paper to feast my eyes on Amanda, our buxom neighbor and Margie's BFF (that's 'best friend forever' in text lingo for those of you who don't know or have already decided I'm too old to know such things).

"Aloha," I responded in my most neighborly tone.

Amanda reached the edge of the pool and stopped briefly to watch Margie. Today she was doing the Australian crawl with her usual faultless form.

"Did you hear what happened?" Amanda called as Margie drew near, but Margie continued to swim without missing a beat.

"You should know by now that she won't stop for anything, Amanda. Sit down and have some coffee."

I was already pouring her a cup as she circumnavigated the pool and came and plopped into a chair across from me and dropped her bulky Wall Street Journal on the table. Magoo looked up from his chair, wagged his tail twice and went back to sleep. Magoo loves Amanda, but evidently he was tuckered out. Why? I have no idea. Perhaps he hadn't yet had his twenty-three hours of sleep for the day. I put down my paper to give her my full attention. I had to. Amanda's stunning, and when she's around she commands attention.

Don't get me wrong! Margie's no slouch. As you may have already guessed from my brief description, Margie's dazzling. What you might call your basic blonde beauty. Well, no, that's not exactly right. There's nothing *basic* about her and I haven't a clue what 'blonde beauty' really means, so let's start over.

Margie is gorgeous with a capital 'G.' She's got a cheerleader's complexion, big blue eyes, and short curly blonde hair. She's thirty-seven, though I doubt if anyone would guess she's even thirty. At five-foot seven, she's of average height, and has an almost boyish athletic build with broad shoulders and small breasts. A dancer's body is how I often describe it. And unlike most women I know, she's very happy with herself. In fact, I think she's the only woman I know who *is* happy with her herself and hasn't talked of 'nipping' or 'tucking' or 'lifting' or 'augmenting' or ... well you know how it goes. Her eyes match the blue of the deep Pacific on a sunny day and the girl-next-door shine on her face doesn't go away even when she yells, though she seldom does yells. And when Margie smiles, the sun hides in shame. There now I'm gushing.

Although people are quick to assume she wears lots of makeup, the fact is she doesn't. Her lashes are naturally long and thick and her lips are naturally full and red. Her skin as I said is flawless – which is remarkable considering the amount of time she spends in the sun.

I've watched her put on makeup, and it's just a dab of foundation, a couple of swipes with blush-on, a little eye shadow, eyeliner, a moment with the eyebrow pencil, and finally lip gloss or lipstick or whatever it's called. It takes all of five minutes. Tops! Ten if she's dressing for a big night out or a dressy wedding. All the women I know would kill to look like Margie. And all the men I know would probably kill me to get at her.

As far as her dress, Margie dresses the way all men wish women would dress, which is to say Margie dresses the way women wish they had the nerve to dress. Really. I read a lot. And what I read says that the majority of women and men wish they – women -- had the nerve to dress sexy.

Kona's a very laid back place. There's not a lot of fancy dressing going on so daytime wear is generally shorts and a top, a swimsuit, a Mumu, a sundress or some variation of that. Evening wear might up the outfit a notch, but you don't see men in suits or women in evening gowns. Even funerals and wedding are typically 'Aloha' wear – which for men means a nice Hawaiian shirt, shorts and sandals.

Consider yesterday's outfit which was classic Margie.

It consisted of a pale lavender scoop-necked sun dress with white piping, a pair of rhinestone studded sandals (flat), faux white pearl earrings and necklace and a simple gold chain bracelet. She's always got a pair of super dark sunglasses that she either tucks on top of her head or lets sit half-way down her nose so that she can look out over them in a very provocative way. She had her favorite purse, which is a straw bag decorated with a beaded white plumaria and a matching wide-brimmed straw hat with a lavender scarf. A small heart-shaped tattoo on her ankle was accented with a puka shell ankle bracelet, and her nails were mauve, as were her toenails. Margie has closets full of similar stuff, and many of her fashions can be found in those women's wear catalogs that fill our mailbox. She's not into designer clothes and spends quite modestly on her attire.

Now that I've described Margie, you're probably thinking that I must be a real hunk since I'm her husband. Alas, I'm sorry to say that I'm not. I mean it would make sense; a beautiful woman, a handsome man. The truth is my parents gave me the most honest name they could have: Joe. And I'm very faithful to that name in almost every way. I'm just an average guy.

That's not to say I'm unattractive. I had my share of girlfriends in high school and college and they were all cute if not pretty. And my previous wife, Jillian – the one who tried to kill me – she was very attractive and when she got dressed up she was almost beautiful. But I'm certainly not the kind of guy women fawn over.

At five foot ten and a half, I'm a little taller than Margie – who, out of deference to me, never wears heels that make her taller than I am. I've told her it's no big deal, but still she's always careful. She's got a fair number of pairs of shoes with five and six inch heels – shoes she used to wear when she was married to Frank –who tried to kill me – who was about six three. I asked her once why she hadn't gotten rid of those shoes with high heels if she wasn't ever going to wear them. "Are you saving them for your next husband?" I asked. "Of course not," Margie answered with just a hint of insincerity, "I'm hoping you'll grow."

I try to keep myself in shape – especially since I married Margie – but at forty-one my stomach muscles are starting to give way to gravity. My hairline, as you'd suspect, is slowly starting to recede. Either that or my forehead is getting larger. Most people would call me trim, and Margie never mentions the small love handles I obsess over in the bathroom mirror. I have dark brown hair and brown eyes and a pleasant oval shaped face. I would prefer that my nose were a trifle smaller and my lips a bit thinner, but I'm not heading for the plastic surgeon. I'm starting to find that it's easier to read things at arm's length, but otherwise my vision is still 20/20.

Margie told me one time when I asked her why she married a brown shoe like me that I have a Tom Hanks quality. I asked her if that meant I looked like Forest Gump. She just laughed and didn't answer. Forest Gump wasn't all that bad was he?

So that's Margie and that's me. A bit mismatched in the physical realm, but we laugh at the same jokes and generally like doing the same things and being with the same people and I sure like her and she sure seems to like me. So what more could either one of us want? Nothing. Right?

In contrast to Margie's Nordic features, Amanda is a dark Mediterranean beauty with a bronze complexion, huge brown eyes, and a head of lustrous chocolate colored hair which she generally wears piled on top of her head in some astounding manner that defies explanation. I'm always amazed at women who wear their hair that way. How, I ask myself, is it possible for someone to perform that task behind their head while looking in a mirror? I have trouble shaving!

Amanda's a little taller than Margie; actually, she's three inches taller. So in her stocking feet she's five ten, and since she's not self conscious about her height, she often wears five-inch heels which puts her eye to eye with her husband, Pete, who is six three.

More classically shaped than Margie, Amanda can best be described as Rubenesque, which is not to imply that she is fat by any means. Only that she has more cushion than Margie, especially up front. Amanda has the largest non-enhanced hooters I've ever had the pleasure to meet. Don't ask me how I know they're natural, that's a whole other story!

And before you jump to conclusions about my chauvinism, I should point out that there is one characteristic of Amanda that is even more impressive than her bosom: her brain. Without a doubt Amanda is *the* smartest person I have ever known (notice I did not say 'woman'). She reads four different newspapers each morning – two of which are the Wall Street Journal and the New York Times and she finishes the Sunday NYT crossword *before* breakfast. Take it from me you do not want to play Scrabble with her or any other game that requires a sharp mind and steel-trap memory, unless of course she's on your team.

There is one small blemish on Amanda's imposing list of physical and mental faculties however: her glasses. Amanda's eyesight is terrible and she wears the thickest glasses you've ever seen. She flinches at the mere mention of contacts, which it seems she tried once and had to be sedated before they could relax her enough to open her eyes to remove them. Margie's vision in case you're interested, is a perfect 20/20, but she does own a pair of fashion glasses that she wears when she thinks she needs to look 'brainy.'

It's my firm opinion that everyone should have a neighbor like Amanda. But of course if they did there'd be no need for men's magazines or National Geographic or porn on the Internet or a dictionary or a thesaurus for that matter.

And so you'll understand why I like to look at Amanda and try like the dickens to always stare at her eyes. Of course she knows she's an eyeful and, like Margie, she wears clothes that draw attention. Today it's a tight black and white tennis outfit, though I have never actually seen her play tennis.

"You're looking lovely as usual," I said when Amanda focused her attention on me.

She dodged the complement. "Did *you* hear the news?" she whispered excitedly.

"Hear what?" I said casually although I knew she was referring to the murder. Amanda is very well connected and knows all the gossip before anyone else. Not that I'm into gossip, but I generally hear about it anyway.

Amanda leaned forward and said with obvious delight. "There's been a murder!"

"Oh, that," I said fluffing my paper and feigning disinterest. "Yeah, we heard all about it."

Amanda jumped back in her chair. Her eyes narrowed. I picked up a slice of pineapple.

"You heard? How? It's not in the papers."

I took a sip of coffee. "I'm not at liberty to say," I muttered. I was aware that I was playing with fire. Amanda can be quite disagreeable when toyed with, so I add: "Margie will not forgive me if I tell you, so you'll have to wait for her."

I glanced toward Margie and took up my paper, holding it low so as not to obscure my view of Amanda.

Amanda was clearly annoyed, yet she seemed to accept my answer and turned her attention to Margie, cutting blade-like through the calm water.

"Doesn't that bother you?" She asked with a tinge of annoyance in her voice.

I followed Amanda's gaze toward Margie, and I assumed she was referring to my disinterest in all things related to aerobics, exercise, or hard labor.

"No," I said. "I have my own way of exercising. I just appear to be a slouch."

"Not that, dummy! Doesn't it bother you that she swims naked?"

This *is* true. Margie swims au natural. Why not? No one can see into our pool easily and she claims to enjoy the freedom. Of course Amanda has known this forever, but this is the first time she'd elicited my feelings on the subject.

I grinned and shook my head both to indicate that I did not find it objectionable and to indicate how poorly Amanda understood the male libido.

"Amanda," I said. "You would be surprised how very few men in this world are bothered by the sight of a beautiful woman swimming naked in their pool."

Amanda opened her mouth to say something, but just sighed and shook her head. She took a sip of coffee and helped herself to a banana from the breakfast platter. She's a frequent guest so she knows her way around.

Margie's idea of breakfast is a large platter of island fruits; most often papayas, pineapples, melons, strawberries, oranges, bananas, mangos and fresh avocadoes. Personally, I'd prefer bacon, eggs and an English Muffin smothered in butter and cream cheese and a donut or cream-filled pastry to top it all off. But I'm too lazy to prepare such a meal and I'd have to make a special trip to the store to get bacon and English Muffins and cream cheese and everything else and I'd also prefer not to anger the local food goddess – a.k.a. Margie—who

22

would put a curse on me if she ever saw me filling my maw with that stuff.

It's not really so bad. Since Margie and I got married and I adopted her diet of fruits, vegetables, nuts and an occasional – very occasional – pizza, I have slimmed down to my college weight. So I can't complain. Breakfast now is a few bits of fruit and fresh ground Kona coffee while I read the local paper: 'West Hawaii Today.'

Amanda finished her banana and asked the question that she'd hesitated to ask before. It's a universal question that women eventually ask all men in one way or another: "Why are men so one dimensional?"

I looked up from my paper.

"Amanda," I said, "surely you should realize that men are one dimensional because it's easy. Men like easy."

"Like easy women?" Amanda quipped.

"Exactly," I responded. "Happen to know any?"

"Several," she said. "But *you're* not their type."

"That's not very nice, Amanda. Why would you say that?"

Margie appearing suddenly at the table between Amanda and me, dripping water everywhere and all goose bumpy.

"What are we talking about?" she asked.

Amanda stared at Margie's breasts which were just at eye level, the nipples standing sharply in the cool morning air. "Nice tits," Amanda offered cattily as Margie picked up her towel and began drying off.

Margie looked down at her small breasts. "Thanks," she beamed, coming over and giving me a peck on the cheek. "We like them, don't we Joe?"

"Yes," I responded enthusiastically. "Very much!"

Amanda rolled her eyes and Margie picked her robe off the empty chair, pulled it on and cinched the tie.

"So what are we talking about really?" Margie said as she poured a cup of coffee, and gestured to top off Amanda's and mine. We both refused.

"Joe says you already know about the murder," Amanda pouted. "*I'm* the one who's connected around here. How did *you* find out?"

"Well," Margie said quite causally as she came and sat on my lap. "We know because... we... found... the... body!"

Amanda's eyes widened, her mouth fell open. She looked to me for confirmation. I nodded in the affirmative.

"Tell me everything!" Amanda howled.

Margie jumped off my lap and got her own chair before she launched into the details of the night before with Amanda hanging on every word.

I pushed back my chair, got up and headed for the house. I left not because I was rude, but because having been present at the discovery I knew what was about to be said and I didn't care to hear it again and because morning coffee and papaya have a magical effect on my colon -- if you get my drift.

I wasn't gone all that long and when I returned I found them discussing the murder and the possible perpetrator or perpetrators.

"I'm betting it was the husband," Margie said emphatically.

"Now there's a pedestrian thought," Amada groaned. "Can't you come up with something more original?"

"It's always the husband, isn't it Joe?"

I made my way to my chair without comment and poured a cup of coffee and sipped it slowly while their eyes watched me.

"Aren't you going to answer?" Margie finally asked.

"I don't recall a wedding ring." I said. "What makes you think she was married?"

"She wasn't wearing a ring," Margie said. "But…" Margie held up her left hand and uses her thumb to move her wedding band and expose the pale skin beneath. "I saw it when they put her on the stretcher. I'll bet the ring was inscribed. With something incriminating!"

I whistled appreciatively. "Sounds like you've already solved the crime."

My comment drew nasty looks from both of them.

"Margie," I said, "you're not planning to get involved in this thing are you?"

"Of course not!" Margie said defensively. "What makes you think we'd get involved?"

"Because I know you. And Amanda!"

"Well, obviously you don't know us well. We're just making conversation, aren't we, Amanda?"

"Absolutely," Amanda said unconvincingly.

"Uh huh," I said and began to ponder exactly *how* deeply they would get involved.

Margie you see is a little possessive about things she finds, and since she was the one that had found the body it didn't seem that out of the realm of possibilities that she might feel it was up to her to track the killer down and see that justice was done.

Unfortunately I had no hope of preventing them from discussing the murder. It was just too tempting. And so long as that was all they did – discuss the murder -- I could live with it. But would Margie be happy just discussing it? Only time would tell.

I decided to get away for awhile.

"Come on Magoo, let's take a walk," I said. "We'll leave these two alone to 'discuss' the murder."

Our Neighborhood

Generally, Magoo doesn't get a walk. He's small and our house and yard are big by Kona standards so he gets what exercise he gets by walking from room to room trying out the furniture and checking for errant doggy treats. When he does get a walk, he's very considerate and doesn't require a leash.

We headed north, walking in the street, since there are no sidewalks in Kona, and I took the opportunity to check out the neighbors' yards to see what was new. There was a new swing set in the Dickenson's yard, which must have been for the grandchildren since Abe and Dolly are into their 60s, and they were finally fixing the pool in the bungalow across the street.

We ran into Han, our gardener, who was working a few houses up and I stopped to chat with him and get updated on Mrs. Han and all the little Hans. Margie knew all their names of course, but my capacity for names is nil. Magoo took the opportunity to do his business and luckily Han had an empty sandwich bag so I got be a good neighbor.

After a few minutes of jabbering, Magoo barked to alert me to the fact that we were on a walk and that we'd been standing still longer than he'd care to, so Han and I bowed graciously to one another and Magoo and I continued on our way.

As I watched the little mutt prance along ahead of me, I reflected on how much of a mystery he still is to us. We came by him – actually Margie came by him – in a curious manner when he was already a full grown dog so he had

26

another life before this one and we sometimes discover things about him that are odd. It's probably the same with adopted children; unless you adopt a baby, you can't know what their previous life was really like.

Magoo, for instance, doesn't like bacon. Now why in the world a dog shouldn't like bacon, I can't fathom. He likes liver, beef, pork, chicken, eggs, turkey... well you get the picture. But fry him up a nice strip of bacon and he sniffs it once and turns away. I, on the other hand, love bacon; not that I get much when Margie's around. She can recite from memory the chemicals, additives, caloric content and nutritional information for bacon. And she generally does recite it whenever she catches me eating some, which doesn't ruin my enjoyment of it, but it doesn't help it either.

Another thing Magoo hates is yelling – or rather I should say arguing. If I yell 'Hi' to a neighbor over the hedge, he does nothing. If I raise my voice to tell Margie that I've already heard the nutritional content of bacon and would prefer not to hear it again, Magoo scoots under the nearest upholstered piece of furniture or under the bed – depending on where he is—and won't come out for a good long while.

I suspect this is a result of being raised in a conflicted household but we'll never really know for certain. Luckily, Margie and I seldom yell or argue, although we have been known to use sign language with one another. Magoo does not understand sign language.

Another of Magoo's quirks is his love of women – a trait I share. He tolerates men, but when a new female comes to casa Thomas, Magoo is always there to welcome her warmly. Sometimes too warmly and he has suffered rejection at the hands of cat lovers many times. He prefers to lie on Margie's side of the bed and sit in her lap and chew her panties if they are carelessly left on the floor. I assume his former mistress treated him better that her male counterpart, but again, it's just speculation.

You should also know that Magoo is something of a hero.

It was just after Margie and I got married and moved into our new digs. Middle of the night, Magoo started barking. We woke up and our first concern was an intruder. I grabbed my Louisville Slugger (which I keep handy in the closet for just such emergencies) and Margie grabbed a size five-and-a-half taupe sling back with six-inch stiletto heel (which was probably a more appropriate weapon) and we tiptoed to the living room. Magoo had preceded us and was now out by the pool barking and chasing his tail. Not that he has much of a tail.

I should confess that the Louisville Slugger is a carryover from my former life in Chicago. Kona does not have the same crime problem as The Windy City, but habits die hard and the Louisville Slugger is my response to the NRA which would have me shooting holes in everyone and everything.

It occurred to me at the time that the mutt has suddenly gone insane and I was about to tell Margie my suspicion when she observed there was a strange glow out there. We dashed outside to discover a conflagration – that's a fire in case you didn't know – blazing on the side of our neighbors' house.

Margie dropped her shoe and dashed toward the neighbor's yelling for me to call 9-1-1.

Well of course I didn't have to be told that. I made the call, and then hustled my butt over to the neighbor's. Margie had already roused Mr. and Mrs. Yang and was comforting them as Mrs. Yang screamed and cried and Mr. Yang just stood there a bit dumbfounded.

The fire department arrived and quickly doused the flames and Margie and I were applauded for our efforts. We made certain, however, that everyone knew that the real hero was Magoo and he got a well-deserved write-up in the newspaper. The Yang's moved out shortly after the fire, but before they did they made a sizeable donation to the local humane society in Magoo's name.

Reflecting on the near tragedy next door helped me put things in perspective. How much trouble could Margie really get into by playing detective after all? It wasn't like she was going to get seriously involved. She and Amanda were just bored and wanted something exciting to do. So once I'd reasoned my way through Margie's obsession, I calmed down. And since I was getting tired of walking, and the sun was warming up, Magoo and I headed back to the house.

Margie and Amanda were still out by the pool, yakking away, so after getting a treat for Magoo in the kitchen, I went and joined them.

I could tell they switched subjects as soon as I got close -- I told you they were not going to let this murder thing slide – and were chatting on about the new neighbors, Stan and Monica from Saskatoon. Amanda was of the opinion that Monica was a bitch and Margie, though falling short of agreeing with that, did think the woman wore too much makeup and was none too friendly.

I slipped into my usual chair and took up the paper to read the foreclosure listings. Not that I was in the market for a foreclosure, it just seemed more interesting than what the ladies were discussing, and I was relieved when Margie announced she was going to go and dress.

For several minutes I sat quietly with Amanda. She read her Wall Street Journal, while I pretended to read the foreclosures. In the background, the distant buzz of a leaf-blower mixed with the sound of a lawnmower.

"You and Pete got any plans for the holidays?" I asked casually after awhile. Pete is Amanda's husband and my bff, if men can have bff's. It doesn't seem right somehow, but I'm out of the loop, so write me. Don't text me; I don't have a cell phone. Neither does Margie. This is one of the many things she and I agree on. Cell phones are just long leashes that prevent one from having any real freedom and they were developed by and are marketed by the devil for evil purposes.

Amanda made an unpleasant snorting sound in response to my question and finished with: "My brother's flying in."

"Really," I said. "I didn't know you had a brother."

Margie reappeared suddenly at the table, 'dressed' now in a pink sundress, with white flip flops, and simple gold cross earrings and a necklace. Her hair was nearly dry, but she fluffed it a few times to hurry it along.

"What are we talking about now?"

"Amanda's brother," I said. "He's coming for Thanksgiving."

"Nicky?" Margie squealed. "Oh, he's soooo sweet!"

I didn't actually see it, but I felt Amanda roll her eyes.

"Perhaps he can stay with you if you like him that much," Amanda said dryly.

Obviously there were unresolved issues between these siblings.

"Well..." Margie started as if she might actually be considering the idea.

"Oh no," I roared a little too forcefully. "No house guests! Margie and I are going to be alone. Just the two of us. It'll be quiet. It'll be peaceful. For the first time in ages, I'm actually looking forward to the holidays!"

Margie's face sprouted that look of confusion reserved exclusively for times when I've made a major faux pas, and Amanda's mug swelled into a self-satisfied smirk. Clearly they knew something that I didn't and as you can imagine that frightened me.

"What?" I asked, looking quickly from one to the other then back to Amanda for help. Amanda, of course, knew exactly what was happening and had all she could do to keep from laughing out loud and spewing a mouth full of hot coffee across the table like Shamu at SeaWorld.

"What am I going to do with you, Joe?" Margie said, shaking her head sadly. "Don't you remember? My parents? We're picking them up at the airport at seven-thirty?"

My mouth didn't actually fall open, but it certainly could have. In any event I was entirely bewildered. To say I'd forgotten about her parents' arrival wouldn't be entirely untrue; you see until that very moment I'd been living under the impression that Margie's mother and father had been dead for years.

"Parents?" I stammered finally in a voice that was only just audible.

"Yes, parents," Margie reiterated, her tone reflecting her irritation with me. "At seven-thirty." She shook her head again and turned to Amanda.

"Men! They never listen!"

A Friend in Need

The Sogol house is only a few steps from ours: up our driveway, across the street and one house over. It's built backwards as compared to our house, by which I mean the pool is in the front of the house surrounded by a large lanai that is open to the street so the view from their lanai

31

is nearly identical to ours except it includes our house and our pool house/guest room roof.

I went around to the side door near the garage and leaned hard on the bell. I knew the door was unlocked, but I liked to hear the bell chime those first few bars of 'Some Enchanted Evening.' It wasn't because I like the tune, but because Pete found it so annoying. Amanda, however, had insisted on it. She's a sentimentalist and loved the tune from *South Pacific* because it was the play that was showing at the community theatre where Pete and Amanda had their first date. So Pete was stuck with it, probably forever.

Eventually I heard a thump, then muttering, then footsteps, and finally the door opened to reveal Peter Sogo -- Amanda's, balding, paunchy, pale, be-speckled husband -- wiping his hands on a dirty towel.

One word escaped me as I pushed past him and headed for the kitchen: "Cookie."

Pete quickly fell in behind me. "What's wrong now?" he offered sympathetically.

As I mentioned, Pete is my BFF or at least he was the buddy I turned to when things get tough and I like to think the feeling is mutual. It's kind of odd that I feel so close to him since we've known each other less than a year – I met Pete about the same time I met Margie -- but we clicked and we've spent many happy hours watching college and professional sports, drinking by the pool, and making trips to the hardware store. Actually they are Pete's trips to the hardware store. I just tag along for moral support.

I reached the kitchen and saw the cabinet doors under the sink were open and repairs were in progress. I don't know why Pete is always trying to fix things. I know he'd like to be handy, but he isn't. He's terrible at it. It isn't a money thing. The Sogol's, like us, have plenty of money. In fact, Pete has his very own helicopter. He was a pilot in one of those wars that are constantly going on in the near to mid east. I had yet to fly with him, however, despite many invitations. It wasn't that I didn't think Pete was a competent pilot. After all, if he flew the way he fixed things, he'd already be dead. The fact is I hate flying. It makes me nervous to the point I have to take those little pills they give you at the doctor's to calm you down before they shove you into one of those MRI thingies. But enough about me.

"Stupid garbage disposal's on the blink," Pete offered by way of explanation for the repairs in progress as I crossed the room to take the big Cookie Monster cookie jar off the counter and set it on the island.

I pulled off the head and extracting two saucer-sized chocolate chip cookies, each in its own Ziploc bag. I offered one to Pete. He shook his head and knelt back on the floor in front of the sink. I unzipped one cookie and took a huge bite. As I chewed I felt the calming effects of refined sugar and cocoa beans surge through my veins. It was exhilarating.

"Milk?" I asked without swallowing.

"You know where it's at." Pete said, sitting down and rolling over to lie on his back and slide under the sink. I went to the fridge and got a carton of milk and came over and sat on the floor next to him. I drank from the carton and munched my cookie.

"Could you hand me that thingy?" Pete's hand reached out from under the sink. I looked about at the pile of tools strewn on the floor, selected what I thought might be the appropriate 'thingy' and placed it in Pete's hand. I unzipped the second cookie and began to devour it greedily.

"Margie's parents are coming?" I said matter-of-factly, although it certainly was anything but matter-of-factly to me.

Pete came up quick, bumping his head. "Shit," he howled as he pulled himself from under the sink and rubbed his forehead. "The Squabbles?"

I began to choke, and Pete pounded me on the back till I could breathe again. I thanked him, and then repeated his evaluation of my impending guests in a voice quivering with apprehension: "The Squabbles?"

Pete dove back under the sink. "That's what Amanda and me call 'em."

I heard a tool drop.

"Say could you hand me that clampy looking thing?"

I found something that looked 'clampy' and handed it to Pete. I leaned against the cupboard and stared across the cool tile floor. I would have gotten a third cookie, but my legs didn't seem to want to work at the moment.

As I sat there on the floor with Pete and wondered why Margie had never mentioned her parents and why they should be referred to as 'The Squabbles' -- as if it needed more explanation than that – back at my house Amanda and Margie had come to an agreement on what they were going to do to solve the mystery that had landed so considerately in their laps.

Thanks to Amanda's connections in the police department, they had learned several pieces of evidence. One thing was that the dead woman's name was Julia McMan. The second thing was that she was on the faculty at Collette College in Louisiana. And the third thing was that she had not been sexually molested – a fact for which Margie and Amanda where grateful. As you may note, this wasn't much information to begin a murder investigation, but it was more than anyone else had at the moment. The local paper was preparing a story that read 'Mystery Woman Found Dead on Kona Fairway.'

"Two hours," Amanda said as she gathered up her Wall Street Journal and headed for the door. "We'll meet back here in two hours and compare notes. Agreed?"

"Okey doke," Margie piped with her usual enthusiasm. "But don't say anything to Joe. He's happier when he only thinks I'm doing something he disapproves of than when he knows I am."

"Mum's the word," Amanda said and tapped away happily toward home and her computer and the infamous, all-knowing Internet – which in Margie's opinion, like cell phones, is a tool of the devil.

Margie picked up the morning breakfast dishes and returned to the house. Unlike Amanda who was certain the answer could be found by Googling the right combination of words, Margie didn't have any clear idea how she was going to research the dead woman. As noted above, the only real pieces of information they had were her name and that she was on the faculty at that college in Louisiana. Not much to go on. What was she doing on the island? That seemed to be the first question to answer. But what else?

Not to be discouraged, Margie did what she often does when she wants to do some serious thinking; she headed to the bathroom and our big Jacuzzi.

As she soaked and listened to the Beach Boys (she's a big fan and claims she actually partied with them way back when), it occurred to her that both she and Amanda had overlooked something of significant importance. Women have friends!

Not that men don't have friends, of course, but a women's friends are different. A woman's friends are family. Even closer than that, they're a combination therapist, marriage counselor, physician, and what-have-you. Women tell their friends everything. And so it occurred to Margie that if she could only talk to Julia's friends – you'll note she was already on a first name basis with the victim -- she might learn a great deal.

So who were Julia's friends? That's not the sort of thing you can find on the Internet. Well, I guess you can find such things on Facebook or one of those other social networks, but what was the chance Julia was on those? Had Detective Lo already talked to her friends? Would they cooperate?

Margie left the tub and found her robe, wrapped her head in a towel and headed for the living room. She was still dripping water when she got connected to the chairman of the geophysics department at Collette College where Julia was on the faculty.

She reached Dr. Moot, a pretentious sounding bore, without too much trouble, but he wasn't helpful at all and transferred Margie back to his secretary, Abigail Swain. Abigail is a name you don't hear much anymore but it's got a certain punch to it don't you think? And Abigail as it turned out was very helpful. Having only just heard of the murder she expressed genuine shock and dismay. Dr. McMan was well liked according to Abigail, and hadn't an enemy in the world with the exception of that 'silly grad student' who was sleeping with her husband.

Abby – as she was now known to Margie, since they had become instant BFFs -- gave Margie quite a bit of information and the names and numbers of three of Julia's close friends that she knew about. There were loads of others, Abby swore, but she didn't have names and numbers for them. And so Margie rang off with the promise to keep Abby informed about the progress of the

36

murder 'investigation.' Note that Margie actually used the term *investigation* in reference to her search for information. A sure sign there was trouble ahead. What form it would take could not have been grasped at the time.

The first call was to a woman named Mary Kohl who was an old college roommate. It was five hours earlier in the Midwest so Mary's machine picked up and Margie left a message.

The second call, to Cindi Alba, a girl whom Abby claimed had worked with Julia before she'd come to Collette, also got a machine and again Margie left a message.

The third call was a charm. Margie connected with Nance Dorfman who Abby described as Julia's friend since childhood. Nance picked up on the third ring, her voice raspy and choked with a cold and post nasal drip.

Margie introduced herself and explained why she was calling and after some initial hesitancy and cautiousness, Nance opened up. I won't bore you with all the information Margie obtained since much of it is not germane to the murder. It was just stuff like Julia's first crush, her first prom date, and so on. But Margie is one shrewd cookie and rather than try to direct the conversation, she just let Nance spill her guts, and jotted down anything that might be relevant on a big yellow legal pad.

Forty minutes later, Margie heard the telltale clicking noise on Nance's line that signified an incoming call and took the opportunity to stop– with an invitation to call her back anytime about anything.

After she hung up, Margie turned her attention to the legal pad and made a few notes as she reviewed things. She looked at the clock above the mantel. Twelve minutes till Amanda returned. Just enough time to throw something on.

Bad Guys Too

Of course Amanda and Margie weren't the only people interested in the murder. There were also those who would prefer no one learned anything about it.

On the other side of the island Kanoa sat on the stump of a Koa tree under the shade of a large eucalyptus and ate his lunch slowly. He'd been chasing wild pigs up and down the hills all morning and he was tired. He'd heard them close by several times, but hadn't managed to get near enough to kill one with the club. But he would. Kanoa was a skilled hunter, and when he put his mind to a task, he succeeded.

Kanoa's meal consisted of fish and poi, which had been the staple of Hawaiian cooking from before his ancestors followed the glow that Pele – Goddess of fire – lit on Mauna Kea from Polynesia a thousand miles distant and settled on the Big Island, which in Hawaiian is pronounced *Havaii*.

At six-foot three and 300 pounds Kanoa was an imposing figure, even for a Hawaiian. His bulk was all muscle, and as you can imagine, he stood out from others.

Unfortunately, Kanoa -- whose name in Hawaiian means 'the free one' -- was not a happy man and he did not feel at all free. He had let fill his heart fill with anger, and you could see anger in his eyes. It was the anger that men have when they think they've been cheated; when they think their lives might have been better 'if only.'

The 'if only' in Kanoa's life, was what he saw as the rape of Havaii by the westerners and the overthrow of the monarchy in 1893. It was an anger instilled in him by his mother and his father who had, like him, lived poorly, disenfranchised by circumstance and the greed of those who came to Havaii early on.

Kanoa believed he was descended from chiefs. This was something his parents told him; though in truth he was not and was in fact only a little more than half Hawaiian. His great grandfather on his mother's side had been Samoan, and his great grandmother on his father's side had been Chinese. Even had he known this, it would have made no difference. He had been born a Hawaiian. He'd lived his life as a Hawaiian. And Hawaii belonged to him and his heirs and not to those whose skin was white or yellow or black. His parents had told him that if it had not been for the invaders they could live as their ancestors had. They would have a home by the ocean and eat freely of turtles and fish and mangos and poi.

Kanoa had never managed to learn the truth about Hawaii. About the chieftains (Ali'i) who ruled with fierce power and controlled every aspect of the lives of their serfs, which was the blood that flowed through Kanoa's veins. Had he lived two hundred years earlier, he might have been killed for coming into the woods to hunt food; he would have been clubbed and his body thrown into the sea so that his soul would forever wander. He would not have been allowed to hunt or fish, but instead he would have spent his days in back-breaking labor keeping the taro fields cleared or stocking the fishponds for the royals and their alii or carrying wood for them or building walls for them or losing his life in wars for them. And his only reward would be to sleep in a tiny shelter and eat poi twice a day.

But Kanoa had never learned that. He had seen a movie when he was fifteen with Mel Gibson in it. He liked Mel Gibson because he had made a movie about a great warrior who had taken on the English – William

Wallace. But in this movie – it was called 'Mutiny on the Bounty' but Kanoa had forgotten that -- the ship which Mel Gibson sailed on had been greeted by happy, beautiful, healthy natives. It didn't matter to Kanoa the movie took place in Polynesia. For Kanoa, this was the image of Hawaii he held, a Hollywood image, one that never existed. But it was the one he chose to believe because it was splendid and beautiful and much more fulfilling than the life he was leading and because he wanted to believe it with all his heart.

In keeping with his vision, Kanoa had become a member of a group devoted to restoring the Hawaiian monarchy overthrown in 1893. Kanoa was actually a part of a very small splinter group that advocated a violent reclamation of Hawaii. It was such a small group that it was nearly invisible. The police knew of its existence but paid little attention to it since they had not found any evidence that the group was involved in violent acts. As long as they talked big, nothing would come of them. But Kanoa knew the police were very wrong.

Sitting on the stump and eating his meal, Kanoa thought how wonderful it would be when they had triumphed.

Although he had yet to take a wife, Kanoa imagined the day when he would bring his young sons out into the forest to hunt with him and how he would teach them the skills his father had taught him, and his fathers' father had taught before that.

Though he was a clever man, and intelligent, Kanoa was naive to imagine that someday the people who lived and worked in Hawaii would leave. They had the power: politically, socially, and economically. Returning Hawaii -- even a part of it -- to native Hawaiians was as likely as returning the Americas to the American Indians. The time had passed. Most Hawaiians knew that, accepted it, and moved on with their lives. But Kanoa could not.

Kanoa read the papers. Violent minorities in other parts of the world were making changes. Al-Qaeda had taken on the U.S. with acts of terrorism and sent the nation into a depression. Kanoa envisioned performing similar attacks but he did not realize how futile they would be. You cannot hide well on an island; it is too small. You need the vastness of Afghanistan and the protection of Pakistani, Iraq, and Iranian Muslims.

Still, he felt that one day he and those like him would make a mark. But to do that they would need money. And money Kanoa had discovered was not so difficult to obtain. There was lots of money on the Big Island – if you knew where to look.

Where to look, was in the drugs: ICE, crystal meth, marijuana, cocaine, all were sources of money. Easy money.

His Hawaiian heritage frowned on the use of drugs other than for medicinal use or religious ceremonies and the fact that most of the clients for his drugs had some Hawaiian blood in their veins, saddened him. But he rationalized that no true Hawaiian would use drugs – only the weak, the impure, or the mixed-race Hawaiian's would do so. And as for the whites and other non-Hawaiians that lost their homes and families and even their lives to the drugs, Kanoa felt nothing. No, not nothing really. He felt gratified. He felt gratified that they should experience what it was like to lose everything and have nothing.

These were his thoughts as he sat on the stump and ate his lunch until he heard the Jeep. He could hear the Jeep long before he could see it and watched indifferently as it crawled the last few yards up the makeshift road. Even four-wheel vehicles had to drive slowly on that road. He'd left it that way on purpose. If they couldn't bring vehicles up to the shack, they'd have to come on foot. 'They' being the authorities, the feds, or anyone else.

The driver of this Jeep was a man named Duncan Snell. He was a haole [pronounced: *howlee*], which is the name Hawaiian's use to refer to anyone not born on the islands. Duncan was tall and wiry and had a huge scar down his back where they had operated to fix a spine that looked more like the letter 's' than an 'i.' He had longish, dirty blonde hair and a scraggly beard. He had big hands and big feet and big teeth when he grinned, which was most of the time.

If you sized Duncan up quickly, you'd think he was a slightly deformed half-wit. But you'd be wrong. Despite his physical deformity, Duncan was strong; Kanoa had seen him pick up a man twice his size and slam him to the ground.

Duncan was not a half-wit either, though he played the part when it suited his purpose. He was shrewd and smart and had been trafficking in drugs since he was sixteen and had never spent a night in jail, though many of his associates were doing hard time.

Kanoa had been introduced to Duncan through a friend and although Kanoa hated Duncan he needed him. Duncan was the man. He had direct contact with the 'big guy,' who paid them money and for whom they worked. Kanoa had never met the 'big guy' and figured Duncan hadn't either. But he had heard him talk to him on the cell phone.

With Duncan was a man named Kracker. Kracker was not a haole, but he was not Hawaiian. He was Asian. Mixed Chinese and Japanese. He was small and slightly built. When he fought it was with a knife or a machete or a gun. Kanoa could tolerate Kracker. At least Kracker ate poi.

Kanoa left his seat to meet the visitors when the Jeep finally reached the parking spot under a big Koa tree and Duncan turned off the engine.

Kracker waved. Duncan grinned. The men exited from either side. Kracker went to the back of the Jeep, Duncan walked toward Kanoa.

"How's the pussy," Duncan called as he walked. It was Duncan's standard greeting.

Kanoa thought it stupid and crude but he gave the answer Duncan liked. "Wet and willin'."

Duncan smiled and slapped Kanoa on the shoulder. "We got a problem," Duncan said as he loosely turning Kanoa with his hand so that the big Hawaiian started walking with him toward the shack.

"What' that?" Kanoa asked. He wanted to brush Duncan's hand off his shoulder but he didn't.

"Our buddy got hisself jailed," Duncan said.

Kanoa looked at Duncan's face. Duncan was still grinning.

"Feds?" Kanoa asked.

"Naw," Duncan said. "Police think he dusted his wife. Without that little cock we got nothing."

Kanoa shrugged. "Not my prob'em. I bring the beans and move the stuff. That's what you ask. That what I do."

They had reached the door of the shack and entered. Duncan took his hand off Kanoa's shoulder and went to lean against a burlap bag of coffee.

"This the Kona?" Duncan asked, patting it gently.

"Yeah," Kanoa answered. "It's all Kona."

Duncan looked about as if calculating the volume. "How much?"

"Just over six." Kanoa said.

"Thousand?"

"Yeah."

"Nice." Duncan crossed his arms over his chest. "You know anyone on the Kona side could help us with the problem?"

"Do what?" Kanoa asked.

"Spring our friend," Duncan said.

"Hire a lawyer," Kanoa said.

"He already did that," Duncan said.

"What else was you thinkin'?" Kanoa asked.

"I don't know. That's why I'm asking."

"You can't bust 'im out. Island's too small for that shit. Anybody breaks out 'a jail or prison they jus' get caught again. No place to run. No place to hide. It's an island."

Duncan fingered his beard and looked up at the thatched roof.

"The big guy is worried and that makes me worry. Which should make you worry."

"Kanoa not worry. Nobody figure t'ings out. Da cops is stupid."

"Hey. Don't underestimate 'em. They may be dumb as shit, but they got lots of time to screw around and make trouble. We don't need trouble."

"So what you gonna do?"

"I'm not sure, but I think you and I ought to take a drive over to Kona and look around. You know some place we can stay over there?"

"I got a cousin live mauka."

Duncan dug out his cell phone. "Give him a call."

Kanoa ignored the invitation. "Got no phone, but I always welcome. Lemme get a few t'ings."

Kanoa started to leave.

44

"No phone. I'll bet he ain't got a crapper either," Duncan said with distain.

"He got a crapper," Kanoa said. "Big log out back."

Kanoa cackled as Duncan pocketed his phone and sneered.

Kracker appeared at the door with two coffee bags. He entered and dropped them on the floor then went back out. "Two hundred. Want to weigh it?"

"Later," Kanoa said. "Where' the supplies?"

"Jeep," Kracker answered.

"I'll give you a hand," Kanoa said, and Kracker and Kanoa left the shack to Duncan as he was just lighting a roach.

That's Cute?

While Margie was occupied with her search and Amanda Googled everything she could think of, Pete and I sat with our drinks out by his pool overlooking south Kona. The *Wind Skiffer*, the island's popular snorkel cruise ship, was just returning from its morning voyage, which meant it was about eleven thirty.

I took a gulp of scotch – which wasn't nearly as therapeutic as the cookies -- but more manly. Pete nursed a local beer.

"You really didn't know her parents were alive?"

I'd already admitted this, yet Pete insisted on asking again.

"She's never mentioned them. They weren't at the wedding. How was I supposed to know?"

Pete whistled and shook his head. "You didn't tell *her* that did you?"

"I'm not stupid!" I shot back.

I thought to myself, and then asked aloud: "What else do you suppose she's 'forgotten' to tell me?"

"No way to really know," Pete said with a tinge of awe in his voice. "It's just the way she is."

He took another sip of beer.

"I remember when we first moved here, Margie thought she'd invited us to dinner. Of course she hadn't, so we didn't show up. Well that upset her and she figured we were rude people so she gave us the cold shoulder. We thought she was snooty because she wouldn't talk to us. It wasn't till the Nolte's house blew up six months later that we started talking and figured out what had happened."

Pete took a deep breath. "Actually, though, I think it's kind of cute."

"Cute?" I said with astonishment. "I don't think you know what that word means. How about annoying? How about disconcerting? How about frightening?"

"Well," Pete started, "having a wife who doesn't tell you every little thing is better than a wife who tells you everything...in great detail...till you're so sick of hearing about it you just want to..."

I tuned Pete out. I'd heard this tirade before – from both sides. The truth is, Margie's 'forgetfulness' is one of many things that make her interesting. I don't know about you, but I enjoy people who have a quirk or two, just so long as the quirk isn't being totally nuts. But I must insist that Margie's 'forgetfulness' isn't cute but it *is* annoying. Annoying as hell!

The truth is Margie is capable of having a passionate conversation with anyone about anything without including that person themselves in the conversation. To put it another way; Margie has conversations that occur only in her head. Oh, she thinks these talks really happen, but of course they don't, and trying to convince her otherwise is a losing battle fraught with relationship danger.

The first time it happened to me was about the money. I knew when we met that Margie was my financial better. She and Frank had a nice place here in Kona and I assumed an equally nice place in L.A. – which was home for them. I also knew that Frank's life insurance had paid off the house in Kona, the car, and all the other bills – Margie told me this. Of course the insurance company fought to deny the payment because they said Frank died during the commission of a felony, but eventually they had to shell out because Margie's attorney pointed that Frank was never convicted of a felony; he died before there was a trial.

What I didn't know, and what Margie had 'forgotten' to tell me – although she'll argue to the death that she did tell me – was that she herself was worth millions!

Obviously Frank was as clueless about it as I was. If he had known about Margie's money he'd never have tried to kill me. He could have won half of her fortune in any divorce settlement. So when I found out, I felt kind of sorry for poor Frank and Jillian. But not all that much.

Of course finding out Margie had twenty million dollars was nicer than finding out her parents were coming to stay for Thanksgiving!

"I wish Margie had a diary I could read," I said, suddenly aware that Pete had ended his tirade against Amanda.

"That would be useful," Pete acknowledged. "Have you looked for one?"

In fact, I hadn't. "I guess I'd better put that on my 'to do list.'" I said, sipping my scotch.

"I suppose I should be happy her parents are alive. Family's important. I mean... How bad can they be? Honestly?"

I looked over at Pete optimistically. He was trying to put on a poker face but he's got a lousy poker face. You could tell he didn't want to answer me but I waited. Pete can't leave a question unanswered.

"Well," he finally offered, "I wouldn't call them horrible."

Unfortunately I was hoping for something more consoling.

"You call them 'The Squabbles,'" I reminded him.

"Yeah, well, they have a little problem with each other."

"So they fight all the time?"

"Not all the time, just..." Pete said quickly then paused. "Yeah, pretty much all the time."

I gulped down the remainder of my scotch and stared ahead.

"I suppose they're staying through New Year's," Pete said.

I shot forward in my chair and looked at him with astonishment. He wouldn't meet my eyes.

"That's...that's... six weeks?" I stuttered. (Please don't be impressed; anyone could have done the math.)

"That's how long they stayed last time."

I set my glass down, stood up and started for the house.

"Hey, where ya' going?" Pete called.

"Cookie!" I said, staggering forward. I wondered briefly if there were enough cookies on the whole island to soothe my concern.

Eventually I got my fill of cookies and Pete and I tired of the pool and retired to the amusement room where we watched a pathetic college football game. It was so pathetic I won't name the teams out of respect for the students at those schools and the fear of libel.

Meanwhile back at my place, Amanda was feeling pretty cocky when she breezed in the door. She'd managed to unearth quite a bit of information about Julia and her husband and the conference – which is what brought her to the island in the first place -- and whatnot on the Internet. But when Margie unveiled her information, it simply blew her away.

"How did you find all this out?" Amanda demanded as she scanned the legal pad and Margie's copious notes.

"Oh," Margie said. "I just made a few phone calls."

This was true enough, but it didn't seem believable. The fact is Margie had gotten lucky. So when Margie saw how badly Amanda felt, she filled her in on the details of how she'd acquired the information, which probably didn't help much but did make it seem more palatable.

While Pete and I were watching football, Amanda and Margie spent the time comparing notes and prioritizing information looking for clues and a path to follow to pursue the next lead.

The problem was that while they'd managed to gather a lot of information in a short time, it wasn't all that relevant and there certainly wasn't any clear path of action.

"What we need," Margie argued, "is more information on the time and place of the murder and whether or not Julia's husband has an alibi."

"And how to you propose we get that information," Amanda asked.

"I'm not sure," Margie responded. "I think we need to question one of the insiders. That's what the police do.

They find a suspect and grill them and work the case from the inside out.

"How do you know that?" Amanda said.

"Perry Mason," Margie said. "And Agatha Christy. I know we won't find that on the Internet."

Amanda took some offense to the reference to the Internet, but said nothing.

Little did they know at the time that fate would soon play a role in finding them the ultimate insider.

After the horrible game I mentioned had ended, I headed home and found Margie in the kitchen loading dishes in the dishwasher. Magoo was there as usual, hoping something would fall from the sky – or off a countertop. Amanda was leaning against the counter. They both were silent and looked guilty when I entered so I was certain they had been discussing the murder. I decided not to call them on it since they would just deny it and I didn't feel like arguing.

"Who won?" Amanda asked with no real interest in her voice.

"No one," I said honestly. "They stunk so bad both teams had to do fifty laps around the stadium."

"Really?" Margie was quite amazed at this.

Margie's not into male team sports. She's very athletic and plays individual sports like tennis and swimming and stuff, but football, baseball, and especially basketball are a mystery to her. I apologized to her for the exaggeration and confusion.

The phone rang and Margie went to answer. Amanda and I followed along. I because I wanted to find out what Margie was planning for dinner and Amanda probably because she didn't want to be left alone in the kitchen.

"By the way," I said to Amanda as we walked, "I'm supposed to tell you we're going to Home Depot to get a part."

Amanda rolled her eyes. She does a lot of eye rolling. She's got great eyes for it.

"For the disposal?"

"I guess," I said. "I'm just the helper. I really don't have any pertinent knowledge."

We found Margie in the living room sitting on the arm of the sofa; she looked anxious and tapped her foot nervously. These, I had learned, were not good signs. Whoever was on the other end of the phone was upsetting her and it soon became apparent who that person was.

"Dad!" Margie's tone was emphatic. "Dad! Listen to me. Getting mad is not going to help. Just settle down."

It occurred to me that now was an opportune time to ask Amanda a question that had gone unasked far too long.

"Why is Pete always fixing things?"

Amanda shrugged and shook her head. "I have no idea. Maybe it makes him feel manly."

Her tone clearly showed her dislike for Pete's avocation.

I pondered her response as Margie attempted to get her father to listen.

"Dad! Dad! If you do that, they will... Dad! Dad! Put mom on the phone. Yes, mom. Please just settle down and put..." She must have succeeded in getting mom on the line because the next words were: "Mom? Mom, can't you get him to... NO! Don't call him that. He hates it when you..."

It didn't appear to me that Margie's mother would be able to resolve the problem, whatever it was.

"I don't fix things and I feel manly," I confessed to Amanda.

"Pete had a distant father," Amanda offered in lieu of a real explanation. "I suppose I'll eventually need a plumber. Know anyone?"

"No," I said truthfully. "Margie may."

It seemed that Margie had lost her connection.

"Hello? Hello? Hello?" Margie hung up the phone and looked up depressed.

"Problems?" I asked, trying not to sound cynical but failing badly.

"We got cut off. They're stuck in Honolulu. Dad lost it with the airlines and now the TSA is holding him. I need to call Dallas."

"Dallas?" The reference escaped me.

Margie picked up the phone and started to dial. "Dad's attorney," Margie obligingly clarified with a hint of 'you know that, I told you before.'

Of course this was something I didn't know.

"What a shame," I said in what I hoped was a consoling tone. I felt it was best if I left before I learned too much.

"Well, I'm off to Home Depot," I said brightly and headed for the door.

Margie started: "I'm going for a run just as soon as ..."

Her conversation with me was interrupted by the party she was calling. "Hello. Yes. This is Margie Thomas, Maxwell Moore's daughter. I'd like to speak to Steve Davern. It's urgent. Very, very urgent."

With great care, I shut the door behind me before any of the craziness could escape.

For many men, warehouse-sized hardware stores are a source of comfort where male hormones can run and mingle with tools and building products and whatnot.

52

For me, however, such places are a confusing jumble of items that beg the question: *What on earth is that for?*

Pete is at home here -- at least he pretends to be at home here based on the number of trips he makes in a week. I am not handy and have no desire to be handy. I'm very intimidated by handy people. It's as if they have a gene that's missing from my chromosomes.

We were standing in the plumbing aisle at the moment – at least that was my assumption -- and Pete was holding some old parts and looking around. I was focused on Pete.

"There holding them in Honolulu," I emphasized. "They'll never get on the evening flight. It's at least a twelve hour reprieve! Why don't you and Amanda come over for dinner and drinks to celebrate?"

Pete wasn't paying much attention to me; he was trying to find parts.

"I don't know. Whatcha' havin'?" Pete asked distractedly.

"What do you want?" I asked, seeing an opportunity to engage him.

"Steak," Pete said flatly.

"You know Margie won't let me cook steak," I said. "How about mahi mahi?"

"Fish? Don't you ever get tired of that vegetarian crap?"

"It's not so bad," I lied. "I thought you liked fish?"

A young clerk, maybe fifteen with a buzz cut and a tattoo on his neck tried to pass by. Pete confronted him and held up the parts in his hand.

"You got any of these?"

The clerk took the parts and turned them around 180 degrees.

"Yeah, over here," he said. "But I think you gotta buy they whole thing."

He led us up the aisle. I was still working the barbecue idea. "So, what do you say?"

"I don't know," Pete stalled. "Let me think about it."

The clerk stopped in front of a rack of boxes. "Here 'ya are."

Pete looked down and grimaced. "Eighty-eight bucks?"

I thought I had a deal maker idea. "I'll make long islands," I said. "You know what happens when Amanda drinks long islands."

Pete took the box off the rack, turned and twisted it and examined the label.

"What time you want us there?"

I returned from my excursion with Pete to find a bland, white four-door vehicle that screamed 'Rental Car' parked in our driveway. This did not bode well and my immediate fear was that somehow Ma and Pa Squabble had escaped Honolulu and were already here—which would have been physically impossible since I'd only been gone an hour or so. Still, I'm a worrier, so I worried.

I entered the house cautiously and found Margie in the living room still in her running togs, holding the phone, tapping her foot nervously.

"Whose car?" I said softly, though I was certain I didn't want to know.

Margie raised her finger to ask for silence. I obliged. It was apparent she was talking to someone at the Honolulu airport. I only heard one side of the conversation, but it seemed terse.

"Okay. Okay. Yes, I know he's difficult. I'll get him to do it. No. Yes. Of course. Tell me about it, I lived with him for eighteen years. No. Okay, I'll hold."

Margie put the phone against her chest and looked at me quizzically. She'd obviously forgotten my question.

"Car?" I asked. "Whose?"

"Oh, that's Trisha's." Margie motioned in the direction of the pool. "Go keep her company. I made a pitcher of long islands."

I looked at my watch. "It's half-past four. You never make drinks before five," I said.

Margie put the phone to her ear and waved me along. "Just…" but she didn't finish. She was back talking to whomever. "Hello. Yes. That's the problem. I know…"

I crossed the living room, picked up the pitcher of drinks and glasses waiting on the serving tray, and headed out to the pool. I was confused and nervously expectant.

As I exited the house, I spotted the justification for the early libations. It was not the dreaded parents – which I already knew based on the phone conversation taking place.

At the table by the pool sat a thin, pale brunette no more than twenty-five dressed in a green sleeveless top and cream colored shorts. Her face was hidden by long brown hair and her knees were pulled up onto the seat of her chair and against her chest. She was toying nervously with a lock of hair.

She looked up as I approached, and I could see she'd been crying. I offered a smile and a cheery greeting.

"Aloha. I'm Joe, Margie's other half. You look like someone who could use a drink."

I put the tray down and started to put ice in a glass. Trisha continued to play with her hair. She'd yet to acknowledge me. Her gaze was far away.

"You're Trisha?" I said. Of course she was, but I had to say something.

Trisha looked up and opened her mouth to speak but before any words could escape, her lower lip began to tremble and a second later she started bawling. Big time!

"What did you say?" Margie snapped as she swept past me and gathering Trisha in her arms.

"I didn't say anything." I pleaded, opening my hands and shaking my head innocently.

"There, there. It's all right." Margie cradled Trisha and gave me an undeserved look of contempt.

"It's been a tough day. Why don't you lie down? Come along."

Margie helped Trisha to her feet and guided her toward the pool house at the far end of the yard. Magoo tagged after and I poured a long island, took a deep draught and held up the glass.

"Who the hell is Trisha?" I asked aloud, but the glass refused to answer.

An Unwelcome Guest

A bit later I caught up to Margie in the kitchen where she was cutting carrots with the passion of a French Revolution executioner.

"Who is Trisha?" I asked, trying to be nonchalant.

"Nobody," Margie said without looking up. "I found her down by Kahalu'u when I was running. She was just sitting there looking out at the ocean, crying."

Margie is a soft touch and I wasn't surprised by this reply, but I wanted more info.

"What was she crying about?"

"Oh, nothing really," Margie answered.

Nothing? That didn't ring true. People didn't sit and cry over nothing.

Margie continued to cut carrots. There were already enough for most of the island's residents and then some.

"It's her boyfriend," Margie finally admitted. "I invited her to come up and stay with us a little while, till everything gets straightened out."

"She get thrown out?" I quizzed. "He cheat on her?"

"No. Not exactly," Margie said, still paying close attention to the carrots. There was something about the way she said it and the fact that she didn't look me in the eye that had me nervous and suspicious.

"Is there something you're not telling me?" I like to be direct when I can be.

Margie finally quit cutting and started dumping carrot chunks into the colander.

"Well, okay. If you must know, her boyfriend got arrested."

"Yike," I said. "What'd he do?"

"Is that really important?" Margie said, turning toward me and putting her hands on her hips in a defensive gesture. "She's depressed. Her boyfriend's in jail and she's got no place to go. Can't we just leave it at that?"

"I could," I said, "if it wasn't obvious you're hiding something from me. Come on, what is it? What did he do?"

I suspected he'd been arrested for drugs or something serious, but I really wasn't ready for what Margie told me.

"Well," Margie said, turning back to cutting more carrots. There were now enough to pave the streets of Kona. "He got arrested for killing his wife."

I stood quietly a moment, stunned.

"You mean the woman…"

"Yes, yes. The woman we found on the golf course." Margie finished.

I flapped my mouth noiselessly then asked: "What on earth possessed you to bring her here?"

"Well, I couldn't just leave her," Margie argued. "She was crying!" Margie beheaded a few more innocent carrots.

I looked over my shoulder to make sure we were alone.

"Margie. Really," I begged. "This is not something to get involved in."

"Well, I'm not going to throw her out! Is that what you want me to do? Just throw her out?"

"No, that's not what I want you to do."

Actually it was exactly what I would have liked to happen. I sidestepped: "We'll get her a room ..."

"No we won't!" Margie chopped carrots that may or may not have symbolically represented me.

"Be reasonable Margie. She could be involved in the murder!"

Margie stopped cutting and said softly. "She's just a little girl, Joe."

I took a deep breath. I decided to try reasoning with her. It had never worked in the past, but I'm all for positive thinking.

"Little girl? She's sleeping with the victim's husband. Where I come from that's not a little girl! Look. I resigned myself to the fact that you and Amanda were going to do a little sleuthing with this murder thing. But this goes way beyond that. If detective Lo knew she was here and you were getting involved he would be very unhappy. There's such a thing as interfering with a police investigation you know."

Margie shook her knife angrily. I took a step back. Obviously Margie was passionate about her position.

"I don't give a frigging turd what detective Lo thinks. They made an arrest. As long as I don't step on their toes with respect to Kenny there's nothing they can do."

I crossed my arms in a hostile gesture. "How do you know that?" I asked, and then added: "Who's Kenny?"

"The suspect. I called Cynthia."

"Cynthia? Now you're calling our lawyer? Margie, that's the definition of involved!"

The phone rang and Margie put down the knife and made for the door.

"We'll continue this later," she said firmly.

Stymied for the moment, but unwilling to let it go, I followed Margie into the living room.

Just as Margie picked up the phone, the front door opened and Amanda breezed in followed by Pete, who carried a bottle of scotch and a bag of dinner rolls. Magoo rushed to welcome them.

Margie was soon pleading with dear old dad again. "Dad! Dad! Okay. If that's what you have to do, just do it."

Amanda swooped in close to me and whispered excitedly in my ear: "They arrested the husband!"

Normally it would have given me great joy to pop Amanda's 'I know something you don't know' bubble. But at the moment I was disinterested.

"I know," I said obnoxiously.

Amanda's eyes narrowed. I knew what she was thinking: *How can he know? This is my news.'*

"Who told you?" Amanda demanded.

"Margie."

Amanda cast an evil eye toward Margie who was trying to find privacy by walking out to the pool with the phone as she continued to argue with dear old dad who I couldn't wait to meet. Actually I could wait. I could have waited a very long time I'm sure.

"I know, Dad. Please... No, Dad. You've ... Dad! Don't be so... Dad, are you listening to me?"

Amanda demanded more information: "Where did she hear?"

"Trisha told her," I said truthfully.

Amanda's eyes said it before she spoke: "Who the hell is Trisha?"

"The mistress," I said, though actually since his wife was dead I guess she was no longer technically a mistress.

Okay, I admit it. I was playing Amanda like a pike on a minnow. It was not nice but it was fun to be on the giving end as opposed to the receiving end for a change.

Pete finally heard something of interest. "Who's got a mistress?" he asked, coming over.

"That's what I said." I offered.

Amanda was not so easily confused.

"Where did Margie meet her?"

"In the pool house," I lied. But it was an innocent lie.

Amanda gave up on me; she turned to Pete as I headed out toward the pool and Margie. I thought I should keep tabs on her conversation.

"Who's in the pool house?"

Pete shrugged, noted the open bar, and crosses over to start mixing drinks, leaving a flustered Amanda standing alone.

Twenty minutes later as I was tending the grill and Pete, with drink in hand, was supervising, I turned to spy on Amanda, Margie and Trisha who where behind us in the pool house.

"We're in trouble here, Pete" I said.

"Naw. It's okay. I like 'em blackened," Pete said happily, oblivious to my true meaning.

"Not the fish, Pete! The murder."

Pete was distractedly playing with a knob on the front of the grill. "You got a loose knob here, Joe."

"Leave it, Pete." I tried to get him to focus. "We've got to do something before it's too late."

"They're just talking," Pete offered.

"Have you ever known them to 'just talk?'"

Pete shrugged and continued to play with the knob. Once Pete is onto something, he stays with it. Getting him *onto* something isn't easy.

"You know it's impossible for Margie to keep her nose out of other peoples' business," I said. "She's not built that way. Amanda's the same."

"Where do you keep your screwdriver?" Pete would not let the loose knob go.

"In the garage, Pete. There's a big toolbox…"

Pete was already hoofing it to the garage. I turned again to look at the three women in the pool house. They were talking nonstop and I was certain I knew what they were talking about.

Our pool house – it's more of an elaborate cabana really -- is furnished with a big four-poster bed, a kitchenette with an under-counter refrigerator, a sink, a wet bar with two stools, a couple of small wingback chairs -- one with a hassock -- and a small steamer-trunk coffee table. The whole thing is open to the yard, but lacy drapes, tied back during the day, can be closed at night. We often use it for guest or on hot evenings when having walls around you is just too confining.

Amanda sat on a stool at the counter with a glass of long island ice tea. Margie lounged in one of the wingback chairs with a fruity drink in one hand and flipped through a fashion magazine with the other. Trisha lay on her stomach on the bed with her head hanging over the edge and her long hair down, obscuring her face. Her legs swung back and forth idly. Tammy Wynette/Celine

61

Dion sang in the background. Magoo was on the bed with Trisha, but he was just snoozing.

Amanda, who hadn't been there when Margie first quizzed Trisha, was playing catch-up. She'd heard the condensed version of Trisha's story from Margie but wanted to hear the whole thing from Trisha.

"Tell me what you know, Trisha, and don't leave anything out," Amanda said.

"Again," Trisha moaned. "I already told the police and Margie. It's not that much."

"Come on. I might hear something that'll help get Kenny out of jail."

Trisha sighed and turned to lie on her back, her head still over the edge of the bed so her face was upside down. "Okay," she said and began her account of what she knew so far.

She explained that she had followed Kenny to the island without him knowing. She'd been upset that he was going with his wife to the conference, but he had told her it was really to visit a 'friend' he had up near Waimea. He did not plan on spending any time with 'her.'

The conference Trisha referred to was the annual International Geophysical Symposium and Conference which was being held up at Waikoloa and at the volcano, on the other side of the island. Kenny's wife, the late Professor Julia Longly-McMan, was a keynote speaker and considered *the* foremost researcher in the fields of mineral physics, rheology, heat flow and volcanology. What exactly that meant, Trisha didn't know or care. She just knew that Julia was a total bitch and Kenny put up with a lot from her. Of course, we're only hearing one side of the story.

In any event, Trisha had rented a room under an assumed name: Katie Morgan. It wasn't till the police questioned her that she discovered her pseudonym was that of a famous, or infamous, adult film star. "It seemed like such an innocent name!"

In any event, when she contacted Kenny and told him where she was, he was upset at first, but then calmed down and came to visit during conference hours when his wife was busy. Trisha had noticed that Kenny seemed distracted and on edge and he kept stepping outside on the lanai when he took phone calls, but she assumed it was because he hadn't planned on her being there. Overall, he really hadn't spent much time with her until the night Julia was killed.

On that night, Kenny called and told his wife that he was stuck up in Waimea because he'd had too much to drink and was staying with his friend. Of course he was actually spending the night with Trisha.

"He seemed more himself that night," Trisha offered. But they had celebrated a bit too much and Trisha figured she passed out about ten. Kenny was there when she awoke about noon the next day, but he was just getting ready to leave.

"That was the night we found the body," Margie said.

Trisha said she'd spent the day in the room nursing a hangover and waiting for Kenny to return. He'd told her he'd be back about dinner time, but when the knock came on the door it wasn't Kenny but the police.

"I think they traced his cell phone traffic to find me," Trisha explained. "That's when I found out they'd arrested Kenny and taken him to jail."

Trisha relocated to the *Kona Islander* so she could visit Kenny, but they -- the police -- wouldn't let her see him or even talk on the phone. And that's when Margie found her crying on the beach.

"And now I'm here," Trisha finished.

"How much of this did you tell the police?" Amanda asked.

"I didn't have to tell them much," Trisha answered. "They seemed to know most of it."

"Do you have any idea who his friend was up in Waimea?" Amanda asked.

"Not really," Trisha said. "He just said he as an old college buddy. But it didn't sound right, and he never gave a name."

"Did you ask?"

Trisha shook her head. "When you're in a relationship like mine, there's a lot of stuff you don't ask. I didn't want to be like his wife."

Amanda thought a moment. "Do you have any idea how the body got here?"

"No," Trisha squirmed. "It sounds so bizarre."

"Any ideas about who would want to kill her? Did she have any enemies?"

"I told Margie that I think she had a lover, but Kenny never said if he knew one way or the other. They stayed together because Collette College is a very conservative institution and if they got divorced, one of them would have lost his or her position. Most likely it would have been Kenny since he was not as good at kissing up to the mucky mucks as Julia was and she had the better credentials."

"You told the police Kenny was with you all night and they still arrested him?" Amanda asked.

"Yup," Trisha sighed and turned to lie on her stomach again, her long hair again obscuring her face. "They said that since I was asleep he could have left and come back."

"That doesn't seem right," Margie said, still turning pages.

"No kidding," Trisha said.

"There must be something we can do," Amanda said.

"You'd think," Trisha said. "But what? Kenny's got a lawyer but he's no help."

Trisha rose and excused herself to visit the bathroom.

As soon as she was out of earshot, Amanda asked Margie if she thought Trisha was telling the truth.

"As much as she knows, yes," Margie said. "She told me the same stuff she told you. It doesn't sound rehearsed."

Margie stopped turning pages: "You know what. Let's take Trisha shopping after dinner! She told me she can't stand the thought of going back to the hotel and she's got nothing to wear. What do you think? That'll cheer her up. It always cheers me up."

Amanda sat up, suddenly alert: "That's a great idea! I need some new sandals anyway."

Margie gave a self satisfied smile and looked over her shoulder to where Pete and I stood over the grill.

Dinner was nearing completion so I sent Pete to tell the ladies and when they followed him back I noticed Trisha's demeanor was notably upbeat and they all looked guilty.

What have they plotted now?

Margie announced they were going shopping after dinner.

"Oh," I said innocently, trying to read the meaning behind Margie's sudden shopping urge. Margie, as a rule, isn't much of a shopper, except in catalogs, as I've already told you. But Margie had her poker face on and her poker face is good, real good.

"Trisha needs a few things," Amanda offered.

"Of course she does," I acknowledged.

They all rushed away to the house to get utensils and plates and whatever other fixing Margie had prepared for dinner.

"Pete," I said as soon as they were out of earshot. "This is serious!"

Pete was kneeling under the grill, still absorbed with the knobs. He had returned from his trip to the garage with a kitchen butter knife having failed to find my toolbox in the garage despite it being bright red and having TOOLBOX stamped on it in big, black block letters.

"What?" Pete asked.

"They're going shopping!" I said.

"That's what women do." Pete said logically.

"That's what they do when they need to be alone to plot things!" I countered.

"So what are ya gonna do?"

"I don't know," I said truthfully. " Maybe..."

"Why don't you just turn her in?" Pete said casually.

Pete caught me off guard. "Who Margie?"

"Naw. The girl. Do the police know she's here?"

I tend to forget that Pete can be something of an idiot savant at times. I smiled. Of course they didn't know she was here! But would they care?

Pete stood up grinning and holding a knob from the grill, a look of great accomplishment on his face. An instant later, flames shot high into the air.

"Whoa!" Pete yelled as we jumped out of the way. I grabbed Pete's drink and threw it on the flames. It extinguished the fire, but soaked the fish.

Carefully, we moved back to the grill and stared suspiciously down at our dinner.

I had had misgivings about the dinner, but as it turned out we had a good time. There was little conversation which is pretty unusual for a Thomas/Sogol dinner party. I didn't bring up the impending visit from Margie's parents, and nobody mentioned the murder – which I found peculiar since I knew it was on everyone's mind.

We mostly discussed the weather – which was perfect as always – and the appearance of the *Northern Star*, the cruise ship that had pulled in an hour or so ago. It was noted that the *Northern Star* was spending more time on the Kona side than usual and Pete explained that that was because it was raining and storming on the Hilo side and the poor weather was expected to continue through the week.

The ladies ate quickly and Margie started to gather dishes as soon as they were done.

"The fish was excellent tonight, Joe. What did you do?"

"Nothing really," I said, looking up innocently. "I just used Pete's secret ingredient."

Margie cast a suspicious look at Pete and from the corner of my eye I saw Amanda eye me warily. I can't read minds but I'm sure she was thinking *'Who's he kidding. Pete burns water!'* It was kind of her not to challenge me though.

Amanda got up to help Margie and so did Trisha. "It was a very tasty meal," Trisha offered. "Thank you very much."

At least she had manners.

Loaded down with plates and glasses, the ladies headed indoors and Pete, always a slow eater even though he generally offers the least in terms of conversation, continued to munch away.

"We're off!" Margie called from inside and before I could yell 'have fun' I heard the front door close.

As soon as they were gone, I stood and picked up my plate and Pete's as well. Pete looked up as if to object, but then let it slide. Pete is a most agreeable person.

"Come on," I said. "We've got a call to make to the police."

Pete did as instructed and got up and followed me and five minutes later we were in the parking lot of the Kona Shopping Center where – for some strange reason -- they still have pay phones. On the mainland the advent of the cell phone has made pay phones all but extinct, but here in Hawaii they're still around if you know where to look.

I took the phone from the hook and thrust it at Pete. He pulled back as if I'd tried to hand him a black adder.

"Why do I have to make the call?" Pete asked.

"Because Detective Lo might recognize my voice," I said.

"What if they trace the call?"

"It's a pay phone, Pete. We'll be gone in two seconds."

I held out the handset; Pete squirmed. I was beginning to think he didn't want to help.

"If you don't want to do it, just say so."

"I don't want to do it," Pete said.

I shot my 'some friend you are' look his way, shoved coins into the coin slot, and roughly punched the numbers. Yes, I do know the phone number of the police station.

Pete, relieved of any stress, buried his hands in his pockets, rocked back on his heels, and ogled a pretty blonde walking by.

As I waited for someone to pick up, I had a sudden shock. Margie hadn't said where they were going to go shopping. But before I could panic I heard "Kona precinct. Detective squad. Amado speaking."

I responded in my best falsetto. "Ola! Me speaky pleas De Tek Tive Lo? Is berry impotant."

Pete stepped back and looked at me sideways. I knew my fake accent was bad, but to be dished by Pete was a new low. I really didn't care.

Certain I'd just get shuffled to voicemail, I was startled to hear Lo's distinctive growl. "Detective Lo."

"Ola. De Tek Tive," I stammered. "I tink you like know girly friend de man who kill wife stay Margie Tomas."

He didn't quite get it so I repeated myself twice until he finally understood.

"Margie Tomas. Si."

The detective tried to get me to identify myself, but I was too cool.

"Who 'dis?" I said. "Jus a fren'."

I slammed the handset down and bolted for the car. Pete stood for a moment then sprinted after me.

As we squealed out of the parking lot, Pete stated the obvious. "If Margie ever finds out, you're a dead man." To which I responded: "If Margie ever finds out, YOU'RE a dead man!"

After ratting out Trisha, Pete and I returned to my house and sat in the big wicker lounge chairs and watched a basketball game that neither one of us really cared about and sipped the last of the 'tea' and longed for the nerve to smoke a cigar. Of course neither of us even had the nerve to buy a cigar – such is the lot of men in modern America.

A couple hours later Margie and Amanda and Trisha returned with an alarming number of bags. Amanda and Pete said goodnight and Trisha said she was tired and went to her room (a.k.a. the pool house), so Margie and I headed for the master bedroom and although it was still a tad early for bed it felt to me as if it was long overdue. It had been a stressful day to say the least.

As we changed for bed, I felt a little disappointed that nothing had come as a result of my call to Detective Lo, but I'm a big boy and used to disappointments. I wasn't about to give up, however, so I decided I'd try to get Margie to listen to my side of things one last time. As you know I was pretty unhappy with our house guest.

"You say you're not going to get involved, and then you get involved," I started.

"She's just sleeping here," Margie countered as she slipped into one of her flimsy little things that remind me of the lingerie the pinup girls on those Vargas cards wear.

"See. That's involved," I pointed out, entering the bathroom and taking up my toothbrush.

"It is not," Margie insisted. She too entered the bathroom and she too began brushing her teeth.

"Yes it is." I spit.

"No it isn't," she spit.

It seemed to me that our discussion was beginning to take on the format of a third grade 'did too' 'did not' melodrama.

I was about to try a new tactic as soon as I finished flossing when the phone rang. Margie looked at me expectantly; I returned the look. Margie was already in her nightie, I pulled at the hem of my boxers as if to say *I'm still in my boxers*. Margie knew she had to go.

"He's your father?" I called after her, since I was certain I knew who it was that was calling.

"I just talked to him," she shot back from the doorway.

I turned to Magoo. "Well, at least there's one argument I won."

I reentered the bedroom and I heard Margie pick up in the living room. "Hello?" she said with her usual perky manner. "Oh, hello detective," the tone turned frosty.

I stopped buttoning my pajama top and tiptoed to the door so I could hear better.

"What can I do for you?" Margie continued tersely.

"Yes, that's correct. Ms. Ryan is staying with us. How did you...?" Margie's tone swung back up. "Really?! That's wonderful. Yes, I'll tell her. Thank you very much!"

The grin I'd been wearing slipped away. *What was that all about?*

I heard Margie running through the house and I left the bedroom as Magoo tore past me to chase after Margie.

As I entered the empty living room, I heard shrieks from the pool house. *What the...?*

Margie suddenly appeared sprinting toward me, her face flushed with excitement. She streaked past me toward the bedroom without breaking stride. Magoo, yipping, was in hot pursuit.

"They're releasing Kenny!" Margie yelled. "I'm giving Trisha a ride to the police station."

For a moment I stood dazed, unable to comprehend what had just happened, then I turned and followed her quickly back to the bedroom, where Margie had already put on a top and was pulling on shorts. I was amazed at how thrilled she was.

"She's got her own car, you know," I said sensibly, certain it would do no good.

"She's not up to driving. Anyway, I want to meet Kenny." Margie put on a bracelet and earrings.

"You said you weren't getting involved."

"Don't be silly, I'm just giving her a lift." Margie looked in the mirror, fluffed her hair, and began to head out the door.

"I'm not waiting up for you!" I threatened.

"That's fine. I might be awhile," Margie called back. "Isn't it exciting?"

I flopped on the bed, nearly hitting Magoo, who had decided he wasn't up to more running.

"Well, old fella," I said, giving him a pat on the head. "At least we're rid of Trisha!"

No Room at the Inn

Like most men, I'm a creature of habit. I wake up every morning to the same sounds and smells and sights. For me, it's when the sun reaches high enough to reflect off the hibiscus bush outside the bedroom window and throw enough light into the bedroom to see clearly. That's about six thirty, give or take fifteen minutes depending on the season. There's also the sound of birds chirping and distant leaf-blowers and lawnmowers from the caretakers at the golf course. And last but not least, it's the smell of fresh brewed coffee wafting through the house.

After yesterday, I yearned for the morning's normal activities and a satisfied grin spread over my face as I slowly rolled out of bed, found my robe, and headed for the hot cup of Kona coffee and the newspaper that I knew await me in the kitchen.

True to form, the Kona brew was there. I poured a cup, picked the paper off the center island, and headed out to the pool as I did every morning. I was scanning the headlines as I walked through the living room when I suddenly realized I was not alone. I looked up and discovered a strange man in my path.

He was a few years younger than me and a few inches taller, with glasses, sandy hair – slightly receding – and prominent ears. He approached me with his hand out.

"Kenny McMan," he said in a husky voice. "You must be Joe. Glad to meet you."

It took him a moment to realize my hands were full and to drop his own.

"Oh, sorry; of course. Damn nice of you to open your home to Trish and me. That Margie. She's absolutely wonderful!" he continued as he hustled past me and picked up a set of keys from the table next to the door.

"I was just on my way to fetch some cream. Can I get you anything?"

Too stunned to speak, I just stood there frozen. He took that as a no, and opened the door.

"Okay then. Back in a minute."

He shut the door and left me standing in the middle of the room. It's been a long time since I cried, but at that moment I felt like I just might.

As I ate the cookie I watched Pete, who had something disassembled on the kitchen island and was closely inspecting a part from whatever it was. I had no idea what it might be.

Pete shoved the part at me. "Does that look right to you?"

I didn't answer. Pete examined it again. "What did Margie say?"

"She's not getting involved." I said mechanically.

"Well that's good isn't it?" Pete picked up another part and started to examine it.

"Pete! She's just saying that!"

"Yeah, right. Could you hand me that whatchamajiggy there?"

73

I looked behind my chair at a litter of tools, took one at random and handed it to Pete. Pete started to object, then just took it.

"She claims there were no hotel rooms."

"Well maybe..."

"On the whole island?"

I shoved the remaining half of the cookie in my pie hole and mashed it hard. I began to unwrap a second cookie.

"I've got my own troubles ya know," Pete said. "Amanda's brother is coming."

"Oh, yeah," I said sincerely. "What's he like?" I was tired of my problems and thought I'd focus on Pete's.

"Nicky? He's an 'Acktoor.' Thinks he's God's gift to women. Very self-absorbed."

Pete fiddled with the part and then added: "What's with The Squabbles?"

"Shit! I almost forgot. They're coming today!"

Pete held up another part. "That look okay to you?"

When I returned from Pete's I found Margie in the living room on the phone. I stopped to listen, but Margie turned away. *Ah, dear old dad.*

"If you don't apologize, they're not going to let you on the plane. You have to apolo... Dad! Please! Dad! Put mother on ... No! Just put ... Mom! Can't you... Mom! Stop calling him names! It's not going to help! Hello? Hello?"

Margie clicked the receiver a dozen times and let the phone drop back in its cradle. She looked up at me.

"We got cut off," she said, but her voice lacked conviction. She took a deep breath and forced herself to smile.

"They'll be here though. Dad loves the holidays. And they're dying to meet you."

"And I'm dying to meet them as well!" I said with as much sincerity as I could muster. It wasn't much.

We stood silently, each of us absorbed in our own problems. It was clear things were not going my way, so I asked Margie if we could talk.

"Okay, what about?"

"Not here," I said. "Someplace private."

I turned and headed for the den. Margie shrugged and followed me.

"Margie," I said when we were alone and I'd closed the door. It's funny, but I'd never even noticed that room had a door till just then. "Margie, I thought you promised you weren't going to get involved in this thing?"

"I'm not," Margie said.

"What do you mean 'you're not.' The prime suspect and his mistress, excuse me, girlfriend are living in our house!"

"Joe! The police let him go!"

"That doesn't make him innocent! That just means they don't have enough evidence to hold him."

"Well..." Margie stared straight through me. I could hear the wheels going. I prepared myself for her answer. "I don't think he's guilty!"

Margie crossed her arms.

"What's that suppose to mean?"

"Just that. I don't think he did it. I believe Trisha's story." Margie dropped her arms and softened her tone. "Have you even talked to him? He's very articulate. And he seems very nice. He's trying to figure out who killed his wife. It's not like he's cast her aside or anything."

I started to speak, but Margie cut me off.

"He was talking about her and he started crying. Do you hear me; he was crying. Real tears. Do you think murderers cry over their victims?"

75

"I don't know what murderers do and I don't want to find out. I want them out of the house."

I shot a steely look at Margie.

Margie returned my look. I tried to make myself look stern. I have trouble with stern. Margie knows I have trouble with stern. Margie crossed the room, reached up and put her arms around my neck, pulled herself up, and planted a big full-mouthed kiss on me.

I stood my ground – which is to say I kept my arms crossed and tried not to respond. Margie's an excellent kisser, and it was really nice, but I was seriously conflicted. One part of me wanted to sweep her up, carry her to the bedroom and… well, you can finish the sentence if you're over eighteen in most states. Another part of me was upset with her involvement with the murder and the house guests and wanted to punish her for not seeing things my way and refused to kiss her back. In reality, I think most of me resented the fact that since I was a man I was not going to be able to punish her. Men are not built that way. So I did the best I could. I just stood there and let her kiss the hell out of me, which I thought should get my point across!

Margie released me somewhat, stepping back but leaving her arms around my neck. I could smell her perfume and I could taste her lipstick – bubble gum flavor. She looked deep into my eyes for a moment with her beautiful blue orbs. Then she smiled sweetly.

"It's really too late, Joe, I already promised them they could stay till the police find the killer. But I promise not to get involved." Then she kissed me lightly on the lips again and started to go.

"But you are involved!" I yelped.

She knew she was lying, of course. But it was no use in my saying so. Margie opened the door.

"Oh, by the way, since we seem to be having a large crowd anyway I invited Amanda and Pete and Nicky to join us for Thanksgiving. Won't that be wonderful?"

Wonderful was not the appropriate word. *Please, somebody just shoot me!*

"I'm ordering pizza for lunch!" I heard her yell to those outside. "What kind do you want?"

After Margie left, I sat down on the sofa to review what had happened. I licked my lips. Privately, I admonished the traitorous part of my anatomy that was enjoying the bubble gum flavor more than seemed necessary. I took a deep breath.

Okay, so she wasn't going to be a pushover. Well neither was I. I waited a moment in the den so that Margie would know I wasn't pleased with the outcome of our discussion. But I didn't wait too long. I wanted to make sure she ordered a Hawaiian pizza (that's pineapple and Canadian bacon in case you didn't know) which is my favorite.

I sipped my scotch and watched Kenny across the table as we waited for lunch, trying my best to ignore Margie's disapproving glare. I knew I was drinking too much on an empty stomach – where the hell were those pizzas! -- but I didn't care. I'd accept the consequences later.

I was trying to figure Kenny out. He looked like an honest man – so did several serial kills I've seen on Court TV– and he appeared to be genuinely distraught over the death of his wife. They were 'real' tears in his eyes, but something wasn't right and although a part of me wanted to figure out what that was, a larger part of me was saying 'be gone!'

Fat chance of that happening.

One thing that bothered me about Kenny was that he did not seem to be what I would call a professorial type. He was smart all right. You could tell that from listening to him for just a few minutes. But he didn't look how you'd expect. Kenny was a <u>skootch</u> over six feet, and he was well tanned and athletic looking. My recollection of college professors was short dumpy men with bulging stomachs and thick glasses. Things might have changed since I was in college I guess, and of course I should have guessed he was no slouch. After all, Trisha was a very attractive young woman.

But I didn't like the way he kept eyeing Margie and Amanda – who was visiting more than usual since the murder. I know, I should be used to men ogling both of them, but to me he was still a suspect in his wife's murder and his mistress/girlfriend was sitting right next to him. I had him pegged him for a sleaze ball and I was determined to keep a close eye on him.

The conversation around the table was about the murder of course and I was the only one not involved. Not because I had nothing to say mind you but because I was morally, ethically, and spiritually against getting involved in the thing. As I said, however, it was a minority opinion.

Margie, who as you'll recall had only minutes ago promised not to get involved, seemed to be the ringleader.

"Was there anyone at the conference who was threatened by her work?" she asked Kenny.

Boy was there! Kenny dashed off a list of more than a dozen colleagues at various universities and research facilities who would have been happy to see Julia dead. People she'd 'borrowed' ideas from or whose ideas she'd ridiculed. Julia, according to Kenny, was a tenacious researcher who was also a shameless self promoter, and in addition to the professional people, there were any number of companies as well as whole countries that would have been happy to see her career abruptly ended.

Julia's research, according to Kenny, struck at the very foundation of any company or country that profited by controlling access to energy: oil companies, electric companies, mining companies, you name it. Kenny claimed that Julia was very close to finding a solution to the energy problem by making it practical to drill into the earth's mantle and tap the unlimited resources there. Anyone whose profits would crumble if unlimited energy were available simply by drilling a hole into the earth was a viable suspect according to Kenny.

This all seemed a little farfetched to me, but it was bolstered by Trisha's affirmative nods at each point. Trisha had said earlier that she didn't know much about Julia's work, so I assumed her nods were to support her lover. They carried little weight with me, but Margie and Amanda seemed to have become instant believers.

And despite my vow to stay out of the whole matter I wanted to ask: *So why wasn't Julia being guarded like the Hope diamond?* But I didn't.

Minutes later, the conversation was interrupted by the doorbell.

"I'll get it!" I said graciously, since I was certain it was the pizza delivery person. (You have to say that now because sometimes it's a man and sometimes it's a woman, but to me they'll always be 'the pizza boy.')

But Margie was already up and headed to the door.

"I'll get some plates and forks," Trisha said getting up quickly.

"I'll visit the ladies room," Amanda added.

So suddenly it was just me and Kenny staring quietly and slightly uncomfortably into space. That's what guy's do when there are no women around to direct the conversation and the television is not tuned to some sports event. Real men don't talk. Everyone knows that.

Trisha returned first and passed out plates, napkins and forks, and Amanda reappeared as well. I was just thinking *what the heck is taking Margie so long?* when she appeared with two pizza boxes and dropped them in the middle of the table.

"Do you know a man named Sam Belmont, Kenny?" she asked.

Kenny looked up, surprised. "Why, yes. Of course. He's been my wife's collaborator on virtually every paper she's published in the last ten years. Why? How did you...?"

"The police just arrested him," Margie said, "for killing Julia."

There was stunned silence. I reached across the table and found the box marked 'H' – which is how they mark the box for a Hawaiian pizza -- and opened it and pulled loose a thick, gooey piece and dropped it on my plate. I was famished.

I was about to take a bite when something stopped me. I looked up to find everyone glaring at me, and not agreeably.

"Pizza?" I said, offering the box to the others.

Magoo came over and sat back on his rump to beg. He was the only taker.

Don't Worry, Be Happy

Sam Belmont was almost sixty, but he was still lean and active and handsome. His hair had grayed to that salt and pepper mix that women seem to find especially appealing. He was a biker – no not that kind, the kind that wears those silly pants and teardrop shaped helmets.

He was also the head of the Department of Geothermal Science at a very prestigious California University whose abbreviation was not UCLS, so you know he wore a very large helmet.

Actually his helmet was large because his ego was monumental. Most people found him to be a self-centered bore and hugely arrogant, which only goes to show that in America anyone can make it to the top.

He wasn't feeling particularly arrogant at the moment. In fact he was feeling incredibly non-arrogant sitting in the small holding cell trying to wipe ink from his fingertips with a dry paper towel.

When they first arrested him, he scoffed at the idea that they had any evidence at all, but later, during the interrogation – what was that man's name? Detective Lew or something – when he'd ticked off the circumstantial evidence they had, Sam began to squirm. He should have just clammed up of course. But he was innocent and he thought that if he told them what he knew they'd just let him go. That, in retrospect, had been a terrible mistake.

It was no big deal that he was screwing Julia. Heck, half the professors he knew were screwing students, grad students, post-docs, research assistants, or colleagues. And he wasn't worried that Anna, his wife, would find out. She'd caught him before. She was never going to give up the prestige that went with being the wife of a department chair at that California University I can't mention and she'd told him that. For all Sam knew, she was screwing someone on the side. She certainly wasn't screwing him!

And it was no big deal that they'd found the angry emails on his computer from Julia. She'd been mad before when he'd 'borrowed' her ideas and incorporated them into papers without giving her credit. That's how you stayed at the front of your profession for Pete's sake. As he'd done in the past, he'd assuaged her with wine and love and pretty baubles. It always amazed him that even highly intelligent women were easily mollified by small pieces of glassy stone – if it was the right stone.

Of course without Julia to attest to the fact that they had made up, the emails did look incriminating. But that was not the biggest problem.

The biggest problem was that they'd found traces of blood in the trunk of his rental car.

He'd explained, of course, though he found it embarrassing to confess to that detective and his associate, that he liked sex in unusual places. And he liked sex in risky places. In fact, it was a big part of the relationship with Julia that she and Sam enjoyed the same kinky sexual fantasies.

It was harmless. But it was kinky. They'd had sex in airplane bathrooms of course. Who hadn't? And they'd done it in cardboard boxes, some just barely large enough for two people to squeeze into. They'd done it in a refrigerator – unplugged of course and without a 'death' door – that's what they used to call the old style refrigerators that actually locked.

None of those had been terribly risky. But they'd done it once in the cabinet at the front of the lecture hall during one of their colleagues' classes. That been spectacular! And they'd done it in a tool shed during a garden party at yet another colleagues' house. They'd done it lots and lots of places. And that's what he'd had to tell the detectives. They'd done it in the trunk of his rental car one night after dinner while it was parked on the street and they could hear people walking by and talking. Julia had skinned her knee while getting situated. It wasn't much of a scrape, but still it had bled a little. And that's where the blood came from.

He hadn't appreciated the smug look on the detectives' faces nor the sarcastic 'uh-huhs' he'd received. It was the God damn truth! Only he'd never mentioned Julia's passion for small, public places to anyone. And she always told him she'd never done anything like that with Kenny. So it was just his word.

So where did that leave him? Had she had another lover with whom she'd done it? If so when? And how could he find out?

He wished he had a pen and paper to jot things down. He'd already contacted an attorney – one recommended by a friend. But he had to fly over from Honolulu so he was going to be a few hours getting there. In the meantime, Sam had to sit and wait. And worry.

Reap What You Sow

The arrest of Professor Belmont came as quite a surprise since Margie and Amanda had no knowledge of him before his arrest.

Kenny got grilled as to who he was and what his association with Julia was. Since you've already read the previous chapter and know the Professor's background, I won't repeat that information. Suffice it to say that Kenny told Margie and Amanda a version of the truth, but not the whole truth. And so Margie and Amanda really only knew that Sam and Julia were involved professionally and intimately and perhaps that wasn't a good combination. I tried to point out that now that the police had arrested someone other than Kenny for the murder, we could all forget about it, but my voice was drown out by the call to know more about Sam Belmont.

In any event, it was all too much for me, so I made my escape, and the only place that made sense to escape to was Pete's place.

We were in Pete's garage and I was leaning against a large green tarp that covers his classic 1954 Cadillac Eldorado Convertible, white, with lots of chrome and big red leather seats. It's covered because Pete won't drive it. It's an investment, he says. Personally, I would drive it. Amanda would drive it. And unknown to all of us, Margie had driven it from Kona to Waimea in just under an hour and fifteen minutes! (That's really good time, just in case you're wondering.) What's the point in owning a car like that if you don't drive it?

Anyway, Pete was sitting on the garage floor inspecting the undercarriage of a lawnmower.

"Amanda told me," he said. "You're going to have meat aren't you?"

"I don't know," I said honestly.

"Thanksgiving without meat is…unpatriotic."

"I'll make sure there's meat. Turkey probably. Margie doesn't hate turkey."

"Could you hand me that thingamajig?"

I reached down into a jumble of tools and handed Pete one at random. Pete looked at it as if to reject it, then took it and began tapping on the bottom of the lawnmower.

"I don't like that Kenny guy," I said. "There's something slimy about him. I've caught him ogling Margie a dozen times already."

"I guess you're not going to like Amanda's brother then," Pete said, setting the tool aside.

"Why's that?" I quizzed.

"He slobbers all over Margie."

I considered his comment a moment. "Great! Maybe it'll keep Margie from getting more involved in this murder thing."

"Then again it might not," Pete said.

For a few moments Pete puttered and I just stared.

"You know," Pete offered. "When Amanda gets a head of steam up on something I'm not too keen on, I try to throw her off track."

"Like how?"

"I don't know, tell her something like 'I think we should start a family.'" Pete looked up at me. "You got an edger?

"I loaned it to you."

"Really?" Pete turned and looked into the mass of clutter that is his garage. "I wonder where it is?"

Pete, as usual, was not much help so after watching him for an hour or so I went home.

When I entered my house, I saw Margie and Amanda and Trisha out by the pool and so I headed for the kitchen. Where Kenny had gone I didn't know and cared even less. Unfortunately the phone started to ring and Margie yelled for me get it. I didn't want to get it because I figured it was her father, but I didn't want to explain to Margie and Amanda why I didn't want to do it so I picked it up.

"Hello," I said bluntly.

"Mr. Thomas?" asked an exceedingly sultry female voice.

You know imagination is a funny thing. Sometimes it's hard to image anything and other times the slightest clue starts the old imagination ball rolling out of control. This was one of those later times.

Although she'd only said my name, the voice dripped with such sensuality that an image sprang to mind of an

85

exotic beauty with full red lips and long dark hair. Where that image sprang from I haven't a clue, but there it was.

"Yes," I said, lowering my voice to make it sexier.

"This is Desire Wildo. I'm executive secretary to Mr. G. Peter Ryan. I understand his daughter, Trisha, is a guest at your house."

The voice was an aphrodisiac. I felt my knees wobble and sweat formed on my upper lip. My imagination had kicked into high gear and the image of Ms. Wildo – what will she do? – crystallized as a drop-dead gorgeous Polynesian woman dressed in one of those tight-fitting black oriental gowns decorated with golden hand-stitched embroidery, her long silky hair pulled up on her head and held in place with large chopstick-like pins. She is a vision, but her demeanor exudes an all-business attitude.

I swallowed hard. "Yes she is" I answered haltingly. For some reason I pictured Ms. Wildo itching the tip of her nose with a long manicured nail and smiling, fully aware the effect her voice had on me.

"May I speak with her?"

My pits were wet and I was breathing as hard as if I'd just climbed Mount Hood.

"Of course," I responded and placed the phone down on the table.

"Trisha, there's a Ms. Wildo on the phone for you."

Trisha looked up at me as if I'd just told her of a death in the family.

"I don't want to talk to her!" Trisha stated flatly as she pulled her legs up onto the chair and hugged her knees. It was the same defensive posture I'd seen when I first met her.

"Who is that?" Margie asked Trisha softly.

I answered for her: "She's Mr. G. Peter Ryan's secretary," I said.

Amanda and Margie looked at one another conspiratorially. I had no idea why, but the implication didn't escape me so I wasn't surprised when Margie said: "Tell her she's not here."

Margie rose and stood behind Trisha and held her shoulders protectively.

"I ... I think I already said she was here."

"Well, tell her you were mistaken!" Margie's snapped.

Margie almost never snaps, so I knew she was serious.

I made my way back to the phone and gave the news of my oversight to Ms. Wildo, who thanked me politely and hung up.

I made my way back outside and found that Trisha was just disappearing to her room.

I was glad to sit down. I was still a little shaky from my conversation with Ms. Wildo but I pulled myself together.

Margie shook her head at me as if I'd done something wrong.

"What?" I said, but Margie and Amanda were already trailing after Trisha and it wasn't until bedtime that I got any answers.

As it turned out, answering the phone and telling Ms. Wildo that Trisha was at our house was the wrong thing to do.

"Nobody told me she didn't want to talk to her father," I said defensively.

That was the truth, and I was about to bring up the serious lack of communication that was in place at the moment but decided this was not the time to get into that. I was hoping to get lucky—it had been awhile. And, yes, I was still sweating a little from my encounter with my mental image of Ms. Wildo.

"Well why do you think she hasn't called him?" Margie said.

"I assumed…" I started. "I mean really. How was I supposed to know that?"

"You don't know who G. Peter Ryan is?"

Margie finished undressing and stepped into her nightie. Here was my opportunity, only…

"Of course I know who G. Peter Ryan is. But nobody told me she was the daughter of the third richest man on the planet. I didn't even know her last name!"

Margie shook her head at me in disgust at my stupidity. I stood my ground. Suddenly the doorbell rang.

It was kind of late for us to receive visitors, so we exchanged looks of unease. Once again I was in my boxers and Margie was in her nightie. Margie sneered at me, grabbed her robe, and stomped from the room. I continued to undress, my chances of getting lucky having just stomped out of the room with her.

"Shouldn't you get up and bark or something?" I snapped at Magoo, but he just rolled over for a tummy rub that he was not going to get. If I wasn't going to get lucky, neither was he!

The relative quiet of the night was suddenly broken by loud voices and the sound of confusion. Magoo jumped up and ran from the bedroom barking savagely – actually twelve-pound dogs cannot bark savagely, but don't tell Magoo, he thinks he's a pit bull.

What now?

I took a deep breath and donned my robe, found my slippers, and started for the bedroom door.

The ruckus had reached a crescendo by the time I entered the living room where I found a scene straight out of an old *I Love Lucy!* episode.

The whole place was illuminated by a single living room lamp and the swirling blue lights atop a squad car parked in our driveway, the front doors were open wide and the doorway was filled with a veritable gaggle of folks.

On this side there was Margie and Magoo, who was dancing and barking and chasing his virtually nonexistent tail ferociously. On the other side of the door were Detective Lo and two uniformed officers – big guys, real Hawaiians – who filled the space and blocked the large door completely.

Behind them, standing on tiptoe at times and twisting and bending to see past the officers were a very distinguished looking gentleman and a classy looking lady who was certainly his wife. I knew Detective Lo and the two officers. The other two characters I assumed were Margie's parents Maxwell and Catherine Moore, who were, at the moment, trying like the dickens to push their way into the house past the officers at the door. They weren't making any headway.

Margie, in the thick of it all, was trying her best to sort everyone and everything out while welcoming her parents.

For your enjoyment, I thought I'd capture the feel of the moment by transcribing as best as I can the following conversations which were intermixed and overlapped so much that I'm certain I can't recall them properly, but I'll give it the old college try.

"Mrs. Thomas," Detective Lo said in his usual unflappable manner. "I need to see Ms. Ryan."

"Of course detective, in a moment, if you'll just step aside ..." Margie had managed to reach through the 'blue shield' and grasp one of her parents' suitcases. She was trying to pull it through but not having any luck.

Detective Lo wasn't having any of it. He was there with a purpose and he wasn't about to budge until Margie paid attention. "Please, Mrs. Thomas…"

"Mom! Dad!" Margie ignored the detective. "You should have called. We could have picked you up…"

Margie's Dad barked back. "We wanted to surprise you, Margie. But what the hell is going on?" Mr. Moore was trying to feed the suitcase through the officers, but they weren't budging and even though Margie had the handle on her side and pulled with all her nearly one hundred pounds of feminine muscle, there was no progress.

"Ohhh…" Margie groaned. "Detective if you'll just …"

"Mrs. Thomas!" Lo asserted himself again.

"Why do you want to see her?" Margie asked, still pulling on the suitcase. "Here, Dad let me…"

"Mom! It's so good to … You look wonderful."

"Thank you dear. What's going on Margie? What are the police doing here?" Margie's mother was sharp. She noticed the cops right away.

Margie grabbed a different suitcase and tried to slide it between the two uniformed officers who also refused to budge.

"I'll explain later, Mom. Officer if you'll just…" Margie yanked hard and suddenly and quite miraculously the suitcase popped through. Unfortunately, her success was completely unexpected so Margie wound up on her ass in the foyer.

"I can't tell you that Mrs. Thomas," Detective Lo said, in response to Margie's question. He must have thought Margie was paying attention now, but I could have told him she wasn't. She was more concerned with suitcases.

"Oh, that's heavy. What's in there?" Margie said, getting up off the floor and wrestling the escaped luggage out of the way. The sole score of the game so far.

"But Margie, when did you get a dog?" Margie's Mom again, oblivious to the police blocking her entry. "He's adorable. What's his name?"

"It's Magoo, Mom... Officer if you could just..." Margie reached through and found the handle of yet another suitcase.

"Mrs. Thomas. This is important." Detective Lo was beginning to realize he in no way had control of this situation. "Can I have your attention for just a moment?"

"Magoo? What's that? Oh, Margie, it's a madhouse. Is there trouble? Goodness. Here, I brought you candy." Margie's mother again. She could switch subjects faster than Jesse James could draw a six shooter.

Mom passed a box of candy between the officers at which time Margie seized the opportunity to grab Catherine's arm and started to pull on her, still the officers wouldn't budge.

"Thanks, Mom, that's very nice. Officer, will you please... just a little so..."

As Margie pulled, Catherine lowered her shoulder and lunged. She must have played linebacker at some time in another life, because a second later another miracle occurred as Catherine popped through the police line and into the house. She grinned triumphantly, straightened her dress, touched her hair, and turned to give the officers a cold snub. Another score for Margie!

Now it was Dad's turn. "Margie, you would not believe the incompetent morons in Honolulu."

"Dad, that can wait. Let's just get you inside."

"MRS. THOMAS!" Detective Lo had actually raised his voice. "I must insist that you..."

"See hear, mister whoever you are. You can't talk to my daughter that way…" Dad, who I felt had been holding back till this point, was now wading in.

"Dad. Don't." Margie pleaded. "I can handle this. Detective, as you can see my mother and father have just arrived and…"

"Margie, have you got any ginger ale?" Margie's mom again. "My stomach's in a twirl. Your father's impossible."

Margie paused to handle this latest crisis. "I don't think I have ginger ale, but we have Dr. Pepper."

"Oh, that's fine. If I remember the kitchen is right over …"

"No mom, that way," Margie coached her to turn back. "Dad. Dad. Just leave the suitcase. Officer if you could just… Where the hell is Joe?"

I was there of course, but standing back out of the way were an errant suitcase, guest or bullet would not hit me. I was concealed behind an open bookshelf, you know, one of those things made up of open squares that let you set up books and knickknacks and the like. It's always been a handy place to spy on folks in the living room. Not that I'm into spying. I've only used it a couple of times before and that's because Margie insists on letting the Mormons in for coffee!

"I don't want to interrupt your reunion Mrs. Thomas," Detective Lo said calmly. "If you could just go and get Ms. Ryan…"

"Just leave that Dad. Joe can help with it later."

Margie reached through the cops at the door and grabbed her Dad's arm. She pulled, he squirmed; together they broke through the blockers. In my opinion the cops were getting lazy.

Dad dusted himself off.

"Mrs. Thomas!" Lo was back to raising his voice.

Having rescued her parents, Margie was finally able to focus on the detective's request. It had not occurred to her earlier that had she done things in reverse order things might have gone more smoothly. But then Detective Lo wasn't completely blameless. What was that saying about the immutable object meeting the immoveable force?

"Okay. Okay," Margie finally caved. "Just a minute."

At that moment, Amanda appeared behind the officers in her short-short robe, her hair all messy and cold cream or some such dotting her face.

"Margie. What the hell's going on? I was in the tub..."

"Oh, Amanda, I don't know..." Margie shook her head.

Amanda spotted Margie's parents and waved. "Hi, Mr. Moore. Hi, Mrs. Moore. Remember me?"

Mr. Moore nodded and waved back. "Of course I remember you. You're Amanda, the stripper."

"No. I'm the neighbor..." Amanda corrected.

Catherine started to pull at her heavy suitcase.

"Amanda, could you help Mom with that?" Margie said, forgetting that Amanda was on one side of the police line and mom on the other.

Amanda presses up against one of the officers blocking the door and cooed softly. "Do you mind…"

The officer looked at Amanda, smiled, and stepped aside. Amanda melted into the room like butter off hot bread. Margie did a double-take and groaned.

"Thank you," Amanda said, giving the officer a flirtatious finger-wave.

"Dad, please stop that..." Margie pleaded.

Magoo had taken hold of Maxwell's pant cuff and was growling as Maxwell dragged him around the entryway like a mop.

"Mom that's too heavy. Amanda, could you find Joe? I..."

The fact of the matter was I had given up and headed for the kitchen to make a pot of coffee. The way I saw it, we would need a big one. Of course, the confusion continued without me.

All the noise brought Kenny and Trisha, looking quite disheveled, in their robes out into the living room — it appeared at least someone in my house might have gotten lucky — but they stayed tucked out of sight from the police.

And about that time Pete made an entrance from the pool side, eating a dish of ice cream. He smiled and nodded hello to Kenny and Trisha, who politely returned the acknowledgement.

"Mrs. Thomas. I'm losing patience..." Detective Lo finally barked. Personally I'm amazed he hadn't lost it sooner. I guess being a detective takes a good deal of patience.

Kenny 'Psst!' Pete to ask what was going on, but of course Pete didn't have a clue, though I'm sure the drama of it all captured his attention.

"Haven't a clue," Pete offered. "Maybe the police brought Margie's mom and dad." It was as good a guess as any.

Finally Kenny decided the police may have been there for him so he told Trisha he'd better see what they wanted and stepped forward. After all he'd been their guest only a few hours earlier, and it was likely they wanted to see him again. So Kenny stepped out in the open and approached the door. "Are you looking for me, detective?"

"Kenny!" Margie scolded, then turned her attention to more important things "Oh, Mom, make dad stop with the dog." Dad was still using Magoo to mop the floor and by the look of things both he and Magoo were enjoying themselves.

"Kenny, he wants to talk to Trisha about something but... "

"Is Ms. Ryan with you Mr. McMan?" Detective Lo shouted.

Kenny started "What do you want with her..." but unfortunately at that moment Trisha peeked out from her hiding spot and Detective Lo spotted her.

"There she is, make the arrest," Lo ordered. And before you could say 'what the hell is going on,' the officers pushed past Margie and Kenny and had Trisha 'in custody' as they say.

Margie stomped her feet angrily. "What are you doing? You can't break in here and start arresting people."

Margie sounded sure of herself. I was impressed – even from the kitchen.

Of course it didn't do any good. The officers had Trisha in handcuffs and were leading her to the door.

"Margie, who's she?" Catherine asked. "Why's she being arrested?

"It's all right mom, I'll take... Amanda! Where's the phone. I've got to call Cynthia..."

As the officers exited, Pete finally had an opening.

"Hi, Margie. Hi, Mr. Moore. Hi, Mrs. Moore."

Maxwell scowled at Pete. "Who the hell are you?" he demanded abrasively.

"Don't swear Maxwell," Catherine said. "That's Joe, Margie's husband."

Amanda handed the phone to Margie.

"No, Mom. That's Pete, Amanda's husband. You remember... Where the hell is JOE!"

Outside, Trisha was being helped into the waiting squad car.

"Don't worry, Trisha," Margie called. "I'm calling Cynthia. We'll have you out before you can say ... "

I think she was going to say 'Jack Robinson,' but Cynthia must have picked up on the other end because she turned her attention to the phone: "It's Margie..."

"Don't tell them anything," Kenny yelled across the room.

"Don't tell them anything about what?" Mr. Moore asked.

It was at this point that I reentered the living room sipping a cup of hot Kona coffee, quite pleased with myself for having NOT gotten involved.

"Joe! Where have you been?" Margie snapped.

As a rule, Margie does not snap, but I felt that under the circumstances a snap was justifiable.

I smiled and held up my cup. "Fresh pot if anyone's interested."

What's Good About It?

It took some time, but eventually everyone and everything got sort of sorted out and those who had homes to go to went home and those who were guests got to the guest rooms and those of us who actually lived in the house found their way to the master bedroom and the king size bed.

Of course after Trisha's arrest it took Margie longer to settle down than usual. And although it was never made clear to me how, Trisha's arrest was clearly my fault. But eventually I was allowed to fall asleep – even after two cups of Kona brew – and I slept the sleep of the innocent.

Unfortunately one cannot sleep forever. Well, technically one can but that's called dead and things weren't quite that bad -- at least not yet.

The morning came as it always does. The chirping of birds, light reflected off the hibiscus and the distant sound of leaf-blowers and lawnmowers and someone swimming in the pool.

I actually felt a grin begin to spread over my face before it died and was replaced by an anxious frown. There were strangers in the house!

I rolled out of bed, found my robe, took a deep breath, and headed for the bedroom door to face the inevitable. *Well at least it can't be as bad as yesterday*, I said to console myself. I am, by nature, an optimist. Yeah I know it's stupid but that's the way it is.

Approaching the living room with caution I found it quiet and empty. I walked through to the kitchen, crossed to the counter, and poured a cup of coffee. I picked up the paper off the island and headed out to the pool. Things were looking up!

The coast was clear outside and Margie was swimming laps as usual. This morning however she was wearing a conservative, black, one-piece swimsuit. Well, actually it wasn't all that conservative. It was cut up high on the thigh to show a lot of hip and low in back. Plumbers show less crack.

I watched Margie casually as I navigated to the table, gave Magoo a scratch, settled into my usual chair, leaned back, and began to read.

Before I'd finished the front page headlines, which noted that Sam had been released and Trisha had been arrested, something we already knew of course, Margie had completed her laps and appeared at the table vigorously drying her hair with a towel.

"How'd you sleep?" she asked pointedly.

"Fine," I offered, wondering if something had occurred after I took my pill and drifted off to lala land.

"Something new?" I asked, eyeing the swimsuit.

Margie looked down and pulled the Lycra with thumb and forefinger, letting it snap back. "This?" she lied, "I've had it for ages."

"Of course you have. So what happened after…"

The relative calm of the morning and my question were disrupted by the sound of a door slamming. A moment later Catherine made an abrupt exit from the house looking mad enough to devour a small child.

"That man is impossible…" she cried as she descended on us. Her voice sent Magoo to look for a sofa to hide beneath. Magoo, as you'll recall, hates yelling.

Either Margie had gone deaf overnight or she was attempting some sort of physiological bomb diffusion method, for she sang: "Good morning, Mom" as sweetly as if her mother had just announced we were all going for cake and ice cream.

"If he thinks he's going to wear that ... that... Oh. Whatever it's called. It looks like a damn slingshot!"

There was a moment of silence. Margie offered cautiously: "A Speedo?"

"He looks like a fool..." Catherine spat as she dropped into a chair. She had yet to acknowledge my presence, for which, under the circumstances, I was thankful.

As if on cue, Maxwell made his appearance. He was as a matter of fact wearing a Speedo. But it wasn't nearly as small as Catherine made it out to be, and although I'm told he's pushing sixty-eight I thought he looked damn good in it. There was even a twinge of envy on my part, since my gut would have made less of a fashion statement.

Margie tried to start things off in a positive way and sang: "Aloha, Dad."

But Catherine had her own agenda. "Will you put something decent on!" she bellowed.

Maxwell looked down at himself. "I'm decent," he declared and gave Margie a kiss on the cheek which made Margie beam.

He looked over the table. "Coffee? Wonderful." He slid into a chair.

"You look like a fool," Catherine repeated.

"You're just jealous because you can't wear a bikini anymore," Maxwell shot back.

It was probably the wrong thing to say. Catherine growled, "Agggh," and got up and stormed into the house.

Margie turned to Maxwell. "Dad?"

Maxwell glanced at Margie then away. He sipped his coffee and stared at the high bushes. Margie crossed her arms and tapped her foot. Maxwell ignored her. Margie continued to tap. I buried my nose in my paper and waited.

I had to give Maxwell credit. When Margie taps her foot at me, I fold pretty fast. He held out quite awhile but finally he caved too.

"Okay, okay. I'll wear the stupid trunks," he said, getting up and heading back to the house.

Margie slid into a chair and poured coffee.

"You might want to think about patenting that foot tapping thing," I said appreciatively.

Margie smiled and for a moment peace reined. But only for a moment.

"For God sake, do that in the bathroom," Catherine's voice carried from the house. "I don't want to see..."

A door slammed again and Catherine stormed across the living room and disappeared into the kitchen.

Margie lost her smile and looked at me sadly.

"I think I'll take mom to the farmer's market."

That seemed like a good idea till I realized the consequence.

"And leave me alone with your father?"

"You'll be fine," Margie said unconvincingly as she started for the house.

"Just a minute, Mom," she called and then stopped. "I forgot to tell you, Kenny moved to a hotel."

Good news at last!

"Really?" I sang. The day was looking up.

"Yes," Margie said. "Frankly I don't know what Trisha sees in him. He seemed so..."

"Slimy?" I offered.

Margie grimaced. "He isn't that bad. Anyway, it's a good thing he decided to go. It's going to get pretty crowded what with Shelly and Mark and the girls arriving today."

I choked on my coffee and Margie had to come and slap me on the back. When I was able to breathe feely again, Margie gave me a sideways look.

"Don't tell me you forgot *they* were coming?" Margie chided.

"No," I lied. "I remembered. I just swallowed wrong."

It was a lie of course. I knew nothing of them. *Shelly? Girls? Mark?*

"Margie! Where do you keep the bread?" Catherine screamed from the kitchen.

"I'd better go," Margie said reluctantly. She kissed me on the forehead, and scampered away.

I watched after her a moment, then said to an empty chair. "I'm looking forward to meeting Shelly and Mark and the girls. Aren't you?"

I went back to reading my paper and Margie and Catherine left for the farmer's market. Maxwell eventually reappeared in a standard pair of swim trunks -- Hawaiian style: black background with a large floral pattern -- and pulled up a chair at the table across from me. He poured another cup of coffee and took a sip while quietly perusing the place.

For your edification, I think it's my duty to describe Maxwell a bit now.

Maxwell, Max, Dad, Pop, whatever you call him, is a very distinguished looking man. He's built solid, like a boxer – a heavy weight – but doesn't have much of a gut, as I've already said. He's well tanned and carefully groomed, and he looks like a man who has weathered many a season and survived quite well. He's got steely blue eyes and a bit of a pug nose and carries himself well and he's got a 'friendly' fatherly look about him, though I hadn't had the opportunity yet to get to know if that was just his persona or his true nature. I guess you might sum up his appearance as handsome and confident.

"This a new house?" Maxwell asked abruptly while I was still in my paper.

"No," I started and let the paper droop before I realized what he was asking. "Yes!" I said. "Margie used to live up the street with Frank. She sold that place. We bought this together."

"I thought so." He lifted his cup. "Kona?"

"That's all we drink. It's the best."

"Got a real zing to it. I'll have to take more home this trip."

101

Maxwell leaned back and surveyed the yard. "I never really cared much for Frank. Never around. Always working. I always thought he married Margie for the money."

I smiled and let the paper drop to the table. Here was a chance to get on Maxwell's good side.

"As it turns out," I said with a big Cheshire cat grin, "He didn't know about the money."

Maxwell perked up and leaned forward. "No kidding?"

"No kidding."

I explained briefly about Frank's ignorance and Maxwell leaned back and cackled. "We'll I'll be... He never...?"

"Never had a clue. I guess Margie 'forgot' to tell him."

We shared a quiet laugh. It seemed that things with Dad were going pretty good, so I decided to make small talk and gather some vital information.

"I understand Shelly and Mark and the girls are arriving today."

"Yep. Can't wait to see 'em. You met 'em yet?"

"No. I haven't had the pleasure."

"Mark's a bit much," Maxwell offered. "But Shelly likes him, and he spoils Bridgette and Barbie."

"Let's see..." I feigned. "Shelly? How many years between ..."

"Shelly's three years younger than Margie. Got married a good ten years before her though. Bridgette's 14 and Barbie's 13. But God they act older. Kid's today. Christ they grow up fast."

"Don't they. It was Bridgette's birthday...?"

"A week ago last Sunday. The 14th. Her golden birthday."

"Of course. Well I'm certainly looking forward to meeting them. Margie talks about them all the time. All the time."

We fell silent. I picked up my coffee mug and had just raised it to my lips when Maxwell asked:

"So, Joe, what do you do?"

There it was. *The question.* Caught mid-sip and unprepared I continued sipping as my brain shifted into high gear. Nothing came to me. If Margie hadn't told him I didn't work, I certainly didn't want to be the one to. He'd just voiced his opinion about Frank. At least Frank had a job. I was just a…just a… boy toy!

I tried to continue sipping but the thing of it is you can only sip for so long. Finally, I had to come up for air.

"Didn't... didn't Margie tell you?" I stalled.

Maxwell chuckled. "You know Margie. I'm sure she'd say she did, but..."

I was sweating now. I had to come up with something. My eyes searched back and forth; I knew I had only seconds before he'd sense I was stalling and get suspicious. Then I spied a paperback open on the table.

"I'm a writer," I said flatly.

It wasn't a bad lie. I did know how to write and I had written. I've written checks, notes, even an occasional report. I was hoping he wouldn't pursue the matter, but if you ask anyone, you'll find I'm not a lucky person.

"Really? What do you write?" Maxwell asked.

Oh, shoot. I was trapped. Cornered. Caught. I tried to think my way out. It was too early to think that hard and my head began to hurt when all of a sudden my luck changed, or at least I thought it might have changed. For at that moment I spotted Amanda coming towards us. Magoo jumped down from his chair and ran to greet her.

103

He likes Amanda, and the feeling is mutual. She bent down, picked him up, and cuddled him.

I quickly sidestepped Maxwell's question. "Aloha!" I shouted to Amanda enthusiastically.

Amanda slowed and looked around. It was apparent that she was uncertain what to make of my exuberant greeting.

"My, don't you look sumptuous," Maxwell joined in, standing up as Amanda made her way over.

Of course his observation was dead on. Amanda smiled and twirled in her clingy red sundress. She did look sumptuous, but then she always does.

"Mahalo, Mr. Moore."

"Please, call me Max. Come on, sit down and let us have a look at you. Coffee?" Maxwell poured a cup before Amanda could answer.

"Oh, there it is," Amanda said, picking up the book on the table. "I was wondering where it had got to."

Amanda found a seat and got Magoo adjusted on her lap. "So what are you boys up to?" she quizzed after taking a sip of coffee.

"Oh, we're just getting to know one another," Maxwell said as he sat back down. "Joe was telling me about his writing."

Amanda looked at me and raised an eyebrow. "His writing?"

She was looking at me with fresh appreciation. Obviously, she didn't think I could come up with such an impressive lie.

I entreated her with my eyes not to blow my cover. In hindsight, it would have been better had she done so on the spot, but as I mentioned Amanda is smarter than I am so she used her great intellect to punish me. Why?

Because she finds it amusing!   She's really not as nice as everyone says she is.

To my regret, she jumped on the bandwagon with both feet. "He really is an excellent writer, don't you think?" Amanda queried.

Maxwell was taken aback by Amanda's question.

"Well, I've never actually... Margie didn't tell me... Joe, what do you write exactly?" Maxwell finally sputtered.

Before I could answer, Amanda volleyed. "Murder mysteries!"

I said she didn't play tennis but she certainly knew how to hit a ball hard and put a lot of spin on it! I slumped in my chair. Daggers shot from my eyes at her but she repelled them with her superpowers and kept on going. She was having a blast!

"In fact," Amanda added. "This is one of his books!"

Amanda handed the paperback to Maxwell, who took it and flipped through the pages as Amanda and I sat silently exchanging words with our eyes.

What are you trying to do? My eyes asked.

I'm just trying to help. Her eyes responded insincerely.

I'll get you for this. My eyes burned.

Amanda's eyes feigned terror.   And laughter.

Maxwell finally looked up, confused. "But it says the author is ... Kimberly Shoulton."

"Oh," said Amanda fanning the air, "that's Joe's pen name. Mysteries sell *much* better if they're written by women. Don't ask me why."

"Really?" Maxwell said turning the book over. "I had no idea."

Amanda rose. "Well, I really should be going."

Maxwell held out the book.

"Oh, keep it, Mr. M. It'll give you a chance to see what a wonderful writer your son-in-law is."

Maxwell looked back at the book, puzzled. I stood up quickly.

"Let me walk you out, Amanda," I said, barely able to control my anger and wondering what the penalty for murder was in Hawaii and whether I could plead self defense.

Before I could take a step, however, Amanda skittered away all bubbly. "Don't bother, Joe. I know the way," she said cheerily.

I plopped down in my chair and stared at the book that Maxwell had opened and was now reading.

How was I going to get out of this?

I sat on the bed and Margie stood with her hands on her hips looking down at me. A memory of fifth grade and Mrs. Kincaid flashed through my brain. Not that I hadn't done anything stupid since the fifth grade, only that I'd had a crush on Mrs. Kincaid, and now that I thought about it Margie did bear a slight resemblance to my fifth grade teacher. But I digress.

"What on earth possessed you to tell him you were a writer?"

I was going to say it was all Amanda's fault, but that wasn't exactly true. I started the lie and Amanda just climbed on board.

"I didn't want him to think I was a gold digger. He said he thought Frank was only interested in you for your money and..."

Margie sat on the bed next to me and put her arm around my shoulder.

"Joe, Joe, Joe," she said consolingly. "My dad has thought that about every man who's ever looked at me."

I perked up. "He has?"

"Yes, he has," Margie laid her head on my shoulder. "And do you know why?"

The idea of sudden redemption leapt forward. "Because he married your mother for money?" I asked hopefully.

Margie groaned. "Noooo. My father's a self made man. Why would you think...?

"Never mind," I said. "I was just hoping that... Just tell me what you were going to say."

"What I was going to say was that the reason my father thought all the men were gold diggers was because they *were* all gold diggers!"

"But Frank didn't know you had money," I reasoned.

Margie gave me a strange look, then obviously she remembered that in fact we had discussed the fact that Frank didn't know about the money. She continued: "But he knew my father had money. Lots of money. You didn't know I had money till after we were married and you didn't know my father was rich till I told you about him after the wedding."

I was going to correct her about the 'told you after the wedding' part since as you know I hadn't a clue about her parents until the other day, but I thought that might be a bad card to play at the moment so I simply asked: "So how does that help me?"

"I don't know," Margie answered. "I just wanted to let you know that I don't think you're a gold digger." Margie rose and started for the dresser.

"So what did you tell him you wrote?"

I slumped forward and let my face fall into my hands.

"Amanda told him I was a mystery writer."

"A mystery writer?"

"Named Kimberly Shoulton."

Margie fell silent. I peeked out at her. She was shaking her head in disbelief.

"Kimberly Shoulton!" Margie repeated. "She's written like fifty books!"

I fell back on the bed and stared up at the ceiling. Magoo came over to lick my face. It was nice of him, but this timing was bad. I pushed him away.

Margie started toward the bedroom door, still shaking her head.

"Kimberly Shoulton," she repeated. "Kimberly Shoulton?"

I wanted to shout. *It's Amanda's fault.* But I knew it would do no good. Magoo started to lick my ear. I didn't have the energy to stop him.

After Margie left, I lay on the bed and tried to think what I should do. It took me almost an hour, but eventually I hatched what I considered a credible plan to cover my deception – no it didn't include telling the truth. Like any politician worth his or her salt I knew the best way to cover a lie was to continue to lie – so I pulled myself off the bed and started out.

I snuck out of the house and when I returned two hours later I snuck back in and made a beeline from the front door to the den carrying a large box that contained the ingredients of the plan I'd concocted.

After locking the door behind me, I dropped the box on the sofa and pulled a smaller box from it that contained the key ingredient: a software program called 'Hard at Work.' I booted the old computer and installed the program without too much swearing and without sweating blood.

The salesclerk had demonstrated how to get the thing going and within moments the computer speakers sang with a 'clackity, clack' noise that mimicked the sound of someone tapping on the keys of a keyboard. There were variable length pauses, as if some thought might be occurring now and again. And the sound of repeated backspacing, which I've notices is far more common among computer users than it should be, gave it that air of authenticity that made me buy it. I adjusted the volume and stood back to appreciate how genuine it sounded.

I was about to head back to the box on the sofa when I heard the doorknob rattle and a tapping at the door.

"Joe?"

It was Margie.

"Yes?" I responded without making any effort to go to the door or open it.

"What are you doing?"

"I'm writing," I said quickly, then added. "Don't bother me."

There was a long pause.

"You're writing?" Margie's voice sounded incredulous and I imagined her staring at the door as if it might be possessed. Had I actually been writing I might have taken offence to the tone.

"Yes. I'm writing," I reiterated. "That's what writers do."

"Why is the door locked?"

That was a good question but I had a ready response. "I always lock the door when I'm writing."

I heard a sigh and then Margie's footsteps retreated.

Alone again, I moved back to the sofa and dug in the large box. This time I extracted a book. I held it up. On the cover was a handsome man in blaze orange sloughing through high grass carrying a double barrel shotgun with a big black lab at his heels. The title read "The Hunting Detective" and the writer was Kimberly Shoulton.

I opened to page one and sat in the big armchair and began to read.

Up Mauka

Kanoa's cousin's place was exactly what Duncan had expected. It was typical old country Hawaii, not much more than a shack really, with a rusted corrugated roof. The kind of place few tourists ever see, but home to many Hawaiians.

Duncan was accustomed to discomfort. He'd lived in the jungle in South America and Central America, as well as the back country in Mexico. Still, he preferred creature comforts. He was worth a couple of million dollars, but his money was hidden and he was satisfied to wait a few more years till he retired to spend it. He had a place all picked out in Belize where living was cheap and the weather was hot and moist and the women he felt were much like the weather.

Kanoa was his normally stoic self. One word answers to questions and no humor. Duncan couldn't figure him out. He wasn't like anyone else he'd worked with in the drug trade, but Duncan didn't waste much time thinking about it.

"We got to go meet the guy down in Kona," Duncan said as he climbed into the passenger seat of the Jeep and set a large blue and gold day pack on the floor between his feet. "He wants lots of folks around. Nervous I guess."

Kanoa didn't like being Duncan's chauffeur, which is basically what he was. But Duncan didn't care what Kanoa liked. Duncan never drove himself to a meet. He'd learned that in Ecuador. Keep your eyes free to watch things and your hands free for your weapon, which today was a semi-automatic rifle that sat on his lap under an old shirt so anyone looking into the Jeep wouldn't see it. In Ecuador, they always shot the driver first, so it was hard to find drivers. Duncan was glad that Kanoa had no knowledge of things in Ecuador.

The meet with Kenny was to take place at the end of the pier in town. Kanoa was to be stationed far away so he couldn't hear the conversation when Duncan met with him. He was supposed to be a lookout just in case someone had followed Kenny, but Kanoa had no clear idea who he was looking for or what to do if he spotted someone suspicious.

When they arrived, Kenny was already at the end of the pier with a camera, pretending to take pictures. A day pack identical to Duncan's sat near his feet. Duncan took his day pack and walked out within talking distance of Kenny, but not so close so as to appear to be with him. He dropped his day pack next to him so the two day packs were almost side by side. To the casual observer it would appear that two strangers had just struck up a conversation. Kanoa stood near the entrance to the pier and pretended to watch the swimmers and snorkelers and skim-boarders.

"You got sprung," Duncan opened the conversation. "Glad to hear it."

"I'm still a suspect, but I don't think they're tailing me," Kenny offered. "At least I haven't noticed anyone following me."

"You won't notice 'em," Duncan said. "They're good at it. But I didn't see no one, so I guess you're right."

"What happens now?" Kenny asked.

"We go about our business jus' like before," Duncan said. "'Cept we be a little more careful," Duncan grinned. "Meaning you make sure you' alone before you visit."

"I had no idea she…" Kenny stopped while a couple moved past them.

"I hear your pussy got herself jailed," Duncan said. "Too bad for her. You ain't plannin' to rescue her are you?"

Kenny shook his head. "Is that what they want to know? Whether I'm going to risk everything for a piece of ass? I can get that anywhere. She was just a means to an end. I have the ends, I don't need the means anymore."

"Glad to hear it," Duncan said. "I'll pass it along. One more question though. That couple you was stayin' with, how'd you come to know 'em?"

Kenny grinned. "I didn't. Neither did Trisha. The blonde's a soft touch. Took Trisha in because she was crying down by the beach; they let me stay because Trisha was there. The husband wasn't happy with either of us and I'm sure he's glad we're gone."

"Your girl didn't tell 'em anything?" Duncan asked.

"She told them what she thought she knew. Like probably everyone else on the island with time on their hands, they're playing detective. But what they know isn't worth diddly." Kenny took a few shots with the camera.

"Don't worry about them. They're clueless."

"Anything else?" Kenny asked.

"Nope," Duncan said. "Jus' be careful like I said. In this business if you make people nervous you could find yourself ... unhappy."

Duncan picked up Kenny's day pack and walked away, giving Kenny a little wave just in case anyone was watching.

Back in the Jeep as they climbed the hill to Kanoa's cousin's place, Duncan shared a single item with Kanoa: "We need to keep an eye on those folks that took our guy in. I don't think our buddy is the bes' judge of people. You know anyone does landscapin'?"

Kanoa thought a minute. "I got a uncle work down at som' the condos. He got a truck."

"That'll do, buddy," Duncan sang. "That'll do nicely."

More of the Same

I hid in the den pretending to write while I read and scanned Shoulton books as fast as I could till Margie called me for lunch.

Lunch went rather well. Dad complained once about the lack of meat – actually there was meat, if you consider fish meat and tuna fish sandwiches a healthy lunch, which Margie does and evidently so does Mrs. M. because she told Maxwell to stop complaining about food all the time. Dad was about to respond when Margie cut him off by sharing the latest news on the murder and the details of Trisha's arrest.

It seems that the quick release of Professor Belmont and the sudden arrest of Trisha was due in no small part to the legal prowess of one Ernie Baum (Sam's attorney) who pointed out to Detective Lo that Sam's rights had been violated by the delay in his being read his Miranda rights and the discovery by the sheriff's office in Ashford Louisiana (where Collette College is located) of Julia's secret diary which substantiated Sam's version of their romantic trysts and also provided details of an encounter with Trisha in which she – Trisha -- threatened to kill Julia.

"You know, Joe," Mr. M. said as he examined what appeared to be a potato chip, but which was actually a taro chip and which I personally can only enjoy when smothered under a generous helping of guacamole dip, of which there was none because Mrs. M as it turns out is allergic to avocados . "I was thinking what an amazing stroke of luck it is to have a murder occur right at your doorstep, you being a mystery writer and all."

I had a mouthful of sandwich so before I could respond, Margie helped me out.

"Actually, Dad, Joe's very excited about it, aren't you Joe?"

I swallowed and started cautiously with "Well…"

But Margie took charge again. "He's been gathering information ever since it happened, haven't you Joe? In fact, I wouldn't be at all surprised if he solves the crime before the police!"

My eyes pleaded for her to stop, but she avoided me.

"You've already developed some theories about what happened?" Maxwell asked, setting down the taro chip and picking up a carrot stick, which seemed safer and more familiar.

I looked from Margie to Maxwell. *Here would be a good time to jump in, Margie.* But it was clear she was through and was going to let me take it from there.

"It's still a little early," I managed.

"I'm an avid mystery fan you know." Maxwell said. "Did Margie tell you that? I've read all the Perry Mason's and Agatha Christy's." Then afraid he might have offended me he added: "But I'm certain you have as well."

I started to sweat. I hadn't read any of those. I still had 47 Shoulton novels to get through!

Thankfully Margie decided to take pity on me and come to my rescue.

"Actually, Dad, Joe tries not to read other writers. He's afraid it might influence his own writing too much."

Maxwell considered her comment a moment. "Very smart!" he said decisively and rose from the table.

"I'll be anxious to hear your views on the murder as things develop, Joe. Well, I think I'll take a nap and let Joe get back to work and you and your mother go shopping or whatever. We don't have to be at the airport for a couple of hours do we?"

"The plane doesn't land till five," Margie said. "Mom? Do you fell like doing a little shopping?"

"Yes I do," Catherine responded. "I want to find a little something for the girls when they arrive."

Margie said she knew just the spot. A funky little shop in Kona that sold locally made jewelry and art, and Mrs. M. picked up the leftovers and headed toward the kitchen and Margie stood and began collecting dirty dishes.

Maxwell leaned toward me and said conspiratorially: "Ever notice that women spend more time shopping than men spend watching sports but they insist we're the ones with the addiction."

He gave me a wink and headed for the house and what I suspect was a very pleasant nap.

After Margie and Mom left, I returned to my lair and managed to down two Shoulton books before Margie knocked at the door and informed me it was time to change and head to the airport. I tried to make an excuse, but it was no use. Margie informed me through the door that if I didn't get in the bedroom and get changed she would tell Pete that I had driven his Cadillac while he and Amanda were in Honolulu and we were watching the house. Well, of course, it had been Margie who had driven the car if you'll recall, but the threat was enough to dislodge me from my den.

I caught up to Margie in the bedroom where she was in her bra and panties and putting on a funky white dress that had a white ruffle around the neck and polka dots of various sizes and colors and a red satin sash at the waist.

It was designed for a teen, so on Margie it looked deliciously naughty.

I was of the opinion that what I was wearing was just fine for picking people up at the airport and told Margie so, but she informed me that after we made the pickup we were taking everyone to dinner at Huggo's before coming home.

Huggo's is my favorite restaurant, but it didn't make it any less upsetting. *Would I be able to show my face after the Squabbles et al had eaten there?*

Huggo's is not a fancy place, but since it appeared everyone else was 'dressing up' for the occasion I figured I should too. I stripped to my boxers and was putting on a pair of tan shorts exactly like the ones I'd just taken off when Margie looked over at me.

"Don't you have anything else?" she asked.

"I have these," I said reaching into the drawer and pulling out a third pair of identical shorts.

Margie closed her eyes a moment. I think she was praying.

"Never mind," she said recovering. "Now remember, let Dad have the check."

"I don't have a problem with that."

"And don't tell Mark he's talking too loud. He only talks louder."

"Okay."

"And when Shelly asks if she looks fat, just shake your head no and look sincere.

"I can to that."

"And don't wear socks with your sandals. You'll look like Mark. Mark *will* wear socks with his sandals!"

"I never wear socks with sandals!" I protested.

"Oh, by the way," Margie said finally – at least it sounded like the last item though I can never be certain.

"Shelly and Mark are having a few problems so they've rented a hotel room and so just the girls are staying with us in the pool house."

I wasn't too happy about that.

"It sounds to me like we've just become 'teen' sitters," I moaned. Teenage girls – the few I've had experience with – scare me.

"Don't worry. Mom and Dad and I are all very excited about getting to spend more time with the girls. You won't have to do any 'teen sitting.'"

I won't spoil it for you, but you can probably guess she was wrong.

Margie went to the closet and picked out a bright Hawaiian shirt for me that complemented her outfit. I know this because she told me so. She even started to help me buttons it, although I've been able to button my own shirt for quite some time.

"My family's kind of a lot isn't it," she said.

I shook my head negatively and tried to look sincere. Margie kissed me.

"You're very talented, Mr. Thomas. Save it for Shelly."

Margie kissed me again, then turned away, took one last look in the mirror, fussed with her hair a moment, twirled, and left the bedroom. I sat on the bed and finished buttoned my shirt and wondered how Margie had blossomed from such a distressing family tree.

Ten minutes later we piled into the Volvo wagon and started out. We'd barely made it out of the driveway when Mr. M. informed Mrs. M. that she had put on too much too much perfume and it was making him nauseous. Mrs. M. responded that her perfume was far less offensive than his aftershave, which Mrs. M added was much too feminine for a man to wear.

The idea occurred to me that I could escape by opening the door and throwing myself from the vehicle but before I did Margie came to the rescue by turning up the fan, cracking the windows, and telling Mom and Dad that she had found, through Amanda, new information about the murder investigation. This drew their interest and we were temporarily saved.

The new information had come from Amanda's generally reliable informant and was of the form that Trisha had not been arrested only because of that entry in Julia's diary, but also because of an entry in Trisha's diary in which she had wished Julia dead and admitted to the fact that she'd thrown a stone bust of Sir Isaac Newton at Julia's head during a department gathering a week earlier.

As I'm sure you know, in police lingo this is known as motive and intent, and it occurred to me that this one more reason not to keep a diary. But that reminded me that I was supposed to be looking for Margie's diary so I could keep abreast of everything before it happened and stop playing catch-up.

"Well, I'm glad that's over," Catherine said. "And to think you let that girl stay at your house! You could have been murdered."

"It's not really over, Mom," Margie said. "I don't think Trisha did it; she was way too upset about it all. But I will admit it doesn't look good. It just means she had motive. It appears she also had opportunity – since she doesn't have a good alibi for the night Julia was murdered, especial since Kenny told the police he had gone out, which meant that she was alone and could have...oh you know what I'm trying to say.

"But they don't have a time and place and they haven't found a murder weapon, and the police think that Trisha must have had an accomplice since Trisha is hardly capable of hauling around a body that outweighed her by twenty-five pounds."

"The husband must have been in on it," Catherine said.

"Why does everyone always want to blame the husband?" Maxwell waded in. "Maybe she had threatened to tell her lover's wife about them? After all, isn't that why they arrested that other guy? There had to be some reason for him to be playing around."

"Men don't need reasons," Catherine assured him.

"Well, I think they do," Maxwell volleyed.

The conversation was beginning to travel a familiar route, so I weighed in. Under the circumstances – being a famous mystery writer with a murder having literally 'fallen' in my lap -- I had come to the realization that I had to get involved in these conversations even if I was dead set against them.

"In '*The Detective Wore a Daisy*,' my fifth book, (I hadn't read the book, just a brief synopsis) I had the victim murdered by her brother over a quarrel they'd had years earlier that had subjected him to public humiliation for which he'd carried a grudge which eventually drove him mad."

There was a moment of silence.

"Did Julia have a brother?" Maxwell asked.

Margie was quick to respond. "I don't think Joe was suggesting this murderer had the same motive, Dad, only that there are many motives for murder. Right, Joe?"

"Absolutely," I said.

The murder conversation continued along these lines until we arrived at Honokohau, the small boat harbor, at which point I successfully switched the subject to deep sea fishing – which it turns out Maxwell was an avid fan of. He spent the remainder of the drive talking about his fishing exploits and I had to agree to go fishing with him and Mark. I didn't want to agree, but as I said, *I had to.* Thankfully I was able to wrangle a seat for Pete although I don't think he had any more interest in fishing than I did, but I certainly didn't want to spend the day alone with Dad and my as yet unknown brother-in-law. Margie and Catherine meanwhile found a new subject of their own to discuss: shopping. Imagine that.

We arrived at the airport just a few minutes before the plane was due. Mark and Shelly and the girls were on United flight 302 direct from San Diego where, I had just recently discovered, they lived.

The Kona airport -- code KOA for you travelers -- is a cluster of mostly open buildings that serve as the terminal. Because it's almost always warm and dry in Kona this works great.

The airport, however, is located on a stretch of lava desert and the black lava combined with the asphalt runways and tarmacs raise the temp a good ten degrees from ambient. So it was close to 90 as we stood in the shade and waited. But still, with the trade winds, it was comfortable.

"When's the flight land?" I asked, even though I knew we were on time.

"They'll announce it," Margie said a bit irritably as she dug in her purse and from which she eventually pulled her tiny digital camera and handed to me. I took it and started to focus on her. I love taking Margie's picture; she's so photogenic.

"Not me. My sister," she said, striking a perfect pose all the same.

I took her picture as the loudspeaker announced the arrival of Flight 302 at Gate 7A.

I checked the small screen of the camera to make sure the battery had life in it and then we waited and made small talk for a few minutes until a stream of passengers began filtering through the security doors.

Finally Mark and Shelly and the girls came through and Margie yelled at me to take a picture, which I did. Several of them in fact. None of them keepers I'm afraid.

I'm a firm believer in first impressions and I've gotta say that the Marshall's did not make a very good first impression.

Oh, they were a nice looking family. Mark was tall and had that lankiness about him that screamed 'RUNNER,' but he was losing his hair and had opted to shave his head completely, which made him look gaunt and tired. Shelly was not lanky. Not that she was fat. She had what I like to think of as 'round' edges, and she didn't look at all like Margie. She wore her long dark brown hair straight, but pulled back by her sunglasses which she wore on top of her head. She had big brown eyes and was either very well tanned or had a naturally dark complexion. Unlike Margie, Shelly was fairly top-heavy – a trait I realized she shared with her mom. In fact if you'd stood Margie and Shelly and Amanda in a line, I'd have picked Amanda and Shelly as the sisters based on looks alone.

The girls, Bridgette and Barbie, were a combination of their parents of course. Both had dark hair and the older one, Bridgette, wore her hair like her mom's but she had streaks of blue in it. She too was well tanned or had a dark complexion and had her mom's brown eyes. Although she was only fourteen she was already well developed and in my opinion her tank top was too racy for her age. Barbie was more like her dad. She was lean and fair and wore her hair in what I think is called a Bob, which means it was cut straight just below her chin. She

121

had no bangs and her hair was streaked with bright red. Like her sister, she was dressed in a tank top and short shorts. Call me old fashioned, but shouldn't young teens wear clothes that *don't* attract pedophiles and other perverts?

As Maxwell had warned, neither one of girls looked their age and I thought perhaps that's what happens when you give your children names that are in common use by strippers and porn stars.

But while they passed muster on physical appearance, the Marshalls lost quite a few points on attitude and behavior.

"I will *never* fly that airline again!" were the first words out of Shelly's mouth even before she greeted Mom and Dad and Margie. And Bridgette and Barbie were continuing an argument that must have started earlier but the only part of which I heard was "did too" "did not" and that sort of thing. Luckily Catherine had brought trinkets for them, which ended that battle but began a new fight over who got which one. Mark, for his part, was quiet and smiled nicely as if oblivious to everything going on around him. I thought perhaps he'd benefitted from Prozac. I pegged him for the absent father so common in American families.

Despite all this, we managed to shake hands and or kiss cheeks and or give and get leis and when that ended I volunteered to give Mark a ride to pick up their rental van while the rest of them waited for their luggage.

I know you're probably thinking I did it to escape, but that's not true. It's the sort of thing I generally do. I'm a nice guy; ask anyone.

Since it's only a short ride to the car rental lot, I didn't learn much about Mark. Only that he thought his job was in trouble, he thought his wife was having an affair, the girls were too much to handle, he was seeing a therapist, he might be in love with his therapist, his therapist was a man, and his father had announced he was leaving everything he owned to some fanatical religious sect that believed Jesus Christ was an alien.

The only thing Mark learned from me was that I was good at repeating the words 'I'm really sorry to hear that.'

Mark got his van and I followed him back to the airport where he picked up Shelly and the girls and I picked up Margie, Maxwell, and Catherine. You know it's funny how fast things can change. I was actually glad to have Maxwell and Catherine in the car again, considering the option that is.

Dinner was far less stressful than I'd anticipated, mainly because I ordered vodka Martinis and --when Margie wasn't paying attention -- a Porterhouse steak with baked potato, sour cream, and butter.

At first the conversation centered around the girls who were busy texting friends back home and not paying any attention to the grownups or the spectacular view of Kailua Bay. I learned that they liked boys – lots of boys – had stolen the car on two occasions, were doing poorly in school, and thought that the current president was Calvin Coolidge. Why they thought the current president was Calvin Coolidge no one knew, but we all agreed it was quite interesting.

I noted that Mark and Shelly were very cordial to one another and based on what Margie had said earlier about the state of their marriage, I assumed they were doing so for the benefit of Mom and Pop and the girls. Mom and Pop however where not so cordial. Catherine insisted on telling Maxwell that ordering the lobster was a bad idea because it always gave him gas and stomach pains. Whereupon Maxwell told her he was old enough to

123

decide whether he wanted gas or not. Catherine volleyed back that if that were the case he could sleep on the sofa, to which Maxwell replied he'd be happy to since at least he wouldn't have to listen to Catherine's snoring. I could go on, but I'm sure you get the picture.

In an effort to diffuse the battle between Mom and Dad, Margie brought up the murder. Everyone, except the girls who were busy texting as I've already told you, was eager to get the 'inside' scoop on it.

As we ate, Margie provided information and answered questions. I kept silent except to order martinis and devour my steak and suck the bones until everyone else had finished. I was still of the opinion that Kenny was the evil doer, but those at the dinner table were clearly against me; the majority of votes siding with Sam, though we knew little about him. Trisha, it was generally acknowledged, was completely innocent and should be released immediately. Margie was particularly upset because although she wanted to visit Trisha, her attorney – Trisha's attorney that is -- had contacted our attorney and told her that she would not allow any visitors for at least the next few days.

When the bill came, I did as promised and let Dad have it without a fight. There had been enough fighting after all. I noted that Mark made no attempt whatever to grab it.

The ladies excused themselves to go to the power room, which is what ladies do after dinner as you may have noticed. They do it in groups, which you also may have noticed. Why? No one knows. At least no *man* knows. I think the women know, but it's a very well kept secret.

Of course the girls didn't go, they were still texting and once the ladies were gone, the table seemed empty and quiet, which made me quite unhappy. Why? Because as the local host I felt it was my responsibility to make conversation which was going to be difficult because my lips were numb from the martinis. I may need to look into AA after the holidays.

Mark, however, took this opportunity to slide down by Dad and me. It was clear there was something on his mind that he wanted to share and he didn't want to boom it across the big table.

"I've got to say," Mark began. "You're not really thinking outside the box on this murder thing are you?"

"How's that?" I asked reluctantly. I really wasn't in the mood to go down the murder trail again this evening but I saw no way to avoid it without being rude.

"Well, if you ask me you're overlooking a very significant detail. Here you find a body in the middle of the fairway with a hole in her head. And according to the coroner she has fallen some distance out of a clear blue sky. There's no record of a plane or a helicopter having flown in the vicinity at the time, and everyone thinks it's a puzzle as to how she got there."

"It's not?" I asked, again with reluctance.

"Well, I'm just saying I think you've got to explore the possibility that this wasn't your typical murder."

"You think it might have been a suicide?" I know that was a snotty thing to say, but my senses were blurred by alcohol.

Mark laughed and leaned into the table and spoke softly. "Don't be silly, Joe. All I'm saying is you need to consider that this young woman wasn't killed, but abducted. And the hole in her head wasn't caused by a bullet, but by aliens probing her mind for information of some sort. It happens all the time."

125

Mark leaned back and put his arm over the chair next to him.

"I haven't heard of any cases out here in the Pacific, but in California -- and especially in Nevada and Arizona -- there are any number of documented cases of people having been abducted and probed – though I can't say I've heard of any deaths in this manner. Still I think it's worth considering."

Mark's ravings were interrupted at that point by Shelly who returned to the table and announced she was dead tired and that she needed to lie down. Mark agreed, pushed his chair back and stood up. He raised an eyebrow in my direction, which I interpreted to mean 'think about it.'

"All I'm saying is that you need to think outside the box. Don't believe everything the police tell you. There are loads of government cover-ups every day, right Dad?"

I looked at Maxwell who looked at me uncomfortably but said nothing.

"Well, we'd better go." Mark knocked the table three times, turned and started off with Shelly. The girls didn't seem to even notice that their parents were leaving.

I'm not sure how long Maxwell and I sat without saying anything, but it was long enough for Margie and Catherine, who had finally emerged from the ladies room, to start back toward the table. Maxwell broke the silence.

"He's in charge of the whole West Coast division. Does a decent job of it, too. But you probably noticed he's squirrelly as a bedbug – if I'm not mixing my metaphors too much."

"How long has he been a believer?" I asked sympathetically.

"I found out at the wedding reception when he told me they were honeymooning in Mexico to view the Mayan ruins and look for evidence of alien influence."

"So Shelly's a believer as well?"

"I assume so," Maxwell sighed. "God, I hope the girls don't catch it."

When we finally got home, I headed for the bedroom. It had been a long day and I planned to tuck myself in early.

But before I had a chance to get my sandals off, Margie appeared and informed me that Amanda's brother, Nicky, had arrived and that we had been invited to stop over and say hi.

I wasn't anxious to meet Amanda's brother, since Pete had spoken poorly of him, and so I told Margie I was tired and asked if it couldn't wait till morning. Margie insisted it would reflect poorly on her if we put it off. I also got the impression that Margie was excited to see Nicky, and there was a bit of me that was wondering exactly what Pete had meant when he said that Nicky 'slobbered' all over her. Still I was reluctant.

After a bit of convincing – Margie threatened to blow my cover and expose me for the fraud I was – I decided it was the neighborly thing to go and meet him this evening. You probably noticed this is the second time Margie has blackmailed me today. It's not typical of her and I hope she stops. It's very annoying.

Mom and Pop volunteered to stay with the girls – I wish I'd thought of that – so Margie and I made the short jaunt over to Pete and Amanda's.

We went in the front way, which is to say we climbed the steps from the street up to the lanai and pool area and found Pete and Amanda and a strikingly handsome man who I assumed was Nicky and a very attractive blonde woman sitting by the pool with drinks.

Evidently, they didn't hear us arrive because they were still chatting away until suddenly Nicky spotted us.

His reaction was quite dramatic! "Margie!" he screamed and ran at us and grabbed Margie around the waist and picked her up in the air and spun her around as if she were a little girl.

Margie laughed and kicked until he put her down.

"You look absolutely fabulous!" Nicky crowed at her, then turned and sang over his shoulder at the others. "Doesn't she look absolutely fabulous?"

"You look pretty fabulous yourself."Margie said with a throaty laugh.

"Oh, paaleeeeze," Nicky fawned, pressing his palm to his chest.

He grabbed Margie's hand and began to lead her away. "You've got to tell me everything you've been up to. Everything!"

But before they'd taken two steps Nicky stopped and turned to me.

"Goodness," he said, apologetically. "You probably think I'm terrible."

Nicky came at me and put out his left hand which I took and shook clumsily with my right -- he was still holding Margie firmly in his right.

"You must be Joe. It's wonderful to meet you. Sis and Pete have told me all about you. Come on, join us," Nicky took my arm and guided both Margie and me past Pete and Amanda and right up to where the mystery woman was lounging.

"Joe, Margie, this is Angelica Marroni, the love of my life."

Angelica smiled and looked embarrassed. "Please," she said, "just call me Angie."

Angie tried to get up. In fact she tried three times to rise but she kept falling back into the chaise and giggling.

"You'll have to excuse me," she said finally after sinking back into the lounge. "I can't stand. Nicky had to get me bombed to get me on the plane and Amanda's been feeding me drinks since we landed. If I don't remember meeting you tomorrow, I'll apologize tonight." She held up her glass in a gesture of salutation and we returned it with a wave and an 'aloha,' after which she took a long pull on her drink and finished with: "God it's beautiful here."

Amanda gave Pete an openhanded backhand to the chest.

"Pete, get up and get our guests a drink," she said with a noticeable speech impediment. Obviously Amanda had been drinking more than usual; she never speaks to Pete that way.

Pete opened his mouth to respond, and then pulled himself up.

"Come on, Joe. You can tell me if I'm doing it right." Pete headed inside and I fell in behind.

When we returned, I noted that Nicky had pulled up a chaise lounge for Margie next to his and she and he were chatting away a mile a minute. I delivered Margie's drink and pulled up the last of the lounge chairs next to Pete at the far end of the conversation.

Pete leaned over and whispered to me: "I told you he slobbers all over Margie."

As I've already told you, Pete is my best friend and he's actually quite smart – even if he can't fix things – so I was a bit surprised he hadn't picked up on Nicky.

If you've been paying attention, you've undoubtedly come to the same conclusion as I had: Nicky is definitely gay. His word choice, his mannerism, his dress – his clothes were impeccable and there wasn't a hair out of place on his head. Everything about him screamed 'I'm gay!'

I could understand how Pete might have missed these signals since Nicky has a very masculine appearance, even if his pants were tight and his shirt was open three buttons down and he wore lots of man-jewelry. I had acquired what I considered to be fairly accurate 'gaydar' from my stint working on the loading dock of a furniture store during one summer in college. Evidently, Pete evidently hadn't had such an opportunity.

Once I'd determined that Nicky was gay, I began to speculate about Angie. She was a very good looking woman, a little big for my tastes. By big, I don't mean fat. She was just tall and sort of 'manly.' She had long blonde hair, a well toned figure, big boobs. She looked like she could be a movie star's girl friend, but there was something about her that didn't seem quite right. Was she just his fag-hag?

Time would tell.

As usual, it was a perfect Kona evening and we sat and drank and watched the moon out over the ocean and mumbled this or that. Margie and Nicky were the only ones who had anything resembling a conversation and whenever I caught a snippet of it, it seemed to be about Nicky and his exploits despite his earlier pronouncement that Margie should tell him absolutely everything she'd been up to.

Eventually the hour grew late and the conversation slowed and Angie fell asleep and began to snore so we called it a night.

On the way home I attempted to verify my suspicion about Nicky with Margie.

"Well, I guess I don't have to worry about Nicky stealing you away from me," I said casually.

"Whatever are you talking about?" she said.

"Pete told me that he slobbers all over you. I figured -- you know, that he had eyes for you. He's a very attractive man. A successful actor. Blah, blah, blah. You know."

"Joe, you should know by now that I'm not interested in attractive, successful men. Anyway, he's gay! Didn't you notice that?"

"Yeah, I got that. But I don't think Pete knows."

"I'm certain Pete doesn't know. And let's hope he doesn't find out. According to Amanda, Pete's a bit of a homophobe.

"Pete? Really? I never would have guessed."

"That's what I love about you. You're a lousy guesser."

"So what's the deal with Angie? What makes an attractive lady like her hook up with a gay blade."

"You don't know?" Margie's tone smacked of disbelief.

"Know what?"

"She's a he," Margie said.

"No kidding!" I said, and blew a whistle. "I knew something was odd about her but..."

"And under no circumstances are you to tell Pete!"

I agreed and we walked a little farther. Then I remembered something Margie had said.

"Exactly what did you mean when you said you weren't interested in attractive, successful men?"

My Ex BFF

Morning came in the usual way with leaf blowers buzzing, lawn mowers whirring, birds chirping and plants clacking. I made my way to the kitchen without encountering Margie or anyone else and found the coffee unmade and my paper missing. I suspected vandals and then remembered her parents.

With great reluctance I made my way through the living room and saw the three of them – Margie, Maxwell, and Catherine – out by the pool. Maxwell had my paper.

As I neared them, the conversation grew audible.

"I know it's not good for me, Margie. But couldn't we have eggs and bacon just once?" Maxwell asked.

"Dad, it's not good for you," Margie responded.

"I just said that," Maxwell shot back.

"Oh, leave her alone, Maxwell. You're always stuffing yourself," Catherine said wading in.

"I do not stuff myself!" Maxwell said. "I haven't gained a pound since we were married. Which is more than I can say for some people."

I said a prayer that the phone might ring or a house might explode, but no such luck.

"Mom. Dad. Please," Margie begged.

"Well I'm not going to sit here and be called a fatty," Catherine huffed.

"Dad doesn't think you're fat, do you dad?" Margie said hopefully.

There was a pregnant pause.

"Dad?" Margie pleaded again.

Catherine stood, tossed down her napkin and stomped past me without a word on her way into the house. Margie slumped. Maxwell continued to eat.

I reached the table and took up my usual spot, sans paper. Margie looked up and tried to welcome me with a smile, but it came out badly and looked more like a sneer, which I'm sure she didn't mean, but which hurt all the same.

"Do you want a banana or some papaya?" she asked as I poured myself a cup of coffee.

"I'd prefer eggs, please, with bacon!" I said boldly.

"See!" Maxwell shouted enthusiastically.

Margie's eyes shot daggers at me and I wilted.

"Just kidding. I'd love a banana."

I sipped my coffee and ate my banana and watched Maxwell read my paper.

Later, when I was hard at work in my office (yes I was working hard; I was reading Shoulton books just as fast as I could) Margie knocked on the door and reminded me that we were going to visit Trisha in jail.

'Reminded' is probably the wrong word since I'd never heard of this itinerary before, but considering the option would be to spend the morning with the girls and The Squabbles, I looked at the journey to jail as a reprieve.

We took the Volvo and I drove. Margie sat with a basket of cookies in her lap. I was a little irked at this. Margie never made cookies like that for me. The best I got was shortbreads. It wasn't that she didn't want me to have them; it's just that they weren't healthy for me. That irked me too.

Once again I tried to reason with her. "You keep telling me you aren't getting involved, and then you get involved." I said.

"I'm not involved," Margie said. "I'm just going to make sure Trisha's okay. Why can't you be supportive about this?"

"Because this is dangerous stuff. A woman was killed!"

"Don't be so melodramatic!"

133

"Melodromatic! Margie, do you know what that means? Listen Margie..."

"Turn here!" Margie snapped.

I hit the brakes and turned hard left.

"Margie, it's..."

"Pull in up there."

I did as I was told and pulled the car into the parking space next to the door of the police station.

"There's such a thing ..." I began but Margie was already out of the car.

"You think you can ignore me, but you can't," I called after her.

We'd already been at the station ten minutes getting the run-around about how we weren't on the visitor list Trisha's lawyer had left and that they'd have to get the okay from Trisha and her attorney before we'd be allowed to talk to her. I'm certain Margie wanted to ask why she wasn't informed of this when she'd called, but she knew that would just get her started so she sat stiffly in the hard guest chair with her hands in her lap and a Mona Lisa smile on her lips.

The phone rang.

"Detective Lo," detective Lo said sharply. He cast a glance at Margie as he listened.

"I don't know why they want to visit. That's none of my business. Do you want to put them on the list on not?"

Obviously he was talking to Trisha's lawyer.

"Okay, I'll let you talk, but keep it short." Detective Lo handed Margie the phone.

Trisha's lawyer was very polite, and Margie told her that we just wanted to talk to Trisha as friends, to see if she was all right and needed anything. She promised we wouldn't talk about the case and wouldn't ask Trisha to say or do anything that might be construed as illegal.

After she'd made the promise, Margie handed the phone back to Detective Lo who told the lawyer he had to have a faxed copy of the revised list initialed by her before he could admit us. He hung up.

"She said she'll fax it right away. Would either of you like a cup of coffee? Some water?" The detective was trying to be cordial, but he was not especially successful.

"No thank you," Margie said. I nodded in the negative.

The fax came through and Detective Lo took us out into the squad room and turned us over to a desk sergeant who took us to an interview room and told us to wait. He left and ten minutes later Trisha was escorted in by a female police officer.

Trisha looked pale and miserable dressed in jailhouse dungarees until she saw Margie, then she smiled and the color came back into her face. Margie tried to lift her spirits with a grin and a hug and a sincere "hang in there," but it was obvious Trisha was depressed. She looked at me, and nodded hello, but I could tell she didn't care whether I was there or not.

"Margie, it's so nice of you to come. I didn't think anyone..." Trisha sighed and slumped in her chair; tears formed in the corners of her eyes.

"It's okay, Trisha," Margie said, taking her hand and patting it. "You'll get through it. We all know you didn't do it."

We sat down on the opposite side of the table. The officer left us alone.

Trisha choked back the tears. "Who's we?" she asked, looking up at me suspiciously. She must have guessed that I wasn't 100 percent certain she was innocent. But I didn't say anything.

"Me and Joe and Amanda, and... Well, all of us."

A smile broke over her face and a tear let go down her cheek.

"Thank you, both of you; I was beginning to think..."

Margie stopped her. "Don't talk that way.

"How are they treating you?" Margie asked.

"Okay, I guess." Trisha said. "I've got my own cell. It's..." she teared up and couldn't go on for a moment or two.

"Did you talk to Kenny?" she asked. Then before Margie could respond she answered her own question. "He doesn't care. He hasn't tried to see me. No letter. Nothing…

Margie patted her hand again to break the spell "I've been trying to reach him, but we keep missing one another." This was a lie. Kenny wouldn't take the calls. I would have told her she was ahead of the game by cutting Kenny out of her life, but it wasn't my call to make it was Margie's and she just skated by it.

"I made you some cookies. They wouldn't let me give them to you in here. They said they'll put them in your cell."

"Thank you," Trisha said, her attention someplace else.

"Mac nut and fudge," Margie added.

"You heard about the diary?" Trisha looked down at her hands in her lap. "I didn't really threaten her. She just laughed at me. Do you know how infuriating it is when someone who you're really, really mad at just laughs at you?"

Margie looked at me. "Yes, I do."

I felt offended, but let it slide.

"That's why I threw that bust at her. I didn't try to hit her," her voice rose. "If I'd wanted to, I would have. It looks bad though. It proves intent. And I had

136

opportunity. But I didn't kill her! I hated her, but I couldn't kill anyone.

Margie patted Trisha's hand. "I know, Trisha."

As you'll recall, the 'diary' in reference was Trisha's diary. It was a very complete diary according to our informant and contained an account of an altercation between Trisha and Julia in which Trisha supposedly said 'If you don't give Kenny an amicable divorce, you're going to find yourself dead! And I know just the people who can make it happen.' The diary entry was just two days before Julia came to Hawaii and six days before she died. It was pretty incriminating evidence. In legal parlance I think they refer to it as death bed incrimination or something like that.

It was also clear from the diary – again according to our sources – that Julia had laughed in Trisha's face, enraging her to the point at which she threw a large stone bust at Julia's head which missed but broke a large glass water pipe and flooded the small lab in which they were arguing. There was a confirming report in the college files about the broken water pipe – which had been attributed to the simple bump from a ladder being used -- but no police report. Julia had also documented the event in detail in her diary but never called the police.

I was curious about the glass plumbing though and did some checking. Sure enough, laboratories often use glass plumbing. It handles corrosives better and is helpful in spotting potential clogs before they occur. You learn something new every day, don't you?

In any event, the diary was bad news for Trisha, and it looked like she was going to be in jail until someone else confessed, someone else had better motive and opportunity, or the trial ended with a not guilty verdict. Bail had been denied because of her father's wealth and the prosecution's argument that once she was free her father could easily whisk her off in his private jet to any of a dozen countries without extradition agreements with the U.S. where she might live a perfectly wonderful and opulent life beyond the reach of the U.S. legal system.

"Listen," Margie said in a hushed voice. "I just promised your lawyer that I was only going to talk to you about how you were and nothing about the case. But we need some information to help us figure out who did kill Julia and why. So you can't tell her what we talked about. At least you can't if you want me to be able to come and see you again."

"Oh, no. I won't tell anyone. I'll just say you asked about everyday stuff," Trisha said.

"Good. I'll send you over some things, so you can say you asked for a few items. Is there anything special you want?"

"Only the cookies, and you said you already brought them."

"And I'll send more tomorrow. Now listen. I...we need to know more about your relationship with Kenny."

Trisha's face paled and stiffened. "I don't ever want to think or talk about..."

Margie patted her hand again. "Yes we know, he's a real prick, but we need to ask you anyway."

Margie gave Trisha a moment to let her anger subside. "Okay. What do you want to know?"

Margie launched into a whole series of questions about Kenny and her: how they'd met, how she'd decided to do research with him, what kind of research they were doing, Kenny's relationship with Julia, and so on. I could tell Margie was trying to be indirect so Trisha wouldn't have a clear idea of what information was really the most important.

We only had twenty minutes, but we covered a lot of ground and when the officer reappeared to take Trisha back to her cell, we'd learned a quite a bit, though it was going to take awhile to sort it all out.

"I hear you're going to see my father." Trisha said flatly as she stood up.

"Yes," Margie said. "He called and said he'd like to talk to us. Do you want us to tell him anything for you?"

"No," Trisha said. "Just look out for him."

"What do you mean?" Margie asked.

"Just be careful," Trisha said and stood up. "He's not a nice man."

Trisha cried and hung onto Margie for a minute till she promised to visit as often as possible.

Two minutes later as we climbed back into the Volvo, Margie voiced her dismay at Trisha's relationship with her father. "Isn't that sad? She doesn't think her own father is a very nice man."

"Well," I said. "She knows him better than we do. I think we should take her advice and be careful." I didn't bring up the fact that I'd never been informed we were going to meet Trisha's dad, and this didn't seem like a good time to bring it up.

After our return home, Margie called Amanda and invited her over. Maxwell and Catherine had taken the girls off somewhere, so we had the place to ourselves and were sitting around the pool eating a light lunch and drinking ice tea. Real ice tea. I was privy to the following conversation because a) I like to eat lunch, b) I don't like to eat lunch alone, c) I like to sit by the pool, and d) Amanda was wearing an especially tight tank top.

Amanda seemed distracted when she first arrived, but then she started to ask questions.

"So what did you find out?" Amanda asked.

"Well, for one thing," Margie responded. "Trisha said that Kenny had no funding for his research until after she'd been working for him for almost a year. What do you think that means?"

Amanda thought a minute: "Maybe Trisha said something to her father about Kenny's research that made him take an interest in it."

Margie nodded in agreement.

"I wished I'd thought to ask Trisha whether she'd talked to her father about Kenny's research, but we didn't," Margie said. "I'll ask next time.

I did ask if her father was upset that she was dating the man whose wife might have ideas that could jeopardize his energy holdings. Trisha said that the only reason her father disliked Kenny was that he was older and married."

"What did she say about Kenny's research?"

"I didn't ask her directly. I just asked her in general terms about what applications there were for Kenny's research."

"And..."

"Well, as I understand it Kenny found a way to attach the scent molecules of one thing onto the molecules of another thing. The example she used was an orange. An orange has a very pungent aroma which is caused by ... oh, I don't remember. Anyway, you can isolate those molecules and then attach them to something else to make it smell like an orange, but the scent molecules of the thing you're adding the orange smell are still there so you get something that smells like orange *and* whatever it is being added to.

What Kenny was working on was a method to neutralize the original scent molecules so that they had no scent at all. Then you can add the scent of anything you want and no one will know the difference."

"Why would you want to do that?" Amanda asked.

"Trisha said there's a whole host of reasons. Food companies could use it to make food additives smell better. And the perfume industry could use it to make cheaper perfumes. Stuff like that."

"Well," Amanda said. "That doesn't seem very helpful. Where does that leave us?

"I haven't a clue," Margie said. "Maybe we'll get some information out of her father when we see him."

"You're going to see her father!" Amanda was taken aback at the news. I was thankful that I was not the only one who had not been informed of the meeting.

"Yes, didn't I tell you," Margie looked off into the blue. "Oh, that's right, I told Joe, not you."

I coughed my objection to the truth.

"Are you okay?" Margie asked.

"I'm fine," I said and picked up a taro chip.

"There's something odd about Mr. Ryan's lack of involvement in this whole thing." Margie said.

"What do you mean?" Amanda asked.

Margie looked at me, took a peach from the fruit plate and bit into it before answering.

"If your daughter was in jail and you were one of the richest men in the world, what would you do?"

Amanda thought a moment. "Bust her out?"

"No. He can't bust her out. But it seems to me he could get her out."

"Did you forget?" I asked. "The judge refused bail."

Margie gave me a hard stare. "No I didn't forget. But what's that all about? The only evidence they've got against her is that diary. You think that's enough to hold her without bail?"

"You're right, Margie," Amanda said. "I remember a guy in Seattle that killed his wife and baby and they had

141

everything but a signed confession and he got out on bail."

"Wait a minute," I said. "Her bail was denied because she was a flight risk. Her father has a private jet and ..."

Margie butted in. "They could just take away her passport. She's not going anywhere without a passport. And besides, her father's not going to ruin his reputation – a reputation he guards like a frigging virgin – to help his daughter escape a trial any freshman lawyer could win. There's more to it. I know it."

Margie's gaze drifted off, which generally meant trouble, and since we were already involved in poking around in a murder investigation I assumed her gaze had even more impact than usual.

At that moment, there was a commotion at the door and Mom and Pop and the girls burst in.

"I have never been so embarrassed in my life," Catherine hissed.

Mom and Dad and the girls had returned from their trip up to Waikoloa where the girls had had an opportunity to swim with the dolphins. Evidently it didn't go well.

"I only asked her if they were real! My God, Catherine, they were the size of cantaloupes, surely other people have asked her the same question," Maxwell's response illuminating the basis for the present clash.

"She was mollified! Don't you understand anything about... And you didn't even try to apologize."

"What for? It was just a question."

The girls had already scampered out of site to their lair in the pool house, and Catherine seemed headed for the guest room with Maxwell dogging after her. Clearly this tussle was going to continue but thankfully it wasn't headed our way.

Even so Amanda and Margie both jumped to their feet.

"I just remembered a phone call I have to make," Amanda said, fleeing the scene as if she'd just nabbed the Hope diamond. "Talk to you later, Margie."

"I guess I'll go referee before things escalate," Margie moaned and dragged herself toward the house.

"I'll stay out here and shoo flies off the fruit," I called.

"It's the least I can do," I said to Magoo, who cocked his head at me and then went to follow Margie just in case she was going to the kitchen.

I lingered by the pool for a bit then made my way quietly to the den and hid in there and read while the computer typed away. I was deep into a very interesting murder in which a deranged husband slaughters his wife's entire family in a secluded cabin in the northern part of Wisconsin --an interesting premise don't you think?-- when the phone rang and without thinking I picked up the extension in the den. Usually I let Margie get the phone; it's never for me anyway. This time I was wrong. It was Amanda, and to my surprise she wanted to talk to me.

"Have you seen Pete?" she asked. I could tell from the sound of her voice this wasn't a casual question.

"No. I haven't seen him. Is something wrong?"

There was a long silence.

"We had a fight. He stormed out last night and hasn't been home since."

"Pete stormed out? Why didn't you mention this earlier?" I tried to imagine that, but couldn't. I mean the leaving part I could imagine, but the storming part? I whistled.

Amanda ignored my question. "Are you repeating me?" Amada's voice was testy. She paused. "It was over Angie," she added quietly.

"He found out?" I asked.

"You know about Angie?" Amanda asked with a hint of relief in her voice. She was probably glad she didn't have to explain.

"I guessed and Margie corroborated. But how did Pete…"

"They were … he saw them…" Amanda was having a hard time with this. Finally she blurted it out: "He saw them in the shower together."

I whistled again.

"Will you please stop that?!" Amanda barked.

"Of course Pete got all nutty about it and said it was immoral for two men to … well, you know. He said he was going to tell them to leave. I said he wasn't going to do any such thing and that he was a homophobe and… Well… We both said a few more things and then he stormed out."

"Did you check the garage?" I realized immediately how insensitive that sounded.

"That's not funny, Joe! I've called every place. He's nowhere. Could you find him?"

"I'll take a look around, Amanda," I promised. "Don't worry, he'll show up." I hung up and shook my head. *Pete stormed out? I'd really like to have seen that!*

I found Margie hiding from her parents in the bedroom and told her what had happened then grabbed the car keys and headed out, glad to have a mission that would get me out of the house for awhile.

Of course the first place I checked was Home Depot, which is where Pete spends most of his time when he's not at home. But his car was not in the parking lot and he was not in the store.

Next place I checked was the video arcade where Pete holds the record on most of the video games. He's not the best repairman, but he's got lighting fast reflexes. That turned up nothing.

The ice cream shop was a long shot, but it allowed me to get a double scoop of raspberry swirl in one of those big waffle cones. McDonald's and Subway and Taco Bell where also long shots, and no, I did not partake of food from those places – unless you count French fries.

Another hour of cruising around Kona and I was ready to call it quits. Amanda should have put one of those GPS locators in his car if she cared that much.

I arrived home and was climbing out of the car when I heard a 'tink-tink-tinking' sound from the garage. That didn't seem right, so I went back to the car, leaned in and pressed the garage door opener which slowly opened to reveal Pete, sitting on the garage floor surrounded by lawnmower parts.

"Hey," Pete said without looking up.

"Hey," I said and ambled over to lean against Margie's Miata. I looked at Pete. Pete looked down at the clutter.

"I can put it together," he promised.

I really didn't care if he could since we had a gardener and he brought his own equipment. The lawnmower was a holdover from the previous owners.

"Let's go get a drink," I suggested.

Pete wiped his hands on a rag – which looked suspiciously like an old sweatshirt of mine -- and pulled himself off the floor. We climbed into the Volvo.

The best place to have a drink at that time of day – or actually any time of day -- is Huggo's. And it was early enough that there were a few tables left for the sunset watching crowd and late enough that I didn't feel like an alcoholic, which is to say it was four-forty-five.

We got a table by the water, ordered drinks and pupus and quietly watched the nightly entertainment set up until our stuff arrived.

I had a beer and Pete had a Whaler's Tail, which is basically eight kinds of booze and a shot of mango juice (to take the edge off) served in a glass the size of Indiana. A pineapple wedge the size of a large Frisbee finishes it off. By comparison, the lime wedge shoved in the neck of my beer seemed trivial. A platter of nachos sat between us looking like Mt. Vesuvius after the eruption.

"So," I said, carefully testing the waters. "I heard you and Amanda had a tiff."

Pete gulped half his drink before coming up for air and a helping of nachos.

"You might call it that." I could tell from his tone, he was still mad about it.

"She's worried about you," I said. "Don't you think you should give her a call and at least let her know you're all right?"

"Screw her!" Pete drank the rest of the Indiana-sized drink and motioned the waitress for another.

I was shocked. Pete was not the swearing kind. In fact, I couldn't think of another time I'd heard him swear (unless you count 'shit,' 'fuck,' or 'damn' after he'd injured himself while fixing one thing or another). I'd heard Pete and Amanda argue, but never swear at one another.

"Did she tell you *why* I left?" Pete asked after filling his mouth with nachos – it was not a pretty sight.

"She said it concerned Angie."

"Angie! Fuck! She's no more an Angie than I'm Betty Lou!" Pete's voice was getting loud; we were drawing

146

attention. I motioned him to lower his voice. He responded by clamming up.

His second drink came and he guzzled half of it. By my calculation, he had enough booze in him now to start a fight with anyone in the place.

Pete looked at me sternly through watery eyes. "You don't think it's wrong for two men to...? Jeez. I get sick just thinking about it," his speech was noticeably slurred now. Passing out didn't seem out of the question.

"So don't think about it. It's not like they're trying to convert you," I said.

Pete took a big sip through one of the three straws in his drink.

"So you think it's okay?"

"I don't have a problem with it," I said honestly.

"But I do, and Amanda should respect that!"

Pete took another hit. He looked at me hard.

"It's her brother. What's she supposed to do?" I asked.

"He's not my fucking brother!"

"You don't have any brothers."

"What the hell does that have to do with it?"

"I'm just saying..."

Pete struggled to his feet.

"You God-damn liberals are all alike! Everything's fucking okay with you guys. Welfare, abortions, queers! Everything's okay!"

I stood up to face him. For a moment I thought he was going to take a swing at me, but then he just turned and staggered out of the place leaving me standing alone at the table with a couple dozen eyes looking my way.

It occurred to me that I should go after him, but I stopped myself. I was mad. I'd never thought of Pete as a bigot and frankly I figured he could go screw himself.

Damn closet republican!

I stayed a Huggo's to finish the nachos and have another beer to calm down so it was dark by the time I returned home.

As I pulled into the driveway I discovered my way was blocked by a strange car. When I tried to maneuver to the left of it, I heard metal scrapping on rock.

"Shit! Shit! Shit!" I cursed and pounded the steering wheel. *That car better not belong to another suspect!*

As I entered the house I heard voices in the background arguing. Guess who?

"It's not my fault if you forgot your snorkel gear," Catherine chided. "I'm not your mother."

"You packed yours! How hard would it be…" Maxwell's voice trailed off.

There was no need to hear more. I stepped cautiously around the corner and pushed open the door to the den. I noticed the light was on so I was thinking that Margie had been in there, but after I entered I stopped cold.

I was not alone. There on the sofa bed was Angie, propped up reading one of my Shoulton books.

"Hello," she/he said sweetly sitting up. "You must be Joe. I'm Angie."

Evidently she had forgotten we'd met earlier, but that didn't really matter. I was too shocked to answer and just looked blankly into the corner of the room for a moment and then, zombie-like, I turned to leave.

"Margie!!!" I bellowed loud enough to rattle my fillings.

I found my lovely bride in our bedroom holding a pillow, a blanket, and sheets in front of her, and before I could ask my question, Margie answered it.

"She doesn't have any place to go! She had a fight with Nicky. I'm sure they'll work it out in the morning."

I wagged a finger at her.

"Absolutely NOT! She...he...she is not staying here. We have too many house guests now. I won't have it!"

"Joe, don't be unreasonable." Margie said.

"No!" I insisted. "I'm not going to cave on this one, Margie. I'm serious. Enough is enough!

Margie dropped the bedclothes on the bed under which Magoo had already scrambled.

"Fine. If that's the way you feel, then you tell her she's got to leave."

"You're the one who invited her!"

"And you're the one that wants her out."

I'm no good at throwing people out and Margie knows it. So I fumed a moment that Margie had called my bluff.

"You t think you're going to win, don't you, but this time I won't back down!" I said and stomped from the room. Behind me, Margie stamped her feet on the floor.

I found Angie just as I'd left her, sitting and reading.

"Isn't Shoulton the best?" Angie said looking up as I entered.

"Angie," I said abruptly, ignoring her comment about Shoulton. "I'm sorry, but I'm going to have to ask you to leave."

Angie looked confused. "But Margie said...?"

"Margie doesn't make *all* the decisions. You'll just have to patch things up with Nicky."

She made no effort to move. She just sat there and looked at me. I was about to reiterate my demand when Maxwell entered behind me carrying a cup of coffee.

"There you go Angie. Anything else I can get you?" he said cheerily, as he delivers the cup to Angie with a big grin. "Hello, Joe. What are you two talking about?"

Before I could answer, Maxwell noticed the book Angie was reading.

149

"You like that book?" he said enthusiastically, clapping me on the shoulder. "Joe here wrote it, you know." He must have noted the look of confusion on Angie's face because he added: "Shoulton's his pen name. They tell me mysteries sell best if the author's a woman."

A carnivorous grin spread across Angie's face.

"So you wrote all these books?" Angie asked. She/he put his/her hand on his/her chest. (*Note to the reader:* I'm getting tired of this she/he, him/her crap. From now on let's just call Angie a 'her' and let it go at that. Okay?)

"Goodness me. I had no idea!" Angie pretended to be impressed.

From the other side of the house, Catherine called for Maxwell.

"What is it?" Maxwell snapped loudly.

"Where did you put the camera?"

"What do you want the camera for?"

"What?" Catherine said.

"I said what do you want the camera for? It's almost bedtime," Maxwell howled.

"In the bedroom? It's not here. I looked."

Maxwell snarled and started to leave. "I didn't say it was in the bedroom. I said it's almost bedtime," his voice trailed off.

With Maxwell gone, it was just Angie and me, and I didn't like the way she was smiling.

"So you're the famous Kimberly Shoulton." Angie said.

"Well," I said. "I don't generally..."

"Cut the crap, honey." Angie cut me off, her demeanor turning from sweet to sour and her voice changing to one much too masculine for her current attire. "I met Shoulton at a book signing six months ago."

I stood frozen like a deer in the headlights.

"I don't know what you're trying to pull on dear old dad, but I'm not going anywhere, unless you want to explain why you're pretending to be something you're not. Capish?"

Angie snuggled into the sofa, dropped her eyes and returned to her book. I nodded and then just stood for a moment, unsure what had just happened. Eventually I realized I'd been dismissed, so I tucked my tail between my legs and took my leave.

Back in the bedroom Margie was overjoyed to hear I'd changed my mind.

"I knew you couldn't do it! You're just too nice to be mean."

She picked up the bed clothes and some towels she'd added and headed toward the door smiling.

I sat on the bed, exhausted. I let myself fall back and stare at the ceiling. Magoo, who had come out from under the bed, hopped up on the bed and sauntered over and licked my face.

"Thanks, buddy," I said. "At least I can count on you."

A minute later Margie reappeared, closed the bedroom door and lifted Magoo to the floor. She climbed on the bed and straddled me.

"Good boys deserve special presents," she said as she began to unbutton my shirt.

Hey, this could work, I thought and I was just thinking that things weren't so bad and that everything might work out after all when my hopes were dashed by the sound of a crash from the guest room followed by: "Now look what you've done, Maxwell! Can't you be careful? Honestly...."

"Well who leaves a glass on the edge of the toilet for God's sake..."

"Well, where am I supposed to..."

It was at this point that Margie gave me a quick kiss and jumped out of bed.

"Later," she said. "I'd best go and referee."

"Referee all you want," I said aloud, but not loud enough for Margie to hear. "They don't need a referee, they need dueling pistols."

Mrs. M.

The master bath had become a sanctuary for me since the guests arrived. It was the one place I could be alone without fear of intrusion – except from Margie that is – which is perfectly all right with me since much of the time when we're together in the master bath Margie is wearing her birthday suit which is my favorite outfit of hers. But I digress…

In any event, I was in my sanctuary, toweling off after an especially long and hot shower, when Margie, all dressed up to go out, poked her head around the corner.

"Where are you going?" I probed nervously. I didn't like it when Margie went some place because if often meant that I was to be alone with one of the inmates.

"It's Wednesday," Margie responded as if that were enough information, then spotting the perplexed look on my face added: "I'm going to read to the second graders?"

Margie reads to the second graders up at Mahalakaliki Grade School one day a week. She also reads to the old people up at the Kona Care Center every now and then. She loves doing both these things and I'm sure the children and the old folks love her doing it. Margie puts a lot of energy into everything she does so I'm sure she reads with great passion.

"Of course," I said. "I forgot. And what are we reading?"

"Dickens," Margie said

"Any particular Dickens?"

"*A Christmas Carol*, of course."

"Is that permitted in public schools?"

"Joe, I don't think anyone is going to complain about *A Christmas Carol*. It's not just a Christmas story, it's also a story about sharing and caring and thinking of others."

"Of course," I said, lathering up my face for a shave. I'm a blade man; electric razors seem too modern. I like the feel of cold steel against my skin and the excitement that comes with the danger of bloodletting.

"Can you keep an eye on Mom while I'm out? Dad's gone off with Shelly and the girls to snorkel and Mark's gone off somewhere…"

Blood spurted from my face where I'd just nicked myself. I grabbed for tissue paper to stop it.

What had she said? Keep an eye on Mom? Think fast, Joe.

"Maybe your mother would like to tag along with you; help out?" I blurted.

I was not eager to spend any quality time with Mrs. M. Although she seemed like a nice enough woman when she wasn't squabbling with Mr. M., or criticizing Margie, or looking at me like I was a big lay-about, Truthfully I'd hoped to avoid getting really close to either her or Mr. M.

"I already asked, and she's not." Margie's face disappeared. "Oh, and I'm going to stop and see Trisha on the way back."

As you'll recall, Margie had promised to visit Trisha as often as she could and bring her homemade cookies. I complained that she never made those things for me and

153

her response was: "I will when you're in jail." I seriously thought about doing something to land me in jail; I was that desperate for cookies.

I guess I should have just considered myself lucky that I didn't have to accompany her to jail.

"Just a minute!" I called after her and a second later Margie's face reappeared. "What am I supposed to do with her?"

"Just grab a book and go out by the pool and sit with her. You don't have to *do* anything."

Yeah, sure. I'd heard that before.

Margie's face disappeared again and although I called after her a second time, it did not reappear.

I tore off another piece of tissue and slapped it on my face to stop the blood. I looked at myself in the mirror. *Be strong.*

So as to spend as little time alone with Mrs. M as possible, I dawdled in the bathroom and took my time getting dressed – polo shirt, shorts and flip-flops, same as yesterday but different colors.

Eventually I had to make my way out to the pool where I found Mrs. M. with her nose in that book of hers: *Kill, Kill, Kill* – which I was pretty sure was a murder mystery.

For my read, I brought along a civil war book describing the battle of Bull Run and the realities it brought to the Civil War. I'm not generally interested in such things but my great grandfather had taken part in that battle and so when I ran across it at the library, I grabbed it. The writing was good, and thankfully, the author didn't dwell on the horrors of the time.

"Before I get settled, can I get you anything, Mrs. M.?"

Catherine looked up from her book. "No thank you, Joe."

154

I sat down and opened my book.

"Oh, maybe a glass of ice tea, if you have it," Catherine said lazily.

I got unsettled and fetched ice tea for both of us and also brought along a plate of leftover cheese and crackers in case we got the munchies.

It occurs to me that I haven't described Mrs. M. to you. Perhaps you're not really interested, but I'll do it anyway. It's good filler.

Mrs. M, Catherine, Mom, whatever you choose to call her, looked like a mom, but not in the frumpy dumpy sort of way. In fact except for the fact that she was a dozen or so pounds overweight, she looked quite young for her age. Actually, I think the word I'm looking for is matronly. My dictionary says it's *a woman, especially a married woman of middle age or later, who has had children and is thought of as being mature, sensible, and of good social standing.* That seems about right.

Her blonde-brown hair is cut fairly short, curled and heavily frosted, a feature shared by many women of her age, and it fit her quite well. I tried to imagine her with long hair and failed.

Although I'd never been told as much, I assumed she'd had a facelift. The assumption was based on both the surprising lack of crow's feet and the general tightness of her face, which didn't seem to match the more creased look of her neck. Sorry Mom.

It was easy to see where Margie had gotten her bright blue eyes and both Mom and Margie had the same small, nearly lobe-less ears. I think I mentioned earlier that Margie appeared to have inherited her father's nose; a more feminine version of course.

Unlike Margie, Mrs. M. dressed conservatively and seemed to know exactly what to wear for any occasion.

Of course being wealthy and traveling with three large suitcases helps in that regard. I could continue about her nails and such, but you've got the picture. If you need more help, think Jane Fonda with a few more pounds and you're pretty close.

Anyway, I got comfy again and was about to start chapter eight of my book: 'Blood of Brothers,' when Mrs. M. offered up a tidbit I couldn't resist.

"Have you ever seen any pictures of Margie when she was young?"

Putting a finger in my book to save my place, I tried to remember, but couldn't. "I've seen her college photos," I said.

"Younger?" Mrs. M. asked.

I looked up from the book and reflected. "No. Can't say that I have."

In fact now that I thought about it I was sure I hadn't because when we were looking at the photo album my mother had put together for me, I'd asked to see her childhood photos. She'd dodged the request by telling me how cute I was. I wasn't cute, I was a nerd. But I grew out of it. I think.

"And you probably never will."

Of course Mrs. M.'s comment caught my attention and after a few tics of the clock I realized she wasn't going to be forthcoming.

"Why's that?" I asked finally.

"Because she was a fatty." Mrs. M. looked up from her book over her readers and caught my eye and winked knowingly.

Now this information was new and the fact that Margie, sleek as a greyhound, had once been a 'fatty' intrigued me; but there was something else afoot that piqued my curiosity even more. *Why*, I thought, i*s good old mom digging up dirt that Margie obviously wants to remain buried?*

I chose my next question carefully. "How fat was she?"

Okay, it wasn't the kind of question I needed to think long and hard about, but I had it on good authority that fat kids grow up to be fat adults even if along the way they manage to slim down. I tried to picture Margie in a Mumu. I drew a blank.

"Well, let's just say she was larger than a bread box."

"But there are no pictures of her?"

"She's taken them all and either hidden or destroyed them."

I pondered that bit of info: *Margie a fatty; I'd like to see that!*

There was still an hour or so to kill before Margie's return, so I pursued the current topic, since it seemed a fruitful one, and concerned a subject upon which I had an infinite quest for information and about which I seemed to know so little.

"So what else can you tell me about the young Margie of whom I know so little?"

For the next hour plus, Mrs. M. filled in all those years when I was a small boy in Chicago and Margie was a small girl in L.A. It turns out that not only was Margie a 'fatty,' but she was also a tomboy and had an imaginary friend – who she blamed any and all trouble on.

According to Mrs. M., Margie wore pants and t-shirts and had her hair cut short and for a brief while Mr. and Mrs. M. were concerned about her sexual orientation. But Margie eventually got her period and immediately went absolutely gaga over boys. She let her hair grow, began wearing 'slutty' clothes –Mrs. M.s words, not mine

157

– and started taking ballet lessons. According to Mrs. M., Margie was a star at ballet – if a little on the chunky side.

Ballet didn't last long, however, and Margie discovered horses, as so many young girls do at that age, and took up polo. She was a success at that as well and her team nearly made it to the junior Olympics.

Polo was followed by barrel racing which was followed by dressage and jumping, a sport which Mrs. M was glad she gave up after Superman took a fall and became a quadriplegic.

In her high school years Margie was on the golf team, the swimming team, a cheerleader, a thespian, first chair violin, girl's choir, and on the debate team. She was a straight A student and somehow, despite being the most popular girl in school, managed not to get pregnant – again, those are Mrs. M's words not mine.

I knew about Margie's college years and her stint in Vegas and her marriage, so once we arrived at that point, I backtracked to what I thought were some of the more interesting highlights Mrs. M. had illuminated.

"Margie had an imaginary friend? What was that like?" I queried.

"Oh, she was impossible. She told Amanda everything," Mrs. M. looked up at me over the rim of her readers again as if to make sure I understood that Margie's closest friend shared the same name as her childhood imaginary friend, something I picked up on right away.

"I'd go past her room some evenings and she'd be chattering away at great length about some boy or an assignment or some upcoming event as if she was on the phone with a friend, but she wasn't. It was always Amanda. We considered counseling for her, but since she seemed well rounded and had loads of real friends, we made some inquiries and got assurances that having an imaginary friend wasn't anything to be too concern with. I'm not sure that was good advice, because as I'm sure you know that although Margie doesn't appear to actually talk to her imaginary friend anymore, she does seem to forget who she's told what to."

"I've noticed that," I said.

"As I said, Margie blamed her imaginary friend for everything. 'I'm late coming home because Amanda got drunk and threw up on herself, so we had to wait while her clothes got clean at the Laundromat.' 'It wasn't me! Amanda broke the lamp.' 'I think Amanda farted.' It was like that all the time. She tried using that excuse even when she came home from college for visits." Mrs. M. paused. "Does she still do that it?"

Well that was a good question. "I'm not sure," I said. "She blames Amanda for lots of stuff, but until now, I'd just assumed it was the real Amanda. I guess I'll have to pay closer attention."

"That's a good idea," said Mrs. M.

I got a little more info on Margie's vast accomplishments in and out of school during her younger years but by the time Margie returned, we'd fallen silent and were reading quietly.

I heard Margie's car on the drive and a moment later Margie entered the house and slammed the door behind her. Margie never slams doors so I assumed something was wrong.

"What's the matter," I said, springing up from my chair and heading indoors.

"They wouldn't let me see her!" Margie yelled and slammed the bag of chocolate chip cookies she'd brought for Trisha onto the floor. I winced with the image of those perfectly yummy treats being transformed into a pile of crumbs. "I've been taken off the visitor's list!"

Margie stomped toward the bedroom and I followed after. She was already stripping down and pulling her running clothes from her drawer when I arrived.

"I need to burn off some anger before I kill someone," she said by way of explanation.

A good husband knows when to talk and when to listen. Since I consider myself a good husband I sat on the bed and waited as Margie undressed and redressed. By the time she was tying her running shoes, she seemed to have calmed down a bit. I wanted to ask why she'd been taken off the visitor list, but I thought it bad timing and in truth I was quiet happy with the turn of events since as you'll recall I didn't want her anywhere near the murder suspects.

"How did it go with my mother?" Margie asked, skipping the subject of her anger and breaking the silence.

"Great," I said.

"Really?" Margie seemed legitimately surprised. "What did you do?"

"Nothing really. We just talked."

"What did you talk about?" I could tell Margie was suspicious that we might actually have something in common to discuss.

"Oh, not much. You mainly."

"Me?"

"Your mother says you were a fatty when you were young. Is that true?"

Margie looked at me oddly for a moment and then started to chuckle.

"She's still telling that one?" Margie looked at herself in the mirror and fluffed her hair.

"So it's not true?" I asked, a little confused that Mrs. M. should be telling fibs about her own daughter.

"I was not a fatty," Margie said. "I was at most eight pounds overweight, but Mom never let up on me about it till I became head cheerleader in my junior year. To Mom, fat is as bad as it gets. She was a model before she and dad got married. I told you. Remember."

She had not told me, hence I did not remember, but I nodded my head as though I did. You may remember from my description of her that Mrs. M. wasn't exactly svelte so I had to verbalize my concern.

"But," I said, "she's carrying a dozen extras and I haven't heard her mention a diet."

"And you won't," Margie snipped. "Mom's pounds are not the same as my pounds, or your pounds, or Dad's pounds. They don't exist."

"So why did she tell me you were a fatty? And why have you hidden all the pictures of your youth?"

"She said that?" Margie looked forlorn. "Well, in the first place, I haven't hidden all the pictures of my youth. I'll be happy to show them to you at any time. As to why she told you I was a fatty, I suppose it's because she's jealous of me."

This caught me off guard. "Jealous of you? Exactly why would that be?"

"Well for one thing, my relationship with my father."

"And that would be…"

"I have one! Mom's jealous because I have a very healthy relationship with my dad. She's been jealous of that for as long as I can remember."

"You have a healthy relationship with your father?" This seemed a reach to me.

"Of course, I do! Think about it, Joe. Who did he listen to when he was stuck in Honolulu? Me. Who got him to change into more suitable swim attire? Me? Who got him to… Need I go on?

161

What she said was true -- as screwy as it sounded --
and I must have let the confusion show on my face,
because Margie came over and took my chin in her hand
and shook it a little.

"Well?" She said. "Am I right?"

Her hand smelled of that yummy coconut lotion she
wore and I drank it in while I looked into her lovely blue
eyes. Of course she was right! But that wasn't the issue.
Why should a mother be jealous of her daughter's
relationship with her father? And more importantly, why
specifically should Mrs. M. be jealous? The way the two
of them fought, I figured neither one of them gave a hoot
about the other one and that they stayed together out of
sheer malice. It was a reach to think of Margie and her
mom as rivals for Mr. M.s attention.

"So your mother said you were a fatty to get even with
you because your dad likes you better than he likes her?"

Margie sat on the bed and looked up at me sadly.
"Screwed up family?"

I sat next to her and took her hand and held it.
"Screwed up family," I agreed. "And I thought mine was
the only one."

Margie stood up. "I'm going for a long run. See you in
an hour or so. Don't tell mom she's a liar."

"Do I look stupid enough to ..."

"I'm just saying; don't mess with her view of the
world. It can get pretty crazy in there."

Margie left the room, and I sat on the bed and said the
void: "Crazy *in* there? How about crazy out here?"

That night, as I lay on the pillow waiting for Mr. S
(that's the Sandman), I realized that one of my greater or
lesser faults is that I give women the benefit of the doubt
when it comes to almost everything. And I'd done it
with Mrs. M. -- assuming she was the sweet, innocent,

little old 'mom' I'd conjured in my brain.

I guess it's a chauvinistic thing, even though I don't consider myself a chauvinist, but I have a hard time picturing some fresh-faced sixteen year old girl killing her best friend. I always figure there's more to the story than I know. But put some pimply faced punk from the streets of L.A. in the same story and I have no trouble believing he did it!

The truth is, of course, girls *can* be just as dangerous as boys.

New Problems, New Suspects

Margie was unusually quiet on the drive up north the next morning to meet Tricia's father. Normally when we make this drive we're on our way to Hapuna beach for the sun or Hawi for lunch – Hawi is a small town on the northern tip of the island with a few touristy shops and restaurants. We like the Bamboo Restaurant for the food, the hula dancing wait staff, and the local art. In fact, the earrings Margie was wearing were from the Bamboo Restaurant. How's that for a coincidence.

Anyway, as I said, Margie is generally bubbling as only Margie can bubble when we're on our way north. She would have asked me at least five times if I'd remembered the camera, the sunscreen, the this, that, or the other – even though she'd been the one to pack it in the trunk or stuff it in the big beach bag that always accompanied us.

But this time she just watched the road. I would have asked what she was thinking, but it was kind of nice just to drive in silence and look over and see her looking so absorbed. It would have made a great picture. Maybe some other time.

"You're unusually quiet," I said finally.

"Just thinking," Margie said.

"You know that scares me," I said only half joking. "*What* are you thinking?"

Margie wrinkled her nose at me. "Nothing" was all she offered, and we drove on in silence.

We pulled off the highway onto Mauni Lani Drive and stopped at the guard shack where a very helpful gentleman checked us in and directed us toward Mr. Ryan's estate.

The Mauni Lani Bay Hotel is one of the most exclusive hotels on the Big Island. It's situated about 30 miles north of Kona on the beach. It has 350 rooms and a number of private bungalows. The rooms go for about $500 a night depending on location and season. The bungalows start at – well, if you have to ask, you can't afford it. There are also a number of private residences on the grounds in what is known as Mauni Lani Estates, and that was our destination.

We followed a long private road till we came to another guard shack where a second guard checked us in and we drove along a private drive a few hundred yards till we crested a small hill and could see the house. I thought at first we might have taken a wrong turn, because the structure in front of us looked much more like one of those boutique hotels that are becoming so popular than a private residence, and I wondered briefly what it was like to be a gazillionaire and have everything you wanted. Probably not as much fun as you think.

We pulled up in front, and a young man came out to take the car and we climbed the stairs and walked along the well manicured portico to massive Koa wood doors.

As I reached for the knocker, the door swung open and we were greeted by a dumpy, gray-haired woman dressed in a flowery red and green Mumu.

"Aloha, Mr. and Mrs. Thomas," she said pleasantly. "I am Desire Wildo, Mr. Ryan's executive secretary. Please come in."

I stood there stunned for a moment. *The voice was the same, but...So much for telling a book by its cover! Or a cover by its voice?*

"Mr. Ryan is waiting for you in the library, please follow me."

We tagged behind Desire through the house, past a pool and a courtyard with exotic birds, two large fountains, a koi pond and a very large statue of King Kamehameha, till we reached another set of Koa wood doors. Desire knocked briefly, opened the doors, stepped aside, and bowed us in.

The library didn't resemble the rest of the house at all. The paneling was dark from ceiling to floor and it had the air of a New England library, not a Kona room at all.

As we entered, I spotted three men grouped together at the far end of the room near large louvered doors that stood open and let what light there was into the place. The view outside was of yet another pond and fountain and a large green space and then the ocean.

The men, who had been talking, stopped and turned as soon as we entered. One man was quite tall, maybe six-six. He was lanky and balding, but his hair was dark and he looked to be in his mid thirties. He was dressed in casual clothes – a Hilfiger golf shirt, shorts and sandals – but he looked uncomfortable. I had the impression that he was out of his element and would have been happier in a three piece suit and tie. He, I was certain, was not Ryan.

Another man was Asian. He was short and stocky and wore a Hawaiian print shirt. He had long tan slacks and woven sandals. Expensive woven sandals. He had a large gold chain around his neck and a pendant of some sort

165

hung from it. He also had a gold and jade bracelet and ring and a slave tattoo high on his arm that was partially obscured by the sleeve of his shirt. He had a drink in his hand, which looked like scotch. I was interested. He was clearly not G. Peter Ryan either.

The third man, who by the time I'd taken inventory of the others, was headed toward us with a wide grin on his face and an outstretched hand was certainly Ryan. I recognized him as much from his pictures as from his confident manner. He was a smaller man than I'd assumed, but he had the magnetic personality I'd anticipated. Every really successful person I'd ever met had the ability to make me feel at home instantly as if I were an old, dear friend. Ryan did that and more.

He attacked Margie first, taking her right hand in his and covering them both with his left.

"My God," he gushed as he pumped the heck out it. "Trisha said you were beautiful, but..." He shot a toothy grin at me. "You're a very, very lucky man." He held Margie's hand until she pulled at it, whereupon he let go immediately but continued to admire Margie for a beat or two. The guy had perfect timing.

"Thank you," Margie said. She was used to compliments, and I could see that Ryan felt he had to up the ante if he was going to impress her.

"Do you model?"

"I did a bit in college," Margie answered.

This was going to be fun. I anticipated his next question.

"Why did you quit?"

"I wanted to dance."

"You're a dancer?"

"I used to dance in the chorus line at the Golden Nugget."

He looked impressed, but I was surprised he wasn't squirming. Usually by now the man would be squirming. A model, a Vegas dancer. Most men were intimidated.

"I used to know an Alicia Rand; I believe she danced at the Golden Nugget. Did you ever run into her?"

At the mention of the name, Margie's face brightened. "Alicia! Of course I knew her. She was one of my best friends!"

Jeez this guy was good. I stood quietly and watched and listened as the two of them spent a few moments reminiscing about a mutual acquaintance I'd never heard of. But Ryan didn't let it drag on. He had an agenda, as all men of his type do, and after a few Q and A's he moved the conversation in my direction.

"Is that where you met....Vegas?" he paused, took a step in my direction, thrust out his hand and took mine just as he'd taken Margie's. "...it's Joe isn't it? Or do you prefer Joseph?"

His handshake reminded me of Father Tom's back at St. Francis of Our Lady of Peace in Chicago where I had been a regular and an altar boy. It was warm and firm and comforting. He must have been great at funerals.

"Joe's just fine," I said, pulling my hand ever so slightly and noting how skillfully he released his grip. I wondered briefly how long he would have held it if I'd let him.

"We met on the island actually," I said, assuming he already knew everything about both of us including my sojourn as altar boy for Father Tom.

"It's really wonderful here. Absolutely wonderful," he was enthusiastic and loud.

Then in an instant his voice changed and he was the concerned father whose daughter was in jail charged with murder. "If only the situation were different." He looked away into a corner of the room. It was a nice touch, but I wasn't convinced it was authentic.

"Come in, come in," Ryan threw an arm around Margie and ushered her toward the other two men who waited smiling. I lagged behind.

"This is Jason Hilton, my chief legal counsel."

The tall man gave a quick, courteous nod and smile. He took Margie's hand and said 'nice to meet you' then took my hand and repeated the phrase. His hands were huge and I suspected he played basketball for Harvard or Yale or wherever you went to be chief legal counsel for someone of Ryan's stature before you were even forty.

"And this is Tommy Chow," Ryan said, presenting the Asian man.

We repeated the above with Tommy whose handshake was just right but who couldn't take his eyes off Margie's pert little nipples pressed against the thin fabric of her top.

I was close enough now to see that the pendant, bracelet and ring were indeed jade. Probably worth more than our Volvo, but then you expect someone who hangs with someone like Ryan to be flush.

"Tommy and I go way back," Ryan said. "He's from Honolulu. He came to keep me company while we sort this out. Can I get anyone a drink?"

"I'll have a scotch," I answered a little too quickly.

"Just juice if you have it," Margie said. "Preferably mango."

I expected Ryan to ring a bell and get a servant in there to make the drinks, but he apparently was a do-it-yourself kind of guy and headed toward the bar and started making the drinks himself.

"First, let me thank you for helping Trisha. She tells me you took her in without a thought. That tells me a lot about the kind of people you are."

Ryan brought us our drinks and motioned us to sit.

Margie and I sat on a large leather sofa behind a low coffee table, and the three men sat across from us in large wingback chairs that formed an arc. I felt oddly as if we were about to be interrogated.

"So tell me," Ryan began, "how is Trisha?"

An hour later we were in the car and headed out the drive with Ryan and Tommy Chow waving goodbye like two country gentleman.

"Did you get the feeling we were being interrogated?" I asked.

"Of course, Joe. What did you expect? That was the whole point of the meeting; to see what we knew. Didn't you think it was odd that he pretended not to know that I could no longer see Trisha?"

Hum. I thought, impressed that Margie was ahead of me on this. The thought hadn't occurred to me, but obviously it had occurred to her.

I shouldn't have been surprised since Margie's as smart as a whip – of course she can't do math – but generally I consider myself the more cerebral of the two of us – brainy if you will -- whereas Margie would make a great shrink. She can feel your pain before you know you've got any.

"So, how did we do?" I asked. "I noticed you kind of danced around the Kenny issue. Why didn't you tell him Trisha asked you to get in touch with him?"

"He already knew that, Joe. Otherwise he would have asked about him. "

I was getting trounced. Of course, Margie was absolutely right. It wasn't what he asked that was important; it's what he didn't ask.

"And he never asked how we found the body or how we think it got there," I said, pleased with myself for catching on.

"Exactly!" Margie crowed and then added: "Joe, I think we've got to figure out how the body got there. There's no way Trisha could have put it there by herself. She's not a pilot. I checked."

"She doesn't have a pilot's license," I said, getting the cranium cranked up to full speed now. "But she's been flying around in daddy's planes since she was a baby. She may not have a license, but she might be able to fly a plane."

I glanced as Margie. She was admiring me with that look she has for me when I've said the right thing whether it's a complement or an observation.

"You might be right," she said and fell silent.

It was a quiet trip home and we arrived just before noon to find the place empty. Amanda left a note to say she'd taken Mom and Dad up to Waimea and dropped the girls off with their mom and dad at their hotel – bless her heart. I was delighted with the prospect of spending time alone in the house.

"I'm going to put on my suit and go for a swim while the pool is free," I said. "Care to join me?"

Margie begged off. "No thanks, I've got some sleuthing to do."

I was disappointed not so much because Margie didn't want to take a dip, but because she'd chosen sleuthing over me. I'd survived worse disappointments, however, and ran to change.

It was about an hour later when Margie found me in the bedroom jumping up and down on one foot while I tried to clear the water from my ear.

"Where have you been?" I asked.

"It took me eight phone calls, but I tracked Alicia down," Margie said. "She doesn't know Ryan. She's never talked to Ryan. But she was thrilled that I called."

"So Ryan did some digging into our pasts," I mused. "I wonder what else he's been up to.

"What did you think of Tommy Chow?" I asked. I had found Mr. Chow quite intimidating and his big toothy smile for all its wide white expanse seemed cold, sinister.

"Didn't I tell you? When he shook my hand, the hair on the back of my neck actually stood up!"

"I can believe that," I nodded.

I know one thing," Margie said finally. "I wouldn't want to be alone with him in a room."

"Me neither," I said.

"All in all, it doesn't seem like it's been a fruitful day. We got more questions than answers," Margie said. "But something tells me that somewhere in all this there's a clue or two, only we just can't see it yet."

"Yeah, you're probably right," I said. "But there's one thing that really worries me, Margie."

"What's that," she asked.

"The list of suspects. It just keeps on growing?"

"That's the way it is with murders," Margie observed. "What we need is to find a definite link between Ryan and Julia."

I cleared my throat. "Like Trisha?"

"No. That's too obvious. We need to find a different link."

Margie told me she was off to share what we'd discovered with Amanda.

"Maybe she'll have a different perspective," she added.

"I'm taking a nap," I said, but Margie was already gone.

As I lay on the bed, I considered how Margie might go about investigate one of the world's richest and most private men. I expected trouble. I didn't know how it would arrive, but I knew it would.

I must have fallen asleep, because when I awoke, the room was hot and it only gets hot when the sun is just overhead – about one o'clock.

I got up for a cool beverage, found my way to the kitchen where I checked fridge and found a few leftover pieces of pizza – pepperoni and black olive – and a cold diet soda.

I took my snack out by the pool, followed by Magoo, who knew food when he smelled it, and settled into my usual chair.

It was then that I noticed the girls.

They were lounging in the pool house. Bridgette in the fat little tufted chair. Barbie lying on her stomach on the bed.

Evidently, they had been brought home early and left alone, which didn't seem at all odd to me since they were certainly old enough to handle things on their own.

They were both on their cell phones, and neither seemed aware of my presence.

Ignoring them seemed the safe thing to do, since I had little in common with teenage girls and I assumed they would do the same to me, which seemed to be verified when Barbie looked my way and then turned away again.

I popped the top on my soda and began to eat the cold pizza, which as far as I'm concerned is one of life's most exquisite feasts and not one I get to partake of all that often.

And for the next three and a half minutes, life was good.

But all good things must end and in this particular case it ended with a scream, which was followed by a second scream.

As you can probably guess, the screams came from the pool house.

I looked that way and saw the girls standing toe to toe, each with a cell phone in one hand and a fist full of hair belonging to the other one in the other hand.

It appeared there was a problem, and it occurred to me that it wasn't *my* problem. But then it occurred to me that it might be hard to explain the hair loss to their parents. And Margie.

"Hey, hey," I said getting up and heading for the fight, my mouth still full of pizza. "What's the problem?"

The young ladies looked at me as if I was a total bother.

"None of your business," Bridgette shrieked.

"She told my boyfriend I was sleeping with some surfer dude," Barbie shouted. "She's a bitch."

There was a new round of mutual hair pulling and mutual screaming.

"I'm not a bitch, you're a bitch."

"Am not."

"Are too."

I pondered a moment the best way to proceed and finally concluded that since the cell phones had started the problem, they might end it as well.

"Give me the cell phones," I said, holding out my hand.

The girls stared at me as if I'd just asked them to remove their clothes.

They stopped pulling one another's hair. Barbie looked at me, then at Bridgette. Clearly, she was going to take her lead from Bridgette.

"No!" Bridgette said. I could tell she was wondering if I might physically take them.

I continued to hold out my hand.

Barbie let go of Bridgette's hair.

"We'll stop," she said flatly as Bridgette released Barbie's hair.

"I was only telling the truth," Bridgette said in her defense.

"Liar!" Barbie screamed and grabbed a hand full of her sister's hair, and twisting it till she screamed.

Bridgette kicked Barbie and Barbie pulled her hair harder.

Reluctant as I was, I decided I needed to wade in to prevent any real damage. I grabbed Bridgette's cell phone hand and pulled the phone from it. She let go of Barbie and turned on me.

"Give me that!" she spat, her face red with rage.

"No." I said, dropping it into my pocket.

I held out my hand to Barbie, who looked at me, then at Bridgette. I waited. She knew I'd take it, so reluctantly she gave me her phone. I tucked it into my other pocket.

Bridgette was seething. "You wait! You wait till my mother gets back! We'll see who has the last laugh!"

Without saying anything, I turned and went back to my chair. I picked up an old newspaper and pretended to read. Out of the corner of my eye, I watched the girls standing there looking at me, then Bridgette whispered something in Barbie's ear. Barbie smiled and they left the pool house and walked into the main house. A minute later, I heard the television in the guest room blasting out one of those horrible hip hop music videos.

So much for peace and quiet and making friends with Margie's nieces.

A half hour later, Mrs. M. and Shelly arrived carrying loads of groceries – which explained why the girls got dumped here – and they had no more gotten in the door than Bridgette and Barbie ran to meet them. They were too far away for me to hear, but they jabbered excitedly and kept pointing at me. I could see Mrs. M's shocked face but Shelly kept shaking her head and the girls kept bouncing up and down and pointing. Margie made a sudden appearance and the girls turned on her and danced and pointed at me until they made some sort of sign, at which point Mrs. M and Shelly and Margie all laugh heartily.

I was about to get up from my chair and find out what was going on, but then I saw Shelly shake her finger at the girls and they stopped their antics and slipped off unhappily toward the pool house. Mrs. M. shook her head and headed to the kitchen and Margie and Shelly came my way.

"What's the scoop," I said, extracting the cell phones from my pockets and placing them on the table for Shelly.

"They probably want these back." I said.

Shelly laughed and shook her head. Margie just shook her head.

"So that's what got them all excited. You took away their cell phones?"

"It's a long story," I said. "But it was that or watch them pull each other's hair out."

Shelly picked up the phones. "So you didn't expose yourself to them?"

My mouth fell open.

175

"I beg your pardon?"

"Don't worry," Shelly fanned the air. "They're horrible, horrible children. They have no idea how serious such accusations are. I knew they were lying the minute they said it and we eventually got them to admit it. Don't give it another thought. Now, if you'll excuse me, I think I'd better go dish out some punishment."

Shelly started to leave then stopped. "In the future Joe, you may just want to let them pull each others' hair out. If they had to go to school with bald heads they might get the idea their conduct is destructive."

"I'll give that some thought," I said, still shocked by the accusations.

Shelly left and Margie sat down across from me.

"Don't ever, ever, ever leave me alone with them again." I said; then I asked: "How did you get them to admit it was a lie?"

"Oh that was easy," Margie said drolly. "Shelly just asked them to describe it."

She gave me a bright smile and got up and headed for the house.

"You're a stud muffin, Joe, but you're no John Holmes."

I yelled after her: "Yeah, well it's colder than usual today. Did you consider that?"

Margie just laughed and kept going.

Thanksgiving?

Turkey Day – or more respectfully Thanksgiving – arrived despite the prayer I'd made the night before that the world should end in a fiery inferno while I slept.

I hadn't really expected my prayer to be answered since I only pray when things are bad or when I need something. God's a smart cookie and he/she could

176

probably tell that I lacked commitment and sincerity. Be that as it may, I continue to pray as I see fit. But as I said, Turkey Day arrived as usual on the last Thursday of November.

The morning broke and I awoke to noise. Not the familiar distant hum of leaf blowers and lawnmowers and the sound of the plants blowing in the breeze outside our bedroom, but to the noise of a squabble. A real hum-dinger.

It was not, as I first suspected, a Mom and Dad squabble and it took Margie's voice to assist me in determining the participants.

"Will you two stop? The girls will hear you!"

Ah, the Shelly and Mark show, I mused. *This is new.*

The reason I was having trouble identifying the squabblers (or is it squabblees?) was because they had spent so little time with us. But I'd been told that the marriage was rocky, so I was not surprised at the fracas. I was especially pleased that they had left their hotel to come and fight at our house. It wouldn't have been the same if I'd only *heard* about it.

You may be surprised to know this, but I had no interest in the conversation so I rolled out of bed and headed for the shower and the solace of thick tile walls and the acoustical qualities of hot running water. I was all sudsy and warm when Margie appeared unexpectedly, stripped to her birthday suit, and climbed in with me.

"Mark is flying home," she said tightly, picking up a luffa sponge and starting to scrub my back with the vigor of a maid scouring toilets. I yowled in protest but she ignored me.

"He wants a divorce," she said, attacking my back with greater fervor.

177

To save my skin, I slipped away from her and wedged myself into the corner of the shower, expecting to see the water running red with blood. Sorry, I'm only being slightly melodramatic.

"That's terrible," I said since it seemed the thing to say although the thought of at least one of the inmates leaving had me giddy with excitement. Then I noticed Margie's tears and I felt bad that I had not been sincere. So being the sensitive type, I stepped forward, gathered Margie in my arms and gave her a hug.

"It'll be all right," I added lamely, at which point Margie began to bawl uncontrollably.

"No it won't," Margie managed between sobs. "Everyone's unhappy. Everyone's fighting all the time. Nobody loves anybody. Nobody cares about one another. Nobody..." It went on like this for quite a while, but I'll spare you the details.

One of Margie's quirks that I've yet to mention is that she has a tendency to get stuck on a subject every once in awhile and can't seem to break out of it. Sometimes it's something little; sometimes it's something big. The point is there is only one thing that breaks the spell: a new distraction. My mind had been very busy lately with this and that and the other thing, so I didn't have any real brainpower left to think of something ingenious, so I just lifted up Margie's face and kissed her passionately on the mouth.

I was uncertain what her response might be. I figured the options were: push me away, kiss me back, or knee me in the groin.

To my delight she kissed me back. In fact, she kissed me back hard and before I could say 'I am the luckiest guy in the world,' we were making passionate love in the shower – standing up. Yippee! Happy Thanksgiving!

178

As you can imagine, my mood was considerably improved after that shower and when I emerged from the bedroom clean and casually dressed for the holiday, I felt there was little anyone could do or say that would change that.

Boy was I wrong.

As soon as I entered the living room, Shelly dashed over to me, her eyes red and her makeup smeared. It didn't take a genius to see she was badly shaken.

"Did Mark say anything to you?" she asked. "You were talking at dinner. Did he say anything about leaving? Did he tell you why he's so unhappy?"

I shook my head to the negative and was about to back that up with a resounding 'no,' but she was wound up.

I didn't want to drag up the alien thing and of course I thought it poor form to mention that he's in love with his therapist, so I shook my head and started to answer that we hadn't discussed his unhappiness, but again she cut me off.

"He's got no excuse. I'm the one that should be angry. I'm the one who should be leaving. I'm the one that should be..."

I realized that Shelly was following the same pattern as Margie had, getting stuck in gear with no clear avenue of escape. I felt on this occasion however that kissing her was probably not the way to proceed and would probably lead to that earlier option of getting kneed in the groin.

Luckily, Catherine came and rescued me. She bundled Shelly in her arms and directed her out to the pool where Maxwell was sipping coffee and reading my paper. There was no sign of the girls, and I assumed they were sleeping in, which is what any self respecting teen would be doing on a beautiful Thanksgiving morning in Hawaii.

I was standing there in the middle of the living room considered where I might go: the kitchen, where there was probably coffee but no paper and no comfortable place to sit. The pool, where Margie's clan was circling the wagons around daughter number two. The Sogol house, where I might find high calorie pastries and bacon, but which would make it appear to everyone that I was shunning my obligations as host. And finally the den, which of course was off limits because it was currently occupied by a belligerent transvestite.

As I pondered my meager options, the decision was graciously made for me by Margie who skipped into the room cleaned up, combed up, and dressed up. She took my arm.

"I need your help with the turkey," she said with more pizzazz than one might expect. Evidently our 'shower' had helped her attitude as well as mine, so a moment later we were off to the kitchen, which as I've already said had no comfortable place to sit, but which also had no crazy people. So I guess that makes it a wash.

Leaning on the island, I watched Margie as she as she dashed about, getting the roasting pan from the storeroom, setting the temperature on the oven, getting this and that from the fridge and cupboard. She was humming the whole time, though I couldn't catch the tune, and I couldn't help but worry that she was losing it. It seemed to me she was in denial and that she would crack as soon as she had to deal with the crazies again but I decided to live in the moment and at the moment it was just Margie and me in the kitchen enjoying one another.

Though it was only nine o'clock, I opened a bottle of Chablis and we sipped away as we got the turkey stuffed and Margie lined up the side dishes for later. By ten o'clock, we'd finished the bottle of wine, shoved the turkey in the oven, peeled the potatoes, prepped the asparagus, washed the lettuce, and moved the frozen dessert to the fridge to thaw. Amanda was bringing her famous chocolate macnut pie, but there's no such thing as too much dessert on Thanksgiving.

With a fresh bottle of wine in hand, and a plate of cheese and crackers and another plate of freshly sliced fruit, we left the kitchen together to face the family and what I expected would be a somber holiday.

As you might suspect, we got no further than the living room before the shit hit the fan. Damn telephones!

Margie set down the cheese and crackers and picked it up. Her facial expression was all that was necessary to know it was not good news. Margie said only one word: "Uh-huh" (I'm assuming that counts as one word) but she said it four times and each time she said it, she looked up at me and her eyes told me that each time she said it, she'd heard something worse.

It was a relatively short conversation and when Margie rang off, she relieved me of the plate of fruit and bottle of wine and set them on the table and took my hand and led me back to the kitchen.

If I hadn't known that all her family was in our house at the moment – I assume it's all the family – I would have guessed someone had died. So when she finally got around to telling me the news, it seemed anticlimactic.

"Mark's been arrested," Margie said in a barely audible whisper.

"What on earth for?" I babbled. "He's only just left. He hasn't had time to do anything. Was he speeding?"

"He tried to board a flight to Honolulu and they found a stash of marijuana in his suitcase," Margie's voice rose just a hair on the 'marijuana,' but otherwise remained a whisper.

181

I shook my head. "That wasn't very bright of him. "What's the charge?"

"Nothing yet. He's claiming it was Shelly's stash and he knew nothing about it."

Here was a twist. "So he's ratting her out?"

"I guess. I better call Cynthia and find out what to do," Margie started to leave.

"Wait a minute," I said. "How do you know all this? The police wouldn't call to tell you."

Margie smiled a bittersweet smile. "It's best if you don't know, Joe. Just note that Amanda's not the only gal who's well connected."

With that, Margie left me alone in the kitchen to ponder who she was getting her information from and what consequence it might have for us in the future.

Cynthia told Margie not to do or say anything and that the police would probably be calling to talk to Shelly, since it didn't sound like Mark had anyone else who might bail him out. Under no circumstances was Shelly to go to the police station without Cynthia unless she wanted to be charged too.

The call came five minutes later and Shelly went ballistic. Despite the fact that Mark had walked out on her only a couple of hours earlier, she was eager to do whatever it took to get him out of jail.

Maxwell and Catherine were of the opinion that he should rot – which despite my sensitive nature was also my opinion – but Margie prevailed and insisted she call her attorney – which of course she had already done, but only to alert her that we – yes I was invited – were on our way to jail to meet her and see Mark and possibly get him released.

When we left the house the turkey had three hours to cook, so we felt secure that we would make it back in time

182

to turn it off. Though I have to say, I was of the opinion that we had precious little to be thankful for this particular day and hence a celebration seemed a bit odd. But there was plenty of liquor at home and there were at least two desserts to be tasted so I decided I should be thankful after all.

On the way to the police station, Shelly confessed to us that the stash was indeed hers and had it not been for Margie's cool headed reasoning that admitting such a thing might mean the girls could wind up wards of Maxwell and Catherine we got her promise to do whatever Cynthia told her to do and say.

We meet Cynthia in the parking lot. I had talked to her a number of times on the phone, but I had never met her in person, so I was a trifle surprised by her appearance. Cynthia is a slender brunette with choppy hair, a small tattoo on her ankle and three diamond studs in her left ear. This day she was dressed in a neat pantsuit, which seemed warm for the weather. She appeared to be about our age – Margie and mine that is – but acted older. Maybe it was the lawyering that did that.

In any event, she gave us the lowdown on what was about to happen and suggested we may not be able to spring Mark since it was a holiday and no judges were available. But she was optimistic that the amount of marijuana was small enough that Mark would just be given a ticket and an appearance letter and be released on modest bail. He could have been charged federally, since he'd tried to board a plane, so the fact that he hadn't been was a stroke of luck.

As it turned out, it went the second way. Mark got a ticket to appear, we posted bail, and he was released in our custody.

While we were there, Margie got into an argument with the officer in charge about seeing Trisha and it was only by the skin of our teeth, and me physically throwing Margie over my shoulder and dragging her out, that we got out alive. Again, pardon the melodrama.

The ride home as you might imagine was quiet and awkward and it didn't improve much when we got back. It was clear from the get-go that neither Maxwell nor Catherine were going to speak to Mark. In fact none of us knew how to behave.

Margie did her best to act normal, helped by the girls who were now awake and quite excited about Turkey Day and meeting Amanda's brother Nicky, who after all was a Hollywood heart throb according to Bridgette who read People magazine religiously and could recite the American Idol contest winners for the last six years. And since they had slept right through the morning hullabaloo, they were totally oblivious to the fact that their parents were in the middle of splitsville and Dad was being charged with drug possession. As you might imagine no one was anxious to bring these facts to their attention, and so no one did.

For his part, Mark hid out in the pool house with and without the girls. Shelly had taken up a stool in the kitchen, which, because of the impending feast, was now the lair of Margie and Catherine and Magoo. Magoo was only there waiting for some sort of windfall, or to be more accurate 'floor fall.'

I could have gone out by the pool with dear old dad, but I wasn't thrilled about that opportunity. Or I could have lounged in the living room, which was empty except for the occasional passers through. Or I could have sought refuge in our master suite, which was not as comfortable as the living room, but which was private and far from the maddening crowd.

I sought privacy in the master suite.

And so it was that I was lying on the bed trying to imagine the seating arrangement for later that day when Margie entered. I looked up at her and tried to smile. She did not appear happy.

"What are you doing?" Margie asked, her voice tinged with suspicion and resentment. It was clear she thought I was goldbricking.

"I'm calculating the mean distance between fights at the dinner table," I said. "It's complicated calculus, but I think I've devised a way to seat everyone without anyone being within striking distance of a fork or butter knife."

Margie sneered. "Seriously. Is that all you can think to do. Lie on the bed and make wisecracks."

I thought it was, but since discretion is the better part of valor I answered: "No."

"Why don't you go get some olives? I just realized we don't have any black olives," Margie started to leave. "And take Mark with you."

"What?" I scrambled to my feet. "I don't recall the Indian's bringing olives to Thanksgiving."

It was a wisecrack and Margie caught it immediately. She crossed her arms and started to tap her foot.

"Okay. Okay. But why do I have to take Mark?" I was of the opinion that I was still strong enough to carry a can of olives even if Margie was obviously of another mind.

"He needs someone to tell him what an ass he's being and I elected you."

Jeez, I hate it when Margie takes that tone with me. She's not the boss. I'm the boss. Though telling her that is never a good idea. And she was still tapping.

"Okay, okay," I moaned, found my flip flops and headed for the door. "But I'm doing this under protest."

185

Actually, the idea of escaping the madhouse for awhile was fine with me, but I'd rather have done it without taking one of the inmates along.

I collected Mark, who offered no resistance. He'd been 'wet noodled' by his experiences of the day so far and looked as pathetic as an emasculated man can look. Although I was not in the mood to draw him out, I was under orders from Margie so I opened the conversation with something innocuous: "Have you ever been arrested before?"

Okay, it wasn't innocuous, but it was a question.

Mark blinked a few time. "In college. I streaked the chemistry building and got caught on the security camera. They kept me overnight."

Well that was interesting but it didn't seem like a fruitful line of inquiry, so I tried something different.

"Have you told the girls you're leaving?" That felt better. More direct. More likely to bear fruit.

But the fact of the matter is Mark just began to cry. First it was just a stifled snuffling, then a minute later tears streamed down his face uncontrollable and he was choking for air. I pulled the car over, uncertain whether it was in case I decided to flee or because I didn't want to be seen driving a grown man around crying his eyes out.

"I don't want to leave them," Mark sobbed. Actually, it was more like 'I....don't... want ......to ....leave.... them,' I thought I'd spare you the ellipses (which punctuate the gasps for breaths between the tears in case you need more description).

"…but I really don't have a choice. Shelly's impossible. She's got it in her head that we've got all this money. She's constantly buying stuff we can't afford and don't need."

186

"Have you talked to her about it?" I asked bluntly, putting the car back in drive and continuing.

"Of course I have," Mark shot back. His crying jag was over and now he was just angry. "I've talked myself silly. She thinks because she grew up with money, it just falls from trees! But it doesn't. You know that."

Actually in my current situation it sort of did, but I recollected my previous life and wife – the one who wanted me dead – and answered more supportively. "I hear ya buddy. My ex was like that. She could spend two paychecks before you could say American Express." I'm not sure what that meant, but Mark didn't catch on to it. He was worked up.

"Have you any idea what it's like being married to the boss's daughter? No matter what I do, I get no recognition. If I get promoted, it's because of her. If I win an award, it's because of her. I'm sick of it, Joe. I can't keep doing this."

I'd forgotten that Mark worked in one of Mr. M's corporations. I could see where it might make for hard feelings.

"And the fact that Margie's been so successful doesn't make it any easier. Shelly just closes her eyes and says 'charge it.'"

"Have you tried marriage counseling?"

We were in the store now and searching the aisles for olives, which I was certain would be near the Italian seasonings but weren't.

"She won't go. She says it's not a problem. She promises to stop spending then boom she goes out and buys the girls new outfits which they don't need and may not even wear."

I had no new ideas. If Shelly wouldn't change her ways and wouldn't even go for counseling, what was poor Mark to do. Then I remembered the stash.

"She confessed it was her marijuana, does she do other drugs?"

"I honestly don't know," Mark was tearing up again as we made our way back to the car with several cans of olives – different varieties, stuffed and unstuffed, pitted and unpitted, black, brown, and polka dot. I'm just kidding about the polka dots!

"She's also not very... she's not...she doesn't enjoy..." Mark was having trouble getting this one out so I helped.

"She's not much fun in the bedroom?" I took a chance. It's a common complaint for men; I hear it all the time.

"Yeah. Not much at all." Mark repeated.

We both fell silent and finished the ride home without saying another word. Back at the house Mark returned to the pool house and I dropped off the condiments and retreated back to the master suite.

I was lying on the bed again when Margie entered. She didn't have to ask. I spilled my guts about what information I'd managed to collect and told her that as far as I was concerned, I felt sorry for the poor bastard. Life's a hard enough paddle and doubly so when one of the team won't row.

Margie let me finish, then sat next to me on the bed.

"That's very interesting, Joe," she said, resting her hand on my thigh in a very maternal way. "I guess I'd feel sorry for him too if Shelly hadn't told me that he lost fifty thousand last year in Vegas and has a secretary who not only can't type, but apparently doesn't know how to put on underwear."

My mouth fell open. Yes, I know that seems to happen a lot, perhaps I should firm up my jaw muscles.

Margie concluded. "The only reason Dad hasn't fired him is because of Shelly who, for some unknown reason, still loves the s.o.b. Now stop lollygagging and set the place cards for the table since you have this extraordinary ability to 'calculate' who should sit where. Dinner's in fifteen minutes."

Margie left. I rolled over and brooded a minute, then imagined what a more violent man might do to Mark for his tall tale. Eventually I got up and headed for the dining room. Margie had not been kidding. The seating arrangement was going to take time and talent.

Despite my misgivings about the day, I have to admit that dinner went amazingly well. There were some traditions that didn't get observed. For example, it had always been a tradition in my family to go 'round the table and say what we were thankful for, but I thought it best not to bring that up. And the carving of the turkey, which traditionally is done at the table, was done in the kitchen so that there were no sharp knives close to hand.

There was, of course, little conversation beyond 'could you pass the potatoes' or small chit chat such as 'the rolls are yummy.' It seemed odd that Pete wasn't there and of course Angie and Nicky (who I seated on opposite ends of the table) gave each other the cold shoulder. Still, there were no verbal battles at all, this being due in large part to my stellar performance as a seating arranger.

I could tell you how I did it but that would be too easy. If you're truly curious, sit down with place cards and figure it out for yourself! Then you'll appreciate my talent.

After dinner, the majority decided to take a walk around the neighborhood. The minority, which consisted of me, Nicky, and Mark decided to find a place to lie down and sleep.

Nicky headed back to Amanda's to take his nap. Mark retreated to the pool house for his. And I crawled into the huge hammock by the pool, which is deep and comfy and definitely fits that comic's definition of a hammock as 'a net to catch lazy people.'

Enough is Enough!

Morning came with the sound of a distant leaf-blower and lawnmower and voices out by the pool. I climbed out of bed with as much enthusiasm as a man on his way to the gallows, crossed to the bedroom doorway and listened.

"I only had one cup of coffee," Maxwell said loudly.

"Two," Catherine contradicted.

"I know how many cups of coffee I've had," Maxwell shot back.

I turned and schlepped toward the master bath. Another day, another battle.

As I scrubbed in the shower, I was a very unhappy man. It wasn't even the first of December and I was about to crack. I made a mental list of what had already occurred and what was likely to occur. It was a long list, a nasty list. Everywhere I looked there were enemies at the gate! Loads of them! Suddenly, I vented to God the Almighty:

"I can't LIVE like this!"

There was, of course no one to hear me except Magoo who sits outside the shower so he can lick water off my legs when I step out. Why? I haven't a clue. Perhaps he's testing to see if I'm done.

"Magoo," I said. "It's time to take the bull by the horns and do something about all this." Magoo barked his agreement then ran from the room.

After I dressed, I made a phone call to a guy Pete had spoken of a few times, and got a tip as to where to look for him.

I was about to find Margie and tell her I was going out when she appeared carrying an armload of clothes.

"Here's your golf stuff," she said, tossing a pile of sportswear onto the bed and golf shoes onto the floor.

I looked at the pile suspiciously. There was a white Izod golf-shirt, cream colored Tommy Bahama golf shorts, argyle socks, buff colored golf shoes, and a Tiger Woods visor.

"I wasn't aware I owned golf attire," I said. "In fact I'm certain I don't own golf attire because I share Mark Twain's view of golf: 'Golf is a good walk ruined.'"

Margie smirked. "I picked them up for you," she said and crossing to her closet and pulled out a top and shorts which she held up to check in the mirror.

"Thank you," I said, though I didn't mean it. "Tell me, why do I have them?"

"For golfing," Margie said flatly.

"Let's start over," I said.

"Okay."

Margie put back the outfit she was holding up and took out a different top and shorts.

"Am I going golfing?"

"You don't remember?" Margie said with a hint of annoyance.

"You didn't tell me," I said truthfully, fully aware it would do me no good.

Margie liked the second outfit and began stripping down to her undies.

"It was your idea!" she stated.

"My idea?"

"At dinner. You told Dad we should all go golfing."

"I meant in the distant future, like after the next ice age."

"Well he called this morning and got us a tee time."

"Wait a minute," I said hastily, "I may not know anything about golf, but I know you cannot call up any of the golf courses around here and get same day tee-times."

"Unless you tee off between eleven and one," Margie pulled on the short skirt and checked herself in the mirror. She made a face to indicate slight displeasure and took off the earrings she was wearing then dug in her jewelry box for something more appropriate.

"We'll bake!" I protested.

Just in case you don't know the sun is incredibly intense in the tropics between eleven and one, which is why most people find a shady spot in which to rest or nap. Nobody plays golf between those hours – nobody except the crazies.

Margie shrugged and posed in front of the mirror again. She twirled and exited briskly.

"Use lots of sun-screen," she called from the hallway.

I looked sternly at the golf clothes, then at Magoo. Magoo looked up and growled for me.

Ten minutes later, I was dressed like a two-bit caddy and went to join the gang that had gathered at the door for our golf outing. To be more specific, the gang included: Margie and me, Catherine and Maxwell, and Shelly and Mark. I asked Margie why Amanda and Nicky weren't joining us and was informed that they were meeting us there.

Some of us had clubs, others, including me, didn't. I was surprised to note that Margie had a set of golf clubs but kept mum about it. We all *looked* like golfers, but I suspected I was not the only phony.

Angie and the girls watched from the sidelines.

"Now you all have a wonderful time!" Angie said, though I'm sure she was thinking 'you'll all fry out there.'

"It's really swell of you to stay and take care of the girls, Angie," Maxwell said earnestly.

"Oh, it's my pleasure, Mr. M.; I'm not much of a golfer. Besides, we're going to play supermodel while you're gone. Right girls?"

The girls clapped and grinned happily as Angie pulled them together for a group hug. Angie had become something of a second mom to the girls and kept them entertained when Shelly wasn't around.

I gave Margie a look to ask if this was okay; Margie returned my look with a 'she's a transvestite, not a child-molester' stare.

"You don't mind if we rummage around in your closet do you Margie?"

Margie picked up her golf-clubs. "Knock your selves out ladies," she said. "Let's go."

The herd started through the door. Maxwell, second to last in line, turned to me. "That Angie, she's one of a kind isn't she?"

"You've no idea, Mr. M," I said convincingly. "You really have no idea." And I pulled the door shut.

I found that we were going to play the South course at Mauna Lani and I was pretty impressed. Generally you have to be a member, know someone who is a member, or stay at the resort there in order to get to use the course. I knew we were not members, nor were we staying at the resort, so I wondered who it was we knew. I suspected Maxwell had the necessary connections.

Besides being exclusive, I knew that the Mauna Lani golf course is also one of the most difficult golf courses in the world – which was perfect as far as I was concerned since I was sure I would not finish any hole with anything resembling a reasonable score.

I thought you might be interested in the following according to information available on their website:

'The Mauna Lani Resort's two championship golf courses, Mauna Lani North and South, offer a challenging experience to novice and professional golf enthusiasts alike. Mauna Lani has received Golf Magazine's Gold Medal Award every year since 1988 and was host to the Senior Skins Golf Game for 11 years. The courses are masterpieces of design, each strikingly different, yet equally challenging. Mauna Lani Resort South Course, renown as the former home to the annual Senior Skins Game from 1990 - 2000, snakes through the stark, rugged a'a lava of the prehistoric Kaniku lava flow. The challenging South course offers the golfer a panorama of mountain and ocean views. The South Course is also home to No. 15, one of the most photographed over-the-water golf course holes in the world.'

I knew nothing of this at the time, since I'd only found out we were going golfing an hour before and because my interest in golf was nil. As were my abilities.

The last time I'd played golf (I had tried and failed in my college years) was under extreme duress as the result of an invitation from a supervisor who needed a warm body to fill in for a coworker who came down sick at the last minute. It was not a pretty sight and I was never invited back. Nor did I take it upon myself to pursue the 'sport.' I don't consider walking and hitting small balls a true sport. True sports result in physical injury or death!

As promised, Amanda and Nicky meet us at the first hole and we divided up into two foursomes, ladies and gents, and let the ladies tee off first. Shelly, Mrs. M., and

Amanda managed respectable drives halfway down the fairway, but Margie put them to shame! Margie's drive landed on the green but rolled on past and onto the grass on the other side.

"That a girl," Mr. M shouted when Margie's drive landed. He turned to me. "She should have gone pro."

Here was new news. "Pro?" I queried.

"Sure." Mr. M. responded. "Margie had the opportunity but turned it down. Obviously, she's been keeping in practice."

I wanted to correct him and tell him that I had no idea Margie was a star golfer and that as far as I knew Margie had not been near a golf course for as long as I'd know her except for that night when she'd snuck down to my rental condo on the golf course back when people were trying to kill me. But I just smiled and let it ride.

Mark and Nicky both teed off quite impressively—at least by my standards -- and at present they were sitting in a golf cart a few yards down the fairway off to the side. They thought they were safe, but I wasn't so certain. Maxwell leaned on his driver behind me. I'm not sure he was safe either. I was thankful that the ladies had teed off first so Margie didn't have to be embarrassed by my shameful performance.

I took a few practice swings that felt pretty good, but when I swung and connected, I sliced the ball badly and nearly decapitating Mark and ended up in the rough thirty yards down the fairway.

Maxwell stepped to the tee. "Golf's not your game, is it son?"

I retreated and Maxwell took a few practice swings. As I sat and watched him, I thought of Margie and how much it hurt her to see her parents constantly at one another and it occurred to me that this might be an

195

opportune time to find out what the problem was between Mr. and Mrs. M. I was tired of avoiding the subject and thought that maybe if I just asked him directly, he'd find it refreshing and come out with the truth. No I'm not naïve or stupid, I just thought… oh, never mind.

I waited patiently as he finished a magnificent 200 yard drive straight down the fairway.

"That's the way to tee off," Maxwell announced.

Maxwell picked up his tee and started for the cart we shared. I decided it was now or never. *Be direct*, I told myself. *We're both adults.* He was a tough, no nonsense corporate tycoon. I was sure he could handle my questions.

I screwed up my courage and blurted out as casually as I could: "So what is it with you and Mrs. M. anyway?"

Mr. M. evidently missed the heart of my question for he responded in a confused tone: "What do you mean?"

"I mean, do you two even remember what it is you're so angry about?"

Maxwell stopped walking and looked at me a moment – actually, he looked *through* me for a moment.

"Of course," Maxwell said with no clear indication in his voice whether he approved or disapproved of my question.

"And what is that?" I asked expectantly.

"None of your God-damn business," he said without any real malice in his voice, but forcefully enough so that I understood that pursuing the matter would not be fruitful.

I climbed in the cart and Maxwell slipped his driver into his golf bag and slid behind the wheel. He hit the accelerator hard; I grabbed the rail and held on tight. Evidently my question *had* caused tension.

196

The holes ticked by. My game got worse. Yes I'm afraid to say that is possible. The sun beat down, and I wondered why anyone would think this game enjoyable.

We were on the 14th hole and the end was in sight. I watched Mark hit his ball onto the green but it rolled back into a sand trap. Suddenly it occurred to me that perhaps I was asking the wrong person about what the deal was between Mr. and Mrs. M.

"At least you're near the green." I said consolingly. My ball was somewhere in the rough about 100 yards away.

We strolled along the fairway together quietly for awhile, then I figured: *What the heck.*

"I don't suppose you know why Mr. and Mrs. M. can't get along?"

I expected little, so his casual response came as something of a shock.

"Sure," Mark said. "Mr. M. slept with his secretary."

My mouth dropped open and it took a few steps for me to snap it shut.

"When?" I asked after I'd regained my composure.

"Twenty-six years ago."

I stopped walking and then, after I'd had time to digest his remark, had to run to catch up.

"Twenty-six years ago? But that's ancient history. There's got to be more to it than that."

"Nope. That's it."

"But, why didn't she just divorce him?"

"Shelly says it's because she loves him."

"She loves him?" That seemed implausible. "You've got to be kidding."

We reached my ball and I took up a stance.

"She loves him, but she won't forgive him?" I said.

"Shelly says it's because he won't apologize."

I came out of my stance and leaned on my club.

197

"Wait a minute. You're telling me that Mr. M. slept with his secretary twenty-six years ago and that Mrs. M. has been mad at him ever since but not because he slept with his secretary but because he won't apologize for sleeping with his secretary."

"Spooky huh?" Mark shrugged.

"And he won't apologize because?"

"He'd have to admit he slept with her!" Mark seemed slightly astonished that he had to explain that part.

"And if he admits he slept with her?" I pursued.

"He's afraid Catherine will leave him!"

It was worse than I feared. I shook my head.

"You're not serious."

"Welcome to the family," Mark said.

I took a swing at my ball which I topped and sent across the fairway to the rough on the other side. On the green, Maxwell waved his putter and yelled: "Hit it this way, Joe! This way."

The 15th hole of the Mauna Lani golf course is their signature hole. It's thirty feet above the ocean and runs parallel to it. To hit the green, you have to hit the ball across a small bay. It spooks a lot of people – and sells a lot of golf balls -- so we piled up with the ladies who were still trying to get off the tee there.

Margie was about to tee off and I came over to watch. She looked up and smiled.

"How're you doing?" she asked.

"Aced every hole," I said.

Margie smiled. She knew a liar when she saw one.

"Actually I think I set a new record for the course. The wrong record. But I found out something important."

Margie took a practice swing. Her form appeared top notch.

"What'd you find out?" her voice lacked any real enthusiasm.

Margie got ready for the real thing. She started…

"That your father slept with his secretary."

I expected that the timing of my delivery would unnerve her, but Margie's swing continued uninterrupted; the ball leapt into the air straight for the pin 230 yards away. On her follow through, however, the driver slipped from her hands and twirled end over end into the ocean below.

"Damn." she cursed, looking up at me.

"Sorry," I said, "I didn't mean to…"

"Oh, it's not your fault Joe, it's just that that's the second driver I've lost today. I relax too much with my swing. Who told you about Dad?"

"Mark," I said truthfully. I couldn't think of any reason why she shouldn't know.

"Well, that's what I told Shelly."

"You mean that's not what happened?"

"It could be? I told you before, it's a mystery."

I pondered this information as Margie asked: "Did he also tell you why they can't get past it?"

"Yes." I said. "Is it true?"

"It's as good a reason as any."

"So no one really knows?

"My Mom and Dad do. But I don't."

And you made it all up because…?"

"I made it up because when we were kids Shelly asked. What was I supposed to say?"

Margie started walking off the tee. "Welcome to the family, Joe."

I put my arm around Margie and gave her a hug and walked with her to the green. I decided to take a pass on

199

the 15th hole to save the Pacific Ocean from being filled with useless golf balls.

I wanted to take a nap when we got home, but I still had pressing business with Pete so I told Margie I was going to look for some new shorts, which delighted her, but I don't think she really believed me. Still, she knew I needed my space, so she didn't try to stop me or suggest she come along so that I wouldn't come back with something she wouldn't be caught dead letting me wear!

The truth was I was going a mission to change things! The revelation in the shower that morning an and the insanity of the situation between Mom and Dad had me riled up. And while I might not be able to change things, I sure as hell was going to give it a try – if not for my own sake, then for Margie's.

Just in case Margie and company decided to go some place while I was gone, I took the Miata and headed for the airport. I hadn't driven the little car in quite a while and thoroughly enjoyed the ride. I got checked through security and made my way to hanger #5.

I entered the hanger and spotted the big helicopter Pete's friend had said would be there on the far side.

As I got close, I heard the sound of someone tinkering with metal parts and I spotted Pete on the other side of the chopper surrounded by hundreds of parts both small and large. He had a three-day old beard and his clothes were dirty and rumpled. He must have heard me coming because he looked up. He didn't look happy to see me.

"Whad're you doing here?" Pete said harshly.

"I came to make peace," I said stepping closer.

"Yeah?"

"Yeah."

"You gonna apologize?" Pete asked, his tone a little less abrupt.

"No. I didn't do anything I'm willing to apologize for," I said.

Pete returned to assembling or disassembling whatever it was that lay in pieces around him.

"I didn't come to start the fight over," I said. "But I'm curious, how long do you plan to stay here?"

"Long as my house is 'occupied,'"

"Yeah, well, I'm about to join you?"

Pete looked up. I continued.

"I can't take it either. And it's not 'cause I'm a homophobe."

"What'd you call me?"

I raised my hand to ward off his anger.

"I take it back. Listen. You want to get rid of Angie and Nicky. I want to get rid of the Squabbles and all the others. It occurred to me we might help each other and get rid of 'em all."

Pete scratched under his arm as he pondered my offer. Lifting his arm released an amazingly pungent odor and I waved the air. Pete grinned.

"I could use a change of clothes," he admitted.

"And a long shower," I added.

He was quiet a long time, and then finally he asked: "So what's your plan?"

It was clear he was ready to bury the hatchet, so I pressed forward.

"I don't really have one. I thought maybe together we could ..."

"I've got a plan," Pete said suddenly and with enthusiasm.

Pete had a plan? I looked at all those loose parts that will never go back together. *Could Pete actual have a plan with any hope of success?*

Since I had zilch, I decided to hear him out. "Okay," I said. "Let's hear it,"

Pete began: "Let's just suppose..."

For the next five minutes I listened intently to Pete's plan as he sat cross-legged on the floor amid his latest repair effort. I nodded my head in appropriate places and smiled when he did. Finally he made an end to it with "...and then they'll leave for sure."

I rubbed the stubble on my chin as I digested Pete's plan. Of course it was totally unworkable and would require more finesse and luck and brains than either one of us possessed, but in the interest of mending our friendship, I responded with passion:

"You know what, Pete? That's just crazy enough to work!"

Pete lifted his arm for me to hi-5 him, but the stench was so great all I could do was fan the air. Pete dropped his arm apologetically.

"Our rental unit's open starting today," Pete said, "and I'll bet Amanda's all but forgotten about it. I'll move in tonight. Can you sneak in my house and get me some clothes?"

Pete and Amanda own a small condo unit that they rent out. It had been Pete's before they were married, and Pete takes care of renting it and fixing up things (of course he doesn't really fix them up, but he hires the people that do fix them up). Because Pete took care of everything it was below Amanda's radar. It seemed a logical place for him to hold up.

"It's too dangerous to go sneaking around your house," I said. "I'll pick up some stuff for you at Costco. Write down what you need and your sizes, unless you want me to guess."

Pete found an old piece of paper and a pencil stub and began jotting things down. A minute later he handed it to me. "And don't get nothin' fancy!" he said.

I looked at the list and pondered: *What might be too fancy for Pete?*

I stopped at Costco on the drive home and got the stuff for Pete – nothing fancy as requested, although I did look for something fancy just to see what was available. And while driving and shopping, I formulated my own plan of action – simple, yet elegant. I'd share it with you, but since you're going watch it unfold I thought I'd just let you observe and appreciate my mind at work!

It was dark and past dinnertime when I arrived home and I found Margie folding clothes in the bedroom with Magoo lying on my pillow. I chased him off. There had to be *some* boundaries!

"And where have you been?" Margie snapped.

"I told you I was going shopping," I said curtly. Evidently she'd forgotten about giving me space. Had there been more fireworks while I was gone? I decided not to ask. What good would it do?

Margie looked around. "I don't see any packages?"

"I couldn't find anything I liked," I lied and picked up some of the stuff that was mine and crossed to my dresser and started putting it away.

Margie continued folding quite vigorously. "I could have used some help around here. Things are getting..."

"I saw Pete today," I interrupted purposefully.

Margie stopped folding. "And what did he have to say?"

"I didn't talk to him," I said. I paused a moment. "He was with some redhead." I used a redhead because both Margie and Amanda hated red heads for some reason. Actually hate is the wrong word. They despised them. I don't know why, it may have been envy. Almost every man I know likes redheads – a lot. Anyway, all I know is I heard them talking about it once so it seemed the thing to say.

Margie froze. I continued to put clothes away.

"Where? Who was she?"

"Huggo's. Never saw her before. She didn't look like a local. Probably a tourist."

"What were they doing?"

"Having a drink."

"And you didn't go over?"

"Hey, the guy took a swing at me!"

"I should tell Amanda."

Margie started to leave the room.

"I wouldn't," I said casually. "It was probably innocent. Pete's no Don Juan as you well know. You'll just upset her."

Margie stopped. "You're probably right," she said and came back and folded another pair of underwear and a few more towels.

"Well, I'd better do another load," Margie said with far too much enthusiasm and left the room with the empty clothes basket.

I couldn't help but smile. I knew what would happen next and sure enough, twenty seconds later when I tiptoed to the bedroom door I heard Margie's voice in the living room…

"I know! I can't believe it either," Margie's was empathetic. "Okay. I'll try to get more information. But what if…"

I didn't have to hear Amanda's voice to know who Margie was speaking to. I returned to putting clothes away and looked at Magoo on the bed.

"I'll go to hell for this," I said. "But what the heck."

Magoo, who knows nothing of heaven and hell, wagged his tail and rolled over for a tummy rub, which I happily obliged.

Why Can't It Ever Be Easy?

The early dawn light was just bright enough to allow me to read my paper. The coffee, which I made especially strong, tasted even better than usual, and I was enjoying the quite before the leaf blowers and lawn mowers.

Out of the corner of my eye I saw Margie enter the living room and look outside. She spotted me and crossed the living room in my direction. She said nothing till she was next to me.

"You're up early."

I looked up and noted that Margie, who is always the first out of bed and is generally half way through her laps when I arise, looked decidedly different this morning; her hair was squished to one side and there were creases in her face from the folds in her pillow. Still, she had a certain *femme du suare* about her (don't bother to get out your French dictionary; I made that up just now).

"The early-bird catches the worm," I quipped.

Margie put her hands on her hips.

"What's wrong with you? You never get up early and you never say stupid stuff like that."

I held out my cup. Margie puzzled a moment then reached for the pot and filled it. She filled a cup for herself and sat down.

"I was thinking about Pete last night when I was trying to sleep," Margie said. "Where's he sleeping do you suppose?"

"Could be anywhere," I lied. "He's got a lot of friends."

"Friends?" Margie was taken aback. "Who?"

"Oh," I said. "Fishing buddies, flying buddies, old surfing buddies.

"Surfing buddies?"

"You didn't know Pete's a surfer?"

"A surfer? Pete? In the water? He can barely dog paddle!"

"I've never actually seen him surf, but..."

The calm was suddenly broken by the sound of a door slamming. Margie and I looked at one another.

"Sounds like your 'rents are up," I said casually. "Isn't today the day you're taking them whale watching?"

Margie slumped and laid her cheek on the table. "Oh, God, I forgot about that."

I slurped my coffee and returned to my paper. Margie pulled herself up and headed for the house. Of course I felt sorry for her, but I had my own problems and my own plans.

Later that morning, I was feeling pretty cocky concerning how quickly Margie and Amanda had swallowed the bait with regards to Pete, so I moved to my next plan of action which was to get Angie out of my house. And as far as I could figure there was only one way to do it – fix things up between her and Nicky.

So while Margie was getting ready to take mom and dad out, I went to find Angie, who, because it was still early, I found her in the den reading one of my books. She looked up when I entered and didn't look at all happy to see me.

"What do you want?" she asked irritably.

"I want to start over. I think you and I got off on the wrong foot." I said with as much sincerity as I could muster.

She appeared skeptical.

I launched into my explanation of events – the long version, which included how I first meet Margie and how we'd almost been killed, which by itself is sweet enough to bring tears to most people's eyes. How I'd discovered Margie had parents. How Margie kept bringing home dangerous people. Like I said, the long version.

When I finally shut my yap, Angie sighed and said: "You poor, poor dear" in that feminine voice she used on everyone but me. I think if I'd been standing closer, she would have given me a hug, so it was just as well I wasn't close because I'm not too sure how I'd have reacted to that.

"So I was thinking," I continued. "Maybe if you told me why you and Nicky had a fight, I could help and you could go back to Amanda's and I could have my little den back and there'd be just a little bit less stress on both of us."

A tear streaked down Angie's cheek.

"You sweet, sweet man. I've been wracking my brains to figure out what on earth Margie sees in you and now I understand. You're a real gem."

I accepted her compliment and she launched into an explanation of her relationship with Nicky – with a lot more detail than I was comfortable with -- but I listened attentively and tried not to remember the stuff that was personal. I'll save you from the same embarrassment I endured and just gloss over that part. The thing of it is, when she was all done she refused to tell me why she was on the outs with Nicky and politely suggested that I ask him.

"And you can tell him from me, that if he wants to apologize he better make it more convincing than that stupid spiel he gave in 'Heaven's Hole.'"

I've got to admit, I was taken aback by her attitude. Why, I mused, do people have to be so difficult with one another? It was clear she wanted an apology. And it was clear that an apology would be accepted if it was sincere. So then why couldn't she just tell Nicky that? And why did it always take an intermediary to patch things up?

Of course, I knew it wouldn't help to share my thoughts with her so I thanked her for listening to me and I took my leave and headed across the street to Amanda and Pete's with the hope that Nicky would be more responsive.

I found Nicky alone by the pool working on his tan/carcinoma. I decided to take it slow since I hadn't spent any real time with him, and our meetings had always been as part of a larger group.

I pretended I'd come to see Amanda and was told she'd gone grocery shopping – which I already knew because she'd called Margie to ask if she wanted her to pick up anything. Thoughtful isn't she?

Thankfully Nicky had manners and offered me a glass of lemonade, which I accepted and got for myself from the small port-a-bar under the large striped umbrella.

I pulled up a chair near him and started some idle chit-chat about what it was like being a Hollywood hunk and how much I'd liked the scene in 'Heaven's Hole' when he apologized to 'what's her name.' He agreed it was one of his best scenes and delivered a rousing replay from his chaise lounge. It was very impressive, and very, very odd.

Everyone likes to talk about themselves and Nicky, being egocentric to begin with, took the bait. We spent a good twenty minutes talking about him.

I listened attentively and waited until he mentioned Angie in passing at which point I asked about how they'd met. Thankfully, Nicky gave a much less detailed description of their relationship than Angie had and when he finished, I asked the simple question that I'd come to ask when I first came over a half hour ago: "So what's got her so P.O.ed at you?"

Nicky brooded a moment. Clearly he was not happy with being asked such a direct question, especially since the response might put him in a poor light, and so he did what Angie had done, he passed the buck.

"I really think you should ask 'her' that. I'm still fuzzy on exactly what ticked her off."

Well there it was. Nicky was just as happy as Angie to avoid the problem, and I was getting nowhere.

With no clear idea how to proceed, I lied and said that I had to go because Margie was waiting for me. Nicky said to give his regards to her and I pushed myself off the lounge chair and headed inside to put my glass in the sink. I had a secret plan to borrow a cookie, so I was surprised to find Amanda had returned from grocery shopping.

She asked what I was up to and I told her Nicky and I had been talking. Amanda asked how Pete was and I told her that I didn't know, which was a lie. Technically it may not have been a lie since I didn't know exactly at that time what he was doing, but I don't suppose such a slim excuse would pass muster with St. Peter.

I got my cookie and was headed for the door when it occurred to me that Amanda might know the answer to my question so I asked as nonchalantly as possible: "I don't suppose you know why Angie's so pissed off at Nicky?"

Without looking up from the grocery bag she was unpacking, she answered: "He told her he thought she needed a girdle."

Well what do you know about that?

I thanked Amanda and beat a hasty retreat home. So what it all came down to was this: Nicky had suggested that Angie might think about wearing a girdle! Who'd a guessed?

I know what you're thinking; I should have confronted Nicky with the information and suggested he apologize. But nothing's that simple. I needed time to think things through. And maybe I needed assistance from someone who is smarter and more in tune with crazies than I am. Of course I'm talking about Margie.

At home I found Margie out by the pool with her dad who had pissed off Mrs. M -- who had gone to hide in her room. The whale watching trip had been postponed for obvious reasons. Lucky Margie!

I pulled up a chair and had a cup of coffee since I couldn't think of anywhere to go and I wanted to ask Margie about the girdle issue. The nieces were milling about whining about having nothing to do and although we tried to ignore them it was hopeless. Eventually their whining succeeded in Margie promising to take them snorkeling at the City of Refuge. I thought it a bad idea to give in to them and thought it even worse when Margie announced that 'uncle Joe will go with us.' So much for being asked!

I knew it would do no good to beg off the trip, especially since I wanted a favor from Margie. No not that kind of favor – get your mind out of the gutter! I was interested regarding the correct method of getting Nicky and Angie back together if you'll recall.

An hour later, as we traversed the serpentine Queen Kaahumanu Highway toward the City of Refuge, I opened the conversation with Margie while the girls were busy texting on their cell phones and listening to their mp3 players. There was little chance they'd hear us and since they were totally self-absorbed anyway it was unlikely they would tune me in if they did.

"So, Margie," I said. "I found out why Angie and Nicky are on the outs."

"You mean the 'girdle' thing?"

Did everyone on the planet know what was happening but me?

"Yes. The girdle thing. I know it's a terrible thing to say to a woman," I paused. Of course Angie wasn't really a woman but for purposes of the conversation I let it slide.

"Anyway, what I was wondering. Is there no road back? Nothing Nicky could say or do that would smooth things over?"

"What did you have in mind?" Margie asked.

I wasn't ready for that response, but I forged ahead. "You know, like flowers. Candy. Money."

"Is that what you think women want?"

It was clear from the way Margie phrased her response that I'd taken a wrong turn. Whereas I had envisioned a solution to a single problem, Margie was delving into the philosophical differences between men and women, you know the old 'men are from Mars, women are from Venus' thing. As we all know, the differences are significant. Furthermore, as a male, I have always felt inadequate when it comes to the complexities of the female psyche. In fact, I believe all men feel inadequate with respect to that, although quite a few will tell you that they do understand. There are many liars in the world.

I knew I needed to be cautious. One false move and I could find myself in big trouble, and I didn't want any trouble. I had enough trouble.

"You know I don't know what women want. When was the last time I got it right?"

Margie chuckled in agreement. "Why do you want to help Nicky and Angie? I thought you shared Pete's view of the homosexual world."

"Who? Me?" I stammered. "I'm no bigot. I'd just like to get Angie out of my den so I can go back to writing." I realized my mistake instantly and corrected. "Back to pretending to write."

"Well, if you're serious. The first thing you have to do is find some way to make Nicky jealous. He's holding all the cards. He's the big movie star. He's not going to cave. He might send flowers – actually he already has. But he's not going to crawl on hands and knees and beg for forgiveness."

We had reached the City of Refuge and it was time to unplug and unload the girls, which as it turned out was not an easy task considering they had been 'bored beyond belief' – that's 'bbb' in texting lingo -- only a short while ago.

The City of Refuge is actually *Puuhonua O Honaunau* and is a National Historic Park. It includes ancient Hawaiian temple ruins, fish ponds, sacred burial spots, and petro glyphs. It's called the City of Refuge because in ancient Hawaii there were many taboos (kapu) that if broken could cost you your life. If you managed to make it to the Place of Refuge before you got clubbed to death, however, the priests would cleanse you of your transgression and after awhile you could return home safely. I highly recommend it to any visitor to the Big Island -- a trip to the park, not the cleansing part and avoiding being killed by being clubbed to death.

The snorkeling is best across the small bay from the park, but it's a little tricky getting in and out of the water because of the lava shelf. I showed the girls the best place to enter and how to wait out the waves so you didn't get smashed into the rocks as you got in. Being teenagers, they ignored my advice, but managed through sheer luck and the auspices of guardian angels to avoid any serious injury and in a minute they were happily paddling about the bay.   Okay, 'happily' may be the wrong word since they began trying to drown one another almost immediately.

As for me, I was satisfied to get comfy next to Margie on the rocks in the beach chairs we brought and soak up the sun and the relative quiet. There were only a few other snorkelers around and there wasn't a soul on the rocks with us so we pretty much had the place to ourselves.

I toyed with the idea of engaging Margie in our previous conversation, but decided it was just too nice to be alone with her to mess it up with any discussion that might lead to relationship issues.

Margie, as usual, had thought ahead and brought a book – a murder mystery, of course – so I entertained myself by watching the waves and trying to find shapes in the passing clouds.

Everything was going along just fine. I'd spotted a cloud that looked like a Hooter's waitress. Another that resembled a turtle. And even one that looked exactly like a cloud – Plato would have been proud.

Of course all this tranquility was too good to last, and sure enough the peace and quiet was shattered suddenly by a panicked call for 'Help!' This was not your average teenage yelp calling for attention because she'd gotten seawater in her eyes. This was the real deal!

I dropped my eyes from the sky and spotted Bridgette—who was doing the yelling –slip beneath the waves. I spotted Barbie, a good 30 yards from her sister, her face in the water, snorkeling peacefully, oblivious to her sister's dilemma. Other snorkelers were even farther away; clearly any rescue was up to me.

You know it's amazing what training and a healthy dose of adrenaline can do. Without a thought, I sprang from my chair, dashed across the rocks, and dove in.

I hit the water hard and when I surfaced, I heard a splash behind me. Obviously Margie was in the water as well, and although Margie swims every day and is in much better shape than I am overall, I've got more muscle and I knew I'd get to Bridgette first.

It's odd how time slows down in an emergency. I'd been a lifeguard in college and I'd had to rescue more than one panicked swimmer, so I knew *what* to do. But this time it was different. This time it was someone I knew, and somehow that made it more urgent and scary and so my heart was pumping like the dickens.

I reached the spot where Bridgette had gone under and I dove down. The crystal clear water was a Godsend. I spotted her just a few feet below me, grabbed her hair, and pulled her to the surface where she sputtered and tried to climb on top of me in her panic. Margie arrived and was able to calm her enough so she let me swim her ashore.

We swam to a strip of sandy beach at the City of Refuge where a half dozen people waded out to help bring us in as soon as we got close. Someone had already called 911 and I heard a siren in the distance almost as soon as we climbed out of the surf. A park ranger had a blanket ready, and I wrapped Bridgette in it and made her sit on the sand. I wasn't sure how much water she'd taken in, but I'd seen other drowning victims relapse after they made it ashore.

"You...you...saved my life," Bridgette stammered, shivering beneath the blanket. Margie rubbed her back to help warm her.

"You're going to be okay," I said. I wasn't so certain about myself. My heart was still going a mile a minute.

The fire rescue truck arrived and Barbie finally came up to look around, spotted us on shore, and swam over. I've got to say, she didn't seem all that upset that her sister had nearly drown. She seemed more interested in telling us about the dolphin she saw and the two loggerhead turtles and the "jillions" of fishes.

The paramedics gave Bridgette the once over and pronounced her healthy, but suggested we take her to the Kona Hospital ER on the way home just to be safe. We thanked them and all the passersby who had helped.

By the time we'd collected everything and got to the car I was exhausted and I could tell Margie was too. All I wanted to do was get home, have a drink, and relax. The girls, however, begged to stop at McDonald's, which Margie to my surprise approved and then whined to stop at the surf shop in Kealakekua where each of them got a t-shirt with quasi obscene slogans on them like: 'I Practice Safe Sex...Often!' I was appalled by the purchases but Margie said I should get used to it. If Shelly didn't want them to have them, she could take them away.

Bridgette seemed fine so I suggested we skip the ER visit which would have taken hours – have you been in an ER lately? Bridgette was delighted with that and the girls spent the rest of the trip home texting on their cell phones – whether it was with each other or their friends I have no idea.

We were almost home when Bridgette piped up: "You really don't have to tell our mom about this. She's a

215

worrier. If she finds out what happened she probably won't every let me go anywhere with you again."

"Well of course we have to tell your mother," Margie said. "She needs to know. This isn't the kind of thing you keep from your mother."

"It's just going to make trouble," Barbie said, echoing her sisters concerns. "She might faint!"

Based on my experience with their mom I felt that that wasn't a real possibility.

"And dad will go ballistic!" Bridgette said for emphasis. "He goes crazy when we break a nail."

"Well," said Margie, "they'll just have to deal with it. They need to know and that's that."

The girls fell into an uneasy quiet and I had the distinct feeling there was something going on that they weren't telling us.

We pulled into the drive and the girls made a beeline for the pool house and I made a beeline for the bar.

"I'll call Shelly," Margie shouted. "Make me a tall one. Something with rum,"

The house was empty and I hadn't a clue where mom and dad were or Angie for that matter, but I was delighted not to have them asking questions at least not till I got some alcohol down my throat.

"I'll make Mai Tias," I yelled, pouring half a glass of rum in each of two glasses before I added anything else.

I took the drinks out by the pool and a minute later Margie joined me and took a large gulp before she said anything.

"That's some drink," she said appreciatively.

"Shelly's on her way over. She didn't say much, but she sounded extremely angry."

"Angry?" I said. "What on God's green earth does she have to be angry about? We saved her darling daughter's butt!"

"I don't know," Margie said, "but if she says anything to you, I'm going to punch her right in the nose. You're a hero, Joe."

Margie lifted her glass to me. I blushed. We fell silent and we drank our drinks. And I do mean drank! No sipping. Sipping is for sissies.

Margie made the second round and I'm pretty sure she forgot the mix entirely but I was not going to complain, I was beginning to feel all warm and fuzzy.

We were sipping our second drinks (it *is* okay to sip after the first drink) when I heard a car screech to a stop in the driveway. *Ah,* I thought, *that would be the angry mom!* A second later Shelly came marching towards us, her face set hard and a vein in her forehead popping out. "Where are they?" she screamed.

Margie pointed to the pool house and Shelly changed course and charged ahead. We watched in confusion. I was wondering what she was going to say to them but as it turned out I didn't have to guess. A moment later we heard it all: "You dirty, rotten, filthy, sons of bitches. How could you!" Shelly's voice was just a tad louder than a Boeing 747 on takeoff. "You're grounded! For life!"

"But, Mom…" Bridgette and Barbie moaned in unison.

"Don't 'But, Mom' me. Don't say another word!" Shelly screamed. "Not another word."

Silence fell like a thick blanket.

An instant later, Shelly stomped toward us. I could sense Margie tense. I'd had too much rum by then to tense; I was loose as a noodle. We waited patiently for Shelly's tirade. But she reached the table without saying a word. Her face was red and looked as if she was about to cry. She looked at the drinks on the table, picked up Margie's and downed it in one huge gulp, then threw herself into a vacant chair and let the tears flow.

Margie and I stared at one another, uncertain how to proceed. But before we came to any conclusion Shelly stifled her tears and began...

"I am so, so sorry," she pleaded. "They are horrible, horrible girls!"

"We don't understand," Margie said, still confused. "You don't think Bridgette wanted to drown do you?"

"But she did!" Shelly howled miserably. "They think it's some kind of joke! It's the third time Bridgette's done it and Barbie's done it at the beach and at the pool!"

My mind went blank. I didn't know what to say. I stared at her blankly then over to Margie who returned my blank expression. *A joke? They'd done it before?*

Margie recovered first with the same thought I'd had: "We need more booze," she said and made a beeline for the wet bar.

Yes, booze. More booze! But was there that much booze on the planet?

After the liquor ran out and the girls had apologized to me and to Margie, I retreated to the shower and the warm water and wondered how Pete had spent his day. Probably watched golf and football and maybe NASCAR while drinking beer and eating potato chips with gobs of dip. I hoped he'd appreciate what I was doing to help him out. I know I was doing it for myself as well, but he was having fun, and I was... well I wasn't having any fun. Was I?

After I finished coveting Pete's idyllic lifestyle, I spent the rest of my time in the shower thinking about what

Margie had said about the only way to get Angie and Nicky back together.

I was not about to volunteer to be the shill in a charade to make Nicky jealous. Angie was not my type. The problem was, I wasn't sure I knew anyone her type. Then, just as I'd lathered up for the third time, it struck me: Maxwell!

The old guy didn't have a clue about Angie plus he'd already shown a great deal of interest in her. He fawned on her all the time – in a fatherly fashion of course. I decided the idea was worth some further thought so while changing into my standard shorts and shirt I ran my idea past Magoo who wagged his tail and growled his approval.

"That's sort of the way I think about it too," I said.

At dinner that evening I managed to arrange seating so that Angie and Maxwell were together. He, being a gentleman, took great pains to make sure Angie got the salt and pepper and refilled her wine glass on schedule. Yep, I could see that Maxwell had a soft spot for our (make that my) unwanted houseguest, but I realized I'd have to be careful implementing my plan since it was plain as day that Catherine had also noticed his behavior. It wouldn't be good to solve one problem and raise the burner on another – if you'll pardon the mixed metaphor.

After dinner, I suggested a game of Scrabble, which elicited a questioning look from Margie who knows how I hate board games; however it was widely applauded by everyone else as a great idea.

Again I maneuvered seating to get Angie next to Maxwell, and when we divided into teams it was: Maxwell and Angie, me and Catherine, Mark and Amanda, and Margie and Shelly. Amanda, as you may have noticed, had become a virtual houseguest, I didn't mind all that much since at least she returned to her own home each evening and snuck cookies to me when Margie wasn't looking. I'm easily bought.

It was a spirited game as games go, and Maxwell and Angie turned out to be a very competitive and competent team. They high fived a dozen times and I noticed Maxwell wink at Angie twice when he thought no one was watching. For her part, Angie patted Maxwell's knee whenever he made a good move. I don't know what the attraction was for Mr. M., but obviously Angie had her charm. After all, she was the 'girlfriend' of a famous Hollywood movie hunk.

It seemed to me as though my plan had possibilities. But in order for it to work, I had to get Nicky to join us, and I had no clear thought on how I'd do that. Happily, nature took care of it for me.

Just in case you're interested, Catherine and I didn't do so well. Despite my enormous vocabulary and ability to think in three dimensions, there's only so much one can do with a rack of vowels and the letters 'x'and 'z.' Plus, the booze I'd drunk had taken a significant toll on my thought processes. Ah, well. Margie and Shelly turned out to be the winners, which put Amanda's nose out of joint. She blamed the loss on Mark who, like me, kept pulling vowels and stupid consonants from the heap of tiles.

After the game we gathered round the big TV in the living room just in time for the last of Katie Curic. Katie who looks a bit like Margie but without the curls and who, as far as I know, does not swim nude in the pool when her folks aren't visiting. It would make a good news story if she did though, don't you think?

Mark had informed us that he'd heard on the radio that there was rough weather headed our way, so we were anxious to find out what that was all about. Sure enough, the lead story of the local news was about tropical storm Irene which appeared to have changed course and was now headed due East toward – you guessed it – the Big Island!

There hadn't been a good storm on the Big Island for years – or so I'd been told -- so it only made sense that this one should hit when we were filled to the rafters with house guests.

We spent the next five minutes watching graphics and listening to the harbingers of doom discuss the damage that might be expected if a big storm like Irene hit the West coast of Hawaii. Boy, they were sure having fun with it. By the time they rolled on to the second story I was ready to buy a ticket to L.A. and escape! They also suggested the storm was strengthening to the south and might become a cyclone (that's Pacific Ocean lingo for *hurricane* in case you didn't know). The path was still uncertain but it appeared the West side of the Big Island – that's us – was likely to get hit in about 48 to 72 hours.

Well, I have never been through a cyclone nor had anyone else, so we all watched and listened to the dos and don'ts of cyclone survival. We were likely to lose power. No big deal. Almost any storm left us in the dark; we were well stocked with candles. As to cooking, there was always the faithful grill. Fortunately, I'd recently purchased a second LP tank since we had been grilling more often than usual. The important news was that we needed to protect the windows and doors from flying debris. For that we needed plywood and duct tape. Neither of which was at hand, so a trip to the home store was in order.

According to those in attendance, we were also light on booze, ice, and munchies – something even Margie agreed to stock up on God bless her. And so it was determined that first thing in the morning, we would gather again and take care of what was necessary.

As we got ready for bed that night, Margie commented on how glad she was that I'd suggested games after dinner. I told her I had a good time and let her think that I might be amenable to them in the future – which of course I actually wasn't, unless I could use them for my own sinister plans.

An Approaching Storm

Morning came with the usual noises: birds and lawnmowers and leaf blowers and all that, but intermixed with those typical sounds were the whack, whack, whack of hammers and the buzz, buzz, buzz of power saws and the whir, whir, whir of electric drills and of course the occasionally well chosen swear word – which I assumed was the result of misguided whacking.

Reluctantly I rolled out of bed and found my way to the patio where everyone (including Mark and Shelly who had separate rooms at the hotel now but were forced to appear together as if everything was hunky dory for the sake of the girls) had already finished breakfast and was eager to get started. The ladies had been measuring windows and making lists. I insisted on having time to drink a cup of coffee, read the paper, and have a banana, and was given permission for this as long as I didn't dawdle – which was my plan all along. I ate and read and sipped for a good long time until Margie came out and suggested that I'd better get my fat ass off the chair and pitch in or she'd lock me out in the storm. I'm a quick study and she didn't have to repeat her warning twice. I got off my ass and headed indoors where the entire herd was talking at once and seemed to be in something of a party mood.

I'd observed this behavior in Chicago when a major snow storm threatened to shut down the city. I'm not sure what the psychology is behind it but it's a well known phenomenon. I assume the residents of Pompeii had a similar experience, but I've not heard about it one way or another. I think it's the effects of adrenaline. Or maybe it's the fight or flee response – but I guess that's due to adrenaline too isn't it?

As planned the night before, the ladies set off to the local grocery store and filled Angie's car with enough stuff to survive for several months. They told us later the store was so crowded you couldn't move and that Angie had gotten into a fight with a large wahine (that's Hawaiian for woman) over the last can of SPAM. Why Angie wanted a can of SPAM I can't imagine, but here's a piece of trivia: Hawaiian's consume more SPAM per resident than any other place on the planet. Go figure!

While the women gathered food, the men (which included me) took the Volvo to the home store and wrestled with other men for plywood, nails, hammers, drills and materials to seal the windows and tape the glass doors. It was all very surreal as we were just one of many groups doing the same thing.

We ran into Amanda and Nicky at the home store. Nicky was even more useless than I, and we promised we'd come and help secure the Sogol estate after we'd taken care of our place. Pete, Amanda informed me, had not so much as called to see how things were going at the house, which as you can imagine had Amanda in a mood.

Since I'm not good with hammer and nails and the idea of trusting me with a power tool would be catastrophic, I was assigned a roll of duct tape and windows on the West side of the house. We were fortunate in that Mark and Mr. M. were quite the handymen and took care of most of the preparations. Even I managed, after some practice, to apply large 'X's to the windows without the tape doubling over and sticking to itself or some part of my anatomy.

By lunchtime we had made good progress and stopped to rest and refuel. Margie and Catherine made sandwiches and we ate like it was our last meal. Amanda showed up just as we were finishing and announced that her place was all battened down. A work crew had arrived shortly after she'd returned from the home store to take care of everything. She was sure Pete had sent them, but Margie told me later that she'd ordered it done and that I shouldn't tell anyone. Which I didn't. Except you, and you won't tell. I trust you.

I was a little disappointed in that I'd planned to use the time at Amanda's to start softening Nicky with storied about how much fun Angie and Maxwell had had the night before playing games, but I'm a big boy and took it like a man.

Truth be told, I was concerned about Pete 'cause it didn't sound like him to let something like that slip through the cracks. I couldn't slip away to check on him and I couldn't even find the opportunity to phone him what with all the extra bodies around. I found out later that he had hired someone to take care of things, but they'd realized the surf was up and that was the end of it. It's a common problem in Hawaii. Surf's up! Work's down!

After lunch most everyone took a well deserved siesta. Mark and Shelly went back to their hotel room and took the girls with them to torment the adults in the hotel pool, a decision for which I thanked them. Mr. and Mrs. M retired to the guestroom, and I headed for the hammock out by the pool.

Of course I got waylaid, for just as I was passing through the living room on my way to the lanai where the great hammock was calling to me, I heard a knock at the front door. Before I even opened it I knew it was Shuko, our mail carrier. He always comes just after two and he's always on time. I like getting mail, so I'm always glad to see him. It's sort of a Pavlov dog sort of thing.

Shuko's a nice man, about fifty, fifty-five, with a big toothy smile to greet you and warm brown eyes. Like most of the people I know in Hawaii, he seems perpetually happy and glad to be alive.

"Aloha, Shuko," I sang.

Shuko bowed slightly and flashed his teeth.

"Afternoon, Mr. Thomas," he sang back. "Got package for you today."

He held out a thick manila envelope. I looked at it. *What could that be?* I held out my hand cautiously and he laid the package in it.

"Do I need to sign?" I asked, looking carefully at the return address. It was from a company called Dominic Research in Iowa. I had no idea what Dominic Research was. It was addressed to Margie.

"No. No sign," Shuko said. He dug in his bag and pulled out a stack of mail which he also handed to me. It appeared to be the usual mix of bills and bulk mailings.

"Mahalo," I said. "Can I get you an ice tea?"

Sometimes Shuko will come in and have ice tea with us. We know all about him and his wife and their six children – three girls and three boys. But today he seemed to be in a hurry.

"No thank you, Mr. Thomas, I got to finish early. Sammy got a game."

Sammy was Shuko's youngest son, a soccer star and the pride of the Higa family.

"Well, wish him luck from me," I said.

"Mahalo, Mr. Thomas, I tell him," Shuko began walking away.

"Say 'Aloha' to Mrs. Higa," I called as he disappeared.

He waved a hand above his head to acknowledge he'd heard me, and I turned my attention to the package and shut the door.

"What's that?" Margie asked coming to meet me as I entered the living room with the mail.

Like me, Margie has a thing for mail. We both know people who can let mail sit for days without opening it or even looking through it. For Margie and me it's like Christmas morning, we can't wait to tear into it. Even the stuff marked 'occupant.'

"I don't know," I said. "It's from a company called Dominic Research."

"Well open it," Margie directed.

I put down the rest of the mail and opened the package. I pulled out about a dozen thick, slick corporate brochures from various companies. I knew immediately what they were.

"Annual reports," I said. "Thinking of making some new investments?"

Margie does all the investing. She's good at it and enjoys it. I'm a terrible investor; sell low, buy high, that sort of thing. If you want to know which way the market's going just ask me and assume the opposite.

"No," she said as I laid the reports out on the table. She came over and pushed through them. "These are all companies in which Mr. G. Peter Ryan owns a significant stake. I thought we could find a clue in here about him." Margie said.

"In there?" My skepticism was hard to miss.

"Why not?"

"Well, I just..."

"So what did you have in mind, hire a private detective?"

"Well, no, but do you really think..."

Just then, Amanda waltzed in.

"The reports just came," Margie said in response to her unasked question.

Amanda picked up one and quickly fanned through it. "Looks like I won't need my Ambien for awhile. Where do you want to start?"

Margie picked up a report for a company called EEG which I as I understand it stood for Electric Energy Grid.

"Julia was into energy, right? Look for references to other businesses and subsidiaries and any research partnerships the company claims that might be relevant. Make notes in the margins. We'll follow up later."

"Okay," Amanda said and sorted the reports into two piles. She picked up a pile and stood. "I've got to go feed Nicky. He's totally helpless and probably starving. I don't think he even knows how to butter bread!"

"You're coming back for dinner aren't you?" Margie asked.

"Why not. I'll bring 'Mr. Wonderful' along. What time?"

"Cocktails at five; dinner at seven. And tell 'Mr. Wonderful' that if he doesn't come, he'll be persona non grata.

"Okay, but I may start cocktails before five." Amanda skipped up the steps and out the door.

Margie looked at her watch. "We should get back to work."

I objected: "But my nap…"

"You can nap later," Margie said, picking up her pile of reports and heading for the bedroom. "You've got to help me figure out what we can leave in the pool house and what we need to bring inside."

I was going to object, but I knew she was right. It was something we needed to decide together, so I went outside and waited for Margie to join me and in no time at all we figured it all out.

An hour or so later, everyone woke from their naps and/or returned to the house and we spent the afternoon much like the morning with tape and 'x's' and moving furniture from the pool house. We got far less done in the afternoon because of the heat and the fact we were all running out of steam. But by cocktail time we were able to call it quits, having saved the large lanai doors for latter when the cyclone was imminent.

As agreed, Amanda arrived for happy hour with a reluctant Nicky. I heard later she had had to threaten to call the editor of 'Hollywood Trash' if he didn't join us. Of course Nicky kept his distance from Angie and Angie did likewise. The girls however swarmed Nicky so he had plenty of attention. Not that I was worried about him.

Cocktails went well and I suggested we participate in some board games. I was again rousingly hailed for my idea by nearly everyone (Nicky and the girls being the holdouts) and we settled on Monopoly this time. We broke into the same teams as before; Amanda and Nicky forming a new team, and we tried to include the girls but they said Monopoly was lame and just sat around and criticized us until they got bored and left to do some serious texting that they'd forgotten they needed to do.

Let it not be said that Angie is slow. It was as if she'd read my mind. From the get-go, she made a big deal over everything Maxwell did or said, telling him how smart he was and what fun he was and all that. And it was quite evident that Nicky was taking note. The problem was, Catherine was taking note as well, and so too was Margie.

During a break in the play, Angie, rubbed Maxwell's thigh, which caused Nicky to break the pencil he was holding! *That a girl!*

I decided another round of drinks was in order to keep the party going and asked for a pause in the play while I prepared a pitcher of Long Islands. Margie took orders for pizza – a rare treat as you already know—and I place my order for Hawaiian pizza.

Once she'd ordered the pizzas Margie joined me at the bar to help with the drinks – a chore I was perfectly capable of doing myself – but the purpose of which was made clear when she whispered crossly: "I think Dad is getting a little too chummy with Angie."

"Really?" I teased. "I hadn't noticed."

Margie shot me her 'liar, liar, pants-on-fire' look and I shrugged.

"She's just trying to make Nicky jealous," I said.

"Yeah, well I'm pretty sure it's working. But I'm not going to be responsible for my mother. Did you see her face?"

I turned to sneak a peek over my shoulder at the group. Margie was right. Mom was shooting daggers at Angie who was brushing invisible dandruff off Maxwell's shoulder.

"Are you sure neither of them has a clue about who... what.... Angie is?" I asked.

"They're from a different era," Margie said defensively. "They're not looking for it so they don't see it."

"Plus," I added. "They don't see all that well to begin with."

Margie 'accidently' stepped on my bare toes as a reward for my shot at Mom and Dad, but I took it in

229

stride and didn't cry. Margie's a featherweight as you already know, so it didn't hurt all that much. We delivered the drinks and restarted the game.

For at least five minutes, all was going well until Catherine suddenly stood up and pointed an accusatory finger at Maxwell and shouted: "Cheater!"

The phrase 'you could have heard a pin drop' is appropriate for the silence that descended on the room, and for a brief moment I wasn't sure if her reference was to the game or to the chasm between them that had held for all these years.

"He moved eight spaces. Not seven! He should be on our railroad!" Catherine said.

Well that clarified it, though I was still of the opinion that the remark was Freudian in nature.

"I did not," bellowed dear old Dad. "You're crazy."

That's what I found so endearing about Margie's folks. They could stoke a fire faster than a fireman on an old-time locomotive.

"Mom, Dad, it's just a game." Margie pleaded, but her fire hose wasn't big enough for this row.

"She's right," Nicky chimed in. "He was on Vermont. That's seven spaces back."

"He was on Connecticut!" Angie said, coming to her team mate's defense.

While biting accusations like 'was not' 'was too' and such flew back and forth, Margie, Amanda and I shared looks of wonder and dismay. None of us wanted to get in the middle of this so it was serendipity that the doorbell rang.

"Pizza," I cried with enthusiasm.

I was still naïve enough to think that the arrival of bread, tomato sauce, cheese and assorted meats would be sufficient to repair things. Of course I was wrong.

"I'm not eating with a big cheat!" Mom said and stormed off to her room.

"Me neither," snapped Nicky who gave Angie a look of disgust and rose quickly, upending the board and scattering the game pieces. He stalked out of the house past the pizza delivery girl who, unaware of the tempest into which she'd just entered, chimed "sixty-seven fifty" as soon as the door opened and watched in confusion as Nicky blew past her.

Margie ran to the door, handing over four twenties and told the now smiling pizza girl to keep the change.

The remaining troop, Angie, Maxwell, Amanda, Mark, Shelly, Margie and I all looked at one another. Maxwell broke the silence. "I'll have a couple slices of the pepperoni and green olive."

We retired to the pool area and ate mechanically, except for Maxwell who ate like a lion after the kill. And me, who ate like a junk food junky just returning from rehab.

As I savored my slice of Canadian bacon and pineapple, I couldn't help but wonder that my plan had somehow gone horribly wrong. Not only were Angie and Nicky farther apart than ever, but Mom and Dad were .... well ... at war. And it occurred to me that given the overflow crowd with which we were dealing and the current sleeping arrangements there were no longer enough bedrooms to accommodate those factions who objected to other factions.

And deep down I knew it was I would suffer. But the pizza sure tasted damn good.

The Big Bang!

Now you may not think that sleeping outside under the clear starry skies of Kona counts as suffering, but my back informed me that although it could have been worse, it wasn't all that grand.

I opened my peepers and saw the clear blue Kona sky and little cotton ball clouds and wondered what enjoyment the day held for me. None most likely.

I heard someone swimming laps so I assumed Margie was up. And I smelled fresh-brewed coffee, another indication of Margie's presence.

The ache in my back made it difficult to swing out of the hammock to face the world, but I accomplished the chore in due course and staggered, a bit stooped, to the table where I poured coffee and found my paper. Thanks again to Margie. Dad must have been sleeping in.

Grateful that I had at least a few precious minutes to myself before the entourage awakened, I opened the paper and there, staring out at me was a picture of Nicky who it seems had managed to get picked up for DUI the night before just in time to make the morning news. What luck! The thought occurred to me that I might sleep in Amanda's guest room that night, though I knew deep in my heart it would not happen.

I read the article carefully.

Since Nicky was a big star, his arrest was big news. And since Nicky had tried to punch the arresting officer, it was even bigger news. And since all this had happened at the most exclusive resort on the island, it was Big, Big news.

I read what I needed, put down the paper, took a glanced at Margie's swimming form (again the Australian crawl) – which was not as enjoyable with the clingy black swimsuit as when she was naked -- and retreated to the house, intending to shower in my big, luxurious master bathroom until all hell broke loose or I ran out of hot water, whichever occurred first.

At the door to my bedroom, Magoo greeted me and I reached down to scratch behind his ears. He showed his appreciation by wagging his tail and rolling over on his back so that I might scratch his tummy as well.

After a few seconds of this, Magoo had had enough and headed out to the pool where he knew Margie would provide breakfast as soon as she finished her swim.

Animals have a way of lifting your mood, and if you're a dog-lover you'll understand that my short interaction with Magoo had me feeling almost human. At least that was the case until I started across the bedroom and heard Maxwell belting out 'Moon River' from the confines of my large luxurious bath.

Maxwell had, as you may have already surmised, usurped the master bedroom after the mêlée with Mrs. M., and Margie had been forced to share the guestroom with Mom, and I, as you already know, had been relegated to sleep in the hammock by the pool.

Arrangements couldn't have been better.

I stopped in my tracks. There was literally no place for me to go now. I was just thankful the coffee hadn't kicked in yet because I thought it might be that I'd have to rescue an old can from the rubbish for my personal use. Of course I could step next door to the Stanley's – our neighbors – but I thought it poor manners to ask to 'borrow' their bathroom when we were on tenuous terms ever since they'd caught Magoo peeing on Mr. Stanley's golf shoes which he'd left outside the front door.

I turned around and was just reentering the living room when I heard the front door open and the clatter of Amanda's sandals on our tile entryway.

"Nicky got arrested!" she blurted as soon as she saw me.

"I saw the paper," I responded apathetically.

Her hands went to her chest and shock filled her generally cherubic face. "The paper?"

Obviously Amanda had not seen the local paper, which is not surprising since she reads the New York Time and the Wall Street Journal before turning her attention to local issues.

Amanda seemed unable to process the information just provided and stood like a deer in the headlights staring at me. She might have stayed that way permanently, had Angie not appeared at the door to the den wearing a bathrobe and looking less like a lady and more like a man to ask in that not so feminine voice that heretofore had been reserved only for me: "WHAT DID YOU SAY?"

She recovered quickly and continued in her false soprano. "Nicky's been arrested?"

"Yes!" Amanda squealed, finally coming to life again. "And he tried to punch a cop!"

At that moment Margie appeared behind me. She'd obviously heard everything and took charge of the situation immediately.

"Angie, get dressed! Amanda, call and find out what the charges are. I'll call Cynthia."

And quick as a flash they scattered, leaving me alone in the living room more certain than ever that there were no available bathroom facilities for at least the next hour.

Magoo came and sat next to me and I looked down. "Good boy," I said, even though he hadn't done anything. And maybe that's precisely why I said it.

I was about to make my way out to the pool where I could at least have some peace and quiet, when Mrs.

Moore showed up in the living room dressed to a T, pulling her large Louis Vuitton suitcase.

Now here is something new, I thought.

"I would like a ride to the airport please," she said calmly. "Where's Margie?"

Unprepared for her sudden announcement, I squirmed a bit and then informed her that Margie was getting dressed.

"Would you please tell her I'd like to see her?" Again the tone was calm and determined.

"I'll get her," I said and retreated toward the master suite where I found Margie in red shorts pulling on a simple white t-shirt with a brightly colored fish of some sort on it and fluffing her hair, which was already drying in the warm morning air. She must have used the sink to freshen up because I could still hear Mr. M. in the shower singing away.

Margie sensed I had something to tell her.

"What is it?" she asked.

I was aware that the facts themselves would have significant impact so as casually as possible I said: "Your mother would like a ride to the airport."

Margie looked at me as if I'd just told her something in Greek.

"What are you talking about?" She asked as she found a pair of white sandals with multicolored rhinestones and ran her fingers through her hair again and began putting on lip gloss or lipstick or whatever they (you?) call it.

"Your mother," I said, "is standing in the living room with a packed suitcase asking for a ride to the airport." *There. That should be clear enough.*

In retrospect I realize I should have waited until Margie had finished applying her lipstick because the news unnerved her such that she not only applied lipstick to her upper lip, but also to a fair amount of her left cheek and the side of her nose.

"What?" Margie repeated, turning to give me that look of hers that says 'what have you done now?' To which I responded with a shrug and the look I give back to her that says 'I haven't done anything, damn it.'

Margie found a tissue and corrected her coloring mistake then rushed from the bedroom as if it was on fire. Had there been a fire in the bedroom I would have stayed. I certainly did not want to go back into the living room.

At that moment, Mr. M appeared from my large, luxurious master bath looking clean as a whistle and dressed for the day. And as a matter of fact he was whistling. He was whistling the theme song from *The Bridge on the River Kwai*.

"Good morning, Joe," he said happily, which was easy for him to say since he had no idea what was going on.

"Morning Mr. M," I said with as much enthusiasm as I could muster.

"What's new?" He asked.

I was certain he didn't want to know, but I felt it my duty to inform him. "Well, Mr. M. Nicky's gotten himself arrested for DUI and taking a swing at a cop..."

"Really?" Mr. M. interrupted, a sly grin slipping over his face. I couldn't tell whether it meant he was glad Nicky had been busted or he didn't think Nicky had the balls to take a swing at a cop. Either way I plunged ahead with the more noteworthy news.

"And Mrs. M. is in the living room with a packed suitcase asking for someone to drive her to the airport."

Reactions are funny things. Some people react like Amanda: deer in the headlight. Some react like Margie: lipstick smeared across the face. And some react like Mr.

M whose reaction was clear, direct and to the point: "What the f...k?"

It was, of course, a rhetorical question and he rushed from the bedroom before I could respond.

Peace at last, I thought, and then *Good God the bathroom is open.* I ran inside as quick as a bunny.

Moments later I was all lathered up and humming Moon River – not because I especially like that song but because it does have a way of sticking with you – when I felt a presence. I opened my eyes to find Margie standing outside the shower stall, her arms crossed, her foot tapping.

I told myself to take it easy; let her do the talking.

"Care to join me?" I asked, certain I knew the answer.

"I hope you're proud of yourself," Margie snapped.

Generally my answer would be 'yes,' for as a rule I am proud of myself except when I lie to Margie after I slip away to the donut shop. But from the tone of her voice, I could tell the correct answer was not 'yes,' at least not if I wanted her to join me in the shower at any time in the near future or the distant future for that matter.

The enjoyment that a warm shower brings was no longer present, so I turned off the water and reached for a towel. I delayed asking the question which I knew I had to ask long enough to dry my face and arms. Margie remained where she was taping and scowling. Actually, scowling is not possible for Margie. She has one of those interminably happy faces that make scowling a physical impossibility. But I got the inference.

"What did I do now?" I asked, confident the answer would be unfair.

"You had to bring out that stupid board game didn't you?" Margie put her hands on her hips. "Why?"

It occurred to me that the answer was 'because I thought it might be fun,' but I knew that wasn't the correct answer. I continued toweling, hoping that my physical actions would somehow soften Margie's mood. It didn't work.

"Well?" she crossed her arms again.

There are times in life when you have to take a stand, tell the truth, and let the chips fall where they may. This, I determined, was one of those times. I stopped toweling and let go with both barrels.

"Well," I said, "I thought that perhaps by playing board games your father would cheat and your best friend's brother's transvestite girlfriend would come to his defense upsetting her boyfriend to the extent that he would drive to a first-class resort where he'd get drunk and play fisticuffs with the local constable, get arrested and thrown in jail. And as an added bonus, your mother would suddenly grasp the fact that your father was indeed a cheat – and not just at board games – get mad and decide she was going to leave him after putting up with endless bickering that has progressed for most of your adult life and seems destined to continue until you bury one or the other of them!"

The thought occurred to me that I should cover the family jewels at this point, but while that might have been necessary with my previous wife, Margie could be trusted to deal with such blunt criticism as an adult. Margie didn't have a violent bone in her body.

As the seconds ticked by and Margie stood motionless, I regretted my bluntness. This was, I knew, a lot to take in—or let out as the case may be.

Margie didn't react right away but there was a gradual softening of the intense stare with which she'd fixed me and her eyes grew moist. Suddenly, as forcefully as a dam collapsing, tears streamed from her eyes and cascaded down her cheeks and her face contorted into an anguished mask of grief.

She stepped forward, wrapped her arms around me, and pressed her face into my neck. Between emotional sobs and gasps for air, she choked out an apology.

"I'm...so...sorry...Joe. You've...been....a...prince...dealing...with... my..crazy ...relatives...and...their... stupid..shallow...baggage, ...and... I've...been...just...terrible. I...don't...deserve...you. You're...a ...saint... and..."

Her stream of recriminations concerning her family coupled with glowing accolades for my patient understanding continued for a while longer, but I won't burden you with the entire text. You get the drift. And it wasn't till I pulled her head back and kissed her passionately that her crying jag faded and we stood lip locked in the shower, me naked, her dressed and both of us oblivious to the world around.

Unfortunately the world *was* still around us and voices from afar brought us back to reality.

"You are too a cheater!" Mrs. M's alto soprano bawled.

"It was just a stupid board game!" Mr. M's baritone responded.

"I'm not talking about the fucking board game," Mrs. M screeched an octave higher than previously.

Margie sank from my embrace. "I'd better go referee."

I held her tight. "You've been referee long enough. Let 'em duke it out!"

Margie paused then put her hands over her ears. "Okay. Just let me know when it's over."

I pulled Margie close and hummed the theme song from the Magnificent Seven. Yes I know that's stupid, but it came to me and what was I going to do? I was trying to shield Margie from some very caustic accusations and block my own ears from what was basically a private dispute that was being argued at the decibel level of an approaching aircraft.

Individual words came through however and I'll not repeat them since to do so would neither further the story nor add dimension to what transpired. I'm certain you can imagine what might have been said back and forth and the emotion that was unleashed.

Eventually, I became concerned that it might go on forever and wondered if perhaps I should intervene when I heard the unmistakable report of a gunshot! *Pop!*

Oh my God!

Margie heard it as well and pulled her hands from her ears. For a split second we stood frozen looking at one another in disbelief, then we bolted from the bathroom with Margie first and me a step behind pulling on my bathrobe as I ran.

Dead Again

Detective Lo was his usual no nonsense self as he questioned us out by the pool.

"And where was the dog?"

"Magoo? He hides under the bed whenever there's yelling. I think it's a guilt thing. He probably used to get yelled at," I said.

"So he didn't bark?"

"Not until later. It was his barking that drew our attention to the pool."

The detective made some notes.

"So you didn't see the shooting?"

"No. I already told you that. Margie and I were in the shower."

"Together?"

I gave the detective a glare. "Yes, together."

"And what were you doing in there together?"

"Listen detective that has nothing to do with anything. I'm willing to answer your questions without our attorney but this is getting a bit voyeuristic and if..."

"Okay. Okay," Detective Lo patted the air.

"So you heard the shot. What did you do?"

"We ran into the living room."

"And what did you see?"

"Mr. and Mrs. M. just standing there."

"You didn't see a gun?"

"No!"

"Did you smell gun smoke?"

I hadn't even thought about that so I turned it over in my mind a moment and looked at Margie. She was still stunned from the events and offered no help.

"I don't think so. I'm pretty sure I would have noticed. The gunshot must have come from outside."

"Do you have any idea who the shooter was?" Lo asked finally.

"No. None. We haven't seen Kenny since you arrested Trisha. I don't know what he was doing at our house."

Lo turned to Margie. "What about you, Mrs. Thomas. Do you have anything to add?"

Margie thought a moment, then came around: "If I were you, Detective Lo, I'd talk to Tommy Chow."

For the first time I could remember I saw Detective Lo's stone-face crack.

"What do you know about Tommy Chow?" Detective Lo asked suspiciously.

"He was with Mr. Ryan when we went to see him," I said, pulling Detective Lo's attention back to me.

241

Lo wasn't satisfied with that so we had to explain our rendezvous with Mr. Ryan and Tommy Chow and what we thought of the whole thing. When we finished, Lo gave us the cold stare: "I could arrest you both for interfering in a police investigation."

"Wouldn't stick," Margie snapped. "You already had a suspect in custody and ..."

"Who told you that?" Lo snapped back, losing his cool.

"My attorney," Margie said sharply.

"Humph," Lo said. "Don't be so sure about that, Mrs. Thomas. But let's get on with it. I need both of you to stay out of this thing. Mr. McMan's death proves there's more going on here than a simple murder. If I find out you're getting involved I will arrest you and then your attorney, Mrs. Thomas, can argue with the county attorney while you both cool your heels in a very uncomfortable jail cell!"

I'm not a homophobe and I don't believe I have any latent homosexual desires, but at that moment I wanted to kiss the big lug! He'd finally laid down the law to Margie. Now she'd have to give it up. Not to mention that things were getting seriously dangerous. We really had no idea why Kenny had returned to our house or why anyone would want to gun him down.

"I've got one last question for both of you," Detective Lo said. "When was the last time you saw Patrisha Ryan?"

"When?" I thought about it a moment. "That would be the day we went to visit her in jail," I said. "I understand she went to her father's place after she was released."

We didn't hear anything from Trisha once she was released. Rumor was her dad had shipped her off

242

someplace where he could keep an eye on her. Margie took it hard of course but I tried to cheer her up by telling her it wasn't Trisha's fault. It helped a little.

"You didn't maybe see her or someone who resembled her lurking around the neighborhood? Driving by?"

"No. I'm sure I didn't." I looked at Margie. She shook her head in the negative. "She would never do such a thing!" Margie added.

Detective Lo said nothing, then: "Okay. If I think of anything else, I'll call. In the meantime, don't take any trips off the island. And that goes for you two as well." He turned to Mom and Dad who were sitting inside on the sofa – on opposite ends of course. "You're not suspects at this time, but you're all material witnesses."

Detective Lo turned his attention to the sergeant at the top of the landing. "Did you check them all for gun power reside?"

"Yes sir. Nothing."

"The sergeant will stay here till the crime scene is cleaned up; I suggest you go to your friend's house till then. Call me if you remember anything – anything at all – about what happened or what you may have seen or heard before or after the gunshot."

Detective Lo handed out cards and made his way to the door where he paused and turned with his hand on the knob.

"I warned you once before about getting involved in murder cases and I'd do it again if I thought it would do any good. But I guess you'll just have to learn the hard way."

And with that Detective Lo left us alone.

As the good detective had suggested, we made our way to Amanda's where we found Nicky and Angie and

243

Amanda sitting around the pool half in the bag despite it being just a little after noon.

As you might have already suspected, Angie bailed Nicky out of jail and it appeared Nicky's bender in the face of Mr. M's attention to Angie had assuaged Angie's anger over Nicky's comment about a girdle for they were holding hands and making goo-goo eyes at one another, which had me thinking it was a good thing Pete wasn't there.

We helped ourselves to liquor and tried to catch up – alcohol wise -- as best we could. No one was keen on talking much. But as they say liquor loosens the tongue and before I'd downed my second scotch, the murder scene and the interrogations were the topic of the day.

Amanda observed how eerie it was that Kenny was found floating in our pool just like the hit man we'd found murdered back when Jack and Jillian (Margie's husband and my wife) were trying to murder us and how spooky it was that Kenny and Julia and the hit man had all been shot right between the eyes.

"What do you think the odds are of that?" Mr. M. commented.

"Haven't a clue," Margie said. "But I'll bet Julia and Kenny were killed with the same gun and by the same person."

We all agreed that that seemed logical but by whom had they been killed? We were no closer to answering that question now than we'd been days ago. We drank quietly for awhile till Amanda's cell phone rang.

Unlike Margie, Amanda carries a cell phone so she doesn't have to run for the house. She just reaches in her bra, pulls out the phone, and flips it open with a flick of her wrist.

"Hello," she said as we all sat waiting to see if the call might be for us.

"Uh huh. Okay. Yeah. Thanks for letting me know." Amanda flipped the phone shut. She took a sip of wine. "They made an arrest," she said.

There was a combined gasp followed by multiple owl imitations: "Who?"

"Sam Belmont, Julia's lover. He turned himself in twenty minutes ago." Amanda paused.

"Did they say why he did it? Or why he was killed at our house?" Margie asked. "It doesn't make any sense."

"Sorry. My source didn't have that information. But I expect we'll find out soon enough." Amanda nodded toward the street where a police car had just pulled to the curb and two uniformed officers stood looking up at us.

We all waved, which in retrospect is an odd thing to do to police officers who you know are on official business and there has just been a murder. But none the less, we did wave. And no, the officers did not wave back. They did however climb the front stairs to the pool and ask for Mr. and Mrs. Thomas.

Margie and I identified ourselves and the officers asked if we would come to the police station as Detective Lo had some questions for us.

We agreed to go but informed them that we had been drinking and would be unable to drive for some time. The politely offered to take us to the station in their car. We agreed and said our goodbyes to those present, leaving Magoo in Amanda's capable hands, and made our way unsteadily to the squad car. Of course the neighbors were watching and it probably looked bad, but I figured we'd straighten it all out later.

It has never been my intention to become familiar with any police station, but we were, I realized, becoming regulars at the Kona precinct – which is a sorry state of affairs if you're a law-abiding citizen who finds himself or herself inundated with murder victims, murder suspects, and assorted relatives of friends who get arrested.

We were escorted to Detective Lo's desk where the detective was on the phone. As we waited, I took the opportunity to look about and noticed what a grim decor the place had. *Jeez,* I thought, *put up a travel poster or something!*

Detective Lo rang off and greeted us politely. He informed us that there was going to be a lineup and he wanted us to view the individuals and let him know if we'd seen any of them before and where we might have seen them.

I asked if Professor Belmont would be a part of the lineup. Although he tried to hide it, I could tell that the news that we knew about the professor upset the detective but he did the best he could and indicated that he'd prefer we knew nothing about who might be present. Margie was quieter than usual and I couldn't tell whether it was because of the afternoon drinking or the circumstances of other things that day.

We followed the detective down the hall and into a small room that seemed to double as a broom closet. There was a single overhead bulb and a large black shade along one wall. I've watched enough police shows on television to know that behind the black shade was a one way mirror and beyond that was a room for the suspects.

"They can't see you or hear you. Just let me know if you can place any of these people. Take your time. Don't hurry." And with that the detective raised the shade.

As soon as the shade went up, Margie let out a gasp. "It's that man from the garage."

"What man?" I asked, totally perplexed by her reaction.

"You know, the man who asked about where Julia's body was found."

Margie's explanation did nothing to jog my memory. "Was I there?"

Margie turned and gave me the 'look of despair' she's saving for me when Alzheimer's has crept into my skull and the only thing I remember is nothing. Then suddenly her expression lightened. "Oh, no, that wasn't you. It was when I took Mom shopping."

Detective Lo intruded. "Could you tell me which man you are referring to, by his number?"

All the men in the room were standing in front of numbers on the floor. There were six of them and all of them were similar in size and shape and age. Two had beards and one was bald.

"Number four," Margie said.

Number four was a handsome man with salt and pepper hair and a somber expression and sad eyes. I wondered if he was the professor.

Detective Lo asked Margie a number of questions about meeting the man, such as how he approached her, exactly what he said, exactly what she said, how he reacted to what she said, how she reacted to what he said and so on. I was pretty bored with it all and was wondering how much longer it would be before we could go back to the party at the Sogol's. I was losing my buzz and I knew it would be followed by a major hangover if alcohol were not administered soon.

Finally the detective ran out of things to ask; he lowered the shade and thanked us for coming. He ushered us from the room and led us back up the hall to the squad room where our uniformed officers were waiting to take us home.

He asked where Mrs. M was and we told him she was also back at the Sogol's. He told the uniforms to bring her back and cautioned us to say nothing to her about what we'd seen. He didn't want her testimony muddled by ours. We agreed and left the station.

Margie was quiet throughout the ride and so I kept any questions I had for her to myself.

As you might guess, Mom was not happy about going to the police station, but we convinced her she'd be okay and after she left we filled the crowd in about what had transpired.

"So, was it the professor?" Amanda asked.

"I assume so," I offered. He wouldn't say.

"Well while you were gone, I did some searching on the Internet," Amanda handed Margie three sheets of paper – printouts from various websites.

I leaned over Margie's shoulder and read. The first article showed a picture of the professor, which provide proof positive that he was indeed the man Margie had encountered at the gas station.

The article said the professor was married – who'd a guessed – and taught a course on "Geodynamics," whatever that was. I skimmed as best I could before Margie turned to the next article. Margie reads faster than she talks. I read slower -- that is I read slower than she does, everybody reads slower than Margie talks! I didn't see much else in the first article of interest.

The second article was about the Professor and Julia working on a joint project – so much for how they connected.

The third article was about the Professor's marksmanship. It was an NRA reprint. The guy was awarded a sharpshooter medal, which explains the hole between the eyes.

While Margie and I read, Amanda took another phone call to which I paid little attention until I heard the words 'claimed' and 'innocent.' When Amanda rang off she filled us in.

"The professor readily admits to having killed Kenny, but adamantly denies killing Julia. He claims he was in love with her and planned to leave his wife. According to my source, however, there's evidence to the contrary – such as rope with blood on it in the trunk of his rental car and duct tape and a pair of handcuffs!"

"Sounds like love to me," Angie quipped. "Kind of makes you wonder what kind of place that Collette College is. A regular mosh pit of sexual infidelity."

Mrs. M returned and we grilled her on her experience which was pretty much the same as ours. She too had immediately picked out the professor.

As you can imagine the sleeping arrangements at Amanda's were tough even though Mrs. M and Mr. M. got rooms at a local hotel – not together of course – and the girls went to the hotel with Shelly and Mark for the night.

Margie and I shared an air mattress on the living room floor. It wouldn't have been too bad except we overinflated it and every time I moved, Margie got tossed off, and every time she moved, I thought I was going to throw up. Eventually we let some air out but that didn't help much because then we both sort of rolled to the center. Eventually we gave up and fell asleep; in my case I think I passed out.

In the morning we found the crime scene tape had been removed from our house and so we thanked Amanda and made our way home.

A Day at the Beach

In the days following Kenny's murder, the asylum fell into something of an unstable routine. Everyone – with the exception of yours truly – seemed to be making the most of their holiday with trips to the volcano, outings for deep sea fishing, tennis, golf, resort hopping, star gazing, horseback riding, snorkeling, swimming, luaus, hula lessons, and what not. Of course most of them couldn't leave the island for one reason or another: material witness, awaiting court date, you get the picture.

Mr. and Mrs. M. where not on speaking terms, which as far as I was concerned was a giant step forward in terms of matrimonial harmony. Shelly and Mark, who had repaired their shaky marriage to a remarkable extent, continued to lean on Margie and me and others to oversee the girls who I discovered were on an extended break from their private school and therefore were able to stay with us through the New Year. Yippie? Angie, at least, was back at the Sogol residence although Pete was not. But I got to sleep on the sleeper sofa in the den and returned to working on my book. Wink. Wink.

I put myself on a flexible schedule, which is to say when the others went out I used the excuse that I needed to write. When the others sat home I found things I needed to do outside the house -- like search for Pete. If I'd kept a diary, this is how it might read: Wednesday -- Slept late; looked for Pete; took in a movie; ate at B.K.; watched girl's V.B. (volleyball); had a drink at 3:00; stopped to watch some tourist get arrested; headed home.

As you can see my days were not very productive, but at least I wasn't sitting around the house getting exposed to more lunatic microbes.

Of course I knew where Pete was. He was living the high life in the condo he and Amanda owned. We regularly watched TV together and ate high-calorie, greasy, and totally non-organic food and drank beverages containing alcohol and hops.

And yes, you're correct; my behavior did not escape the eye of my beautiful bride who put it to me one night as we undressed for bed. (We were able to share a bed one night because Dad had gone night fishing. He'd tried to lasso me into it, but I claimed fear of darkness, which is true. I am afraid of the dark, and sea monsters, and … well I won't elaborate. Mark, technically being an employee of dad's did not fare so well. He had to go and I heard later he'd spent the night throwing up.) Anyway, Margie said: "We're going to the beach tomorrow Joe and I'd appreciate it if you could find time in your busy schedule to come along. I know you think because it's my family that it's easy for me to be around them but it's not. They drive me nuts too. So unless you want to start having sex with yourself, you'd better get on board."

I could tell she meant it because she was totally naked when she finished her speech and climbed between the covers. Generally Margie sleeps in PJs or a nightgown. The only time she sleeps naked is… Oh, you don't need to know everything!

"Well?" Margie cooed. "Aren't you coming to bed?"

I don't know what a nanosecond is exactly but I know it's a lot less than a second and that's how long it took me to strip and join her under the covers.

I pulled her to me and felt her hot flesh on mine.

"I thought you said we should never use sex as a weapon."

"I'm not using sex as a weapon," Margie said. "It's more of a carrot." She cleared her throat. "I see you brought the carrot."

251

As was occurring more and more frequently, I was awakened the next morning by yelling, which is something I prefer not to be awakened to if I can help it.

The yellees on this particular morning were Bridgette and Barbie, the girls, and the topic of the yelling was who had purchased the white jeweled sandals and who had purchased the pink jeweled sandals. I had seen the sandals and to me it was a moot point. Perhaps like Solomon, I should suggest they wear one of each.

Like many of the conversations of late, it could not possibly be resolved without yelling and despite attempts by Margie, Shelly, and Mrs. M, whose voices I heard intermingled with the girls, the discussion eventually resolved to hair pulling and – I believe it's called – bitch slapping.

Ah, youth!

I tossed off the covers and stumbled to the bathroom (which was mine now, at least until Dad returned – you'll recall he now 'owned' the master suite and bath) to find refuge in the shower where the sound of water muffled the yelling. I wondered what would become of me if I were to hop on a plane and escape to Tahiti or Maui or someplace equally idyllic until the tribe returned to the mainland. It was sheer fantasy of course, but it helped me cope.

One cannot stay in the shower forever – or so Margie insists – so I eventually turned off the water and found that the fracas was over and the world was again quiet and sane – well temporarily that is. I toweled off, made my way to the bedroom and began to dress.

I was just putting on my shorts when the bedroom door opened and Margie entered looking mad enough to devour a small child.

Yes I know I said this about her mother, but Margie looked a lot like her mother at that moment so the phrase stays. She slammed the door shut behind her.

"Problem?" I asked philosophically. Okay, I know it that sounds insensitive, but I was feeling insensitive at the moment.

Margie glared at me but I refused to wilt. "The girls are driving me crazy!"

"Oh," I said, "so that's what's happening."

Margie threw herself on the bed and stared at the ceiling.

"Two years ago when they were here, they were wonderful. We cooked, we swam, we painted. I even got them up to run with me." Margie sighed. "What happened?"

I sat on the bed and took her hand. Since I have no real experience with teenage girls, I really couldn't offer much, but I thought I had a clue.

"They're assholes, Margie, plain and simple; they're horrible creatures who will stop at nothing to torment the adults in their lives. They're selfish, self-centered, egocentric, self-absorbed..."

Margie pulled her hand free and sat up.

"Hey! Take it easy. Those are my nieces you're talking about!"

I smiled. Margie's eyes narrowed.

"They're teenagers, Margie. What did you expect?"

Margie pulled her hands into her lap and hung her head. She checked her nails.

"I know. It's just..."

"Hard to accept that for better or worse they're going through 'the change' and will probably be unlikable by any but their own kind for several years to come?"

I stood up and put on my polo shirt.

253

"How come you know this?" Margie asked.

"Ah, you forget. I had nieces by my previous wife. They were pretty much the same as yours, maybe a little more intense and a lot less likable. Probably their aunt's influence."

Margie stood and walked to the door. She put her hand on the doorknob. "I wish I could say this little chat has helped. But frankly, I think I'm depressed now!" Margie opened the door and left.

I looked down at Magoo who wagged his tail and rolled over onto his back, oblivious to the machinations of the human world.

"Depression is a contagious disease," I said, scratching his tummy for a moment. "Highly contagious."

Thus started our day at the beach which included everyone except Nicky and Pete and Magoo (dogs are not allowed on the beach). Movie actors are allowed, but Nicky didn't want to come along. Pete as you know was unavailable and undoubtedly basking in the glow of a rousing college game of some sort – which is where I'd have preferred to be.

It was a fun day. I burned, as usual. Margie and Amanda got their pictures taken by at least a dozen total strangers, as usual. This happens when you look like swimsuit models.

Maxwell (who had returned from fishing in time to join us) and Catherine sat in the shade and read, as did Angie, of course none of them sat together. And the girls tried their best to pick up local boys but Mark and Shelly beat them off.

We returned home just after sunset and ate a light dinner. After dinner we all congregated by the pool – except for Catherine and the girls who had decided to go watch a movie in the pool house. And Nicky, who stayed at Amanda's. And Pete, who was probably still watching college games on TV.

Of course the murders – now plural – rose to the fore.

I'd hoped that after Professor Belmont killed Kenny and confessed, people would lose interest in Julia's murder since it seemed pretty obvious that he'd also killed Julia.

Margie and Amanda *were* less prone to bring the subject up since the Ryan connection wasn't panning out despite hours and hours of poring over annual corporate reports and Trisha had been whisked away to points unknown, leaving one less source of information. Even Amanda's mole in the department had nothing new to add. But that's not to say the subject was dead, only that we were enjoying a respite from the thing.

There were now two schools of thought on Julia's murder, however, one school believed the professor did both murders; the other school firmly believed that Julia was killed by someone as yet unknown and definitely not Kenny or the professor. Those who believed the first school of thought included…me. Those who believed the second school of thought included virtually everyone else. Mr. M. took neither side and had lost interest in the whole thing. As a matter of fact, since his tussle with Mrs. M., he'd appeared quite depressed.

As it turns out, I was not the only one happy that the police thought they had their man of course. Sam's confession took the heat off Duncan and company as well. As long as the cops thought they had the killer locked up, they wouldn't be looking for anyone and if they weren't looking for anyone they were unlikely to discover their little venture in the forest.

Since Duncan had never been told what Kenny's role in the plan was, he didn't care at all that he'd been eliminated. Unfortunately, Mr. Big did care, but there wasn't much to be done about it. Dead is dead.

Kenny's death meant however that the whole venture was going to be dismantled, and although Duncan didn't understand why, he did what he was told to do: begin moving the coffee off the island. That was fine with him. He was thinking maybe it was time to make that move to Belize.

Always the optimist, I tried to steer the conversation toward the weather. The cyclone had fizzled out and was headed back out to sea as so often happens, but the forecast was for periods of high winds and rain and I thought it deserved some discussion. By the way, does anyone need a stack of plywood and a large ball of used duct tape? I'll let you have if at a fantastic price!

"I'll bet Kenny was killed to cover Julia's murder," Amanda said to get the ball rolling on this occasion.

"That doesn't make sense," Angie objected. Angie was quickly becoming a senior sleuth since she had taken over my den and had access to the dozens of novels written by Shoulton. "We should try to find out is whether Kenny and the professor were in anything together? Where they planning something?"

"Like what?" Amanda quizzed.

"I don't know," Angie admitted. "I'm just brainstorming here."

At this point I sounded out about Detective Lo's warning *not* to get involved and was resoundingly thrashed because I was told that they were 'only discussing the murders.' In any event, I was in the minority so the conversation continued.

It seemed to me they were spinning their wheels and Sam Belmont, Professor Belmont, was the most logical choice as far as I could tell. And if it wasn't him, then the field was wide open! And while there had been much activity and discussion and thought about the who, what, where, when, why and how of Julia's murder, there had been little forward motion. They still didn't know who had killed her. They didn't have a murder weapon – although it was obviously a gun of some sort. They didn't know where the murder had taken place. They didn't even know why she'd been killed. And they hadn't yet figured out how the body got onto the golf course. They had however expanded the list of possible suspects to include almost everyone on the island! But I exaggerate. I could have pointed this out to everyone, but since no one took me seriously, I just kept it to myself – and you.

"I think brainstorming's a great idea," Margie said. "If we could find out what they were up to, then we've got the motive. We thought Kenny's motive was because his wife was fooling around and interfering with him fooling around. But that doesn't make sense now."

"Has anyone thought to figure out if Kenny or his wife owed anyone a lot of money," Shelly interjected. Shelly was generally pretty quiet during these bull sessions, but seemed interested now.

There was a pregnant pause.

"Good question Sis," Margie said.

"Shelly's got a point," Amanda agreed. "They could have been in trouble. Maybe there was a big life insurance police on the Misses."

Margie suddenly got up and trotted to the house, returning a moment later with a legal pad and a sharp pencil. She sat down and wrote as she said. "Did the McMahon's owe money? Did they gamble? Was there insurance?" She looked up. "Okay what else do we need to know?"

I thought I had something relevant to add, so I asked: "How long can they keep you in jail for interfering in a police investigation?"

The question might just as well have been a non sequitur. No one even acknowledged that I'd said it.

"Have we thought about a local guy? If it was a local guy that shot Julia, how did he know her?" This was Angie's question.

Margie quickly jotted down 'Julia's local connections.'

"I think it would help to find the scene of the crime," Margie said.

"How are we going to do that?" Amanda asked. "It could have been anywhere!"

"Well, just because it's hard doesn't mean we can give up on it." Margie said. "There must be some clue on the body. Do you know anyone in the coroner's office?"

Amanda thought. "Let me make a phone call."

I suspected Kenny knew who had killed his wife and where, even if he hadn't done it himself. Somehow they must have gotten the body to an airfield. Of course a helicopter could take off and land anywhere.

"We need to know how the body got there," Margie said emphatically. "I'm sure it's an important clue. The police haven't figured it out, or if they have, they're not saying anything. It's too bad you and Pete are on the outs, I'll bet he could make some phone calls around to the local airports and find out if there was anything odd happening the night we found Julia."

The questions continued while I got up for more scotch. I was going to put ice in it, but I thought that was a waste of water, so I just added more scotch then returned to the 'conference' to listen. I should have run away, but I'm a people person.

The group was well into page three before they ran out of questions.

"I think we've got all we can handle for now," Margie declared. "Let's divide up the questions and tomorrow everyone can try to answer his or hers."

Margie's idea was greeted with approval by everyone but me – but I? In any event, I was three shades to the wind by then and wondering how my head would feel in the morning since I could no longer feel it tonight. As you have no doubt noticed, I'd been drinking heavily and I had days earlier come to the decision that I was entitled to one hard liquor drink every day for each house guest. That meant I got seven of them, four for the full time squatters – mom, dad, and the girls – and ½ for each of the part time interlopers – Amanda, Nicky, Angie, Shelly and Mark. Note that I rounded up. I thought this a fair deal, and it already seemed to be helping take the sting out of things.

A Break in the Case

I woke the next morning on the guest bathroom floor with my face pressed against the cold tile. My head felt like one of those blowfish you see now and then at the little stands that sell seashells except the sharp little pointy things were pointing inward.

I clawed my way into a standing position and looked in the mirror. Quasimodo stared back.

With great care, I brushed my teeth. I found aspirin and took a double dose and washed it down with three large glasses of water. This improved my condition considerably. Now I merely felt as if I were on the verge of death. I didn't have the nerve to shave; my shaky hands would have scared me for life.

When I felt well enough to leave the comfort of the bathroom, I found the place empty. This was good because I assumed I'd be getting a lecture from Margie on how bad it was to drink so much and the longer I could put off the lecture the better I could handle it.

Magoo accompanied me to the kitchen, where I found my paper, but no fresh coffee. Obviously Margie had taken it out to the pool.

I pondered the notion of making a pot in the kitchen, but the noise of the coffee grinder would have killed me, so I plucked up my courage and headed outdoors.

To my delight and surprise, the pool area was also empty. Margie was gliding through the water in her usual manner, but otherwise the place was deserted. I grabbed a cup, filled it, and gulped it down –burning my esophagus. Then I filled the cup again and sat down with my paper. The caffeine hit improved my condition such that now I was only wishing I could die.

The paper was full of news of the murder, but nothing I didn't know or care about, so I turned my attention to the daily fishing report – which is a little like reading the sports page, only half of the players are dead. Some of those players, however, were impressively large.

The fishing report led me to the tide predictions which led me to the public announcements. It seemed the county was taking bids for someone to monitor air quality. *Hum*, I thought. *Haven't they been doing that?*

My morning perusal of the paper had me knee deep in 'Employment wanted' and on my third cup of coffee, when Margie finished her swim and joined me at the table. She did not ask about my health but launched into her lecture on how drinking to excess was unacceptable and she hoped that I had slept comfortably on the floor of the bathroom and that instead of drinking coffee I should have a tofu, egg, and buttermilk smoothie – a combination the thought of which made me gag, literally!

Thankfully, Dad showed up and Margie stopped. I'm sure she had more to say but she doesn't like to nag in front of others and if she happens to read this and takes exception to the word 'nag' well that's too bad because when your head feels like it's about to explode and your stomach feels like you've been going six rounds with the heavyweight champ and you're legs and arms and hands are shaky, then having your wife tell you drinking heavily is bad for you is nagging!

After Maxwell came Catherine, who sat as far away from Mr. M. as possible and nitpicked Margie's breathing during the night. Then came Amanda, who had stayed up all night on the Internet researching her questions.

Shelly made a surprise visit to announce that she and Mark had reconciled and were going back to L.A. as soon as they could straighten everything out with the marijuana charge.

There were various levels of jubilation at this news. I was more exuberant than a cockroach in a bag of potato chips. Margie offered her blessings. Mom and Dad were cautious but supportive and suggested counseling was the way to go. As for Amanda, she waited until Shelly had retreated to the pool house to tell the girls before responding with great honesty: 'lots of luck, honey.'

Since it was clear that I was not going to get any peace and quiet out by the pool, I excused myself and headed indoors to the master bath and my luxurious shower. Perhaps the warm water would chase away the last of my miserable hangover.

I was out of the shower, but still undressed when Margie came into the bedroom and announced that she and mom and Amanda were going to take a little excursion and have lunch at the Coffee Shack.

The Coffee Shack is an unpretentious little restaurant/deli off the highway between Kona and Captain Cook. The food is great – mostly sandwiches on homemade bread -- and they always have homemade soup. It's got a spectacular view of the coast, but less than a dozen small tables, so it's best to go early or late for lunch if you want to find a parking spot or get a table.

I had no objection as long as I was able to verify the girls were being cared for. That had been arranged, according to Margie, by Gramps who was going to take them horseback riding up at Waimea.

"What about a car?" I asked. I didn't want to be stranded. Not that walking would have hurt me or my physique.

"We're taking Amanda's Caddy," Margie replied.

"You mean Pete's Caddy?" I whistled. "Does Pete know?" Pete would not like them taking the Caddy.

"What Pete doesn't know won't hurt him," Margie said authoritatively.

I was very much in disagreement with her statement, but Margie kissed me good and left me standing naked in the bedroom in a half excited state.

After she left, I took my time getting dressed and didn't leave the bedroom till I heard Maxwell yelling for the girls that if they didn't get going they'd miss their reservation. I exited the bedroom just in time to wish them well and once the door closed behind them, I trotted to the kitchen and found an extra large Milk Bone for Magoo and then slipped out the back way to Pete's.

The condo Pete and Amanda own isn't far away so I'd decided to walk over – I know I just told Margie I needed a car, but that was totally hypothetical. I determined I needed the exercise more since I was feeling sluggish. If you've been paying attention you know I'd been eating too much, drinking too much, and getting little exercise.

When I arrived, Pete was washing his Malibu in the parking lot. He liked to keep busy and there was nothing broken in the condo, so this was the next best thing I suppose.

"Hey," I said.

"Hey," Pete responded.

"What's up?" I asked.

"Not much," Pete said.

I'll save you the rest of our scintillating conversation since it's obvious it's not going to be of much interest.

As luck would have it, Pete was nearly done with the carwash, so after he got everything towel dried he suggested we take a spin to 'air' dry it, which is something only Pete does to his cars.

I suggested we drive up to Honokohau Harbor and have lunch. We both like their fried fish sandwiches and the beer is served in frosty mugs. Pete agreed and we hopped in the car and took off.

Yes, yes, I know I'd only walked a little way and the meal I was describing probably contained at least 2000 calories, but I wasn't thinking right just then. If I'd been thinking right I would never have gotten into the car with Pete!

Pete is what is known as a *distracted* driver, which means he doesn't pay attention to his driving much when he's behind the wheel. Amanda never lets Pete drive, unless her blood alcohol is above the legal limit of course.

And whenever I'm riding shotgun with him, my foot is pressed hard against the floorboard as if I can stop the car using telepathic powers. Generally, when I ride with Pete, I pepper my speech with phrases like 'I think that car is

263

going to pull out,' 'What's that kid doing on that bike,' 'I thought the speed limit was twenty five here,' and so on.

Lucky for me, Pete is oblivious to the motivation of my comments and never complains about my back seat driving, probably because he doesn't pay any attention to it. Like I said, he's a distracted driver.

Using our combined driving skills, we survived our trip to the harbor and after placing our order for fish sandwiches, fries, coleslaw, and beer, Pete and I sat comfortably across the table from one another and stared.

"Say, Pete," I said finally. "Did you see the Cowboy's game on Sunday?"

While Pete and I did your typical Monday morning quarterbacking, Margie, Amanda and Mrs. M. had arrived at the Coffee Shack after visiting the Place of Refuge and were enjoying salads, sandwiches, ice tea, and the panoramic view of Kealakekua Bay.

"What kind of tree is that?" Mrs. M asked, indicting the huge avocado tree that stood behind the restaurant and shaded it from afternoon sun.

Margie and Amanda looked at it. "I have no idea, Mom," Margie said.

"It looks like an avocado to me," said Mrs. M.

"If you say so. How's your salad?"

"Wonderful. Amanda, would you like to try some?"

"No thanks, Mrs. M. I'm full." Amanda pushed away her half eaten macadamia nut pie and took a sip of her ice tea.

"Remind me to get some of this before we leave Margie. It's wonderful."

Mrs. M reached over and took a bite of Amanda's pie. "Oh, that is good."

"Oh, my, look at that," said Mrs. M. said with a hint of amazement.

Margie and Amanda looked in the direction Mrs. M was looking and saw a large red, white and blue hang glider swoop down from above and soar out over the flat land far below. It turned gracefully and began to rise slowly in a large, lazy circle.

"You'd never catch me doing that," said Amanda. "Those people are nuts."

"I don't think it's that dangerous, Amanda, I ..." Margie's voice stopped short.

"What's that hanging below him Margie? Mrs. M. said. "It looks like a passenger. Is that what it is?"

Margie said nothing. She just watched the hang glider slowly circling on the warm updraft. She knew exactly what it was! It was a passenger, and Margie realized that the question that had daunted them from the beginning had suddenly been answered!

"Margie?" Mrs. M repeated. "Did you hear me?"

Margie gave no response. Her attention was fixed on the hang glider as if it was a hypnotist's fob.

"Amanda? What's wrong with her?" Mrs. M. turned and noticed that Amanda too was staring at the hang glider in the same odd way as Margie.

"Whatever is the matter?" Mrs. M said forcefully.

"Margie? Are you thinking what I'm thinking?" Amanda said quietly without taking her eyes off the hang glider.

"Yes I am," Margie whispered back. "That's got to be how it happened."

"How what happened?" Mrs. M. asked uneasily. Amanda and Margie were acting so odd she was afraid something had gone terribly wrong.

Margie stood up, dug in her purse and pulled out two twenties. "I've got lunch. Come on. Let's go."

Amanda was on her feet already, slinging her purse over her shoulder and dropping her sunglasses onto her nose.

"But I haven't finished!" Mrs. M protested.

"I'll explain in the car, Mom," Margie said as she grabbed Catherine under the arm and physically lifting her onto her feet. "Amanda, take mom to the car. I'm going to find out where that hang glider was launched."

Amanda picked up Mrs. M.'s purse and took her arm. "Come on, Mrs. M."

A minute later, despite her objections Mrs. M. was in the backseat of the car with Amanda at the wheel. Margie jumped in the passenger seat.

"Did you get directions?" Amanda asked.

"The girl said to just follow the road across the street. She says you can't miss it."

"Miss what?" Mr. M. said. "We're in the car now; will one of you please explain what's going on?"

Amanda was already pulling out of the parking lot and had crossed the highway and started up the steep road on the other side before Margie turned around.

"It all makes sense now, Mom. It's really simple. We couldn't figure out how Julia, the murdered woman we found on the golf course, got there. It was as if she'd fallen from space. Everyone said it wasn't a plane or a helicopter. Both would have had to file some sort of flight plan and both would have been heard."

Catherine was quick on the uptake. "So you think she was dropped from one of those... those..."

"Hang gliders. Yes, we do. It's the only thing that makes sense, and that's what we're going to check on."

"Oh, dear. That must have been horrible!"

"Mom," Margie said calmly. "She was already dead. Someone shot her first."

"They shot her *and* dropped her to her death." Mrs. M. shook her head. "People do horrible, horrible things don't they?"

Margie had no reply. She turned her attention back to the road.

Amanda opened up: "You know, Margie, I was just thinking. Can you fly one of these things at night? I mean don't they rely on updrafts caused by the sun heating the ground?"

Amanda slowed down on a tight curve. The road was steep and it had already turned from asphalt to gravel; this was a rural area and the road had plenty of potholes to avoid. Coffee trees lined both sides.

"I don't know, Amanda. I'm hoping someone at the top can give us an answer," Margie said. "There. Turn there."

A sign that said 'Overlook' pointed down a road that was nothing more than two tracks through heavy forest. Amanda swung the big Caddy left and followed it. The coffee trees were gone but they were replaced by taller trees and dense lush green underbrush.

"Are you sure this is the right way?" Amanda quizzed.

"How would I know? If you see Tarzan, stop and ask directions," Margie said irritably.

"I hope there's a turnaround at the end of this. I'm not backing down this road," Amanda complained. "If the Caddy gets scratched, Pete's gonna kill me."

"You can blame in on me," Margie said.

"Yeah, sure. But I have to live with him."

"You're not living with him, remember?"

Suddenly the forest fell back and they found themselves in a small parking area. There were three vans and two trucks already there. Two young men, one a tall blonde with a beach boy build, the other a head shorter and Asian looking, were unlashing a hang glider from one of the trucks.

Amanda pulled the big Caddy over and parked and they started to get out.

"Okay, Amanda. Let's see what gives. Mind if I do the talking?"

"Be my guest," Amanda answered. "If I think of something, I'll chime in."

"I'll wait in the car," Catherine said.

"Okay, Mom. Keep an eye on our purses."

As I've said before, Margie and Amanda always get noticed, so as soon as they got out of the car, they had the two young men's attention.

"Excuse me," Margie said when they were close enough to make conversation comfortable. "Can we ask you a few questions about hang gliding?"

"Yes, ma'am." The blonde boy said politely and offered a warm smile. He had a big sincere smile and held out his hand. "I'm Todd," he said. "This here is Koki." Koki smiled and nodded. "You thinking of taking up hang gliding? I know a good teacher."

"No, not really," Margie said. We were just sort of wondering about how those things work."

"What do you want to know?" Todd asked.

Margie launched into an explanation of how they'd been watching down at The Coffee Shack and saw someone with a passenger. She asked if you really could take passengers and how far you could fly and whether you could fly at night and a few other relevant questions. She purposely didn't mention the murder or her and Amanda's suspicion that the murder victim had been dropped from a hang glider.

Todd and Koki were helpful and polite, though both of them had trouble keeping their eyes off Amanda's chest.

The answers they got were: Yes, if you were good and you had a big hang glider, you could take passengers. In fact they both had been introduced to the sport as passengers on a hang glider. As to distance, you could virtually fly forever if you didn't get tired and run out of thermals to ride on, but practically, you had to have a destination in mind so someone would be there to give you a lift home and you needed someplace flat to land. Beach was always preferable. Rocky landings were to be avoided and so were water landings. Neither of them had flown at night because that was only for really experienced hang gliders and presented a whole new set of obstacles. They did know of one guy who was a 'night owl,' as those who were crazy enough to practice that particularly risky form of hang gliding where known. His name was Duncan but neither one of them knew his last name or where he lived.

"Well, that was informative," Amanda said after they'd thanked the boys and started back to the car, "but we still don't know for sure if it's possible."

"We need to talk to that Duncan, guy. Maybe we should come back here closer to sundown," Margie said.

"Yeah, that's…" Amanda was interrupted as Koki came running over.

"Looks like it's your lucky day, ladies. Here comes Duncan now."

Margie and Amanda turned to watch as a particularly rusted out panel van chugged into the lot and pulled up in an empty slot.

Duncan, of course, recognized Amanda and Margie from the get go. He'd been to their houses and watched them more than once late at night from outside. Under his breath he asked:*"What the fuck are they doing here?"*

Duncan got out of his van slowly and waited uncomfortably as Margie, Amanda and Koki approached.

"Hey, Duncan," Koki greeted him. "These ladies have been asking about hang gliding at night. I told 'em you're the only night owl around. I think they'd like to ask you a few questions."

And as soon as he made the introduction, Koki left with a small wave to Amanda and Margie.

"Night flying?" Duncan looked guardedly at Margie and Amanda and tensed a little. "I gave that up. Too dangerous." In fact, Duncan had flown thousands of pounds of cocaine throughout Latin America doing just that. It was one of his specialties and the reason Mr. Big had hired him for this current job.

"Do you know anyone that still does it?" Margie asked. She noticed there was something odd about Duncan around the eyes, as though he wasn't looking right at you even when he was looking right at you.

"You thinking about taking it up?" Duncan said, avoiding the question and making his way to the back of the van and opening the big doors. "I don't recommend it."

"Well actually," Amanda said. "We're trying to settle a bet."

"A bet?" Duncan said with a spark of interest. "What kind of bet?"

Duncan started to unpack his gear from the van.

"Well we were down at The Coffee Shack and we saw this hang glider carrying a passenger. I said I'll bet it's really spectacular at night and she – Amanda jerked her head toward Margie – said it's not possible to fly at night. I bet her it was. Twenty bucks."

Duncan looked from Amanda to Margie and back again, then he broke out in a big grin. "Looks like you'll be needing a referee on that one.

"Kiko," Duncan nodded toward the two boys Margie and Amanda had been talking to before "already told you there are those of us who fly at night," Duncan paused. "At least we used to. But I don't know anyone crazy enough to take up a passenger in the dark."

"Why's that?" Amanda asked bluntly.

Duncan eyed her. "The thermals ain't good. Can't handle the extra weight," Duncan said flatly. "Now if you'll excuse me ladies, I've got to get my gear set up."

Amanda and Margie thanked him and turned and headed for the big Caddy.

"Not very helpful, was he?" Amanda said.

Margie looked over her shoulder and caught Duncan watching them.

"I'm thinking he knows more than he's saying." Margie said. "And don't look now, but he's watching us."

Amanda kept her eyes forward until they reached the car, then glanced over her shoulder at Duncan.

"Damn!" Duncan's voice carried across the small lot.

"What's the matter?" Kiko called.

"Forgot my God damn release harness!" Duncan yelled, shoving his equipment back into the van and slamming the doors. "Guess I gotta go back and get it!"

Duncan jumped into the van, started it, and took off, shooting gravel as he went.

Amanda started to pull out after him, but Margie put her hand on the wheel.

"Wait. Let's give him a head start. We can't follow him, but we can find out which way he goes on the highway."

"And that will tell us?"

"I don't know. But it's something."

They waited thirty seconds or so and then Amanda started down the road.

"So, did you find out what you wanted to know?" Catherine asked from the back seat.

Margie related what they'd discovered and their suspicions about Duncan.

"You think he's involved?"

"I don't know, Mom. But he acted kind of funny. I can't imagine how he'd fit in with a bunch of college professors and G. Peter Ryan."

"Yeah," said Amanda. "That does seem like a stretch."

They reached the good dirt road and started down the steep incline toward the highway. They hadn't gone far when they saw Duncan's van pulled off to the side with Duncan standing beside it looking at a flat rear tire.

"Should we stop?" Amanda asked.

"Yeah, I think we better. Maybe if we help him out he'll give us something solid we can use," Margie said.

"Good thinking," Amanda said and pulled the Caddy up behind the van.

Duncan looked up and walked over to the car. "My spare is flat too," he said. "Any chance I can get a lift with you ladies to a gas station?"

"Of course you can," Catherine said before either Margie or Amanda could answer. "Climb in."

Duncan went around and opened the passenger door and got in back with Catherine.

"Hello," he said. "I'm Duncan."

"And I'm Catherine. Margie's mother."

"Well, I thought I saw a family resemblance," Duncan said politely and grinned his big toothy grin. "This is sure nice of you ladies."

Amanda started to pull out around the van.

"Just a minute!" Duncan yelled.

Amanda stopped the car. "Did you forget something?"

"Yes, I did," Duncan said. There was an odd tone in his voice. "I forgot to show you this."

Duncan pulled up his shirt and reached down and pulled a large revolver from his waist. He pointed it at Catherine. There were three long gasps followed by silence.

"Bubbles, I think you better put the top up before we get started. We don't want Mom here getting sunburn."

Little Girls Lost

After lunch at Honokohau Harbor, Pete and I went back to his place and watched a couple of college games. They were crappy, but just sitting with Pete and no relatives around did wonders for my state of mind. Pete wasn't the neatest guy as you can imagine, but I fought my Felix Unger urges and just pushed things over on the couch when I needed more space. I figured once Pete moved back home they could just have the place declared a biohazard and seal the doors.

When I finally left for home, I almost felt like there was some good in the world.

The hike home was tougher than the hike to Pete's because it was all uphill and by the time I got there, I figured I'd walked off the fish sandwich, fries, coleslaw and at least one of the beers.

Mr. M and the girls were back from riding, and Shelly and Mark had come over for drinks and dinner. But there was no sign of Margie or Mrs. M.

"They must be at Amanda's," I offered when they quizzed me as to whether I knew their where-a-bouts.

"Nope," Mr. M. snapped. "Called an hour ago and talked to Angie – what a delightful woman. Anyway, she said they were just starting to wonder the same thing about Amanda."

"They must have gone shopping," I reasoned. "They'll be along I'm sure. In the meantime, I can do the bar tending and I know we've got some snack stuff in the kitchen." I use the term 'snack stuff' loosely. Margie's idea of a snack is carrot sticks, celery stalks, cut up broccoli and cauliflower – you get the picture.

As I said, I offered to make cocktails, but everyone had their own idea, so I just opened the bar and let them have at it while I went to the kitchen.

Sure enough, Margie had prepared a platter of veggies in the fridge and I found the vegetable dip to go with it in one of those Tupperware bowls. Since Margie wasn't home to stop me, I got out the kitchen step ladder and climbed to the top cupboard where I keep a secret stash of 'those are not good for you' treats. I had a big bag of Maui onion chips, some Cheetos, and cheesy popcorn.

You would think I had prepared pheasant under glass what with the reception I got when I returned to the pool.

"I hope you don't mind, I invited Angie and Nicky to join us," Maxwell said.

"Not at all," I said. Now that Angie wasn't squatting in my den, I'd forgiven her; and since his DWI and assault, Nicky seemed more human so I decided he was tolerable as well.

"They're bringing crackers and salami and some liverwurst," Mr. M added.

You know, my mouth actually began to salivate. I hadn't had liverwurst since…I can't remember when.

Angie and Nicky arrived with the promised goodies and we all ate and drank till sunset. It was after sunset that I started to get anxious. Margie almost never misses a sunset with me. It was traditional that we had a cocktail, watched the sunset, and kissed just as the last ray of light slipped below the horizon. If you come to Hawaii, you'll see the beaches crowded with lovers kissing just as the last rays of light die. It's very romantic.

I shared my uneasiness with the crowd and suggested we begin a casual search, even though I maintained they would show up any minute with tons of shopping bags and make fools of us all.

As you may remember, Margie does not carry a cell phone, nor I discovered, does Mrs. M. Amanda however does have a cell phone, so Angie tried her number again and it rang over to her answering system.

"That could mean she forgot to turn it on or it ran out of juice or, seeing as how this island is one big mountain, she's in one of those many places where there is no reception," I said.

Everyone agreed with me. Everyone also agreed that the next logical step was to try The Coffee Shack. Margie and Amanda always made an impression whether they travel individually or together, and if they'd been there someone would have noticed.

Information connected me to The Coffee Shack, whose voice message informed me that they had closed five minutes ago. Isn't that always the way?

I decided to call Pete, thinking he might know of another way to reach Amanda. He picked up on the second ring. I heard hockey in the background.

"Ah, they're just shopping," Pete whined. "Give 'em time. They'll come home."

After Pete hung up, I discussed it with the group and we all agreed that Pete was right and that one of them had probably informed one of us what they were up to, but we'd forgotten. I didn't bring up the likelihood that Margie had 'thought' she'd informed me but hadn't – a thought that Mr. M shared based on the look he gave me.

"Okay, it looks like we're on our own for dinner," I said, taking control of the situation. "Any suggestions?"

No one raised their hands, but there were plenty of options: chow mien, pizza, hoagies, McDonald's (this was quickly nixed), grilled steaks, grilled burgers...You could tell Margie was not at home.

The common denominator – which means the item no one objected to – was pizza so I delegated Angie and the girls to order pizzas and headed for the bathroom where I had to recycle the beers I'd had with Pete.

I had just reached the bedroom when the phone rang. *Ah, there she is,* I thought, certain it was Margie. I picked up the extension. It was Pete.

"Hey, Joe," he said. He started a lot of conversations with those brief words. "I was thinking. Why don't you just call On-Star. They can give you a location for Amanda's Malibu. The thing has a GPS function."

I paused a moment trying to decide whether or not to let Pete know that Amanda had taken the Cadillac. I finally decided I'd better tell.

"Ah, Pete," I said. I started a lot of conversations with those brief words. "Actually, the Malibu was being used by your brother-in-law. They took the Caddy."

There was silence on the phone for a moment, then: "I'll be right over," and the phone went dead.

"At least Pete has his priorities straight," I said to Magoo, who was too intent on licking his privates to respond.

A Lady Takes Charge

As you can imagine, the topic of conversation in the small shack would have been escape. However Margie, Amanda, and Catherine were all trussed and gagged with *the handyman's secret weapon*: duct tape, so conversation was virtually impossible.

Their only viable means of communication were grunts, groans, and eye contact. Actually, that wasn't precisely true. Amanda was busy sending Morse code messages by blinking her eyes. Unfortunately, she was the only one who knew Morse code and she had to stop after dislodging an eyelash that had her blinking madly and sending what would have been a very confusing series of dots and dashes.

Margie, who I've already told you is just as resourceful as Amanda, was trying to dislodge her duct tape gag with her tongue and was making good progress until she realized the taste of the glue was beginning to make her nauseous and the prospect of throwing up with her mouth still covered was just plain scary, not to mention disgusting.

Most of the time the ladies were left alone in the cabin, but occasionally they were checked on by a small Asian man with a baseball cap who was missing his front teeth and smelled something like day old cod whenever he came in to get a sack of coffee beans. This was Kracker, of course, so named because he did lots of crack cocaine, and he'd been convicted three times for criminal sexual assault – first degree -- a fact that was thankfully unknown to the gals. Yes, yes, I know cocaine is spelled with a 'c', but Kracker spelled his name with a 'k', now stop being so damn critical!

For the umpteenth time, Kracker entered and looked around. All seemed in order, so he smiled his toothless grin and picked up another bag of coffee and turned to go.

Before he got to the door, however, Catherine suddenly contorted wildly and fell to the floor where she began shaking violently!

Kracker halted and stared hard at her. You could tell he didn't know what to make of this.

Of course Catherine's sudden collapse upset Margie greatly and she tried to scream through her gag, but it came out a groan. And she tried to stand, but her bindings held her. Amanda was no less agitated than Margie but was equally helpless! In the meantime, Catherine continued to convulse uncontrollably!

Finally Kracker dropped the coffee sack and approached Mrs. M. cautiously. Catherine continued to convulse and was now making a gurgling sound. Kracker reached down and pulled the duct tape from her mouth.

"What the matter wit' you?" Kracker asked.

But Catherine said nothing coherent, she just continued thrashing and moaning.

Kracker looked toward the door as if trying to decide if he should go and get help. Meanwhile Margie and Amanda pulled violently at their bindings and yelled into their gags.

Since Amanda was closest to Kracker, he finally reached over and yanked the duct tape off her mouth.

"What wrong with her?"

"I think she's having a heart attack!" Amanda cried. "Please, untie me. I know CPR. Let me help. Please. Hurry. "

Kracker looked at the door again and at Margie, who was frantically pulling against her restrains, her eyes pleading with him to release her so she could help her mother.

From his jacket pocket, Kracker produced a switchblade, its long blade springing free, glistening in the dim light.

"You try anyt'ing, I gut you. Uunnerstan," Kracker hissed sharply as he reached behind Amanda and cut the tape holding her hands.

Once free, Amanda dropped to her knees next to Catherine.

"Her too," Amanda croaked.

Kracker sliced through Catherine's bonds on both her hands and feet and sprang away as if there was danger in staying too close. He watched intently and kept the knife in front of him.

Amanda rolled Catherine onto her back and began messaging her arms and legs which began to shake less noticeably. She lifted an eyelid to reveal Catherine's eye had rolled back into her head.

"She's in shock. We've got to get her to a hospital!" Amanda pulled Catherine to a sitting position and held her close. Meanwhile, Margie, frantic to help, had somehow managed to free her hands and ripped the tape from her mouth.

"Mom!" she screamed, as she fell to the floor.

Kracker turned the knife on her. "Shut up!" he hissed, looking toward the door; fear showed on his face. He didn't know how to handle things, and he was afraid he'd get caught doing something he shouldn't.

Margie ignored him and dragged herself over to Catherine and Amanda.

"Mom! Mom! Say something."

But Catherine just moaned.

Margie turned on Kracker. "It's murder, you know. If she dies. It'll be the same as murder and you'll be responsible."

Kracker said nothing, he just stayed back and nervously switched the knife from one hand to the other.

"Don't you have a heart?" Margie sobbed, tears streaming down her face as she patted her mother's face and hands.

Catherine convulsed again and stopped breathing.

"Oh, my God," Margie screamed. "Mom! Mom!"

She shook her mother's face, trying to bring her around. "Stay with me!"

"Please. At least help us get her up on the table so I can give her CPR," Amanda implored. "Show some human decency."

The truth of course was that Kracker wasn't used to being human being decent or making decisions. But you could tell from the look in his eyes that he was scared and whether he was scared that Catherine was going to die on him and he'd be responsible for it or he was scared of Duncan, the result was he knew was going to be the same – big trouble. And if there was one thing Kracker didn't like it was trouble.

With a flick of his wrist, Kracker closed the switchblade and stuffed it into his jacket. He crossed the room quickly.

"You take her feet. We'll lift her head." Amanda directed.

Kracker knelt to take Catherine's feet.

"Careful," Amanda cautioned.

And that's when it happened!

I could compare Catherine's movements to lightning, but a lightning strike couldn't really compete with her. As soon as Kracker knelt down to take her feet, Catherine pulled both of her legs up to her chin and snapped them straight again with alarming force. She caught the poor bastard square in the forehead with her one-inch heels, and the impact propelled him upward and back onto one of the coffee sacks.

Before Kracker had any chance of recovery, Catherine pushed Margie and Amanda aside, scrambled to her feet, and leapt on top of Kracker like a beast, smashing her right knee into his groin with all her weight.

As poor Kracker, only half conscious, came up off the sack doubled over in pain, Catherine grabbed him by his greasy hair, lifted him up, and ran him into the wall on the opposite side of the cabin where he hit his head with a remarkably loud thud and fell to the floor in a pile of arms and legs. Out cold!

Catherine stood over him panting a moment. She wiped her hands together and then wiped them on a coffee sack and straightened her blouse. She turned to find Margie and Amanda sitting dumbstruck on the floor where they'd fallen.

"Well," Catherine said casually as she fixed her hair, "It didn't appear either of you girls had a plan."

The Rescuers

We were on the landing by the door arguing about how we should proceed with our search for the ladies.

"Maybe we *should* call the police," Mark said for the fifth time.

"We've been through that," Pete snarled. "They aren't going to look for them unless we have some evidence of a crime or they've been missing twenty-four hours."

"Pete's right," Maxwell said. "But I don't think we should divide up. I think we should take as many cars as we have to and head to that coffee house and..."

"It's The Coffee Shack," Pete interrupted. "And if we don't use the transponder, there's not a chance in hell of us finding them. It's like a jungle up there once you're off the main highway.

The *transponder* Pete referred to was one he'd installed in the Caddy after the last two classic cars he'd owned had been stolen. It was basically a safety transponder like those used when planes go down. Pete had modified its frequency so as to avoid problems with the FAA, and the only way to find it according to Pete was with the receiver in his helicopter.

"Maybe we're overreacting. They're not that late," Mark tried calmly.

"I know there's something wrong," I said. "I can feel it. Margie would have called or Catherine or Amanda. Something's wrong and I'll bet my favorite hat it's got something to do with the murders."

I know I don't have a favorite hat, but it seemed like a good line at the time.

"Let's stop wasting time!" someone said. I wasn't sure; it might have been me.

There was a shout of agreement and we headed out the door, leaving Shelly and the girls and Magoo at the house with directions on what to do if the ladies did show up.

Pete and I took the Volvo with me driving. The others loaded into the Malibu. We needed two cars because of the *issues* with which you are no doubt all too familiar by now.

We arrived at the airport in record time and piled out of the cars. I'd spent the twenty miles on the way to the airport wondering how we were going to share the helicopter if we couldn't agree on the auto seating, but I gave up and decided to deal with it as it happened.

"So you're sure we shouldn't call the police," I asked Pete as we jogged toward the hangar where I had found his stinky self a few days earlier.

"They won't do nothing. They'll just tell us to wait till morning or something."

"I suppose you're right," I said. "What's the plan?"

"I told you. After the last Caddy was stolen, I stuck an old transponder in this one. It gives off a homing signal once every thirty seconds. I had to change the frequency so the FAA wouldn't kick my ass, but the receiver in my chopper can pick it up if we're within range."

"What's the range?"

"Depends. In the hills, you gotta be pretty much over it. But along the coast, it's probably ten miles."

We arrived at the hanger and Pete flipped on the lights and hit the button to open the hanger door.

"Okay, push her out," he said, running to the chopper and unblocking the wheels.

We all grabbed hold and began pushing. It was remarkably easy; I'd expected more 'car stuck in a snowdrift' kind of pushing.

Once we got the chopper outside, Pete jumped in and began what I assumed was his pre-flight checklist. Since I'm a flight sissy and had never flown with Pete before and hadn't paid that much attention to the seating arrangements of his chopper, it surprised me to find that there were only five seats. Three in the back and two up front. There being six of us, I knew instantly there was going to be trouble but again I put it off.

I started to climb in the back, but Pete blocked me.

"You. Up front with me. I don't want any of those wackos near me."

I stepped back out and folded the seat down to make the back accessible to the others. Maxwell started in, and then stopped to let Angie go ahead.

"Not her!" Pete said abruptly.

Everyone froze.

"We don't need you," Pete said testily, then in response to the question on everyone's face. "How's she gonna help; she gonna hit somebody with her purse?"

"Now see here, Pete," Maxwell said coming to Angie's aid. "That's no way to treat a lady..." Angie reached out and took Maxwell's arm. He stopped talking.

"I won't need my purse," Angie said. "I've got my feminine charm." And with that, Angie threw herself into the air and let out a blood curdling scream. She came down in a martial arts stance, and before you could say 'Jackie Chan in drag,' she let out another shout, twirled in the air and broke the two by four saw horse next to her with a kung fu chop.

There was dead silence. Pete blinked. Angie straightened her dress and smiled sweetly.

"Okay, you can come," Pete said, "But hurry up; let's get a move on it!"

Angie piled in followed by Maxwell and then Nicky, which left Mark outside.

"Hey, what about me?" Mark protested.

"No problem," Maxwell said. "Angie can sit on my lap; if it won't put us over our weight limit?"

Pete looked at me. I shook my head and mouthed "don't ask, don't tell."

"Naw, we're okay," Pete said and Angie stood up to let Maxwell slide over so she could sit on his lap. Mark climbed in quick.

I was the last inside and after buckling myself in with trembling hands, I said a little prayer that I wouldn't throw up or soil myself or do something even more embarrassing.

Pete pushed a button and the rotors began to turn. Pete handed me a helmet with headphones and motioned me to put it on. The rotors turned faster and faster.

Pete reached out to take the control stick, but I grabbed his arm. He stopped. Something had just occurred to me.

I looked over at Pete, who was looking down at my hand, blocking him.

"You don't do your own maintenance, do you?" I said miserably over the roar of the helicopter, terrified to hear his response.

Pete looked at me, removed my hand from his arm, and shook his head in disbelief. "Are you nuts?" he scoffed and pulled back on the control stick.

I closed my eyes as we lifted quickly into the night sky.

Anybody There?

Back at the forest shack, Amanda cracked open the door and peered out into the darkness.

"Do you see anyone?" Margie hissed from behind.

"Shush," Amanda chided and opened the door further. "I can't see a fucking thing. Sorry Mrs. M."

"That's okay dear, it's times like this that words like that are meant for. I swear like a sailor from time to time. It's good for the nerves."

There was dead silence.

"No one's here as far as I can tell." Amanda opened the door wide and stepped out.

Margie, holding Catherine's hand, followed.

"Damn it's dark," Margie said.

"Where do you think they are?" Catherine whispered.

"Who knows. The bad news is they took the car," Margie said glumly. Even in the darkness, the white Caddy would have stood out and there wasn't a hint of it.

"So we'll walk out," Amanda said. "It was less than a mile to the road then a few more miles to the highway."

"Well, I'm glad I wore my hiking shoes," Catherine said, raising her foot in the darkness but no one could see her heels.

"Yeah, well my flip-flops aren't ideal either, Mom," Margie said. "We could sure use a flashlight. Did you see one in the shack?"

"Nope," Amanda said. "And I'm not going back to look. We'll adjust to the darkness. I can see better already."

"Okay" Margie said. "Let's go."

And they started off with Amanda leading and Margie following behind holding Catherine's hand.

"I sure wish we had the cell phone," Amanda said.

"If wishes were horses, pigs could fly," Margie said.

"It's 'if wishes were horses, beggars would ride,'" Amanda corrected.

"Same difference. I heard it crunch under the tire when that idiot tossed it out. I told you those things are no good."

"Yeah, well…" Amanda started.

"Now girls, let's not…" Catherine interrupted and then stopped suddenly.

They hadn't gone more than a hundred yards when the sound of tires on gravel reached them and flecks of bright light shot through the dense undergrowth like fireflies on steroids.

"They're baaaaack…" Amanda said ominously, mimicking the trailer from a popular horror movie.

"This way," Margie said, turning off the road toward the forest and pulling Catherine with her.

"We can't walk through that!" Amanda protested.

"We'll just go in far enough to hide. They won't know where to look for us. They can't see any better than we can," Margie stumbled and fell forward.

286

"Watch that first step." Catherine stumbled and pushed Margie further in.

"You make it look easy," Amanda said as she tried to follow, but she too stumbled and fell forward landing on top of Margie and Catherine.

"I think this is far enough," Catherine said hopefully.

"No it isn't," Margie barked, pulling Catherine to her feet and stepping forward. "We'll just have to take it slow."

"I thought we *were* taking it slow," Amanda countered. "How about if we try on all fours."

"That's the dumbest...actually that's not a bad idea," Margie said, getting down on all fours. "Here Mom, hold onto my skirt."

And in the impenetrable darkness, Margie, Amanda, and Catherine made their way chimp-like through the dense foliage as the sound of a vehicle drew nearer.

Who Are You Kidding?

We were airborne, but I only knew this because I could feel my stomach knotting up and my palms sweating. I had my eyes shut tight and I was chanting my flight mantra over and over inside my head: *we are not going to die, we are not going to die, we are not going to die.* I didn't believe it, of course, but my therapist said it would be helpful. Stupid therapist!

Pete was busy flying and barking his flight path to whoever was on the ground. And the guy on the ground was none too happy with the fact that Pete hadn't filed a flight plan or that he was flying through commercial airspace without permission.

"Screw you," Pete shouted finally. "You can ground me when I land asshole. Till then, you better warn everyone out of my way." Pete sounded like a pit-bull in a dogfight. It should have given me courage, but I'm not that brave.

My stomach swooped as we made what I assume was a hard left turn, or in aircraft parlance, we banked hard left.

"Hey," Pete snapped at me. "Open your eyes. I need you to watch the transceiver needle."

"If I open my eyes, I'll puke," I said assertively.

"No you won't."

"Yes, I will."

"No you won't."

"Pete, I'm not going to tell you again. I'll puke if I open my eyes. Let someone else look."

"No one can see from back there."

"Then I'll trade places with someone."

"No you won't, Joe. Open your eyes or I'll ..."

"You'll what" I said, certain there was nothing he could do to me that would terrify me more than riding shotgun in a helicopter in the dead of night over rough terrain.

"I'll tell Amanda," Pete said finally. Then he followed that up with: "And you know what will happen then."

I thought a moment. Yeah, I was pretty sure what would happen. I'd become 'Upchuck, Joe,' or 'Joe, the cowardly liar' (a reference to my having lied about being a writer). She'd never let me forget it. Never. It would haunt me forever.

Pete stuck the knife in further and turned it.

"And what do you think Margie would say?"

Damn, this guy was good. I knew Margie wouldn't say anything at all. But what she would she think? What could she think? Joe's a coward, a sissy, a gutless, spineless, whiny, useless piece of meat who's afraid of his own shadow! And who'd blame her?

288

I opened my eyes a smidge and looked out through my lashes. All I could see was the fluorescent glow from the instruments and points of light beyond.

My stomach did a flip flop, but dinner stayed put.

"What am I suppose to watch?"

Pete tapped a small screen in front of me. It had half a dozen horizontal lines and half dozen vertical lines.

"When we get a signal, there'll be a glowing dot. You tell me how far ahead it is and whether to go right or left. The idea is to get the dot to glow right there in the middle of the screen. Then we know it's right below us."

I opened my eyes a little further and found if I kept my focus on the screen, my stomach didn't knot up.

"Okay," I said. "I can do that."

We flew along above the highway that follows the coast for several minutes, and then from the back seat came the question I was dying to ask. "How far is it to the coffee place?"

"We're coming up on it now," Pete shot back. "I'm going to fly over, then start making loops till we've covered ..."

"I got a beep!" I shouted. "Go left" "Go left!"

Pete banked left and headed inland soaring higher as the landscape rose sharply.

"That's not good," Pete muttered.

My heart leapt into my throat. "What's not good?" I choked out, expecting the worst.

"It's pretty thick down there. Going to be hard to find a place to set down. I might have to let you guys rappel to the ground."

Rappel? Like navy seals? Yeah, sure, like that was ever going to happen!

'Ping!'

"There's another one, straight ahead," I shouted excitedly. "A little to the right." My eyes were wide open now watching the dial. My adrenaline had kicked in. Fear was no longer my copilot!

Pete pulled the stick back and we rose steeply.

"It's too bad there's no moon tonight,' Pete said unhappily. "That would help. Especially if you have to rappel."

Yeah, like that was ever going to happen!

I was mentally keeping track of the time since the last *ping* by counting my teeth, which took me roughly thirty seconds. It would have taken me exactly thirty seconds, but I had my wisdom teeth pulled as a young man.

'*Ping.*'

The dot was nearly dead center. "We're here!"I shouted and looked down and to my right, but all I could see was black on black.

Come Out, Come Out

From their hiding spot in the forest, Margie could see the car drive slowly into the small clearing made by the road.

The Caddy stopped twenty feet from the cabin and Duncan's van pulled in behind. Duncan got out of the Caddy, leaving the lights on, and went back to the van as Cho stepped out.

"So what we do now?" Cho asked.

"Like I told you. We wait till the big guy calls back. I left a message." Duncan flipped open his cell phone to make sure he hadn't missed the call. "Sometimes it takes awhile. Come on. I got a bottle in the cabin. We kin pass the time with the ladies." Duncan chuckled softly and started toward the cabin.

"Don' drink," Kanoa said, falling in behind Duncan. "Bu I like da ladies."

Margie turned to Amanda. "Do you think we can make it to the car?"

"We'd have to take the van. It's blocking. Do you think they left the keys?"

"I don't know. Maybe we should stay put like we planned. They don't have a clue where we are. Will they look or will they run?"

"Let's stay put," Catherine whispered. "I'll bet they'll run."

A moment later, Duncan pulled open the door of the hut.

"What the fuck!" he yelled. "How the hell did..." His voice trailed off as he entered. There was another shout from inside. "Idiot!" Duncan yelled.

Kanoa had just reached the door and stood shaking his head. "I say no leave 'im. He's no smart."

"Sounds like the thieves are having a falling out," Amanda said merrily. "I feel so sorry for them."

"Shush," Margie said. "We've got to be quiet."

"Then I shouldn't scream," Catherine asked, "because a snake is climbing up my leg?"

"There are no snakes in Hawaii, Mom," Margie said tersely.

"But there are centipedes," Amanda's voice quivered slightly. "It probably won't bite you unless you try to brush it off, Mrs. M."

"That's very comforting, dear. I'll try to remember that. In the meantime, I'm going to scream quietly." And for the next several seconds, Mrs. M. made a deeply muffled heart-wrenching sound that no one had ever heard before. A sound which was broken only by gunshots -- *bang, bang, bang*-- coming from the cabin.

"Oh, dear," Catherine said. "Do you think they killed him?"

Margie and Amanda stared at one another in the darkness.

"I'm guessing the answer is yes, Mom" Margie said.

"Okay, what do you think we should do?" Amanda asked.

But before Margie could answer, the sound of a helicopter could be heard coming in low over the trees.

"Do you suppose?" Amanda asked.

As the ladies watched, Duncan and Cho rushed from the cabin. Duncan ran to the Caddy, shut off the lights, and dove under the car. A second later, the helicopter appeared overhead its running lights gleaming brightly.

"It's Pete!" Amanda breathed excitedly. "It's Pete! I know it's his chopper!"

Unlikely Heroes

Pete flipped a switch and the ground below was suddenly bathed in light. I could see the white Caddy clearly through the treetops and an old shack and a rusty old van.

"I don't see anyone," I said disappointedly.

A series of 'me neithers' echoed from the back.

"You can't land here," Maxwell said, stating the obvious.

"Nope. Can't do that." Pete said, holding our position above the Caddy. The transceiver *pinged* again.

Pete flipped another switch and I heard an amplifier hum.

"Amanda! Margie! Mrs. M.! If you can hear me, come over by the Caddy and beep the horn."

Nothing moved below.

"Where could they be?" Mark said. "Do you think the Caddy was stolen and dropped here?"

"Can't know for sure what's happened. But I think at least a few of you need to get down there and see what's up." Pete flew around the spot idly.

"I'll go," Maxwell barked. "I used to climb. I know how to use a rope."

There was another "I'll go too." And for a second I breathed a sigh of relief until I realized that I was the one who had said it!

"That's the way," Pete said punching me on the arm in a brotherly fashion. "In the back. Open that hatch cover and you'll find a rope ladder on the left. All you have to do, Joe, is open the door and attach it to the side. You'll see the grommets."

My ears heard what Pete was saying but my mind did not comprehend. *Open the door? Lean out? Attach the ladder? What in God's name was he talking about?*

Suddenly a large coil of rope landed in my lap. I looked down at it. I understood. I was about to die!

"Hurry up," Pete barked. "We can't stick around here all night."

With trembling fingers, I reached over and found the door latch and pushed it open. Immediately, the sound of the propeller intensified and wind whipped at my face and clothes. I forced myself to lean out. I could see the grommets.

"You'll have to take off your seat belt to attach the ladder."

Pete's voice sounded miles away. *Take off my seat belt? Why would I do that?*

But it seems that at some point my mind had become disconnected from my body and was taking direction from Pete, so I took off my seat belt and got down on all fours. I held the door open with my head and found the tabs on the rope ladder that I was supposed to attach to the grommets, and started to insert the first one.

Suddenly, the whole world rocked wildly; the helicopter lurched to the right and I was nearly standing on my head as the door swung open wide.

"Gotcha!" I heard Pete shout as I felt my belt cut into my stomach and the rope ladder slip from my grasp and fall through space. The world rocked again and I was suddenly being pulled back into my seat as the door slammed shut behind me.

"Caught a sudden gust," Pete explained by way of apology as I sat trembling, eyes fixed, staring straight ahead.

"Where's the ladder?" Pete asked.

"Aw. Jeez. You dropped it?" Pete sounded exceptionally disappointed. I on the other hand was amazed I hadn't followed it to the ground.

"Well, that tears it. We're gonna have to find a place to land and walk in.

Land? Yes that's what we should do. Land. Walk.

My mind was my own again and I quickly buckled my seat belt.

Hide Out

"What did they drop?" Margie asked her voice barely audible above the sound of the retreating sound of the helicopter.

"I don't know," Amanda answered. "But where the hell are they going?"

"Well, dear. I expect that since they couldn't see anything down here, they're going back home," Catherine's voice was calm and maternal. "But we've still got the upper hand here."

"Maybe," Margie said. "But for how long?"

And as if in response to her question, Duncan climbed out from under the Caddy where he'd been hiding and shouted to Cho: "Get your ass over here. We need to find those ladies and get out of here pronto. And bring that big flashlight in there."

Margie pinched Amanda's arm and made her wince. "What's that for?"

"You didn't want to go back in for a flashlight."

"Well, neither did you!"

"Now girls let's not fight. I suggest we find a thick bush to hide in and pray they don't find us."

So while Kanoa could be heard rummaging in the cabin, Margie, Amanda, and Mrs. M. made their way carefully and quietly toward a large dark clump of vegetation which each of them hoped was not already occupied!

Terra Firma

"There," Nicky shouted. "There's a small clearing just to the right."

Pete swung the chopper around.

"Good job," Pete said. "It looks big enough to set 'er down, and it's only a couple hundred meters back to the Caddy. Take a peak in that hatch and see if there's a flashlight or lantern or something. I know I put one in there awhile back, but it could have been..."

"Here's one," Mark interrupted. "And there's a gun too. Should I bring it?"

"It's just a signal flare, but bring it along." Pete had already finessed the chopper into the tiny clearing, which was actually just a turnout on the road, and cut the engine. Blackness enveloped us.

We piled out and I fell to the earth and kissed the ground. I couldn't believe how wonderful it felt to feel the ground beneath my feet again.

"Jeez, Joe, that's really embarrassing," Pete said. "Get up already."

I climbed back to my feet and looked around. The others were staring at me. "What? You never saw a grown man kiss the earth? The pope does it!"

"You ain't the pope," Angie said sarcastically, to which there was general agreement.

"Come on," Pete said, impatient with our obvious lack of seriousness and took the flashlight and the lead and started up the road to the first turnoff and then followed the dirt road under the trees.

The flashlight gave us plenty of light and we marched single file without any real concern for any danger that might await us. Silly us.

Everything Goes Black!

The light from Kanoa's flashlight flooded the landscape and upset Duncan.

"Don't just swing it around," he barked, taking the light from Kanoa. "Keep it on the ground so nobody can see it." Duncan focused the light on the ground.

"They left prints somewhere. Those ladies weren't wearing ballet slippers."

Duncan swept the light back and forth as he walked.

"There!" Duncan spat. "I've got 'em now."

From their blind in the tall brush, the ladies watched Duncan follow their track to where they'd left the road. He stopped and swept the light under the trees. It passed their position, but then swung back.

"Come on out ladies," Duncan called. "You can't hide there long." Duncan turned to Kanoa. "Go get the machete out of the truck. They can't have gotten far. They'll be easy to track..."

Suddenly Duncan stopped and killed the flashlight. "Shush," he hissed and put his finger to his lips.

"Looks like it's just up there," Pete's muffled voice pierced the heavy foliage amid the sound of feet marching on the rocky road just as light from the flashlight twinkled through the brush, revealing their location.

"We've got to warn them!" Margie breathed noiselessly.

"How?" Amanda breathed back. "That guy's got a gun! And he's not afraid to use it!"

Margie felt around on the ground and found a fist-sized rock. "Get down," she whispered, cocking her arm and hurtling the rock as far as she could in the direction of the approaching voices.

The rock crackled and snapped as it fell into the dense jungle.

"What's that?" It was Joe's voice this time.

"Run, Joe, run. It's a trap! They've got guns!" Margie shouted abandoning any hope of remaining hidden and warning the rescuers.

Well, as you can imagine all hell broke loose at that point.

I could describe for you the melee that ensued what with all the yelling and screaming, and falling and swearing, and the hopeless panic that transpired as me and Pete and Maxwell and Mark and Angie all unarmed and confused by the darkness tried to avoid the bad guys and find the ladies and as Margie and Amanda and Catherine stumbled through the underbrush to join us, and how Kanoa and Duncan both armed and dangerous and familiar with the terrain captured and detained us one by one without killing or wounding anyone and only firing half a dozen rounds into the air. But I'll spare you the details.

As it turned out Angie's karate skills were out not that useful against guns. And as for the flare gun, it misfired and very nearly took off Nicky's head.

The important thing is that after about ten minutes of this silliness in the darkness and people falling and hurting themselves, the bad guys had all the good guys rounded up and forced into the cabin where we were bound with the handyman's secret weapon – that is, duct tape – to await our terrifying fate! Of course Pete and I were delegated to drag Kracker's body outside first. I'd never touched a stiff before and I don't intend to again. Pete, for his part, took it better than I did. I expect it was his military experience.

Fortunately for us there was a limited supply of duct tape even for dangerous criminals and what with eight detainees to restrain Kanoa and Duncan ran out, much to their dismay, and had to leave the mouths of their captives unrestrained, hence the cabin was soon as noisy as a kindergarten classroom when the teacher steps out for a smoke.

As Duncan and Kanoa stood off in the corner and mumbled whatever they had to mumble about, we – the captives – kept on talking.

There were, of course, the requisite questions: "How did you find us?" and "Are you okay?" Then too there were the recriminations "Why didn't you bring the police?" or "Why didn't you bring a gun?" And there were also the heartfelt platitude such as "Whatever happens, you know I love you, Joe or Pete or *fill in the blank*."

Of most significance to me and I'm certain also to Margie was that Maxwell turned to Mrs. M. when things had quieted down and told her that he loved her and he was sorry and asked her to forgive him and that he didn't deserve her, and Mrs. M. started to cry and said that she loved him too and thanked him for his apology said that he was plenty good for her and that was why she'd stayed with him all these years. This started Margie to cry who was joined by Amanda and then Angie and even Nicky who was touched by the significance of it all and it made for a very melancholy scene. And had Mom and Dad not been trussed up like two sausages, I'm certain they would have sealed it with a kiss. Personally, I wanted to hear exactly why Mr. M was apologizing, but that didn't seem to be forthcoming and to be honest I guess it didn't really matter.

Their confession led to more confessions and apologies. Pete apologized to Amanda and to Angie and even to Nicky. He also apologized to me and for the sake of completeness he apologized to Mr. and Mrs. M.

Of course Angie and Nicky apologized to one another again and I apologized to Margie for not being more supportive and she apologized for getting involved in the murder to which there was much mumbled agreement and to which she took some offence until Pete reminded everyone that Amanda was just as guilty and before we went further down that road I said it was water under the bridge and we should forget it. Which we did. And, of course, there was the requisite crying and sniffling and "how did we ever get so angry."

I confessed to Margie that I had a secret stash of chips and stuff in the house and Margie forgave me, even though she knew all about it. Mark told everyone that if anyone survived they were to give Shelly this message: 'I love you Shelly and always have.' And so it went until all the confessions were done and we all fell silent and nervously awaited our fate, whatever it might be.

"You'll never get away with this," Maxwell bellowed finally. It was, of course, a very pedestrian comment and fell on deaf ears since both Duncan and Kanoa knew that bad men got away with horrendous things all the time.

"Shut up! All of you!" Duncan finally yelled, putting the barrel of his revolver to Catherine's head which was – as it turns out – even more effective at cutting chatter than the return of the kindergarten teacher.

"Kanoa, keep an eye on 'em. I've got to call Mr. Big and till him what's happening and find out what he wants to do with our little pack of troublemakers." Duncan started for the door. "And don't fall for any fake heart attacks! If they fall to the ground, shoot 'em."

Duncan slammed the door behind himself and went in search of a sufficiently strong cell phone signal to call Mr. Big, which brought him to the end of the road where he discovered the helicopter, which he reasoned would also have to be dealt with.

As you can image, Mr. Big was not happy with Duncan's report.

"You're talking mass murder," Mr. Big said, his voice rising several octaves, after Duncan explained what had happened and suggested that he and Kanoa kill the captives and dump their bodies in the helicopter and then set the helicopter on fire to make it look like a crash.

"So?" Duncan replied, missing the impact of Mr. Big's statement. "What should we do?"

There was a pregnant pause. Actually it was more than a 9-month pregnancy pause; more like a 22-month pregnancy pause, which is the gestation period for an elephant as I understand it.

"Don't do anything," Mr. Big said finally and firmly. "I'll send people up to handle the situation. Just wait for them. You understand. Don't do anything!"

Duncan was happy to oblige. Mr. Big paid him well and if Mr. Big wanted to handle it, Duncan wasn't going to argue. Killing people was messy business and although it didn't trouble him to kill, it was still a messy business

"All right," Duncan said, "only don't take forever; someone might come up the road and find this chopper."

When Duncan returned to the cabin, he was pleased to find things as he'd left them, quite and in order.

"The big guy's sending his people to take 'em off our hands," Duncan explained in response to the look Kanoa gave him.

"Good," Kanoa said, getting up and heading for the door. "You watch now. I gotta pee."

Like everyone else in that sweaty, smelly little cabin, I knew that my brain needed to stay on overdrive to figure out how we were going to get out of this mess. It didn't look promising. Heck, it didn't even look possible. There might be only two of them, but they had the guns and we were all trussed up; just a bunch of sheep ready for slaughter.

The place had been quiet for several minutes after Kanoa left and Duncan was cleaning his grubby little nails with a huge hunting knife and humming softly to himself. I couldn't recognize the tune, but it sounded like an old funeral dirge.

Since I'm always of the mind that doing something is better than doing nothing, I ventured a statement. "The cops are looking for us," I said flatly.

Duncan looked up and smiled. "Oh, yeah? What'd you do? Steal your mommy's purse."

Evidently Duncan thought this funny because he chuckled.

"We didn't file a flight plan. The FAA is looking for our chopper." It was almost true and I've always been told that if you're going to tell a lie, make it a believable lie.

"You the pilot?" Duncan asked, seeming somewhat interested.

"No," I said. "But..."

"Then shut up!" Duncan snapped. "Who's the pilot?"

No one said anything. Duncan seemed to take that as an insult and stood up.

"Okay, let's see," he said and approached Catherine. "You got two ears. You don't need 'em both." He grabbed Catherine's left ear and put the edge of the blade against it. Everyone gasped!

"I'm the pilot," Pete called.

Duncan let go of Catherine and focused his attention on Pete.

"See that wasn't so hard, was it? Where'd you learn to fly? Army?"

"Marines," Pete said.

"Desert storm?"

"Yeah."

"I was there. What a shithole. Hot. Dirty. Full'a stinking foreigners."

Evidently, Duncan hadn't liked his tour of duty, not that I was surprised.

"What kind of range you got?"

Pete fell quiet. Duncan smiled and juggled the knife from one hand to the other.

"Can you make it to Oahu?"

Pete said nothing. Duncan sighed and started toward Catherine. "Everything's gotta be hard."

302

"Not on what's in the tanks now," Pete said quietly.

Duncan stopped and turned. "How about Maui?"

"Yeah, I can make it to Maui? Let the others go and I'll fly you."

Duncan chuckled. "If I want you to do it, you'll do it whether I let these folks go or not."

Kanoa returned and Duncan gave him a hard time for taking so long. The fact that they argued encouraged me. Maybe there was some way to get them at odds with each other. Margie must have had the same idea, for she asked the question on everyone's mind.

"Do you really think you can kill nine people and get away with it?"

It was a rational question and deserved a rational answer. Unfortunately, we were not dealing with rational people. We were dealing with psychopaths who were beginning to get nervous.

"Maybe not," Duncan confessed, "but I can kill you." And he put his gun to Margie's head and made a 'kapow' sound.

"Jus' do it," Kanoa said. "I not sitting 'roun' here much longer. You got a boss but he ain't my boss."

Kanoa lifted the revolver from his lap and aimed it at Pete.

"Not him, idiot, he's a pilot." Duncan cursed. "He can fly us out a here. Start with the women."

There was a collective gasp and we looked at one another disbelievingly.

"Don't start with anyone," Maxwell said. "I'm rich. I can get you as much money as you want and fly you anywhere in the world."

"Sure you can, pop," Duncan chided. "And I'm the Easter Bunny. Shut up or you'll be first."

"He's not joking," Catherine said. "We're loaded. We can get a private jet and fly you anywhere. Anywhere at all."

Duncan scratched his cheek with the barrel of the revolver and seemed to consider this a moment.

"Too damn complicated. I've got my plan. Your money can buy you a nice funeral." He turned to Kanoa.

"Okay buddy you want to start, take 'em down to the chopper one by one and shoot 'em there. That way we can torch it and make it look like a crash."

"Wait a minute," Nicky said. "We're valuable hostages! You can't kill us."

"Sure we can," Duncan said flatly.

Kanoa shook his head. "I thought we was gonna fly out a here? Now we gonna fake a crash? No one gonna believe a crash. Just kill 'em here." Kanoa's trigger finger was obviously getting nervous.

Duncan suddenly lost it. "You know what, Jackass," Duncan lifted his gun and pointing it at Kanoa. "You're a God damn pain in the ass. Gimme your gun. The Big Guy said he'd take care of it. So we're gonna wait for him to do that."

Kanoa's eyes smoldered with hatred as he slowly lowered his pistol and handed it to Duncan. Now it was ten against one, but of course Duncan was still the only one with a weapon.

"Go sit over there where I can keep an eye on you."

Kanoa reluctantly moved over and sat on the ground between Margie and Angie.

Everyone fell silent and for a moment all was still. Then suddenly the silence was broken by the distinctive sound of a distant helicopter.

Duncan cocked his ear toward the sound. "Sounds like it's coming our way."

The sounds of the chopper grew louder and louder till it drown out every other sound and the blades began whipping the air and brush around the tiny cabin.

Great, I thought, *reinforcements for the bad guys.*

Duncan must have assumed the same thing, because he was wearing a smile as big as a slice of watermelon. But it didn't last long. Suddenly the cabin was bathed in light from above, and more light exploded through the window facing the road.

"This is the police," boomed an electronically enhanced voice which I instantly recognized as that of Detective Lo. "Come out with your hands up!"

"Shit!" Duncan spat as he dropped to the floor behind some coffee bags.

"Now you got 'tings fixed," Kanoa hissed. "Stupid houlie! You boss send the cops!"

"Shut the fuck up," Duncan shot back fiercely.

Evidently Kanoa didn't like Duncan's tone because an instant later a hunting knife appeared magically in Kanoa's hand and left it promptly on a trajectory for Duncan's head.

Unfortunately, Kanoa's aim was off and the blade missed the slimy bastard and burrowed itself deep into a post near him. Kanoa swore his disappointment and Duncan responded with lead. Kanoa's head exploded and splattered blood over everything in the cabin.

As you might guess, this was followed by a lot of screaming and yelling and crying, especially among those closest to Kanoa who were eager to get away from the dead man's body. But Duncan was already thinking ahead.

"Hey, copper," he yelled. "You hear that? I just shot one of your buddies. Kill the lights now or I'll knock off another one."

It couldn't have taken more than three seconds before we were once again in total darkness. The sound of the helicopter drifted away.

I felt more than saw Duncan stand and cross the floor till he was standing next to Margie.

"Okay, Blondie, you and me are goin' to make our escape. Give me trouble and you'll wind up like that guy."

My eyes had readjusted to the dim light and I watched helplessly as Duncan cut Margie's bonds and pulled her up. I couldn't see Margie's face, but I knew she had to be terrified.

"Take me," I pleaded.

"Shut up!" Duncan spat. "All of you shut up. If you yell or make a noise and I hear it, I'm gonna slit her throat. You understand?"

There was a murmur of consensus.

"Okay, Blondie, stay close. You do everything I say and you might survive."

I watched helplessly as Margie was pushed toward the door ahead of Duncan. Frantic with fear and anger I pulled at the tape binding me. It seemed hopeless; then I remembered the knife in the post!

Duncan pushed open the door, holding Margie in front. Outside everything was still and dark. They stepped forward, their shadows instantly swallowed up by other, deeper shadows.

As soon as they were gone, I jumped to my feet and hopped to the post. I turned and found the blade with my hands and quickly sliced the tape that held them. I grabbed the knife and sawed through the tape on my ankles with a single motion.

"Here," I put the blade in Angie's hands and then made for the door. I didn't have a plan. There wasn't time for a plan. I just knew I had to do something!

At the door, staying low, I wondered how many police there were and whether they knew Duncan had a hostage or even that they'd left the cabin. I thought I could just see their shadows, Margie's and Duncan's, as they left the small clearing around the cabin and started into the forest.

Then suddenly, there was a flash of light to my right as brilliant as a bolt of lightning and everything was sharply illuminated. My mind registered the image of the police sniper, dressed in black, the strange night-vision goggles covering his face. A millisecond later I heard the rifle's report and saw Duncan's body twist wildly and start to fall forward. Another millisecond ticked by and then there was a second flash of light. But this one was not from the police sniper but from the muzzle of Duncan's revolver.

And in that second flash of light I saw Margie pitch forward violently and then everything went black!

The Final Chapter

It was another perfect day in Kona. Bright morning sunshine, a warm trade wind blowing softly, and far off in the distance the muted sounds of lawn mowers and leaf blowers and even the crash of the ocean surf. I sipped my morning coffee and stared emptily at the flat, calm water in the pool. Magoo lay in his chair watching me.

I heard the front door open and looked up to see Amanda and Pete peer in and then after they'd spotted me cautiously make their way through the living room. Amanda was carrying a big serving tray and Pete was carrying one of those portable coffee carafes and two big mugs. Magoo jumped down and went to greet them as they made their way over; Amanda placed the serving tray on the table in front of me. They stood quite for a moment.

"How are you holding up?" Amanda asked finally.

"I'm doing okay," I said with no real energy. "What's this?"

The tray reminded me of those meal trays you used to get on airplanes. There was a big plate in the center covered by a silver top, an empty glass, turned upside down, next to a small carton of guava juice. There was another small plate holding a big, cherry-filled Bismarck. A small bowl filled with papaya chucks and a single maraschino cherry. Amanda lifted the cover and revealed scrambled eggs with mushrooms and cheese, six strips of bacon, and two slices of toast, cut diagonally, and dripping butter. I smiled weakly.

"We thought you might need something to keep your strength up," Amanda said as she took the mugs and carafe from Pete and filled them both. They settled into chairs across from me. "You look worn out."

"I'm hanging in there."

I looked at the feast. Margie wouldn't approve, especially not the bacon.

I really wasn't hungry, but for Amanda's sake I thought I should make an effort, so I picked up a piece of toast, tore off a hunk and fed it to Magoo. I took a small bite for myself.

"Where is everyone?" Amanda asked, looking about at the empty yard. I noticed her eyes avoided the pool.

"Well," I said, "Mark and Shelly and the girls took a condo down at Kanaloa, and Mom and Dad are staying at a hotel. They're leaving later today. It's pretty quiet here. How're things at your place?"

"Angie and Nicky have gone to stay at the Mauna Lani. Pete, as you can see, has returned…," Amanda cast a disapproving look at him, "…for better or worse, and is already busy turning the guest room into a study, though he refuses to say what he's going to study."

"No more guests for us!" he said enthusiastically, then cleared his throat and said quietly. "At least not for awhile."

"I heard from my mole at the police department," Amanda offered, then waited to find out if I wanted to know what she'd heard. "But maybe you don't really care."

I chewed and swallowed.

"Go ahead. I suppose I should know how it all laid out. Not that I ever really cared," I said.

"Well," Amanda began, "here's the scoop as best as anyone knows for certain. It seems that Kenny knew he was dealing with a bunch of heavy hitters and to protect himself he kept a file with his attorney to be forwarded to the police in the event of his death. It arrived in the mail yesterday morning. Tapes, memos, everything a prosecuting attorney would want. It included a log of his contacts and even some taped phone conversations. Unfortunately, none of it is any good. I'm told that without Kenny to testify, it's all hearsay.

"As it turns out, during Kenny's research on pheromones, he happened upon a chemical that you could spray on virtually anything and mask its scent and make it smell like coffee."

"Why coffee?" I asked. That seemed like an odd scent.

Amanda shrugged. "Nobody knows for sure. The guess is that that's just the way it was. Anyway, Kenny kept his discovery quiet. If he published it, he'd have to share royalties with the college and the company that was providing his grant money.

"Anyway, as luck would have it, Trisha was one of his grad students and after he verified she was indeed the daughter of the rich and powerful G. Peter Ryan, he took her on as a research associate, put the moves on her, and managed thereby to meet the guy. He shared his discovery with Ryan and, according to Kenny, that was the one and only time he was allowed to meet or speak to him directly. After that everything was handled through middlemen.

"There were, of course, many applications for Kenny's discovery, but only one that would really pay off: cocaine. All Kenny had to do was prove that someone could carry cocaine past those drug sniffing dogs without setting off the alarm.

"The test was a huge success, but they still needed a cleaver way to import the cocaine without anyone getting suspicious. Someone came up with the idea to press the cocaine into coffee bean shapes, paint it, and then spray the magic potion over it all.

"Remember all that 'coffee' in the cabin? It was really cocaine!

"Anyway, according to Kenny, Ryan and company took care of setting everything up and Kenny came over to supervise the first shipment under the guise of accompanying his wife to a seminar on the Big Island."

"How convenient that there should be a seminar in her area of expertise on the Big Island," I said, shaking my head and feeding Magoo another piece of toast. As you'll recall, he doesn't like bacon. He does like toast.

"Actually, it wasn't a coincidence. Ryan owns a gaggle of companies doing research in all kinds of areas, including alternative energy, so he simple finessed to have the conference here. How's that for manipulating the system?"

I tried to whistle my appreciation of such incredible resources, but it's not possible to whistle with toast in your mouth.

Amanda continued, "As it turns out, getting large quantities of cocaine to Kona is relatively easy. The cocaine was shipped by freighter and ferried to the island by fishing boats. Drug enforcement is pretty lax here since it doesn't make sense to smuggle drugs onto the islands and then to the mainland where they get checked thoroughly. They decided to make it Kona coffee because Kona is usually flown to the mainland whereas regular coffee takes the slow boat, and they didn't want to wait for the profits.

"Now some of the rest of this is speculation, so take it with a grain of salt."

I nodded my acknowledgement.

"Kenny's wife – even though she was having an affair with Professor Who Ever – must have wanted to catch Kenny with Trisha, probably so she could get the lion's share of any divorce settlement, and she followed him to that cabin we were in. Duncan found her sneaking around and killed her. Now, Duncan, as you already know, is an accomplished hang glider and the best guess anyone has is that he planned to fly the body out to sea and drop it. There's a very rugged stretch of coastline just south of here and he probably figured that between the rocks and the fish and all the body would just disappear. Unfortunately, the wind must have blown him off course and it was cut the body loose or crash with it, so he cut it loose. Which is where you and Margie came in."

"So Kenny didn't kill his wife?"

"Nope. Except for after the fact. He knew who killed her, he just didn't care."

"And Trisha really didn't have anything to do with any of it?"

"Nope. Poor kid probably doesn't even know what a bankrupt moral asshole her father is."

I recalled her warning to Margie and me when we went to meet him. "Oh," I said quietly, "I think she might."

"It made everyone in the plan nervous when you and Margie took in Trisha, but when Kenny got out and moved in here, he realized that we had no real information. As far as Ryan and company were concerned, we were no threat at all."

"So why was Kenny killed here?"

"No one's sure. Maybe Kenny was just hanging around to see if we'd turned up anything new or maybe he was just a Peeping Tom. But Professor What's It had picked up Kenny's trail by then and found him here and did him in. At least that's the professor's story."

"So the professor at least is going to prison?"

"Oh, yeah," Amanda assured me. "He's going to prison."

I thought a minute then said: "So if you and Catherine and Margie hadn't gone to lunch at The Coffee Shack and hadn't seen the hang glider, things might have turned out very different."

"Probably," Amanda said wistfully. "Although we probably would have got to the hang glider eventually."

"And the guys at the cabin?" I asked.

"Except for Duncan, they were just grunts. Muscle. They thought the scheme was to sell regular coffee as Kona coffee. They had no idea that cabin held close to two hundred million dollars worth of cocaine!

"Unfortunately, when we started asking questions about hang gliding, Duncan must have felt he had no other option than to kidnap us. And then when you guys

312

came marching in to find the Caddy, he couldn't think past what he had to do."

"So when did Detective Lo figure it out?" I was stymied. "Why didn't the cavalry arrive sooner?"

"He couldn't arrive sooner, because he didn't figure it out," Amanda said. "He got an anonymous call from an untraceable number telling him exactly – and I mean a GPS location – where the cabin was located and what he'd find there. The speculation is that Ryan and Company knew they could never get away with killing nine people and hope to keep their actions quiet. So they blew the whistle on the guys in the cabin. The best outcome that could have happened for them was that they should all get killed – which they did. Of course, the file Kenny kept put an end to any smuggling operation."

"That's quite a story," I said, taking a sip of coffee. "Quite a story. So is Ryan going to be charged?"

Amanda shook her head. "He and that buddy of his, Tommy Chow, are too smart. All the evidence is hearsay from Kenny's notes and such. They'll never make a case against them according to detective Lo."

We all sat quietly for awhile and drank some coffee.

Amanda's gaze eventually landed on a small leather bound book on the table.

"What's this?" she asked.

"Margie's diary?" I answered quietly, picking it up carefully. "I was looking for something in her closet last night and discovered it."

"Have you read it?" It was hard to tell if Amanda was just curious or angry that I might have intruded on Margie's secrets.

"No. Not yet."

"You know, Joe. There are some things we're not suppose to know."

I looked into her eyes and nodded my head, and then laid the diary back down and looked over at the pool.

"We'll, we better go," Amanda said suddenly and she and Pete stood. "We'll come back later for our stuff and check on you. Okay? Maybe you should take a nap? You do look beat."

"Thanks. That's a good idea," I said.

They turned and I watched them walk to the door. I sat by the pool and fed Magoo another piece of toast and nibbled at a piece of bacon. I couldn't enjoy it really because I knew how much it would upset Margie if I ate it.

After awhile, I got up and went inside. I was tired. Maybe a nap was what I needed.

I walked through the living room and picked up a glass from the coffee table and took it to the kitchen. I was about to put it in the dishwasher when I noticed it had Margie's lipstick on it. I stared at it and wondered briefly if it tasted like cherry or gumdrops, then set it down carefully next to the sink.

I rinsed out the sponge and wiped off the countertops and surveyed the room. Everything was in order so I left and made my way to the master bedroom.

I leaned against the doorway and looked down at the big king size bed.

There was Margie, snoring softly, her tangled blonde curls framing her angelic face and the two bright-white casts that encased her broken arms resting on pillows over her chest. I crossed the room and sat on the bed next to her and brushed a small curl off her forehead. Margie stirred and opened her eyes slowly.

"Hello, Joe," she said and smiled up at me

"Hello Margie," I said, smiling down at her. I leaned over and kissing her lightly on the lips.

314

The smile slipped from her face and she studied me sternly.

"Why do you taste like bacon?"

Epilogue

That afternoon as we drove Mom and Dad to the airport we passed Amanda's and Pete's. We waved at them, but they busy doing cannon balls into the pool, and didn't see us. I thought they sure looked happy and I figured they were celebrating just being alone. It seemed like a good idea.

Since our near death experience in the forest, Maxwell and Catherine had been acting like two teenagers who'd just discovered sex. It was kind of cute, but also annoying. Margie, of course, bubbled with glee every time they said something nice to one another or showed physical affection.

Everyone was amazingly quite on the drive. I'd already told Margie what Amanda had said about the murder, and Mom and Dad didn't seem to care about it one way or the other so neither Margie nor I brought it up. There were a few questions about this and that and of course Mom and Dad gave us a big thank you for letting them stay.

Later, as we waited for the plane, the Moore's sat together holding hands and Margie and I just stood around. Margie drew even more attention than usual what with her arms in casts.

"Isn't it wonderful?" Margie asked as she looked at her parents holding hands.

"Yes. Wonderful." I replied, wondering how much longer before the first class boarding call. I was still a little shell shocked and wondered if Mom and Dad had really buried the hatchet. Old habits die hard.

315

It occurred to me that I had some business to take care of before they left, so I wandered over to where Maxwell and Catherine were sitting.

"Maxwell," I said. "Could I talk to you for a minute?"

Maxwell looked up at me. "Sure, Joe. What is it?"

"In private," I said, and nodded my head to indicate we should stand someplace were Margie and Catherine couldn't hear.

Maxwell followed me a dozen or so steps away and waited patiently while I stammered a bit before finding the right words.

"Maxwell," I finally said. "Before you go, I've got a confession to make." I couldn't look him in the eye, so I watched the ground in front of my sandals. "I'm not writer." I paused to gauge his response. I looked up. He showed no reaction. "I never wrote any of those books," I continued. "In fact, I don't even have a job – though I'm seriously considering getting one, but I didn't marry Margie for her money and I'm not a lay-about despite how it might seem. And..."

Maxwell reached out and put a hand on my shoulder. I looked up and saw that he had a big grin on his face.

"I know that, Joe. I've known almost the whole time. The evening after you claimed to be Kimberly Shoulton I was watching one of those late night programs and Shoulton was a guest. She's a very pretty lady. Doesn't look anything like you," he laughed.

"Why didn't you say something?" I asked.

"Well," Maxwell began, "at first it was because I could tell that your lie made you uncomfortable and I figured that since you'd lied to me you deserved to suffer. Then I decided not to say anything so that I could find out what you were made of. I figured if you were the right kind of guy, you'd eventually get around to telling me, and, well, here you are telling me." Maxwell slapped me on the shoulder.

"You know all the while Margie was married to Frank, I worried about her. But after spending time with you, Joe, and hearing your confession just now, I know I don't have to worry about her anymore." Maxwell held out his hand and I took it and we shook on it.

"Thank you for understanding," was all I could think to say.

The loudspeaker announced the boarding, so we collected Catherine and the carryon luggage.

"What did you say to my father?" Margie asked as we made our way to the security lines.

"I'll tell you later," I said.

We reached the security line and hugged and kissed as was appropriate.

"We'll see you next year," Margie said when the last hug and kiss had ended.

"About that, Margie," Maxwell said. "You know we love you, Margie, but six weeks is just too damn long. How about if we come in February for two weeks next year, when it's gray and cold back home?"

"Okay," Margie said. "We'll see you next February."

I have never wanted to kiss a man before. But by golly if I could have got at him I would have planted one on Maxwell that would have made him swoon.

I waved and Margie would have waved too, but with the casts, all she could do was kind of wiggle her fingers as Mom and Dad pushed through the security line. We stood and watched them till they were swallowed up by the mob of passengers, then turned and started back to our car.

It's funny. All the way to the airport, I'd been excited to think that they were finally leaving and now that they were going I was sort of missing them.

"So," I said to Margie, "what should we do next year for the holidays?" The prospect of having Margie all to myself again was too much. "We could get away. How about France? I know it's not 'the season' but..."

Margie had stopped and was shaking her head and looking at me with that look of hers that says 'you silly, silly man, don't you know anything.'

I stopped talking and walking. "What?" I asked.

"Poor, Joe. You just don't get it do you?"

"What?" I repeated.

Margie said nothing. Then it hit me. It hit me hard!

"They say that every year, don't they?"

"Yup!" Margie giggled. "Every year."

I guess I must have looked pretty beaten down, because Margie stepped up to me, stood on tiptoe, and kissed me firmly on the lips. It tasted like cherry.

"Want to stop for a drink at Huggo's on the way home?" she asked.

"You know," I said. "I think I've had enough to drink this year. Let's just go home and I'll make you some ice tea and we can sit by the pool and decide what to do for Christmas."

About the Author

Mr. Stimmler writes and lives with his wife and two Yorkshire terriers in St. Paul Minnesota. He escapes to sunny Kona each winter and it is getting increasingly hard to get him back on the plane to return home. You can email him at Gerry@idreamofhawaii.com, but don't expect a quick answer, he's very busy working on the next Margie Murder Mystery!